I0818196

Always Adam

Mark Brumby

This edition published in 2024 by
Hit the North
26 Mill Wharf
Tweedmouth
Berwick upon Tweed
Northumberland
TD15 2BP

www.hitthenorth.info

ISBN: 9781068574726

Originally published as Payback in 2013

Also by Mark Brumby
Big Daddy

Dedicated to...

my family, near and far...

'And he forced death upon them unto the hundredth generation.'

Anon
Translated from the Norse: Haken's Stone, Ranulfskelf, North Yorkshire

HIT THE NORTH

One
16:15 - Thursday 3rd June
Fermanagh Mansions, London NW3

I suppose I should have been happy, I'd won the lottery again.

But then again I won it most weeks. Frequently as often as once a day and I gave the laptop's screen a bit of a poke. It seemed to stop the flickering for a while and it was still there, the rancid little email telling me that I'd won US$12m, this time in Colombia.

And that all I had to do in order to collect was to send my bank details to some Hotmail address or another for the attention of one Senor Eduardo Romero Sanchez. But anyone sending me an email that got caught by my spam filter and that was addressed to *undisclosed recipients* and referred to me as *Dear sir Mr Alfred Spencer Beck* probably wasn't going to make me rich in a hurry.

I was going to have to stick to getting rich slowly but intrusions such as that from Senor Romero Sanchez might provide me with a little more material that I could use in my column, the daily comment that had fast become a ball and chain but which paid just about enough to keep body and soul together and I tabbed away from my email account and looked again at the wise words that I'd entrusted to the screen.

I moved the cursor to the 'send' button and it stayed there but this was what paid the bills and I had to be professional, read it back.

I overheard a conversation in the queue at the chip shop the other day as one of the would-be customers was running through her recent childbirth traumas with another.

So much for trying not to start a sentence with a pronoun. I could have been more creative and built the scene but at less than a pound a word they weren't going to get Joyce or Wilde. I read on:

And she was sharing it with the rest of us too because, rather than whisper such intimacies over a coffee in one or other of their kitchens, she was belting it all out at full volume and, if I hadn't been so hungry, she would have put me right off my food.

Well I should have said something of course. 'Learn to write and put it on paper' would have done the trick but she was an ugly-looking six foot bruiser and besides, it was fascinating in a morbid sort of way and, when she said that she'd had to have an 'epidurable', I just had to carry on listening.

And I'd swear that when she said it was still painful someone else in the queue whispered 'good' but I didn't get to hear the ending because my food was ready and I couldn't fumble with the salt for more than a minute or two. However, judging by the girth of the woman in question, I'd have to assume that the youngster was still in there and that he or she was possibly on horseback.

I allowed myself a nod. It would do. I hit *send* then tabbed back to the document that I'd cut the text from and read the column again. It might brighten some poor bugger's morning commute and it got me a few mentions here and there. Kept me on the staff at the paper with the chance to do the odd piece for the financial section but it wouldn't win any prizes.

Still, it kept my Twitter feed buzzing and the hits on the blog up. It even won me the odd sketch-writing gig here and there. I treated myself to another nod, stood up and worked a kink out of my lower back after which, with only a half turn or so, I managed to touch every wall in my living room without moving my feet as it wasn't a very big room and it wasn't a very big flat.

But it was mine and the mildew and damp and the mould and the piles of papers and unwashed clothing gave it the air of a writer's hovel and that seemed apt. It just wouldn't be the same if I tidied it up. Not that there was the least chance of that and I pushed back my chair and stood up. Walked the three or four feet to the corner of the room that was had been creatively called my kitchenette and opened the fridge, checked my dwindling beer stash.

Decorating could wait but a hot shower and a cold beer couldn't and I was due both and preferably in that order so I reluctantly put the beer back, closed the fridge door and shuffled to the bathroom.

**

So you get in the shower and the phone rings. It wouldn't ring for days but there it was now, challenging me to towel off and get to it before whoever it was rang off, and I considered letting the machine take the call but I'd just sent the email and it could be the paper, they might want a word.

They rang on my mobile as a rule but by the time I'd rationalised that it wasn't going to be the office I was already dripping on the carpet with my towel flapping open and the phone in my hand.

It probably wasn't a pretty sight. Still, whoever was on the other end of the line wasn't to know that so I tried to put a bit of authority into my opening line. 'Hello, Spencer Beck?'

It wasn't bad. I sounded busy, irritated and, more importantly, fully clothed.

And the irritated bit at least was accurate though the pause the other end suggested that I'd wasted my effort and that it was going to be my mum. 'Mr Beck, do you know anything about MI5?'

I scowled and turned to look at the phone in my hand. It certainly wasn't my mum. 'I beg your pardon?'

'Mr Beck, Alfred?'

No one called me Alfred but now I'd had it twice in the space of an hour.

I was Spencer or occasionally Mr A Spencer Beck and only the passport office, the tax man and any one of my legion of aunts knew or cared what the A stood for so it had to be something official.

Or maybe family and official. Maybe an aunt had died and I felt a brief flush of guilt for not calling or visiting or whatever. I wiped a few drops of soapy water from my nose and chin and realised that the ball was in my court. 'Speaking?'

'You know what MI5 is?'

The accent was neutral, perhaps mildly Scottish. The silence lengthened until I spoke again. 'Is this some kind of joke?'

That was really rather poor as far as responses go.

But it won me a couple of seconds and I scrubbed my head with the towel whilst wondering what the hell this was about. I nearly dropped the phone but then the voice that I now pictured as being that of a west coast Scotsman was back on the line. 'Call me Simon, Alfred –'

'Call me Spencer, Simon.'

That was better.

Because I had both sounded authoritative and moved to get us away from all that *Alfred* nonsense. Being christened Alfred had been one of several problems that I'd had to deal with since childhood. I'd become a good runner at an early age and a comedian when my legs failed me and Simon continued. I imagined he felt chastened but had to admit that he hid it well. 'Very well, Spencer. Mr Adam Reid; you know him?'

Everyone knew *of* Adam Reid but very few people knew him so that ranked as another stupid question. 'I know who he is.'

'Quite,' said Simon. 'Did you know he's a person of interest, has been under investigation for some time, Special Branch and now MI5?'

This was all new. I shook my head then verbalised my response for the benefit of the phone. 'No.'

Perhaps I should humour the idiot. I had to get the balance right – no need to choke a story off if there was one there. But if this was some bastard from the office on a wind up I had to maintain the right degree of scepticism. 'Would you care to tell me a little more?'

'It's true,' said Simon. He didn't sound like a lunatic. But that meant precious little. Perhaps he was a functioning imbecile? Some bug-eyed moron with his hand down his pants for all I knew. He went on. 'I can get you in to see him but the stories, the cosmetic surgery, the experiments, his attitude towards race? They're based on truth.'

Rubbish?

Quite probably but new rubbish at least; I'd heard talk of surgery but I hadn't heard anything about experiments and there had never been a racial angle. Adam Reid had enemies with agendas, of course. You didn't get to become a zillionaire without annoying someone, somewhere but it was the racism line that had caught my ear, there could be a scandal here.

But even sopping wet and dripping I knew that if this guy was a crank then slinging that kind of mud could end my career. Safest to put the phone down and get back in the shower but what if it there was something in it?

'What was that about race?'

'We'll get to that, Spencer,' said Simon. 'Ask him about Project Onesius.'

'Onesius?'

'Ask him about his human subjects.'

'Subjects?'

I was doing a convincing bewildered but Simon didn't seem to notice. He went on. 'Ask him about Colombia. Ask him about the experiments.'

'The fuck?'

'Don't swear, Spencer. I can get you into one of his company meetings. He's got one at his research centre in Ranulfskelf next week. Some sort of corporate love-fest and I can get Flanagan over, the detective who investigated Adam's little problem in New York.'

It had been more than a little problem. 'Slow down,' I said.

Simon ignored me. He clearly had my measure. 'And listen to this.'

'Wait,' I said.

No reply.

I wiped a few more drops from my chin and saw that the water was pooling where it had dripped from my elbow. A series of clicks on the line, the tell-tale hiss of a tape and something like crockery being moved kept me interested enough to stand there in my growing puddle and I pictured a breakfast table. Perhaps a meeting over coffee and then a voice, 'I told you.'

I strained to listen. The voice sounded familiar.

'There was never any doubt.'

A humourless chuckle; it was Adam Reid.

'It was the fucking Africans...'

Two
11:58 – Tuesday 8th June
Ranulfskelf Hall and Safari Park, North Yorkshire, England

I slipped the car into second and gunned the engine as I came out of the bend. The vehicle responded well. Trees shot past to my right and left and I grinned, I was having fun.

I could front up as the cynical journo again later but I was enjoying myself, I was free.

Well, sort of. Perhaps it wasn't freedom but what I did have were a couple of weeks to do my thing. I had my Press ID, a few quid in up front expenses and the promise of reimbursement beyond that so what could go wrong?

Only the sheep and cows were treated to the sight of a happy hack as I shot through the Yorkshire countryside and fortunately no flies made it into my mouth. I slipped the car into third and then second as I hit the curve and it tightened. The tyres dragged a bit of gravel an inch or two off line, just enough to give me a buzz.

The car was a bit of a weakness and I'd be quick to pick up on it in someone else, of course. I'd see it as the vanity that it was but the Porsche, admittedly only an entry-level Boxster, was a dream to drive. It might not be in the same league as some other motors coming out of Stuttgart but it was good enough for me and, with the hood down and the engine roaring, I could barely make out the wittering of the Satnav as I passed through a section of sunken road, dry-stone walls either side of me obscuring the fields from view.

Another curve tightened into a bend. Then it tightened further and there was a tractor up ahead. But I was outside and past it before I had time to worry about whether the stone walls would rip my doors off and then the road widened, the threatening limestone walls receded to make room for a grass verge and the village came into view, Ranulfskelf.

One road in and one road out. Mentioned in the Doomsday Book, the village was probably somewhat bigger then than it was now but otherwise not much had changed. It was ringed by the same hills on three sides that it had been a thousand years ago and I hit the brakes as I saw a couple of speed-bumps looming up. There was a satisfying crunch of gravel as I pulled over by what I took to be the village green.

I killed the ignition and leaned back into the seat. The Satnav told me that I'd reached my destination but I'd already worked that out for myself. I turned that off as well and had a bit of a look around as the engine pinged and clicked and began to cool.

I nodded. Hoped I didn't look like too big an idiot and I smiled. I'd been writing pappy prose for a middling rag for long enough. It was time for me to step up and get stuck into something really worthwhile.

**

'OK, give me the bones of it,' Sophie Marchant, Business Editor and my boss's boss had said on Friday when I'd pitched the story to her.

I'd put a proposal to her in an email earlier in the day.

And she was seeing me so there was a good chance that she was sold on the idea. But she would still want to see if I had done my homework though I doubted I could tell her anything she didn't already know at this stage. 'Where would you like me to start?'

Sophie peered at me over the rims of her half-moon glasses.

I was sure she didn't need them. They were a part of her act and so was her positioning. I was standing and she was seated.

She gave me her *I eat people like you for breakfast* smile. 'The beginning would be nice, Spencer.'

I smiled back. 'Course, Soph.

Ms Marchant didn't like being called Soph. Story was that she'd head-butted a former male colleague at a party for shortening her name. Of course he'd been clawing at her pants at the time but the newsroom preferred to believe that the attack had been provoked by the name calling and, looking at Sophie, all hard edges and testosterone, I was glad that she was seated.

And there was a desk between us and the door was unlocked and she was in heels and if it came to it I could tip a filing cabinet in front of her but Sophie's smile didn't waver. She was waiting for me to speak.

'Mr Adam Reid,' I said.

I let the silence build but misjudged it and she was in. 'Nice start, Spencer. Mr Adam Reid. No mistakes so far.'

'Stories about him sell papers,' I said. Sophie was older than me but not by much. Still, it wouldn't be wise to try to teach her to suck eggs. And I wasn't going to underestimate her. I'd stick to the truth but keep the possible racism angle to myself. 'People will pay to read about sex, violence and money. We're coming from the money angle. There's the least risk there. It's what we do but I want to look into the other angles and need to do the work to bottom them out.'

Sophie's eyes didn't leave mine. She raised her eyebrows. 'Go on.'

'And if we can unearth anything else, the story will cross over,' I said and I was quite proud of the 'we' bit. I was being inclusive. 'He's not some drug-addled rock star but this could be better.'

'I'm interested,' said Sophie. 'It's got potential. Tell me about Simon.'

Got potential? I took that as an encouragement, warmed to my theme. 'Nor is Adam a bent politician but he's top ten on the rich list, his money will be what people are interested in –'

Sophie made an irritated sort of gesture and cut me off. 'I said Simon, Spencer.'

I'd previously decided that honesty was amongst the best two or three policies with regard to Simon. 'I don't know him well.'

Sophie's nose twitched. She scented blood. 'How well is 'not well'?'

'Never met him,' I said. There was no dodging that and I went on. 'Spoken to him on the phone once but he's got the tapes. He says he'll get Flanagan over from the States, New York detective...'

'Never met him,' said Sophie. She looked up at me again. 'I want evidence that he can deliver something. And if Simon proves to be a dud I want you back behind your desk immediately so best you get him to deliver something. Get the tape, see Flanagan. Just get something up front. Make sure this isn't all a waste of time, Spencer. Is that clear?'

'As crystal,' I said.

'Because you have previous here,' Sophie went on. Her eyes bored into me and I felt my blood run cold. 'We've been here before. Sure, you want a scalp but stick to the facts.'

'Of course,' I said. I tried to hold her eye, but had to glance away. Another reminder that I shouldn't take up poker as a career because she was right, I had made a couple of attempts on Adam Reid before. They'd been relatively mild, diary pieces but I could see how they might have come across as borderline spiteful. Still, the fact that I was here and in Sophie's office meant that she was taking me seriously. She was minded to invest a few days of my time on the possibility that Simon was legit. So perhaps a little bit of confidence was justified and I continued with that in mind. 'Adam Reid's a sensation. He's got an almost religious following. Flunkies are attracted to him like a cloud of flies –'

'To shit,' said Sophie. I think that was a yellow card. 'I know that but I asked for the facts. Save the flowery prose because I get it, I really do. If we ran it, and I hope you heard the word 'if' in there, how would it pan out?'

'I was thinking a serialisation,' I said and waited for the reaction. I was actually thinking about the book that might follow a serialisation. I'd use the newspaper to front run and ride shotgun re any potential litigation re defamation etc.

But that might have shown on my face. Sophie smirked and I wondered if she could see right through me. She would sooner suck on a turd than print something that put her in court opposite a litigious billionaire. She was planning something but I pushed on. 'A day in the life and then segue it back somehow, a reminder of where he came from.'

Sophie made a circular motion with her finger and I continued. 'Then some straightforward chronological copy. Get the basics straight and add the other stuff if we can get it past the lawyers –'

'Other stuff? There is no 'other stuff' at the moment, Spencer. And there won't be until we can prove it...'

'We've got the tape –'

'We don't have the tape,' said Sophie and she was right. 'And it could be bollocks anyway, remember the Hitler diaries? Fifteen year old on a four hundred quid laptop can mix anything you want on a tape-deck or whatever the hell it is kids use these days so just give me the timeline.'

'Father an unstable killer –

'That's the middle, Spencer,' said Sophie. 'We do the day-in-the-life then the childhood, right?'

'I nodded. 'Adam Reid, born in England. Early years in Yorkshire.'

'Parents?'

'Father Professor Sir George Reid. Mother Elizabeth Reid. Adam was their only child, was borne to them late in life. Father around fifty and mother a few years younger. The family moved to the US before Adam started school. They died when he was fifteen.'

'Ah yes,' said Sophie. 'Very unfortunate.'

'Father an unstable murderer. Bumped off Mrs R then offed himself and Adam found the bodies.' I paused. I'd pushed it already and didn't know Sophie well enough to take too many liberties. The boy must have been deeply affected by the deaths and they orphaned him and that was something of a problem editorially if I was going to do a critical piece but one look at Sophie told me that she knew all that. She made the annoying little circular motion again. 'Did he try to revive his parents?

How did he appear to the police? How did he cope, did it spur him on, that sort of stuff.'

I'd been expecting an interruption. I didn't get one and so continued. 'And then did he shut down? Was he haunted by feelings of guilt? Could he have prevented what happened and was it something he'd done or failed to do that sparked the whole thing?'

I stopped but Sophie was still letting me run with it. I took it as a good sign. She didn't look to be asleep so I continued. 'After the deaths he came back to England. The aunt in Yorkshire squirrelled him away and kept him out of sight. Journalists and authors, stockbrokers you name it have been up to check it out but getting through to her is impossible. Now the old bird lives on his estate, Ranulfskelf, and she's as likely to shoot you as speak to you.'

'OK, I can fill in the gaps. Back to the timeline?'

'He didn't attend schools in England, didn't take his GCSEs. He simply didn't bother. Never confirmed but never denied that he got five straight As at A-Level. His Physics paper was said to have been flawless.

'Not good but flawless,' I said. 'Perfect.' I paused both for effect and because there were some things that I didn't need to say. Stick in the word genius every now and again, for example. And I didn't mention the allegations of cheating. I was a realist. Adam was too powerful to be a cheat. Defaming a billionaire was a definite no-go area. It could be a retirement-precipitating event but Sophie seemed to be with me.

'Yes,' she said and smiled. She seemed to have been reading my mind. 'You get that one wrong Spencer and you'll be spending the next decade in the post room.'

And if we both get that one wrong Sophie then we'll both be spending the next decade in the post room. I kept that one to myself as I didn't want her vaulting the desk and butting me with that hard-looking head of hers. 'Of course,' I said. 'Anyway Cambridge is thought to have made an approach but he wouldn't attend lectures although he was happy to take the exams.

'We'll be careful with what's provable but some say that he did sit them but never received his degree. Didn't have the rounded experience of being an undergraduate, they said.'

'Yes, he's got balls,' said Sophie.

So do you, I thought.

I raised my hand to my mouth and Sophie's eyes tracked the movement. 'He was different from an early age.'

'Murder and suicide will do that to you,' said Sophie.

She looked away from me.

She was slightly embarrassed and I pulled at my lip, felt the warmth.

It was a habit I was trying to break but it was a tough one because of the birthmark; the port-wine stain, the abnormal collection of dilated blood vessels under the skin that had shaped me. It had been a permanent eye-magnet.

It had made me different and it still had a hold on me. Forming a triangle between my lip, my left eye and my ear it was a deep purple. It wasn't a good look. It had singled me out and had made me different.

It both attracted and repelled and, in my darker moments, I had considered myself a freak. Nevertheless, I had left it for years and it had only been recently that I had begun treatment to remove it or to at least to reduce its size and intensity.

Not that it had ever threatened my eyesight or my hearing or anything that really mattered. It was a cosmetic disability, they said. Whatever that meant. I could have lived with it but it had touched me in every possible way.

Derision in the playground and pity from my mother's friends. Sly looks from the likes of Sophie and the journalist-with-a-face-for-radio jokes that I knew were being made behind my back. The whole nine yards but I'd taken the plunge and had begun a course of pulsed-dye laser treatment and it was working.

I had been suffering from psychological morbidity, they said.

Funny that. I'd thought I had a larger-than-normal birthmark but they were right. The mental scarring caused by disfigurement was real and I'd been a fool to wait so long to do anything about it and my hand rose to my face once more.

I felt Sophie's eyes follow it and I coughed. I knew I'd been off on one and I returned to the subject. 'There are suggestions that he visited Philadelphia – ...'

'Suggestions?'

'Yes,' I said. That was a fair call. 'We'll be careful with what we can prove but it's believed that he visited the US to play chess. He allegedly forced IBM's Deep Blue into a series of drawn matches.

'Then he hit pay-dirt,' I said and Sophie nodded her approval. 'He was seventeen. Not legally old enough to hold stocks and shares in his own name but he invested through his aunt.'

'Proof, Spencer.'

I didn't reply. Sophie was beginning to irritate me. 'He's thought to have developed a programme that arbitraged between globally traded stocks and bonds. I'll add detail in a boxed article but it hedged currencies and took out a tiny but virtually risk-free profit across tens of thousands of transactions.

'He consistently made money. It must have been down to skill, luck or illicit means and it wasn't luck.' I held my hand up and waved down the half-objection. 'Standard line is the man's a genius and his company, Cytokine Capital made millions.'

Yes, millions and then tens of millions and then hundreds of millions of pounds, dollars, Euros, you mention it I thought.

The fund charged investors a fee of 2% per annum just to lodge money with it. It also took an additional 20% of any out-performance. Standard hedge-fund stuff but with a staff of less than a dozen, Adam made a fortune.

The size of the fund was never disclosed but it was rumoured at around £3bn. So it was bringing in the teenaged Adam some sixty million pounds a year in management fees and perhaps five times that much as a performance kicker. 'He cleared perhaps a quarter of billion personally in the fund's first year,' I said.

A quarter of a billion pounds.

It was a few short words strung together. Five grand sounded similar but it wasn't in the least bit the same because a quarter of a billion pounds was money on a grand scale.

Fill a suitcase with ten-pound notes. Then fill a security van with suitcases and you would still be nowhere near. In a year the boy had cleared the value of a thousand decent houses and it took your breath away.

'The fund sold in the UK as well as in North America, the Middle East and Russia. In year two he tapped China and then he closed the funds to new money.

'The fund is still in operation but Adam changed direction. He put his shares in the investment business into trust. It's throwing off tens of millions every year but Adam moved into science –'

'Followed his father,' said Sophie.

OK so I wasn't telling her anything she didn't know. 'Yes, microbiology. Disappeared from view for a year or two. Was written off as a crank. Nothing more than a weird punk who couldn't even finish his degree.'

Again I raised my hand to my face. My lip was getting warmer. I continued. 'He may have worked through proxies. Needed big names to attach to his work but he created Zylagene and Zylapharm. Genetic research and exploitation companies respectively and he brought them to the UK stock market as conjoined or twinned stocks around four years ago.

'I know you know about the twins,' I said but Sophie gave me her 'indulge me' gesture so I filled in the gaps. 'He initially couldn't find a broker. The companies were too esoteric. The financial press got a kick out of his apparent failure at the time and even his would-be advisers told him not to go for an Initial Public Offering but he pushed ahead.

'He had made concessions. Insisted the two companies remain

twinned for a minimum of five years but committed not to sell any shares himself during that period so he would be effectively locked in to four fifths of his holding. With those assurances he eventually secured advisors and the shares were listed.

'Came to the market at 16p and private investors liked them. They opened at 45p and closed over 50p on their first day. No more movement but a bit of two-way trade developed later that first week. Some investors bailed out but they continued to rise and, a month after flotation, they broke a pound mark and then the hedge funds got stuck in.

'The shares had momentum and speculators drove the price further. The chat rooms were alive with gossip and then came the story in The Digest of Molecular Biology...'

'The DMB,' said Sophie. 'Go on.'

The DMB, fuck yeah. We all know about the DMB, Soph. At least we do now. I continued. 'The shares had been listed for six weeks. No-one had heard of the DMB at the time and when it did start to have an influence, they blamed the hedge funds for planting stories but they were genuine. The journal knew its stuff.

'The technical jargon didn't make it very user-friendly. It was no-words-of-less-than-four-syllable-type of stuff but there were follow-up articles and then we got it, we really got it.

'Put what Zylagene had achieved in simple words and it was a real earthmover. The company had made a quantum leap. It had moved our understanding of cell structure to a new level.'

Sophie's eyes seemed glazed. We all had our memories as to what we had done or should have done in those heady early days but I'd been more focused than many others and had bought a few quid's worth shares at just over a pound each.

I hadn't breached any rules and the boffins were insistent, this was something special. There was more knowledgeable buying. A couple more articles and then the shares flew.

They broke two pounds almost immediately and I had nearly

doubled my money. Those in from the start had made twelve-times theirs and the City woke up.

I'd feared they would fall on the next day. I would have sold if I'd been in early enough but I didn't sell and they didn't fall and after holding steady for a couple of hours in the morning they moved higher and finished the day at just shy of five pounds, they had doubled again.

That meant that I'd made more money in a couple of days than I'd made in all of my other stock market forays combined. And I had to pose myself the question as to whether I would feel worse if I didn't sell the shares and they halved or if I did sell them and they rose by fifty percent?

It was a tough call.

And it was a Friday just to prolong the agony but I'd quadrupled my money, had made more than thirty grand. I was staring at a decent motor and a holiday but the fear of selling too early was what had really kept me awake nights.

Sunday dragged. The Press was mixed. Was mulling whether to ride it or take profits but they were only hacks. They knew no more than I did but my nerves failed me and I sold at the opening on Monday morning.

And I wasn't alone. From the grimace on Sophie's face she might have been with me but with hindsight it was clear that the decision to sell had been a bad one.

Of course I knew that now but I returned to my story. 'Anyway,' I said and paused to make sure that Sophie was with me again. 'There were interviews. The press got behind the Boy Wonder and the shares broke a fiver but wobbled after the weekend. Held steady for a couple of hours but then the sellers disappeared and they doubled again on the Monday.'

I think Sophie was biting the inside of her cheek and it made me feel a little better. If I said the next bit quickly enough it might not hurt. 'They closed at ten quid odd the Monday and doubled again on the Tuesday. They became the only UK listed shares of any size to double on four consecutive trading days and Adam Reid was a Sterling billionaire.'

And I had my thirty thou, of course. My little dabble had bought me the Porsche but Adam, still a teenager at the time and little more than half my age, had made forty thousand times as much as I had and he had made much more since.

Sophie seemed to be re-running the *could haves* and *should haves* herself and I wrapped it up. 'At that point, Reid had his investment in Cytokine and had made more than a billion quid in Zylagene and Zylapharm. It took the shares more than three years to double again and they're around forty quid a share as we speak.'

Three
12:35 – Tuesday 8th June
Ranulfskelf Hall and Safari Park, North Yorkshire, England

'What do you mean I'm not on the list?' I said it with what dignity I could muster.

But that wasn't a lot and I knew I was reddening. I could feel the eyes of the others in the queue in front of the pillared stately home on me and I turned my back on their accusing stares. This had to be the critical diary pieces that I'd written coming back to haunt me. Either that or Simon had taken me for a fool. And that would be worse because I'd sugar coated his story for Sophie and she'd signed me off but if Simon wasn't there for me today, then I had very little.

His number had been blocked.

I couldn't ring him back and I was up here in Yorkshire on trust and that might have been misplaced. He'd said that my name would be left at the door. Said I'd have no problem gaining access and I stuck my chin out. 'Check it again please, there must be some mistake.'

It sounded lame. I was pleading already and this guy, in his thirties and tall, heavily built and with what would have been an impressively large nose but for the fact that it had been flattened and pushed back onto his cheek by some traumatic event earlier in his life, was blocking my way in no uncertain manner.

I looked again at his ruined nose and winced in sympathy. I wasn't going to call him Nosey to his face but that's who he was to me. Maybe I was not the man to talk but it was his defining feature and his smart hat and his uniform and his shiny buttons and whatnot didn't do much to distract the eye.

I caught his eye and tried to smile.

I was beginning to think that he'd made his mind up that I wasn't going to get past him but he seemed happy enough to humour me. He ran his finger for a third time down some gold-lettered list laid out on cardboard so thick that it stopped just this side of being reclassified as a plank of wood.

And he seemed to be taking his time. Now that the queue was moving and slowly filing into the building he seemed more than prepared to keep me standing here like some sort of exhibit but after what seemed like an age he raised his eyes and shook his head. 'I'm afraid there must have been some sort of misunderstanding. There's no Alfred Beck on our list.'

'Try Spencer Beck...'

'There are no Becks at all.'

'But Simon assured me...'

'Simon who?' said Nosey. His voice had hardened. His goodwill was draining away as the queue around us diminished and I couldn't meet his eye.

'I don't know.'

Nosey pursed his lips. 'I'm afraid I'm going to have to ask you to leave.'

He reached up and was about to put his hand on my shoulder but that was too much and I took a step backwards. I didn't want to be pushed around in front of whoever the hell was currently observing my predicament. 'You're right,' I said. 'Just a misunderstanding. Please have my car brought around and I'll be gone.'

Nosey seemed to relax. But he didn't leave my side and just as the last of the great Mr Reid's guests filed into the hall the Boxster swept around the side of the building and skewed to a halt on the gravel in front of us.

A marshal, a uniform with less braid got out and shared what looked like a smirk with Nosey before handing him the keys. The metal part of the key was housed in a solid rubber and metal fob and Nosey sprung it, held the glinting metal to the light.

He smiled and lowered his hand. He held the key against the driver's door of the Boxster and slowly gouged a three foot long furrow across it. I think I was in shock but his eyes never left mine as he dropped the keys onto the gravel and kicked them into the grass. 'Have a nice day, Mr Beck.'

**

I let the Porsche's engine idle and took a deep breath. I was on the public highway again, off Adam's property. But only just and my hand was shaking on the wheel and I had to admit it, righteous outrage and all the rest to one side, Nosey had creeped me out.

It was natural enough I told myself. There was an air of menace about the man and I wasn't a fighter. And he'd had backup but he'd left the confrontation with a grin on his face and I'd left it with a damaged motor. That put me one down and I didn't feel happy.

I felt diminished and humiliated and Simon had failed me. True I'd been complicit but Simon had said that entry had been arranged and Adam did seem to be raising his profile, was building up to something.

This was the third of three such meetings and the company was hosting its Annual General Meeting in Cambridge next week. It might even be inviting non-shareholders and there would be another meeting in New York so maybe Reid did need the City, and the journalists who catered for it, more than he had before. He could be looking to raise money or to make an acquisition but his staff hadn't been too pleased to see me, had they?

Still, maybe the trip didn't have to be a total write-off. I might not relish a fist-fight but I was fearless with a pen in my hand and I could work some of this into any piece I was going to write. I could allude to a dark side not least because it was true and I waited for my breathing to steady. I took out my iPhone and fumbled it on to record.

'Paranoid,' I said. The story was forming and re-forming in my mind. But harsh words could be therapeutic and I had to get the poison out because it wouldn't make it into print and I lifted the IPhone to my mouth again. 'Reclusive. Delusional and vicious, a manipulative, racist bastard –'

I rubbed my eyes hard and tried to clear my head. I was out of sight of the Hall, screened by the gently curving avenue of lime trees that lined the drive. The huge wrought iron gates that had automatically closed behind me had expelled me like so much waste and I hit record again. 'Ranulfskelf Hall, sixteen hundred acres. Gardens, labs, safari park and model farm.'

I thought back to what I'd read and sought to meld it with what I could see now. 'Four hundred full time staff. A few hundred seasonal workers. Hall cost six million and restored and expanded is worth perhaps sixty. Forty eight bedrooms. Forty seven more than me and Georgian, listed. Peacocks, fountains and liveried staff. Lavish entertainment. Meal for a thousand. Question; how many chickens, perhaps two hundred, weight of potatoes, number of eggs? Messianic and sparkly-eyed visitors. The worthy and the good bringing their sick to touch the hem of his cloak.'

I stopped recording.

I didn't feel too proud of myself. I was a gently trembling individual apparently muttering into his hand. I'd just have to remember the rest. The glimpses inside the Hall, the tapestries and what looked like several suits of armour, and I slipped the phone back in my pocket.

I nudged the Porsche into first and drove the couple of short miles back to the village of Ranulfskelf itself where I'd taken a room in the Crown. Rooms in nearby hotels had gone already because the discussions and presentations by Adam and his team were due to continue into the evening.

I'd considered driving straight back to London but now I was pleased to have the room as I wanted to work and, as the village signs flashed past me for the second time that day, I took the Boxster down to thirty-five and then pulled sharply into the car-park of the pub. I parked away from the overhanging trees and their accompanying piles of pigeon shit because, as with journalists, where pigeons shit once, they shit often.

**

The Crown managed to look both rural and dishevelled and clean and tidy at the same time and, as I plucked my overnight bag from the passenger seat and walked into the pub, it was pleasantly cool inside.

That's what thick stone walls did for you on a warm day but as my eyes adjusted slowly to the dim interior after the bright glare of the car park it seemed that the pub was deserted. As my vision improved however and some of the larger pieces of furniture became visible, it turned out that one of them was an elderly lady and that she was gracing me with an expectant smile.

I checked in and was given a couple of keys attached to a huge fob designed to deter the forgetful from taking them back home with them and I took the stairs to my room.

Room six was homely and was decorated in the car-boot style that I had imagined. The lampshades had a fifties look about them, old prints lined the wall and the bed was smothered by a layer of cushions. But there was a desk and, after turning the key in the lock, I placed the Porsche keys, my mobile and my wallet on top of the bedside cabinet, tossed my jacket onto the bed, I pulled my laptop from my overnight bag and gave the power button a gentle dig.

**

By 7.15pm, hunger was blunting my concentration and I had to eat. I saved my work, turned off the laptop and covered it as best I could beneath a jumble of clothes before leaving the room and locking the door behind me.

Downstairs there were a scattering of people in the bar. I'd heard a number of cars drawing up but these were mostly locals. The Zylagene crowd still wasn't back and perhaps the day hadn't been a total waste of time and money as I'd laid down almost four thousand words.

Impressive but it had been far too quick. It would be laced with gibberish and bile and would need a lot of work. But it had been therapeutic and if I could edit it later and there should be something worth saving.

I edged my way through the filling pub and walked out into the evening. The sun was a good four fingers above the hills to the west. Dusk was still hours away but I deserved a pint. There were a couple of other pubs in the village that looked attractive and I patted my pocket, checked that I had my wallet with me and the memory stick that I used to back up my work and headed up the gentle hill that defined the village.

**

Two hours later, with the smell of freshly cut grass on the air and the evening pleasantly warm, the midges yet to wake up, I left the Bay Horse.

It was the furthermost pub and nestled on the edge of the village. It had been comfortably busy for a mid-week night and I had unwound nicely, the log fire banked against the upcoming chill and the music complemented the dim and cosy interior rather than intruding upon it.

The pub had been host to a mixed crowd. No golfing pullovers and relatively few moustaches. A younger crowd and no Zylagene rejects but the odd suit dotted around here and there and I glanced at my watch, congratulated myself on making the decision to leave.

I'd have liked to have stayed longer but four pints and it might have been five was enough. I was feeling light-headed and I had a job to do. I wanted to be out of here before six in the morning so I walked the few steps from the pub's door to the pavement proper with a sense of purpose but wham, I was flat on my back.

Jogger, shit.

And he was on the deck too but he was moving more quickly than I was. He was back on his feet before me and I felt a hand under my arm, warm breath on my face and a mumbled apology once I was on my feet.

'It's OK,' I said. I think I might have even apologised myself.

'No, no it was my fault,' said the man and I looked at him for the first time. Forties with a full head of grey hair. Grey sweat shirt, grey trousers. He stooped, picking something from the ground.

He held it out towards me and I took back my wallet. I nodded my thanks and flipped the wallet open. Bit of cash and the cards were still there. Nothing appeared to have spilled out.

'Sure you're OK?' said the man.

His eyes moved to the pub sign hanging over my head and he wrinkled his nose. Yes, I'd had a drink. But I wasn't drunk. I was the innocent party here but I managed a half-smile. 'Yes, I'm fine.'

The jogger raised his head and regarded me strangely before turning and continuing down the hill into the village. He didn't look back and I brushed what dust and grass I could from my trousers then blinked hard. I picked out the Crown's illuminated sign further down the hill. It'd been a long day and I set off down the slope. It was time for bed but then I saw the car.

Rear end pointing up the hill towards me it wasn't just any old car, it was a Boxster like mine and I felt a flush of pride. It was schoolboy stuff but I squinted against the sodium lighting and checked the registration number. The shock stopped me in my tracks because I didn't just have one of those cars, I had that car.

It was mine. My stomach fluttered and I tried to take stock. I'd left the car in the car park at the Crown. I knew I had but if someone had pinched it why had they dumped it only a couple of hundred yards away?

Either I was wrong or a joy rider had taken it and stopped to buy some cigarettes or to have a drink in which case the bastard could come out at any moment and I quickened my step and winced as I registered the deep scratch that now traced a path down its left side but then it came to me.

Nosey's little gift had been on the driver's door, the right side of the car. I ran around the front of the motor and into the road. Checked the driver's door and there it was, the nasty gouge. I raised my hands and must have looked as though I was measuring a fish. I dropped my hands to my side, returned to the pavement.

Some utter shit must have stolen the car and damaged it and now they'd dumped it here. Concerns regarding my insurance flashed through my mind. A central London address was bad news at the best of times but I would be sunk if I lost my no-claims; my costs would rocket.

I had left my car keys on the bedside table but I patted my pocket nonetheless. Just a habit but there was a faint jingling and I reached in and somehow lifted out my keys. I stared at them for a moment and then pressed the remote. The locks popped and I opened the door and braced myself before leaning in.

No obvious damage to the inside. I felt a wave of relief and I climbed into the car, sat down. It was only a couple minutes back to the Crown but, no. That wouldn't be a good idea and I swung my legs out of the car, pulled on the wheel to get a bit of leverage and fell back again. Two solid-looking legs were blocking my exit.

The jogger? He must have either lost something or may have found something else of mine. I gave the legs a second or two to get out of the way but they didn't and I leaned over and craned my neck, followed them up to a large, uniformed body. It was a police officer.

Face like death and I didn't know whether to laugh or cry so I made do with a lame grin but the officer, a mature man of perhaps fifty, didn't smile back. 'Good evening, sir.'

'Good evening officer,' I said. I killed the smile but felt my eyelids droop as I struggled to focus. I felt nervous as I always did when talking to the law. It was bad enough interviewing the buggers and talking to them on my own turf but this one, frowning at me and tilting his head, was doing nothing for my digestion. His nose twitched and he sniffed the night air.

I felt a dread build in me and heard the words before they left the police officer's. 'Have you been drinking, sir?'

Four
23:50 – Wednesday 9th June
Northern Line, North London

The tube train was noisy, unpleasant and crowded. It was nearly midnight and I needed the day to end. I knew that, like every other day, it would last for 24 hours but this one was right up there as one of the worst of my life because I'd been screwed.

The keys hadn't put themselves in my pocket. And the car hadn't adorned itself twice with scratches and then transported itself up a hill into the bargain. No, I'd been sent a message and now I was in the mire in more ways than one.

Of course, the policeman had smiled tolerantly when I'd said I hadn't driven the car. I hadn't scraped it when trying to park but whether he believed me or not was of little consequence as I'd been in the vehicle, the keys in the ignition and I'd been banged to rights. Justice didn't come into it. I'd been drunk in charge and I looked around the swaying carriage of the tube train and realised that this was something that I was going to have to get used to.

The roadside breathalyser had been a formality.

And then I'd failed the test back at the police station and had spent the best part of last night in some rotten little police cell in Hexforth, the nearest market town to Ranulfskelf and then they'd chucked me out as soon as I blew below the legal limit.

It had been getting light. Was around 3.30am and they'd left me to make my own way back to Ranulfskelf but then the Porsche died on me. No-one had slashed its tyres or had a go at it with a sledgehammer and, given the kind of day that I'd had perhaps I should have been grateful for that small mercy but the bloody thing hadn't started.

In fact it hadn't even managed to fart or cough and I'd had to book it into some local sawbones of an auto shop where they'd sucked their cheeks and scratched their heads for hours before saying that they needed to keep it a couple of days and for that I read a fortnight, perhaps a month.

I'd taken the train back down to London. And now here I was on the tube with a bunch of drunks and I managed a shake of my head as we rattled into Camden Town and the couple opposite me roused themselves and struggled to focus on where they were.

They stood up and left the carriage. They looked as though they'd knocked back more this evening than I had in total in the last seven days but I tried to remain sanguine. The setback was in the past, the legal ramifications were in the future and that just left the present and my current task was all about getting home and to bed without further incident.

So keep it in perspective, Spencer. No-one died. And it might even make for an amusing anecdote once the mental trauma had subsided. I could refer to it in the column. Say that it had happened to a friend of a friend but not just yet. It was too raw and I stood up and left the carriage for the crowded platform.

I allowed myself to be carried with the flow and it was a relief to find myself above ground. I tucked my overnight case into my side and walked on, my head down.

I didn't want to see anybody and I certainly didn't want to be seen. I'd slept in my clothes and didn't look my best but shortly Fermanagh Road, home to the rather grandly named Fermanagh Mansions, the 'sixties block where I had my flat, opened up ahead of me and I was home. Fumbling for my keys as I approached the building, I negotiated the lock and took the stairs.

I didn't fancy the lift. It was only four stops on the tube from King's Cross but I'd had enough of confined spaces. I reached my flat and I found myself examining the lock and what was all that about?

It was foolish. Something I'd never done before. I was getting paranoid. I shook my head and slipped the key into the lock and opened the door but didn't walk in. Instead I flicked on the light and waited a second or two but the flat's small hallway and beyond it the unkempt living room stared back at me blankly.

I breathed again and laughed out loud. It broke the silence. Sure, the flat looked as though it had been ransacked but then again, it always did as I wasn't the world's tidiest person. Sundry clutter competed for space on every level surface. I put down the case and pushed it against the wall with my foot. I locked the door behind me and kicked off my shoes.

That was a blessed relief and I put my hand on the wall by the side of the mirror and took a deep breath. I rubbed my eyes. Opened them and blinked away the dancing spots and allowed myself a smile.

I looked like a filthy stop-out and that's pretty much what I was. I hadn't slept for more than a couple of hours in the cold cell. Bags under my eyes, two days' worth of stubble and clothes creased to fuck but I was what I was and I tried to take stock.

Could I really have been targeted or was I the victim of a bizarre set of circumstances? I walked to the fridge and took out a Bitburger and began my traditional search for a bottle opener. There were plenty lying around. It was just a question of finding the one that was the least well-hidden and today's lucky winner was one fashioned out of a Father Christmas. I opened the bottle. Sat down heavily and took a mouthful and noted the flashing red light on my answer-phone.

Simon? He certainly owed me a call but it was probably double glazing or the chance to switch broadband suppliers. Or perhaps the newspaper chasing me up and reminding me of some deadline or another or asking me to ring in for some last minute edits. But they would have caught me on my mobile. I took another mouthful of beer, rose to my feet and walked the few steps to the machine.

Three messages.

A couple of suits needed picking up from the dry-cleaners. Did I want to subscribe to a lifestyle magazine targeting the thirty-something man and inevitably, there it was. I was one of the few people in a London home to be singled out for a free double-glazing survey. Life in the fast lane. I hit erase. The beer was going down nicely and there were a couple more in the fridge but then the phone rang.

The display told me we were 15 minutes into the small hours of Thursday morning and I picked up the handset. 'Beck.'

'There's a mobile telephone taped under your sink.'

'Simon?'

'Correct.'

I held the phone away from my head and looked at it. 'What the fuck's going on, Simon?'

'You heard me,' said Simon. His voice was calm and very matter-of-fact. 'Get a couple of hundred metres away from your flat and ring stored number twenty-six. Do you understand?'

'Simon, you've got to tell me –'

'Do you understand?'

'Yes.'

The line went dead and I looked at the handset. His number had been blocked so there was no ringing him back but it was what he had said that disturbed me; that he had broken into my flat. I glanced around but knew that he couldn't still be here as the shower room door was standing wide open and I'd been in each of the rooms. I gave the telephone my most serious frown and replaced it on its cradle.

This was a wind up. It had to be. Nonetheless, I walked into the kitchen, crossed to the sink and bent down.

There was nothing visible underneath and I reached behind the u-bend and the pipes that led from the plughole. Some slimy filth but otherwise nothing and I rose to my feet, tore off some kitchen roll and wiped my hand.

This was stupid. Of course there was nothing taped under the kitchen sink. Simon was some nut job who'd managed to put me in an embarrassing position with the police and my editor. Nothing more and I looked around the flat, registered the open shower room door. I crossed over to it and looked at the small wash hand basin.

Again nothing to see but I stretched out my hand. The rough plaster behind the sink's u-bend rubbed against my knuckles. Still nothing but then sticky tape and something strapped to the underside of the basin. I took a hold of it, tore it down and stood up.

It was a phone; a Nokia. I wasn't a mobile phone junkie so the fact that I didn't recognise the model meant nothing. It was a little dirty but otherwise it looked new. I stripped off the tape and noticed that the phone was already switched on.

The battery was fully charged so what now?

The events of the past few days formed into an unpleasant slide-show in my head. Mysterious phone calls. Suited thugs. Overactive joggers. Scratched and stolen motor vehicles and the night in the cells and I knew that I was at a crossroads.

I could bin the phone, turn my back on the whole thing and move on. But as a journalist that wasn't really an option so what else, take it to the police and tell them the flat had been broken into?

I'd had enough of coppers for the time being. I looked back at the phone, weighed it in my hand. It seemed ordinary enough. The blue screen blinked at me and I scrolled through the saved numbers to number twenty-six. An eleven-digit number suggested the UK and the 07 prefix meant a mobile.

It would be some pay as you go effort, effectively untraceable meaning that the police would have nothing to go on even if I went to them immediately. Instead, I slipped the phone into my coat pocket and reached for my shoes.

I had to make the call but, even by a journalist's standards, this cloak and dagger stuff was getting a bit tiresome. Simon had dropped MI5 into the conversation as though he was a bit-part player in a Bond film but the fact that he'd broken into my flat suggested he was serious.

**

Outside the building much of the traffic had melted away. I set off towards the tube station. It would be closed but walking towards something added purpose and seemed more sensible than counting out a couple of hundred paces at random.

I reached the tube. I had a quick look around and took the phone from my pocket. I felt foolish but scrolled to number twenty-six and hit call. The telephone was answered almost before it had rung. 'An interesting day?'

I was determined to remain calm. 'That's one way of describing it.'

I could feel the smile at the other end of the phone before Simon spoke again. 'The orders came from Adam Reid himself,' he said. 'Bump you out of line. Screw your car, spike your drinks and set you up with the police. Discredit you ahead of any story you might write, you get the picture?'

The silence lengthened and I felt obliged to end it. 'You have any evidence?'

'Reid has touched your life.'

I needed more and wasn't in a mood to ask for it politely. 'The fuck does that mean, Simon?'

'Flanagan's coming over,' said Simon. 'He'll be with you Friday.'

Five
09:10 – Friday 11th June
Heathrow Airport, West London, England

There were probably worse places in the world but I couldn't think of many and I cursed myself for a fool because I was dancing to Simon's tune and I hated crowds.

Yet here I was, hemmed in with all of these other people like cattle in the busiest international airport in the world. On the busiest day of the week, so how did that work?

I closed my eyes, rubbed them hard. This was just the pits but then something bumped into my leg. Childish laughter and the slop of something hitting the floor. Pink flecks of what looked like yoghurt or ice-cream on my shoes and the bottom of my trousers and then a trolley struck me full on the ankle.

I winced. I tried to imagine myself somewhere else. Somewhere away from toddlers and their yoghurt but there was no getting away from it, I was in the arrivals hall because I was a journalist. Simon had lit my fuse and had given me a New York number and what could I do other than ring it?

The number looked credible.

New York was 212 and it was a matter of record that a Daniel Flanagan had been one of the detectives on the scene when Adam's parents had died. Simon's phone didn't appear to have been blocked for international calls. I'd been tempted to use it but didn't want to run the battery down so I'd rung from the flat.

More expense but Flanagan had sounded the part. Distracted, listening to a ball game in the background, he confirmed that he had spoken to Simon. And he knew about the meetings on Monday and he had agreed to come to London provided I paid for his tickets and my hand moved to my wallet.

It was feeling light already as much of my upfront expense money had already gone on car repairs. Getting the money back from the paper would have to wait but ex-detective Daniel Flanagan was booked on flight AA132, the 9.30pm American Airlines out of JFK, scheduled to land at 9.25am. It had made time in flight and was probably already on the ground and so I gave the packed arrivals hall another once over.

It made for quite a sight this confused ant hill of humanity.

A wall to wall scrum of people, some of whom were waving cards like the one I had in my own hand. I'd found the cardboard in the boot of the hire car and now had Flanagan's name scrawled across it in dark red and I joined in and waved it like everyone else but the river of people ignored me.

And I tried to ignore the weaving luggage trolleys. Not think about them in the same way that I was trying not to think about the Porsche, now officially seriously ill and still in Yorkshire. Or my upcoming driving ban where I'd spoken to Julian Broadbent, university friend and now the put-upon solicitor in our group of friends, who had nothing good to tell me about my current position.

No matter what, he confirmed, I was fucked. I was in for a twelve month ban and probably an inordinately large fine just for being a Londoner who broke the law in the North so it was going to be bicycles and aching feet for some time to come.

And crowds of smelly and unpleasant people and dirty seats on the Tube and buses but I put that out of my mind and concentrated on the near-ten-year-old picture of Daniel Flanagan that I'd printed from the paper's morgue.

He would have changed, of course. His hair could be longer or shorter or gone altogether or a different colour and he would have been well-advised to lose the moustache. He may have put on weight and I squinted, stretched up onto my toes.

Nothing and then I had a possible. Not the first but promising. Middle aged man, mid to late-fifties, perhaps a touch older on reflection. Round-faced, a shade bulky and somewhat shorter than me. Bigger moustache but less hair on top, the man was attached by some sort of strap to an immense suitcase and he looked up and scanned the crowd and I waved the sign.

He clocked it and nodded.

He pushed towards me and, apparently unburdened by manners, he made good progress and then, giving the strap attached to his suitcase a final heave, he was by my side. He made eye contact but looked away quickly. 'Spencer Beck?'

'Mr Flanagan?'

The maths put him at around sixty and he didn't look too bad for it. Weathered features and dark eyes. Flanagan took in the bustling crowd around him and sneered. He looked back at me and registered my face for the first time. I stopped myself from raising a hand to my birthmark and instead offered it to him.

'It's Daniel,' said Flanagan. He coughed loosely. Pulled out a grubby piece of cloth and did something that I didn't want to watch before he stowed the handkerchief away and shook my hand.

'Call me Spencer,' I said. 'Decent flight?'

'Got me here,' said Flanagan. He rubbed the bridge of his nose; the red indentation suggested that he had recently taken off reading glasses. Quite a detective myself I thought. Flanagan caught me looking at his case. 'Empty. Might be fuller going back.'

I smiled. He didn't seem to want to talk. Must be tired and I gestured vaguely towards the outside world. 'Car's over there.'

I'd chosen a small hire car. A three-door Polo and it would struggle with Flanagan's suitcase but we'd cross that bridge when we got to it and we struck off towards the farther of the two short-stay car parks. Had to negotiate a couple of zebra crossings and avoid the odd flying taxi and when we got there I found that the machine had rounded up sixty-one minutes to an hour and a half but I paid the fee without a word. I pocketed the ticket to use on the way out and we manoeuvred what felt like a far from empty case into the back of the car.

I had the thing for a week but I would need it for longer. Still, public transport was for another day and Flanagan opened the driver's door and took a second or two to realise that there was a steering wheel on that side. He glanced up briefly and raised an eyebrow. He circled around to the other side and clambered into the vehicle.

The car started first time and I managed to get out of the car park without incident and headed for the M4 as the game engine struggled to please. I dealt with the traffic and Flanagan coughed noisily and did something with his handkerchief but was otherwise silent and then he began to twitch, threatening to speak. Finally, he did. 'Simon told me you're writing a book.'

Simon should mind his own fucking business.

I didn't answer immediately and made a meal of negotiating a lane-change. Simon had been in my flat. He knew about the car and the drink driving charge and now he was spreading the good word about my future plans. Was there anything he didn't know?

'I'm considering it,' I said. I raised my voice against the noise of the small car as it accelerated and I glanced across at my passenger. There had been no hint of scorn. 'Perhaps a biography.'

Flanagan said nothing for a few moments. He cleared his throat. 'Weird guy.'

'Reid?'

I felt Flanagan turn his head in my direction. 'Him too but I meant Simon.'

I smirked. 'I've never met him.'

Another pause from Mr Flanagan. He was no wordsmith but that suited me. It might save time and he'd had a seven hour flight. He cleared his throat again. Sounded like he had a wet piano lodged down there and he shifted in his seat. 'Mind if I smoke?'

Things just kept getting better.

I didn't like it but hey, it wasn't my car. And I was around smokers all day. I wasn't as anal as some people about it and Flanagan must have gone without on the flight. I winced, opened my window. 'Go ahead.'

Flanagan hitched himself up in his seat and pulled something from his pocket. Eyes on the road, I caught a flash of red. Marlboros and I felt a pang myself. I guess I always would. I'd been smoke-free for a decade but, as Flanagan sparked up, I felt another twinge. He took a drag and looked at me. 'Said you had an interest in him.'

Once a cop. I registered the tip of Flanagan's cigarette glowing red but kept my eyes on the road. 'Reid?'

I felt the American nod. 'So the book's about him?'

Well who else? But I was the bigger man, sarcasm wasn't the way. 'That's right.'

The tip of Flanagan's cigarette traced the movement of his head before he took it from his mouth. He coughed unpleasantly. My car or not, I hoped he wasn't going to spit. 'You're not the first person who's got in his way, Spencer.'

Was he weighing me up? I tried my own 'details, please' shrug. I turned the corners of my mouth down for effect and drove on. The motorway ended and the traffic began to build up. I kept my eyes on the road but registered Flanagan's fidgeting nonetheless. 'You OK?'

He looked at me without turning his head. 'Can a guy get anything to eat around here?'

**

I looked from the smoke curling around Flanagan's face to the huge mural painted on the external wall of the pub behind him. Framed against the wall like that, a horse appeared to sprout from the American's head. It was just before eleven and Haverstock Hill was clogged with traffic. The car was back outside the flat, Flanagan's case was inside the building and we were now standing outside the front door of the local waiting for it to open and I could feel the eyes of passing motorists on us. I turned to the American. 'You've been to England before?'

Flanagan shook his head.

'Europe?'

Flanagan did his upside down smile then coughed into his handkerchief. He examined the contents and I averted my eyes. 'No; went to Niagara the once, never made it to Canada.'

I didn't reply. When in doubt, say nothing. A familiar creak told me that the pub door had just opened. I registered the cigarette in Flanagan's hand. 'You'll need to put that out.'

Flanagan gave me his 'you think I'm fucking stupid?' look but I ignored it and led the way into the pub and through to one of the tables towards the back of the room. Flanagan took his seat and I returned to the bar. I ordered two pints of Pride and a couple of sandwiches. The food would be ready shortly. They'd bring it over. I settled up and carried the beers back to our table.

Flanagan took a mouthful and wiped some froth from his moustache. 'It's warm.'

'It's so you can taste it.'

Flanagan's eyes narrowed and he lifted the beer to his mouth once more. He looked like a bulldog licking piss off a nettle but the beer's taste didn't seem to be preventing him from drinking it. I didn't want a row about the relative merits of English and American beers but I would stand my corner if I had to. 'So what do you make of England?'

It wasn't much but I'd felt I should say something. It was 11.15am now. That made it 6.15am in New York money and Flanagan had been up all night. But he looked bright enough and I was impressed because not only was he awake but he was becoming curious. He looked around but didn't seem inclined to answer my question so I tried another tack. 'You must be tired?'

Flanagan grunted. He raised his glass to his mouth, his eyes above it continuing to take in the pub and I decided to press on and cut the small talk. 'You met Adam Reid.'

Flanagan nodded. I knew that he had. And he knew that I knew that he had but he played it straight. 'Just the once. At the scene, before he lawyered up.'

I'd hoped he might have had further contact, maybe something that hadn't made it into the public record but I kept the disappointment from my face. At least I thought I did. 'What's he really like?'

Flanagan was looking intently at something behind me. It'd been a stupid question but he'd heard me and his face puckered up. 'How much did Simon tell you?'

'Just that you'd met him and had some information that you thought I'd find interesting.'

'So nothing?'

'I guess not,' I said. I'd normally have said 'suppose' rather than 'guess' but this was me trying to make the American feel at home. I'd have to watch it. I'd be imitating his accent next. 'What did he tell you?'

Flanagan was looking at something to my side now. It was a little disconcerting. He took a large mouthful of beer. 'He told me that you were keen to see that justice was done.'

I wanted to send the right signal but this might be slow going. A blind date where the matchmaker had told each of the prospects a slightly different story and I raised my shoulders. I'd have to make the best of what I'd got. 'So tell me about him.'

Flanagan leaned back in his chair. 'Not seen him for over eight years. Not since the investigation wound down but I've always felt that he was close.'

'Go on,' I said. I liked the pub. Liked the beer and was quite prepared to let the ex-cop talk. I put my iPhone on the table. 'Do you mind if I make a tape?'

'Uh-huh,' said Flanagan. 'Never did like those things.'

I made a face. Flanagan watched me closely as I put the machine back in my pocket. No chance to click it on and leave it running out of sight. 'You weren't the detective in charge of the investigation?'

'No, that was Maria Alvarez,' said Flanagan, his glass now almost empty. He swirled what beer he had left and was clearly minded to have another one. 'She was my partner. But I was the first detective on the scene. I was in a rush, was due to see my kid in Miami. When Maria arrived I handed it over and made my flight. I was away over the New Year and Maria had the lead. She was good. Files were kept up to date but the case was going nowhere by the time she died.' He downed what was left of his pint. 'That was the following February.'

'She died?'

'Hit and run,' said Flanagan, his eyes distant. We both knew this but we had our roles to play as we got comfortable with each other.

I'd see him as no mean actor but his upset looked genuine and I lowered my eyes. 'The case was closed?'

I knew it had been but I wanted his take on it. Closed implied solved; what did he think? Flanagan shifted in his seat. He leaned back and rubbed his neck hard. 'Murder-suicides happen all the time. Lots of them feature arson at the end but –'

Flanagan let his words hang. This was his little bit of drama. He wanted me to participate and I played along. 'But what?'

The American traced a shape on the table with his empty glass. 'There was a lot that didn't make sense.'

This was old news. It might just be chaff and I'd heard most it before. 'For instance?'

'Didn't feel right,' said Flanagan. 'I'd worked eight, ten murders a year for a full twenty. He worked for your government you know?'

That hadn't been in the files. 'Adam?'

Flanagan shrugged. Turned down the corners of his mouth at the same time as I realised that it was impossible as Adam had only been a child at the time but Flanagan put it into words. 'No, he was only a kid. His old man. The Professor. His mother too when she was younger. Never got access to the files. Felt wrong shutting the whole thing down so quickly –'

Flanagan trailed off and I weighed up whether to prompt him or not. He slopped the foam around the bottom of his glass. He'd have to be tired and I wasn't sure what another drink would do for him. It might be sensible to slip in a couple more questions before I took that risk. 'The Professor, he fitted the bill?'

'Wife killer?' said Flanagan. I nodded and the American continued. 'He was a possible.'

'I read that you called a profiler in?'

'Yeah,' said Flanagan, studying his glass. 'Woman. Whole string of initials after her name. Full of bullshit. Muddied the waters and pointed us all over the place. She said Professor Reid could have done it. Hell, I could have told her that for the price of a coffee. Push the wrong buttons and it's in us all but she said he was the right age. Was a workaholic, there was some domestic strain and all but I don't buy it –'

I'd registered his use of the present tense. 'But you did at the time?'

Flanagan looked up from the table. He caught my eye and looked away. I could read the signs. Unless he was a better actor than I took him for, this was his penance. He wasn't finding it easy and I had to push. Flanagan expected me to. I think he wanted it to hurt and I filled the growing silence. 'Was the profiler ever asked for her views on Adam?'

'Uh-huh,' said Flanagan, his dark-brown eyes filmy and distant. He refocused. Glanced at me and looked away again. 'He was the only living person in the apartment when the uniforms arrived but nobody wanted to point the finger. Not the profiler, not anybody. And maybe they were right. There was no physical evidence. Still, Maria wanted to see him again but he was a minor and an orphan. It was a sensitive issue and then

Maria died and here we are.'

Flanagan looked at me again, holding my eye for a second or two before finding something else to focus on. I spoke. 'Could you run me through the scene?'

'You've heard it before,' said Flanagan. 'It was all over the TV. There have been books written about it –'

'I know there have,' I said. Felt I had to keep the momentum up and stop him from falling asleep. 'But you were there only an hour or two after it all happened and I'd appreciate your thoughts. You've come a long way to talk to me. I know you've had a tiring flight but this is what you're here for.'

Flanagan was going to talk to me. I was seriously out of pocket on the deal but I knew that he was here to share. It was not yet eleven thirty. 'Let me get you another beer and chase up those sandwiches.'

Flanagan seemed to brighten and he looked at me. Something that I took to be an apology flickered across his face and he smiled for the first time. 'Why not?'

I gave him what I hoped was an encouraging smile of my own and stood and made my way to the bar. The sandwiches would be with us in a minute, I was told and I bought a couple of pints of Chiswick Bitter. Weaker than Pride. I didn't want Flanagan flaking out on me just yet. I took them back to our table and set them down. 'Your very good health, sir.'

Flanagan picked up his beer. Gestured towards me with the glass and took a mouthful. He left some foam on his moustache then wiped it away with the knuckles of his right hand. 'You seen a murder scene before?'

'Only in the movies,' I said.

This was his patch and if he wanted to inject a bit of drama then I was quite prepared to let him. Flanagan continued but did not raise his eyes. He didn't look up. 'They don't show you the smell.'

He didn't continue. 'No, I suppose not.'

'Blood and puke,' said Flanagan. Charming. 'All that bodily fluid shit that's going through your mind but it's different when you're there. And it's not like a butcher's shop. I don't care what they say, it's not sanitised. No white aprons, it's much worse –'

He stopped speaking and I gave him a moment. 'Look, you're tired –'

'I'm OK.'

Flanagan looked at me and for a moment I could see him as a younger man. It wouldn't do to underestimate him. 'Fine; how about you run through it the once and we take it from there?'

I couldn't say fairer than that. Flanagan patted his pockets. He located his cigarettes and took them out. He stood up and gestured towards the door with his lighter, inviting me to join him. 'Sure,' I said. 'Why not.'

**

Outside the pub I didn't partake but I could have killed for a cigarette.

Not literally, of course. Death wasn't my bag but I could feel the draw and would have given a week's wages for a smoke. Flanagan lit up. He was watching me. Didn't seem to take any particular pleasure in my discomfort but he knew I was feeling it. He narrowed his eyes against the smoke and took a second drag before holding up his cigarette. 'Well done, Spencer. They'll kill you.'

I raised a hand to my lips, close to where the skin morphed from a pasty-pink to a darker purple. I was aping Flanagan smoking. I took my hand away and shoved it into my trouser pocket. The American had noticed and he gave me a wry smile but I continued before he could say anything further. 'When you met Adam Reid?'

Flanagan nodded. 'I was the first detective on the scene. Took the elevator up. Uniforms were there already. Couple I knew, couple I didn't.'

'Smell of a fire and blood. Like metal, you know? You could smell it from the elevator. It cut through the smoke and all the other background smells. Hallway was taped off before the apartment. No sign of a forced entry, no evidence of a fight outside or directly inside.'

'The uniforms had it down immediately as a murder suicide and you could see why. Guy kills his wife then fakes a break in before he offs himself. Happens all the time but some of the pieces didn't fit. Glass window in the den broken out, not in –'

I picked up on that, had read the reports. 'That's suspicious?'

Flanagan looked at me and his dark eyes glittered. 'It was what it was. Meant it was very unlikely anyone had broken in. Either they had done but picked up the glass and dropped it all out of the window to throw us off, or the window was open when they entered or they'd come in the door or that someone already in the house had broken it. That would fit with a murder-suicide but why didn't the professor do a better job of throwing us off the trail?'

Perhaps standing in the same room as your recently butchered wife would have clouded his mind, I thought, but this was disappointing. There were too many options and Flanagan continued. 'The uniforms were rattled. Tried not to show it but I knew it was bad. CSI hadn't arrived so I gloved up.

'As I said, nothing obvious by the door. Bit of soot. No bubbling of the paint so I went on into the apartment. Entry hall was a fair size. Few sticks of furniture. Rocking chair, big Christmas tree and five rooms leading off of it. Bathroom, kitchen, den, family room, short hallway to the bedrooms.

'Den was homely. Soft lighting, TV, smaller Christmas tree, coffee table, with the TV remote, couple of glasses. All very normal apart from the blood on the walls.' Flanagan put out his cigarette and deposited the butt in the wall-mounted steel box and we walked back into the pub.

Our table and drinks were undisturbed and the sandwiches had yet to arrive. Flanagan continued as we took our seats. 'Diagonal lines. Very dark. Burgundy almost black, from waist height all the way up to the ceiling suggesting an arterial wound. Meant the victim had to be alive at the time that they were cut.

'Spatter on the table top. Implied a heavy blow with a high degree of force and some follow through.' Flanagan looked at me and I shook my head, needed the detail. 'Forceful impact shoots up a spray. Imagine hitting a melon with a wrench or slashing it with a knife and then pulling your arm back sharply and doing it again, you get the picture?'

I grimaced and Flanagan returned to his beer. He raised the glass to his mouth but did not drink. 'The TV was on when the uniforms got there. Door was open and the drapes were closed. Sofa and two wing-backed chairs, the nearest facing away from the door into the centre of the room, the TV.

'Sofa was against the wall, to my right. Coffee table was in front of it. Equal distance from the seats. A leg in plain view at the far end of the coffee table. Belonged to the late Professor but he wasn't going anywhere so I took my time.

'Chairs had some kind of floral pattern on beige but the nearest one was discoloured. Had to be blood. Could see from the way the uniforms were glancing towards it that the victim, Adam's mother, was still seated in it so I walked in and gave the scene the once over.

'She was well-dressed. Serene. Classy and no sign of a fight. No defence wounds, no broken nails, no upturned furniture. Slashed throat kind of spoiled her day but otherwise nothing.

'I had the uniforms put a couple more lights on and checked on the Professor. I thought he was burnt. The room stank of singed hair but that was the dog –'

I didn't know anything about a burnt dog. 'The dog?'

Flanagan grimaced. I'd thrown him off his stride. 'It was beneath the Christmas tree. Thought it was discarded clothing but it was the dog all right. A first for me but we'll get to that in a minute. I moved from Mrs Reid to the Professor.

'His clothing was purple black. The light wasn't good but the carpet underneath and around him was sodden. He'd bled out where he lay. I remember putting my shoe covers on and touching the body for the first time.

'No dignity in death, Spencer.' Flanagan raised his eyes then lowered them to the table. He took a drink from his glass and looked away. 'But there was very little veining. Blood settles towards the bottom of the body. It shows how the victim was positioned initially if it's moved post mortem but the Professor didn't have much blood left in him, it was all in the carpet.'

I didn't know if I was meant to say anything. I wondered briefly whether I could switch the iPhone on to record without Flanagan seeing me but it wasn't worth the risk. I took a mouthful of my own beer and waited. Presently Flanagan continued. 'Most of this is all there in the report but I'm telling you it like I saw it –'

'Please do.'

I gestured for Flanagan to go on. 'White male, the Professor was tall. On the floor of course but I made him at six two, perhaps six three. His eyes were open. Vacant and filmy. Even though he'd been dead for only a couple of hours. Lips were drawn back.

'No obvious injuries to the face or the head. Same for the neck and upper chest. Just the knife in his abdomen. I remember touching it.' Flanagan raised his eyes and then glanced towards the front of the bar as the doors opened. 'I had the gloves on, wanted to see if it moved.

'But it didn't. It was embedded past the blade. An inch or so of the hilt had been pushed inside the body. The wound was very low. Between the abdomen and the groin. Legs folded under the body but that wasn't unusual. Victim must have collapsed. Kind of folded inwards and down.'

I pictured the wound. 'Is it common for suicides to stab themselves in the gut?'

Flanagan looked at me and the seconds stretched. 'Maybe if they were dressing it up as a murder, or if they wanted to suffer, they were sorry –'

'But up to the hilt, in the groin?'

Flanagan lowered his eyes and nodded. 'They'd have to be very sorry to do that, I agree.' He fell silent, surveyed the bar then continued. 'His hands were covered in blood. All his own and they were otherwise clean.

No major injuries but there were needle marks on his right forearm.'

'He had a habit?' I hadn't meant to interrupt but this was new to me.

'That's what I figured,' said Flanagan. 'He had either practiced this at some length in front of a mirror or he was telling the truth. 'Some medics do and they can function. No problem with clean gear or needles. And they have access to product. The guy was left-handed so it didn't set alarm bells ringing. In fact it strengthened the murder-suicide theory. Addict. Wife telling him to get clean and the guy snaps. Get the picture?'

Flanagan looked up once more and drained his glass. The second hadn't lasted very long and I didn't offer to buy him another. Not yet, anyway and I prompted him instead. 'Go on.'

'At that point, I thought I had the picture then I remembered the kid. Uniforms had called Child Services and I was kind of disappointed, wanted to speak with him first but he was out of touch –'

'They'd taken him?'

'No, he was still there. In the living room but Child Services were already with him and he was a victim himself, an orphan not a suspect –'

'But you saw him?'

Flanagan nodded. He reached for his empty glass but let it lay. 'Living room was large. Light carpets. Big wooden table with ten or twelve chairs, a room for entertaining. More casual seating around the walls and wall-lights. Another Christmas tree, four or five uniforms, most of them female. Two women from Child Services and the boy.'

Flanagan fell silent and I let it build before speaking. 'And your impression?'

'Big for his age but dressed young,' said Flanagan. 'He was hunched, head down. Hands on his knees, feet pointing inwards. Purple and black footprints tracking around the couch.

'More blood on his sneakers and stains on his knees. A smudge on his face, something matted in his hair but no blood spatter that I could see. He heard me at the door. Raised his head and looked directly at me.'

'And what did you make of him?'

'For years,' said Flanagan. 'I didn't know what to think.

'But Maria thought he did it?'

'She did.'

'She thought he did it?'

'She did,' repeated Flanagan. He took a drink from his glass and then he said it, he opened up. 'And God forgive me but I think she was right.'

Six
12.15 – Friday 11th June
Haverstock Hill, London NW3

Flanagan had had his moment of drama and I'd cracked. Had been to the bar to pick up our third and what I swore would be our last beer and had got served quickly. The pub was still relatively empty and they apologised about the sandwiches.

They would bring them across and I returned to the table with the two beers, looked at Flanagan and he continued. 'But who knows?'

'The physical evidence was consistent with the obvious theory; that Adam had stumbled in on a murder-suicide but Maria saw it differently. Saw Adam killing them both, changing his clothes and then staging the discovery.'

Flanagan picked up his beer, lifted it to his mouth and took a sip. He was slowing down. That was no bad thing. He wiped a little foam from his moustache and shifted in his seat. He was going to continue his monologue but I beat him to the punch. 'So why did you change your mind?'

I looked at the man, tried to read him. He could just be some lonely ex-cop who wanted to talk but I was hoping it was more than that and Flanagan looked at me. 'The records don't tell you everything.'

I made what I hoped looked like a 'go-on' pout. Flanagan regarded me oddly but he continued. 'There was too much blood.'

That surprised me.

I gestured with my beer glass. It was meant to encourage Flanagan to continue and it seemed to do the trick. 'Old man Reid's I'm talking about,' he said. He did not make eye contact. He was staring at the table by the side of his beer mat. 'Soaked deep into the carpet and into his clothes. More in the furniture and still some in the body.'

'He was a big man?'

Half question, half statement and Flanagan raised his eyes. 'That was no secret. I didn't think too much of it at the time.'

His voice had tailed off. He wanted to get something off his chest and I gave him a bit of space. Someone had put the television on in the background and I found myself listening to something about horse racing from Doncaster.

'And the needle,' said Flanagan a few moments later. I gave him my full attention. He took a drink from his glass. The level of his beer barely moved and I could feel another silence coming but a large plate of mixed sandwiches appeared from behind me and was set down on the table and Flanagan roused himself from his trance. He continued. 'You read the autopsy report?'

I nodded.

'Had access to the bench notes?'

'Bench notes?'

'The transcripts of the medical examiner's comments dictated during the autopsy,' said Flanagan. I had heard of bench notes but hadn't come across them in this case and I noticed what I took to be a look of satisfaction on Flanagan's face. He'd scored a point. Had justified his airfare and he bit into a sandwich, his mouth full of egg. 'Notes and observations,' he said. A blob of something white fell from his mouth onto the plate and I tried to make a mental note of its location. I didn't want to eat food that had already seen the inside of Flanagan's mouth. 'They're often very interesting. Medical Examiners know their notes might be subpoenaed and could be read out to a courtroom full of citizens so they try not to say too much but there's usually something in there.'

I set down my glass. 'And in this case?'

'I'll get onto that,' said Flanagan. He sniffed at the half-eaten sandwich in his hand and took another bite. 'The puncture marks on Professor Reid's right arm were fresh.'

Flanagan finished off the rest of the sandwich and looked at the plate. I saw that this might become a race as he picked up another something with ham in it and I winced, waited for him to speak. Presently, he wiped his mouth. 'He wasn't a junkie. No history and the track-lines weren't old enough. No substances in his bloodstream; a little alcohol, nothing heavy –'

It was coming back to me. 'Doesn't heroine decay in a dead body?'

'It metastasises,' said Flanagan. I took that as a yes while the ex-detective picked at his front teeth. He examined something that had lodged under his finger nail and then put it in his mouth. 'Most drugs do. But the alcohol was still there and then there was the needle itself.'

I leaned forward in my seat. 'Go on.'

'The M.E. said that it had been expertly inserted. Guess it's what you'd expect from a medical man but it tore the skin when it was pulled out...'

'So he was on a high?'

'Might have explained it,' said Flanagan. 'Only he wasn't on a high. No drugs. Not even a bruise.'

I frowned. 'You said it tore the skin?'

Flanagan looked at me, gave me the dead eyes. 'Dead skin might tear but it doesn't bruise.'

I tried to hide my confusion but I thought I could see where this was pointing and the American continued. 'None of this was ever written down.'

The pause gave it away. This was Flanagan's big one. He was paying for his passage and I didn't spoil it for him. 'Go on.'

'Bench notes quote one of the observers,' said Flanagan. 'Junior guy on secondment from Senegal. Heavy accent and all. Said Reid could have been alive when the needle went in but dead when it came out.'

I raised my eyebrows. It was for Flanagan's benefit. My mind was moving ahead. 'You spoke to this man?'

Flanagan shook his head, returned to his story. 'He went back to Africa and I left the department. Haven't been able to trace him but the bench notes are there. Microscopic tearing of the skin and no bruising –'

He was drifting, repeating himself, holding his beer glass to his mouth, not drinking and I tried to move things on. 'So where was the needle?'

Flanagan looked up from his glass then looked down as he spoke. 'Good question, Spencer. Drugs might metastasise but stainless steel needles don't.'

Flanagan wanted to do this slowly and I felt that I should offer something. 'And a dead man didn't remove it.'

Flanagan spoke without raising his head. 'Evidence can get moved. There were what, twenty or thirty people in and out of that room in the few hours after the deaths and there was a small lab in the apartment. Plenty of needles in the place and a sharps box.'

'Sharps box?'

'Clinical waste disposal. Some of it gets incinerated but needles, scalpels, shit like that go in the sharps box.'

'Any blood?'

Flanagan looked up. 'On the used needles?'

I nodded.

'Blood on all of them. Professor Reid's and some from the wife.'

'They were both at it?'

I'd spoken too quickly, had to be careful. Wanted to keep things moving but didn't want to get ahead of myself. Lines built on Flanagan's brow and when he spoke, it was directly to the table. 'Scientists often use their own blood or tissue samples in their work. It's quick, simple. Sample's always consistent. Comes from the same donor and there's no permission needed.'

'Could you tell how fresh the blood on the needles was?'

'No,' said Flanagan. He hesitated, scratched his moustache and continued. 'Sterilizing machine was still warm. Few needles in that too.'

I let that sink in. 'So we've got Professor Reid working in the lab the day after Christmas?'

Flanagan sneered but I continued. 'What did Adam say?'

'He didn't have to say anything.'

'How quickly do those machines cool down?'

Something approximating a smile flickered across Flanagan's face. 'Pretty quickly.'

I ignored my beer. I had to close off the options. 'Could someone have been helping the Professor, cleaning up after him?'

Flanagan rolled his shoulders from side to side. I took it as a maybe. 'It's possible.'

There was something on the man's mind but I was going to have to dig to get at it. I chose the direct route. 'There's more?'

Flanagan looked at me but quickly averted his eyes. 'Why did the Professor live so long?'

'I'm not with you,' I said. I had to say something but felt a buzz of anticipation. I patted my phone in my pocket but made no attempt to try to record the conversation. 'Something was out of the ordinary?'

Flanagan appeared not to have heard me. He threw me a glance but talked to the table again. 'No problems with the woman. Throat cut from behind. Thyroid cartilage, windpipe, carotid artery, jugular vein all severed and the vertebrae deeply scored. A single, powerful stroke. Cut from her right to her left, left handed assailant.'

'The Professor?'

'Like I said,' said Flanagan. 'Left handed assailant...'

'Adam?'

'Also left handed,' said Flanagan. 'Mrs Reid didn't leave her chair. She was dead in seconds, almost instantly.'

Flanagan looked at his beer glass. 'Get any water in here?'

I pushed back my chair. Flanagan must have a bladder like a horse.

Probably dehydrated from the flight. Piss would be like orange syrup but I was relieved that he was moving from beer to water and I crossed to the bar. Collected a glass of tap water and returned to the table, set it down.

Flanagan mumbled something, couldn't manage a thank-you. He raised the glass to his mouth and drank the best part of half its contents and then placed it back on his beer mat. 'But the problem was never Mrs Reid,' he said. He belched softly into his hand. 'She was murdered, no doubt about that. Problem was always the Professor. The suicide. A single, deep stab wound to the lower abdomen – '

'The same knife?'

Flanagan's eyes were no longer focussed but the interruption didn't seem to have thrown him. 'Forensics said so. Kitchen knife. Son said he hadn't seen it before but he was a teenager. Probably didn't know where the kitchen was let alone what knives were kept there.

'Knife was serrated, black-handled. Heavy piece of kit. It was still in the body. No need to go looking for it. Blade was nine inches long. The Professor wasn't carrying much spare weight. It pretty much went right through him.'

I shrugged. 'Terrible but –'

Flanagan swilled the remaining water around his glass. 'In fact it would have gone clean through him but it was angled upwards.'

I couldn't begin to imagine what that must have felt like. My stomach stirred and I waved Flanagan to continue. He was regarding me intensely. 'Would've gone into shock almost immediately. Knife punctured his left kidney, nicked the renal artery, perforated his stomach, pierced his liver. Any one of those individual wounds could've been fatal but as it was, he lived for ninety minutes.'

I didn't ask how Flanagan knew. 'Was he a particularly strong man? Was he fit, would that have made a difference?'

'Some. But not enough to keep a dead man alive for 90 minutes,' said Flanagan. 'Shock and blood loss. It didn't add up.'

I rubbed my upper lip. It felt warm. The blood had risen towards the surface of the skin and I caught Flanagan's eye. The ex-cop was doing a fairly good job of not staring at me. 'How can you be sure that it was ninety minutes?'

'The Medical Examiners, the body was talking to them – '

'I'm sorry?'

'It's what the techs say,' said Flanagan. 'Everything has a voice. Fingerprints and footprints, the scene, the blood and the body itself. The blade punctured Professor Reid's stomach and the contents spilled.

'Stomach acid is corrosive, shit like that corrupts internal organs. The M.E. knows how quickly that happens and can see what damage was pre-mortem when the body tries to start the healing process, and what was post-mortem. He was alive somewhere between 90 minutes and two hours after the assault.'

I nodded.

Flanagan watched me then twisted his lips before continuing. 'And he was close to the dog when it was burnt. The tissue of his wind-pipe and the alveoli in his lungs sustained smoke damage.'

I couldn't see where this was going but Flanagan wanted to continue and I played along. 'Go on.'

'The lungs are like broccoli,' said Flanagan. He looked sagely at his drink. 'They branch and branch and branch and when they can't branch any more they end in small sacs called alveoli. Where the red blood cells take on oxygen, dump the CO_2.'

'And these were burnt?'

'A little,' said Flanagan. He looked away. 'Some of them at least but it shows that Reid breathed in hot smoke and he had to be alive to do that.'

'But he didn't move?'

Flanagan looked at me again. 'Not after he was injured, no.'

'So who set the fire?'

Flanagan grunted. 'Well it wasn't the dog. Least not after it had strangled itself and soaked itself in brandy.' Flanagan's eyes went away, came back again. 'It burnt for a while, poor bastard –'

The silence built for some time before Flanagan posed a question. 'So how did a dying man strangle a large dog?'

It was a good question. Dogs probably didn't like being strangled. Flanagan continued. 'How did he throw the dog's body over to the Christmas tree? Where were the matches?'

More good questions but I had to be careful. Flanagan could be a certifiable loony. He'd made a good case but I simply didn't know if the facts upon which he was basing it were true or not. I'd check what I could but wanted to keep him talking. 'You're sure he didn't move?'

Flanagan smoothed his moustache, looked around the pub. He leaned forward. 'No smearing, he couldn't have moved more than an inch or two but that helped to confirm the time his death.'

He'd got me again. 'How does that work?'

Flanagan lifted his glass. 'Eight pints is a lot of blood. Pretty much all of it was outside of his body and some of it had pooled and begun to dry. M.E. knows how quickly that happens, at what temperature, what humidity, that sort of shit and Reid had disturbed the blood. Some of it anyway, stopped it from congealing.'

'But he never tried to get to his feet?'

'No.'

'Is that normal?'

Flanagan took another mouthful of water. 'When the victim's got a nine-inch blade in their groin there's no such thing as normal. But there's usual and unusual and yes, I believe that he would have tried to stand. Maybe the pain stopped him or maybe he was praying, asking for forgiveness or –'

The man hesitated. I studied him. 'Or what?'

'Someone could have stood over him,' said Flanagan. He swirled the water in his glass again. 'Could've held him down and prevented him from moving.'

'This was,' I said then coughed and cleared my throat. I tried to get the right balance between a whisper and a full blooded shout. 'This was never raised at the time?'

'Wasn't my case,' said Flanagan. It wasn't much of an apology. I didn't push it and he continued. 'And if it was a murder-suicide, where was the note?'

'There wasn't one?'

There had never been any mention of one. But nothing was certain and Flanagan continued. 'Plenty of writing material lying around. Cell phone on the coffee table, laptops knocking around, could have written it out or sent an email or rang their priest, whatever. And then there was the kid. No father wants his kid to see what Adam saw.'

That made sense. Room must've looked like a slaughter house. I looked at Flanagan and waited for him to speak.

'Pretty much ruled out an intruder,' he said. 'As I said, the glass fragments were outside the building, down in the alley. None in the carpet. This was the eighth floor. No fire-escape that side of the building. It would've been difficult to get in and any home invader who makes it to the eighth floor is likely to be a professional. Cool as you like but they don't tend to be killers and there was never any report of any valuables going missing.'

Flanagan's eyes were glazing and I needed to close down the angles. 'Could a murderer have been trying to break out?'

Flanagan seemed not to have heard me but then he shook his head. 'Door was chained when the uniforms got there. Boy said he hadn't done it, there were no other open windows and if the guy left through the broken one then he must have been able to fly.'

The pub was filling. The buzz of conversation filled the air and Flanagan had lapsed into silence once more. I said nothing and presently he leaned forward, continued. 'Crime scene investigators didn't get much more. Only prints on the knife were Reid's but the family entertained in the apartment and it was Christmas.

'There were dozens of latent prints around the place. We never did close them all down but murder-suicide was the favourite from the start. Even the cover up fitted the profile. Intelligent guy lashes out in a moment of madness, tries to cover it up, you get the picture?'

I nodded. 'Any of Adam's mother's blood on the Professor?'

Flanagan raised his eyes and I caught the trace of a smile. 'Only on the blade of the knife. Nothing on his hands. They said the wing-backed chair would have shielded the assailant from the spray so it didn't rule the Professor either in or out.

'But picture the scene, Spencer. Wife dead, boy's upstairs. It's a big enough jump to imagine the Professor thinking clearly again but it could have happened. Man needs his son to have something to believe in. It has to be a random act of savagery to keep the boy sane so he tries to cover it up.'

Flanagan was clamming up again. I bowled him a slow ball. 'Marital problems? Any insurance policies?'

'You know the answers there,' said Flanagan. 'No record of any marital problems. There was insurance, yes, but it would've had to have been a double suicide for it not to pay out...'

'And could both deaths have been both suicides, could one have been suicide=by-husband?'

Flanagan stared at me for a couple of seconds before he spoke. I couldn't read him. 'No,' he said. 'Mrs Reid was murdered. Angle of the wound was all wrong for a suicide and there was no blood on her hands.'

I considered the knife. The size of it and the deeply serrated blade. I shuddered. Flanagan regarded me as he took another drink of water then looked around the pub. 'And then there was the washing machine...'

I was leaning forward into the conversation. My head was spinning. 'What about it?'

'It was running.'

'So?'

'This was the day after Christmas, remember?'

I tended not to wash clothes so I couldn't really empathise. 'Was it on a programme?'

Flanagan looked at me strangely. 'Couldn't tell how long it had been on. Didn't know what length of wash it had been set to but it was strange, it was a mixed household wash.'

I didn't really know what that meant. 'So?'

'Very mixed,' said Flanagan. He clearly knew more about washing machines than I did. 'Coloureds, reds and whites. You see where I'm going?'

Flanagan looked up from his drink, his dark eyes softer. I wasn't quite sure what to say. He'd given me plenty to be thinking about. Too much perhaps but I presumed that he was talking about the washing machine. I knew it would sound bad but I had to speak. 'A woman didn't put the machine on?'

Flanagan leaned back in his chair. 'An adult didn't put the machine on.'

I could see the picture emerging. It could be the story that would make me as a journalist and change my life forever. But I couldn't afford to rush it. I looked back at the ex-cop. 'Professor Reid's hands were uninjured, no defence wounds?'

'Small cuts, nothing that raised suspicion. He could've stabbed himself then pulled at the knife. Least that's what we thought at the time.'

'And now?'

Flanagan shrugged. He was playing it cool. 'Could still be right. He could've been gripping the knife, maybe trying to pull it out. But the fibres –'

'What fibres?' I breathed deeply. I couldn't remember any fibres being mentioned in the reports at the time and Flanagan looked up. I tried not to repeat myself but rules were made to be broken. 'What fibres?'

'The knife was sharp,' said Flanagan. He looked away. 'It would cut rather than tear but the fibres I'm talking about were on the handle.'

I said nothing and Flanagan continued. 'Polyester. Could've been stuck to the knife for hours. Days even but that was unlikely. Dishwasher seemed well-used and there was no match with anything obvious. Didn't come from a dish cloth or any of the oven gloves in the apartment but we were looking in the wrong place.'

Flanagan had faded again. Could be jet lag but I wanted to keep him going. I nodded him on. 'So where was the right place?'

'Footwear,' said Flanagan.

'What do you mean?'

Flanagan looked at me then down at the table. He picked up a beer mat and tapped the table. 'Knife's already in the Professor's gut,' he said. 'Then someone kicks it, kicks it hard...'

Seven
11:22 – Thursday 4th October
9 years earlier
Cavenham Buildings, Park Avenue, New York

In the corner a seated boy sobbed but the books lining three of the room's four walls absorbed the sound and it did not carry.

The boy opened his eyes.

Dazzling blue, glassy with drying tears, they cleared and he looked at the television. It flickered silently by the side of the bed and he ran his finger gently down his nose then pressed hard and winced. It would be worth it they had said, but worth it for whom?

The boy rose to his feet and walked to the too-small pine desk. Tears began to well once more behind his eyes because he knew; she would leave him.

She would die and he would be alone and Adam Reid would cry for her but she would still be gone.

Henrietta. Even the name itself was beautiful. Magical and graceful.

The bond between boy and beast had been there since the beginning, deep and unspoken and never fully understood. He didn't need to understand because it was natural and real but soon it would be gone.

Adam had visited her often.

He had felt the need to be close to her. Even now, though she had become ungainly and the cloud of flies that buzzed around her head had started to pick at the skin he could still picture her kindly, open eyes, her sensitive trunk and her majestic body with its clumps of red brown hair that had so often brushed against him. But now she was going to have to die.

It was inevitable.

They were coming to put her down.

It was for the best, his father had said and, as Adam raised his hand to his face and traced the line of his nose up towards the bridge and pushed at the scar tissue between his eyes, he knew that he was right.

Father was always right. Henrietta's condition was terminal but sixteen was no age and Adam blinked back a tear. He wiped at his eye because he felt a longing to be with her and a bond that he could not describe, even to himself.

Henrietta, like Adam, had been born into a life of isolation and they had so much to share. She had never belonged. She had never had a mate and nor would she for her ancestors had not felt the heat of the southern sun; they had known only the bitter cold of the steppes, the vast tracts of sub-Arctic tundra for Henrietta had no peers that drew breath.

She was a mammoth.

She was a clone and though the word no longer frightened him, a tear slipped from Adam's eye because his father had created her.

He had built her. He had broken down barriers and had done what they said could not be done. He had been years ahead of his time and had breathed life into a long dead animal. He was her maker and her God and now he had condemned her to death and Adam bit down hard upon his lip.

Adam had much to learn but he would get there, he knew that he would. His knowledge might not shield him from the coming pain but he would learn and, raising his head, he sniffed at the air. He felt the man enter the room but did not turn even as a picture of his father began to form in his mind.

He registered the older man moving an arm. Adam waited and then felt the hand, soothing and reassuring on his shoulder.

So predictable.

He shrugged and the hand was gone. A silence and the boy felt the man forming words. 'We have to do it Adam,' said the boy's father. His voice was heavy with regret but Adam closed his eyes and blocked out his father's words as his mind turned once more to Henrietta.

They had not visited her for several weeks. Something had been wrong. He knew that now because she had been distant, forgetful. He had been told she was unwell but still her condition had come as a shock.

'She's dangerous Adam,' said his father and Adam could feel his discomfort. 'To herself and to anyone who goes near her. Even to the people who love her. Her keepers, Adam. Even me. Even you.'

Adam said nothing.

He knew that his father was right and that Henrietta had become paranoid.

Staff had become wary of her, would not go near her and she had become panicky. She seemed to hear things. And she was sensing things that were not there, was hallucinating. Adam's father had told him that she faced a squalid decline. He believed him and the emotions flared within him.

Worry, fear, shame.

Adam felt the tears burn his eyes once more and he turned into the enfolding arms. He looked up at his father, his pale blue eyes almost translucent in the harsher light and he read concern in the older man's face.

He saw pity, too, and he felt a revulsion that he could not explain. He looked away. His tears were drying and he set his face. 'And what about me, father?'

Adam's father stiffened. He shuffled closer. Adam felt the older man struggling to find the words and he did not pull away as his father held his head once more to his chest. 'We'll get through this.'

Adam felt a stab of fear but behind it a sense of something else, of relief. Because what he had to do, he would do. His actions had been made inevitable by forces beyond his control and beyond that of even his father because Adam knew more than they could ever imagine and he would only ever learn more.

He would absorb information. He would draw it in and sift it, whale-like from the waste that surrounded it and retain what mattered and what nourished him. He would collate it and grade it. He would check it against what he knew to be true and weigh it in the court of his mind.

And he would judge.

And once he had judged, he would punish and then he would move on because there was so much more that could be achieved.

They had succeeded with sheep.

That was public knowledge. Somewhere in Scotland and they had made progress with other, lower, animals but they were nearly two decades behind his father and despite the magnitude of their rumoured achievements, the gap was as wide as ever and Adam smiled.

Yes, the scientists were pushing forward the boundaries of science but their feeble achievements were blinding them and preventing them from seeing the whole.

For the moment, Adam would shadow them but when the time was right he would steal the baton and he would beat them to the tape. But he needed his father. He needed the old man to give him what was his by rights and he raised his eyes. 'Father, I need to know.'

Adam's father nodded. His eyes glistened. His bottom lip quivered as he looked away. 'Maybe later, Adam.'

Adam chose his words. 'There is no later.'

He could feel the older man struggle to speak but he did not. Instead, he gripped his son's shoulder firmly. He gave it a shake and then turned and left the room.

As his father's footsteps faded on the stairs, Adam rose to his feet. He reached up and took down a book from one of the shelves and held it to the light where it fell open in his hands. He glanced at the text but he knew the argument well.

Heredity versus environment.

Nature versus nurture and the debate as to how much a person's destiny could be changed by varying their environment. But Adam would treat the arguments with the contempt that they deserved because he knew just who and what he was.

And he knew what he had to do. But he had more to learn and he briefly took in the shelves of books around him. He had read them all and was ready to move on.

The Darwins and the Weismanns had fumbled and groped their way through the gloom. They had stumbled in the right direction and had achieved so much, even in the very early days because, with their children falling victim left and right to typhoid and smallpox, they had focused on the most fundamental of all questions: what made a human being a human being and what secrets are contained within the cell?

Where was the blueprint for life hidden and how did it work?

Religion slowed progress but it fell to these early pioneers to build the path for others to follow and they had asked the right questions.

What made an adult brain cell a brain cell?

How was it guided to do what it did and what differentiated it from those cells that found their way into the liver or the kidneys or the skin?

Adam looked at the open book in his hands. An embryonic cell had sufficient genetic material within it to be any one of a million things and the early pioneers had recognised this. It only specialised when it was ordered to do so but when did this happen and was the process irreversible?

Could the nucleus of a mature, fully differentiated mammalian cell be taught to regress? And if it could, then could it be used to create a different organ, even to become a part of a completely different animal?

It had been the stuff of science fiction at the time but the pioneers had moved on and Adam closed the book in his hand and lowered his eyes. Many questions had many answers but some had only one and he retraced the story in his mind.

August Weismann had held that the genetic information necessary to cause specialisation in a cell was reduced as the cell itself divided. A childish assumption with hindsight but the train of thought was understandable. Each of the cells in a two-cell embryo, Weismann said, held half of their original information. The information then continued to halve until, by the time a living organism had been created, so little information was left in the cell that it had become irreversibly specialised and could never be changed.

Interesting but wrong and Adam raised his hand to his face. The theory had had some supporters. Wilhelm Roux, experimenting with two-celled frog embryos, found that if one of the two cells were destroyed, then half a frog would develop but it was not long before other experiments suggested that Roux's outcome was as a result of the trauma that was inflicted on the embryonic cells rather than proof absolute that the genetic information in the cells had halved.

When two-celled sea urchin embryos were shaken apart rather than cut or bludgeoned into two they developed into two perfectly formed sea urchins suggesting that all of the necessary genetic information had been held in both cells even after division.

Adam's fist closed on the book and his nails dug into the fabric of its cover. He stretched and the bones in his shoulders cracked. He reached up, replaced the book on its shelf and took down a second.

The struggle to learn had continued. By the 1950s, cancer was the target and funding was plentiful. In those optimistic and heady post-war days it was assumed that it would be beaten, that cancerous cells could be re-educated and real progress had been made.

Cancer cells could perhaps be de-nucleated. The disease could be turned in on itself but re-engineering cells opened up new possibilities and the scientists had not been blind to this. Putting cancerous cells to one side, if a donor nucleus were introduced into a de-nucleated cell, the DNA of any resultant embryo would be wholly that of the donor.

Cloning would be possible. Adam could feel the optimism of the age. These were the golden years for science, nothing was impossible. They could nurture organs, extend life or perhaps even banish death and, whilst few openly used this in order to stimulate funding, it was a compelling prospect.

Researchers in Philadelphia spent months introducing donor nuclei into genetically neutered eggs and, in late 1951, they achieved a breakthrough when one of the eggs survived. It resulted in a tadpole but the researchers had never sought to disguise the fact that the cells did not truly come from an adult organism and Adam's eyes narrowed. He was familiar with the problem.

He recognised the sceptics' argument only too well but he knew it to be untrue. Henrietta and the dumb sheep were proof of that but, in the 1950s, the scientists had not been able to repeat their success with adult cells.

That suggested that there had seemed to be a point of no return after which the cells were too specialized and could no longer be used to create a new organism and ambitious scientists began to desert the discipline.

There was no future in it, they thought. They had navigated a backwater and they turned to more exciting and better funded disciplines and even those who had maintained the faith, ultimately declared that cloning from an adult cell was impossible.

Adam smiled; how wrong they were. Some, apparently differentiated adult cells, could be used to clone from relatively easily. But these were invariably sexual in nature and, taken as they were from the sexual organs of the donor animal, they were deemed to be imbued with a flexibility not found elsewhere and much government funding was withdrawn.

But some remained true. Adam respected his father and had built up a picture of his parents' work. Adult cells had refused to divide but then, in the 1980s, in-vitro fertilization changed things and TV screens across the world broadcast pictures of healthy babies, their happy parents crying with joy, for all to see. Globally purse strings loosened once more and Federal funding had become available in the US. It had kept attracted

Adam's father and, ultimately, it had led to everything.

Adam's eyes rested on the book in his hand and he allowed it to close under its own weight. He placed it back on the bookcase and took down another well-read volume.

There would not be a return to the unquestioning adulation of the forties and fifties but science had once again been in favour. The worst fears, those associated with a Brave New World of mind control and cloning, had been put to one side and Adam's father pushed the boundaries of science further than any man had done before or since.

Adam was proud of his father. The fantasists had been concerning themselves with the arrogance of man and whether humans should be allowed to interfere with the result of millions of years of evolution but Professor Sir George Reid had done exactly that.

Of course, the vocal moralists bridled at the idea that changes to the human form could be made to plan. But that had never been George Reid's intention and their fears that Hitler may be brought back from the grave or that legions of glazed-eyed, morally bankrupt but perfect human beings would crowd out diversity, had never come close to being fulfilled but Adam recognised that his father had not been perfect.

Optimism had clouded his vision. His focus had narrowed and he had concentrated essentially on the benefits of therapeutic rather than reproductive cloning. Animals could be genetically altered to generate useful products naturally. Cows could produce therapeutic drugs in their milk, sheep in their meat, for example.

The Professor had been unable to see such a development as anything other than useful to mankind. It would save lives. Animals could be genetically altered to produce material for human transplants and even full organs could be grown within the body of a donor animal and better in a monkey than a rat.

And better in an ape than a monkey and better yet, in something that was even closer to being human, an animal that could share virtually everything with the person conducting the tests. No such animal existed, of course but what if one could be created?

Adam's father had remained well ahead of the regulators and he had continued to advance. He would have made even greater strides and aspired to tame even nature itself but ethics began to intrude and the Professor had moved his family to the wilds of Montana and there, surrounded by its vast plains under its endless, open skies and away from the claustrophobic atmosphere of New York or the research facilities of the West Coast, George Reid had undertaken his best work.

Under the patronage of James Jamieson, the hugely wealthy entrepreneur who had raised and butchered cattle on an industrial scale for almost half a century, the Professor had blossomed. Jamieson had cut up more than a hundred million beast over his career and in a good year he had been responsible for almost a quarter of all bovine deaths in the US but now he owned the largest safari park in the American northwest and wanted to give something back.

He had mellowed in his later years. He had been considering his legacy and made funds available. Henrietta had been born on his land and, a year later, Adam himself had arrived because where others had failed Adam's father had succeeded. He had proved that nuclear transfers were possible and that fully differentiated adult cells could be used to create a new animal.

Mammoth carcasses had been found in the Carpathians Mountains and in Siberia and across the Himalayas and there were cells available. But Adam had to admire his father's persistence because female elephants were not routinely farmed for their eggs and obtaining them could not have been easy.

There were some stores kept and poaching gangs and corrupt zoo officials may have provided other sources but, however it was done, the Professor had obtained eggs and had replaced their nuclei with those from a cell taken from a mammoth.

He had applied an electric current to the cells and had encouraged cell division. He then implanted the resulting embryo into the uterus of a third animal and Henrietta, beautiful one-off that she was, had been carried to full term.

Not a thing had ever been written in any of the major scientific journals and James Jamieson, now a very private man after decades of flamboyance and cheesy TV ads, had stuck to his word and had kept Henrietta's birth a secret. She and her surrogate mother had joined the elephants on Jamieson's safari park but, as the differences between mother and calf had become more obvious, the young mammoth had begun to attract attention. Forced to choose between Henrietta and his privacy, Jamieson had moved her to land he owned in upstate New York where Adam had seen her often.

And she had been happy but now she was not. She was losing her mind and Adam could feel her pain. His blunt fingers closed on the book in his hand and he crushed it. He broke its spine and let the pages spill like the petals of a spent flower on to the floor.

Eight
12:42 – Friday 11th June
Haverstock Hill, London NW3

'So what really happened?'

Daniel Flanagan wiped his mouth, looked at me from under his brows. 'You know what happened, Spencer.'

I looked around the pub. It was beginning to fill and I didn't want to play hide and seek. 'Run it past me.'

'The drapes were closed.'

'So?'

'It was four twenty when I arrived at the scene. The uniforms had been there for nearly 30 minutes. It would have been light outside when they arrived.'

'One of the officers closed them?'

'They know better than that,' said Flanagan. He brushed at his trouser leg. Imaginary ash. Then he scratched his moustache and pursed his lips, nodded to himself. 'Could've been a cosy afternoon in. But I don't see it. I see the killer closing them because this was planned and almost nothing was left to chance.'

Flanagan paused and picked at some crumbs on the plate before him. I realised there were no sandwiches left and that I hadn't eaten a single one. Still, this was Flanagan's big moment. 'Go on.'

The ex-cop looked down, regarded me through his eyebrows.

'Somebody, a man most likely. Probably young and definitely strong, left-handed or faking it gained access to Professor and Mrs Reid's flat. There was no forced entry and there were no reports of the dog barking.'

Flanagan took out his cigarettes and put them on the table but then removed them and put them back in his pocket. He leaned forward. 'The couple were in the living room. Their son was upstairs. All three had eaten. Parents had drunk around a bottle of wine between them by the time the killer took the knife from the kitchen. Perpetrator then enters the sitting room without disturbing the parents, the dog or the juvenile upstairs and cuts Mrs Reid's throat.

He almost smiled and I put down my glass, allowed the violent images to tumble through my mind. 'And then?'

'Mrs Reid's dead but the Professor doesn't know it. He's either not in the room when it went down or it happened so quietly and with so little movement that he didn't see it. Either way he's standing and facing his attacker when he's stabbed in the groin.'

Flanagan lined up his empty plate with his beer mat. 'He's a dead man,' he said. 'Knife slices up into his vital organs. Liver's gone and he's going to die unless he gets to an ER in minutes. But he doesn't die immediately. Slumps to the floor between the sofa and the second chair, probably thinks he's been punched and he doesn't shout for help.'

'Would he have been able to?'

Flanagan said nothing. I waited him out. He pushed his glass around a bit and then spoke. 'He could have shouted, yes. The neighbours might not have heard him. Walls and floors are thick but the dog would. The kid might've done and there was a cell-phone on the coffee table. But he didn't use it –'

'The killer's still in the room with him?'

Flanagan nodded. Coughed hard into his handkerchief and I found something else to look at while Flanagan examined its contents. 'Now Reid's on the floor, knife in his gut.'

I could feel my stomach knotting. I leaned forward in my seat. 'The dog?'

'Wags its tail is my guess,' said Flanagan. 'Professor's struggling for breath but he's got medical training. He soon knows he's in big trouble. Fumbles with the knife. Cuts his fingers but the muscles in his stomach are locking and he can't pull it out.

'The blood and the distension of his abdomen, the shortage of breath and the pain all tell him he's going to die. He's got maybe five or ten minutes left but the killer rigs up a drip. Indentations –'

'You can't be serious.'

I couldn't stop myself. I had interrupted Flanagan's flow. I felt the blood throb in my head as the scene forced its way into my mind and Flanagan continued. 'Indentations in the carpet. Didn't think anything of it at the time and most of the physical evidence has been destroyed now but they're visible on the photographs and I can remember them. Looked like a tripod.'

Flanagan tracked the progress of a young punk, his Mohican almost scraping the light fittings, through the bar. 'There's too much blood. It was everywhere. I'm standing in blood feet from the body and he hadn't completely bled out. You can see from his colour. It's clear even in the photographs but there are four, five litres soaked into the carpet. It's all Reid's but it's been thinned. Saline. Killer's keeping him alive, doesn't want to let him go.'

'The puncture wound, the disappearing needle?'

Flanagan traced the shape of his plate on the table with his finger. 'Professor's got fluids going in. Leaking straight out but they're keeping him alive.'

I looked around the pub again but we were being ignored. Lowering my voice, I leaned forward. 'Why does the killer want to keep him alive?'

Flanagan inclined his head to one side and raised his shoulders. 'Wants to talk is my guess. He needs something.'

Flanagan continued. 'Needle's been expertly put in. A calm hand. Not the hand of someone with a knife in his gut. And the Professor didn't take it out post-mortem and it fits the facts. Would explain why he doesn't move.'

I shook my head. I couldn't believe it although a part of me, the journalistic part wanted to. It was a truly fantastic story and I thought of Adam Reid. 'He couldn't –'

'He could,' said Flanagan, his voice steady. He tried to smile but succeeded only in twisting his mouth. 'You name it, people have done it. And if they haven't done it yet, it's only a matter of time. People can do anything.'

He was right.

But this was no ordinary man we were talking about. Adam Reid was one of the richest and most powerful men in the world. Still, Flanagan didn't look like a delusional idiot but we'd have to cover this ground again and again before I was willing to take it as fact. I tried to keep it going. 'So what happens next?'

'I picture them talking,' said Flanagan. He leaned forward. 'The Professor and his killer. Talking for a long time. Probably more than an hour but at one point it gets heated. Killer tries to use the old lady for leverage but she's already dead so it has to be the dog.

'Maybe that works, maybe it doesn't but either way the dog gets torched. The bones in two of its legs get crushed up and broken. It must have howled the house down and I see this happening in front of the Professor.'

I needed proof and Flanagan caught my eye. He continued. 'He breathes in the smoke, remember? The dog's body must have been only a few feet away but when the uniforms get there, it's over by the tree.'

Flanagan seemed to be tiring but he composed himself and continued. 'Killer still wants information but the Professor's weak, won't last long. Can't move, may be drifting in and out of consciousness...'

Another pause. It wasn't for theatrical effect but I wanted more. 'So then?'

'Reid knows he's going to die,' said Flanagan. 'Lost enough blood to float a ship. Probably knows his wife's dead and he's starved of oxygen and he talks. Might be hallucinating but tells the killer what he wants to know is my guess, gives him everything. But the killer needs more. He loses it, gets angry. Professor might be in a coma by this time. Can't tell him more and the killer lashes out with his foot. Kicks the knife. Throws the dog around the room but the Professor's gone. He's dead...'

The silence built but I did not break it. Flanagan exhaled. 'Then I see the killer stripping naked. He takes the needle out of the Professor's arm. He clears the tripod and plasma bag. All that shit and he puts it with the other waste. Then he fakes the break-in. He means it to look amateurish. It points to the Professor showing remorse. Trying to cover it up and then he puts his bloody clothes and his shoes into the washing machine and turns it on.'

Flanagan leaned back in his chair. 'Killer leaves the room then sometime later Adam comes down and discovers the bodies. Embraces his dead father. Smears his knees and his hands and calls 911. The rest, you know.'

Flanagan slumped back in his chair.

He was either a well-crafted lunatic or I had one of the biggest stories ever to make it into print staring me in the face and I breathed out slowly. I hadn't been aware that I'd been holding my breath and the American rallied. He leaned forward and lowered his voice. 'He did it, Spencer. Adam Reid got away with murder.'

Nine
14:15 - Friday 11th June
Fermanagh Mansions, Belsize Park, London

I handled the two mugs of coffee pretty expertly. Didn't spill above a quarter of either and handed one to Daniel Flanagan.

We were back in my flat. It was early afternoon. I'd been in trouble with the law, I'd lost my car. What's more I'd been drinking again and was in the company of a mad American. Overall, I was a little out of my comfort zone but I would go with it and I nodded at the cup in Flanagan's hand. 'Two sugars?'

Flanagan nodded back and I watched his eyes take in my cluttered abode. I should have felt a flush of shame but I didn't and his eyes came to rest on the aquarium that sat in the corner of the room. 'Nice tank.'

'Just beginning,' I said. I glanced at the aquarium. There was nothing floating on the top. I didn't know much about fish husbandry but knew that was a good sign. I raised the steaming coffee to my lips. It was still too hot to drink. 'Adam was in counselling for weeks.'

It was a half question but Flanagan knew what I meant. He coughed messily. 'Betting is he fooled them.' He took a sip of his coffee. 'I saw him the day it happened, his parents in the next room. I saw his eyes.'

That was a bit dramatic. It felt as though he'd read words like that in a book. I didn't want to antagonise him but it needed to be said. 'The boy was in shock.'

'I ran you through it,' said Flanagan. 'You know what happened.'

That was a bit more genuine. I said nothing but held Flanagan's eye and he did not look away.

He could be mad. Could be another embittered cop but he didn't look as though he was lying. Still, that didn't necessarily mean that he was telling the truth either, let alone the whole truth.

I'd read what details I'd been able to get my hands on and knew that Flanagan had been retired early. He'd been passed over and could be dangerous. I couldn't be sure either way.

'Took a while to put it together,' said the American. He raised his cup to his mouth and sneered at my coffee. 'OJ put the Feds on trial, provided an idiot's guide on how to fuck with them. He screwed their labs and Adam Reid's a quick learner.'

Flanagan paused. He clearly had more and I waited for him to speak. 'They called it 'the DNA wars,'' he said. 'Prosecution thought they had him. Cast-iron case but OJ turned it into a circus, beat them hands down. Jury felt stupid and they blamed the Feds. Then they felt they'd been screwed with and blamed the Feds again.

'Lavender topped evidence bottles, EDTA, scientific names a foot long it was all too much for them and they got angry. They needed someone to blame and like I said, turned out it wasn't OJ. Forensic medicine, science in general got the blame. OJ wasn't alone on the stand. Science was up there. US race relations were on trial. The LAPD, the American justice system they were all up there with him and at the end of the day the people just believed what they wanted to believe.'

Flanagan sighed but I would wait him out. He was off the point and I watched as he took another mouthful of coffee then half stood and took a visual tour of the flat.

Only took him a few seconds and he sat down again. Looked at me and continued. 'And none of this was wasted on Adam Reid. He knew that making a complicated case against him stick would be difficult. My guess is he had his defence off pat before he committed the crime but it never got to trial. Never got close but betting is he would've made a pretty cool witness. Even as a kid he was good but Alvarez was onto him.'

His ex-partner, the one that had died and Flanagan hesitated and looked away. 'She was no fool. She didn't buy it but I guess she was kind of embarrassed, suspecting an orphan and all. Seemed like the easiest thing was to go with the flow and the whole thing went away. Then a couple of years later, her husband sends me her notes and I find out how strongly she'd felt about it.'

'You think he killed her?'

'Hit and run,' said Flanagan a little too quickly. I'd interrupted him again and perhaps made a leap too far but his eyes were on the middle distance. He seemed to have been expecting the question.

'She was pregnant. Baby on the way and I never knew. Just like Maria. She could never slow down.'

Flanagan's eyes clouded further. 'Hit us hard when it happened but her husband fell apart, never recovered. Hector. Nice guy. Lawyer with the DA's office up in the Bronx. Took it pretty bad and who could blame him? Punk that coughed for it died in prison but that didn't bring her back.'

The ex-cop put his coffee to his lips once more but he did not drink. He blew on it and put it back down on the table and patted his pockets for his cigarettes and looked at me for approval. This was a make or break moment. Either he was going to smoke in my flat and fill it full of stink or he wasn't.

But he wouldn't be the first to do that. I could live with it and I nodded. He continued. 'Do I think Adam Reid could have had Maria killed? Sure, could've. But he was in England by the time she died. The file was closed, it was over.'

'You retired without taking your concerns to anyone?'

It was an accusation. I hadn't meant it to sound that way. The man's eyes narrowed and I half expected to get Flanagan's coffee in my face. It looked as though he was considering it but the moment of danger passed and he shrugged, pulled out his smokes. 'Looks that way.'

'Could you tell me why?'

'I lost it a bit after Eileen died,' Flanagan said. He knocked a cigarette out of his packet and sparked up. He looked past me and out of the flat window and continued. 'My wife. My late wife. I was getting it back together a few months after her death but I had my pension to protect –'

I ran the words back in my mind. I had to ask. 'To protect?'

Nothing subtle about that and I watched as Flanagan lowered his eyes, studied the cigarette in his hand. 'Learn a lot as a cop.'

I felt my stomach sink. 'Go on.'

'Little things,' said Flanagan. He breathed deep. 'Back up your brother officer. Right or wrong. And carry a second gun. Might need to give yourself a bit of an edge or need a throw-away and never rely on a single chest shot. Bad guy could be wearing protection. A good leg-shot is better than a bad chest-shot. You want more?'

I had to know what I was dealing with. Something was on its way. I'd never been good with surprises. 'Yes.'

Flanagan drew on his cigarette and his eyes narrowed against the rising smoke. 'You've got to give the evidence a chance, help it along.'

Fuck me, here it comes. I prepared myself as Flanagan leaned forward, a hard edge to his voice. 'Be real, Spencer. I'm telling you how it is.'

'OK,' I said. I had to pull this back. 'I appreciate that. I need to know what happened.'

As speeches go it wasn't the best but it was the truth and Flanagan seemed prepared to continue. He broke eye contact. 'Like I say, you have to watch your brother's back, protect them.'

'Yes.'

'Back them up.'

I could feel where this was going but I needed to hear. 'Back them up?'

Flanagan studied his cigarette. He wouldn't look at me but he said the words. 'Lie for them.'

There it was. He was a liar. Maybe not quite on a par with thief but liar was right up there. 'Is that what you did?'

The smoke had got to him. Flanagan raised his red-rimmed eyes and looked directly at me. 'Perjury they said. Guess they were right. Said that I planted evidence, lied under oath...'

'Jesus, Daniel –'

The words had come out quickly, unplanned. From the expression on Flanagan's face I might as well have hit him but how did he think I was going to react? For a moment the American said nothing then he looked up. 'And I'm not sorry I did it, Spencer. Guy was a pervert and a murderer. A child-killer. You got kids?' He paused, looked around the flat and answered his own question. 'They said I moved one of his shoes from his apartment to the crime scene.

'And I might have done just that but I didn't roll over. Didn't admit it. Why would I but when it came to the fight, my pension and all? I was only a couple of years off, couldn't take the risk.'

I'd met liars. Including some very good ones and my bet was that Flanagan was telling the truth. And that was going to be a problem. Because sourcing anything from an embittered liar was a risky business and an unrepentant liar was probably even worse. And Adam Reid had the deepest of deep pockets meaning that it may well be too big a gamble for a publisher with its balance sheet at stake to take and at the end of the day, if the shit really did hit the fan, then I'd only have myself to blame.

I'd look like a twat.

And although that wouldn't be completely uncharted territory, I didn't want to look like a twat more often than I needed to. Particularly one that was about to be dragged through the courts and lose every penny to his name as well as his reputation, career, you name it and I looked back at Flanagan.

I could feel him reading my face. I'm sure I looked as though I'd trodden in something unpleasant but again, what did he expect? And he'd clearly seen the look before. He took the cigarette from his mouth and knocked a half-inch of ash into the ashtray. He looked to be strangely at peace. 'Believe what you want.'

'Please go on,' I said. I tried to keep my voice neutral and largely succeeded. Because Flanagan could be a walking bullshit fountain but this was the first hearing and I held his eyes until he looked down.

The checking would come later but the silence between us stretched for an age. I was starting to feel uneasy when Flanagan finally spoke. 'Adam left the States a few weeks after the deaths. He was never charged. He was never even a suspect. Case against him just didn't come together and we couldn't keep him in the country.

'His parent's bodies were embalmed. We couldn't stop it once they'd been released. Didn't even try. Then they were disinterred and shipped to England where they were cremated.'

Flanagan looked around the cramped flat. It was a mess but I didn't care what he thought of it. I took the opportunity to drink a couple of mouthfuls of coffee. I wasn't going to help the man out. He could cough up whatever fur ball he had lodged down there without my help.

Flanagan shook his head. He was alternating nodding and shaking and didn't seem able to make up his mind but it looked like some sort of judgement on the place and he cleared his throat. 'Crime scene was corrupted almost immediately. Uniforms. Me and Maria. Child services and the rest were all there within an hour. Crime scene techs themselves afterwards and when they got the place back the family called in cleaners.

'The aunt again. Company that specialised in refurbishing rooms, houses and all after violent crimes. Yeah, these companies exist. Dental plans, pensions, the works and the carpets disappeared, probably burnt. Most of the furniture went too. Place was pretty much stripped and cleaned from top to bottom. Even some of the evidence from the labs was lost.'

'Removed?'

'Could be,' said Flanagan. He lowered his eyes. 'Then Maria died.'

Again the American shook his head. Perhaps it was time for a break but he carried on. 'I had my problem. Terminal problem. Left the force and that was it. The case was already closed by then and no-one was left with any interest in taking it further.

'It was solved. It was a good result. And there were no relatives pointing the finger at anyone. There was just no energy left in it. No evidence and no inclination to prosecute an orphan living thousands of miles away. Hell, Adam Reid never needed any shit hot lawyer to beat us. We didn't even show up for the game.'

Flanagan concentrated on his coffee and I breathed out. It was almost a sigh. This was a roller coaster. And highs and lows were more extreme than any I'd ridden before.

The risks were huge. He could be wrong. Flanagan could be working to an agenda or he could simply be wrong; but the rewards? A story like this would make me. Throw in the fact that we'd be bringing a murderer to justice and I could even feel good about myself. It could be the biggest story in a generation and I had to keep it going. 'So nobody did anything after Maria's death?'

'Why would they?' said Flanagan. 'She was gone. I was gone and Hector was, well he was in an institution for a time. Had a breakdown but that's about right, nobody did anything...'

I looked away. My credibility was going to take a knock after my problems in Yorkshire and I could see it both ways. Maria had lost her life. Flanagan had lost his job and Hector had lost his mind. So a drunk would be moving against one of the richest men in the world relying on the instincts of a dead woman, the word of a liar and the grief stricken suspicions of a lunatic.

What could go wrong?

I had to smile. I had a million dollar cheque but no way to cash it and I tried to backtrack. To reverse things up until it all made sense again and could be backed up by evidence. 'Was it usual for a suspect to leave your jurisdiction so quickly?'

'No,' said Flanagan. He looked up. 'It wouldn't be but Adam was a victim not a suspect. And he was a juvenile. He was an orphan, a minor in a city with thousands of homeless minors and he had relatives in England who wanted him.'

Flanagan held his hands out, his palms upward. What ya gonna do and it made sense. Adam could never have been kept in New York. He'd suffered too much. And how would keeping him in the US have played out on the 9pm news? I changed tack. 'Can we go back a little and fill in some of the detail?'

Flanagan made what I took to be a 'whatever' gesture but fuck him. I might be a drunk. Strictly speaking an alleged drunk but at least I'd never been had up for lying to a courtroom full of people. And he'd flown the Atlantic at my expense. He'd filled himself with beer and sandwiches and my flat with his smoke and now he was drinking my coffee. I continued. 'What was he like when you interviewed him?'

'Didn't interview him,' said Flanagan. He was either sulking or tired. 'Maria did.'

I sighed, tried again. 'What did she make of him?'

'Perfect,' said Flanagan slowly, his brown eyes softer. 'He was genuine. Genuine as fuck, she said. Either that or he'd read the book. Close to hysteria one moment then calm and collected. Perfect.'

'Did he seem, well –'

I didn't know quite how to finish the question. Flanagan supplied the word. 'Guilty?'

I nodded.

'No killer's regret,' said Flanagan. He'd let his cigarette burn down in the ashtray and he took out another. Lit it and took a drag. 'Plenty of the distraught child in him, she said.'

I leaned forward and kept myself in the conversation. 'How did he explain his being upstairs and not hearing anything?'

'He didn't have to explain anything,' said Flanagan. 'Child Services were with him from the start. The family lawyer shows up and everything went through him from that point on. It was a big apartment. Adam was a teenager. Loud music and headphones. TV was on too. First the kid knew of it was when the smoke alarm went off –'

'So how come he hears the alarm?'

I was quite proud of that one but Flanagan chose not to comment. Instead, continued. 'Visual element. Rigged to flash red in the bedrooms. Building regulations. Protect the deaf but they said the alarm was sensitive, had been going off over the holidays. So he ignores it for a while, figures his father will sort it out.

'And that checks out with the neighbours. Kid says through the lawyer that he went downstairs after ten minutes or so but it could have been twenty. Can smell smoke. Thought it must have been something on the stove but then he sees the dog.'

I read the hesitation and filled the gap. 'But?'

Flanagan smoothed his moustache. 'Shape of the apartment, must have seen the parents first. He was never asked to defend his statement but psychologist said he must have blocked it out...'

'You believe that?' It sounded wrong to me but what did I know about trauma? But Flanagan knew more about it than I did and he seemed to be having trouble with it too. He shrugged and I pushed. 'So this is a fifteen year old boy who's closed the curtains and prepared the crime scene. Then he kills his parents, strips naked and fakes a break-in. He puts his bloody clothes into the washing machine and goes upstairs to get changed only to come down again and discover the bodies? All of this while the smoke alarm's going off?'

'That's what I'm saying,' said Flanagan. He knew how it sounded but rose to his feet. 'Neighbours didn't hear the alarm this time but records showed it had been activated twenty two minutes before the kid dialled 911 –'

'Twenty two minutes?'

'We never got to question him about it but he could've had a legion of psychiatrists back him up,' said Flanagan. 'Defence right through from didn't hear it or ignored it to having a blackout post discovery or simply staring at the bodies in shock for a quarter hour or so. So you tell me, how do we make that stick with a minor? We simply couldn't press him.'

The American stretched and walked stiffly into the flat's tiny box room. It doubled as a spare bedroom for guests who didn't mind leaving the door open and sleeping with their legs in the living room. He'd dumped his case there and was back almost as soon as he'd left with a blue file in his hand.

He sat down. He opened the file, spread some papers with his right hand and looked up at me. 'You squeamish?'

'I'm working on it,' I said. 'The official file?'

'A lot of things went walkabout,' said Flanagan without irony. I'd thought it better the man be a liar than a thief but it was beginning to look as though he was both. It just got better. Clearing a space on the coffee table with his elbow, he put the file down.

He seemed to be about to say something but instead he slipped on his reading glasses, half-moon jobbies. He opened the file, took out a photograph. Peering at it over the rim of his glasses, he pushed it across the table and I looked down.

I'd feared the worst. Blood and entrails but it was a head and shoulders shot of a boy. Very much alive and I looked up. Flanagan's eyes had not left my own. 'Meet Adam Reid.'

Ten
14:45 - Friday 11th June
Fermanagh Mansions, Belsize Park, London

'He's fifteen?'

I held the picture away from my face. I'd never seen a photograph of Adam Reid as a child. His privacy had been well-protected and the first file photographs widely available showed him at eighteen. I turned the photograph around in my fingers and rose to my feet.

'Not small was he?' said Flanagan. That was an understatement. Reid had been a big fucker. 'It's a crime scene photo. That's why Adam's not centre picture. Got him in it by accident if you know what I mean. Never hurts to get a shot of everyone.'

Flanagan paused. He presumably wanted me to speak but I didn't. I continued looking at the photo and Flanagan went on. 'He looks pretty much full grown but I guess he'll have bulked up a bit since then.'

Reid must be a big man. Because he'd been a big boy the thick end of a decade ago and I looked again at the photograph. Adam was standing. A slightly built woman had an arm around his shoulder but her hand barely reached around to his neck and Flanagan read my thoughts and leaned over. His finger jabbed at the photo. 'Child Services woman there is around five-three. Officer to Adam's right, couple of feet behind him is six-two.

I peered at the photograph. The perspective could be misleading but

Adam looked to have been six-three at fifteen. He was taller than the man behind him and big. Not fat, just big. 'Was he adopted?'

Flanagan looked at me. He smiled thinly and crows-feet edged his eyes. 'Same question I asked,' he said. 'Looks different. And foster kids, step-kids, adopted kids; they're more likely to be abused and to turn to crime but no, he wasn't adopted.

'Not that we could get DNA,' Flanagan went on. 'Would've needed a court order but Maria checked the hospital records and he was their natural born child.

'Pregnancy was normal, delivery too. Mother was older. Forty-two but that's not exceptional for these types of professional women and baby was heavy, over eleven pounds.'

'Eleven pounds?' I pulled a face. The kid was a whale. I looked at the photograph again then set it down.

Flanagan passed across another and I held it to the light from the window. In it, a smiling Adam was standing easily between his mother and father. He looked a good four or five inches taller than his mother, perhaps the same height as his father, well over six feet but he was younger and I flipped the photo over.

Faded writing suggested a date twelve months before the deaths. Adam would've just turned fourteen. I could feel Flanagan's eyes on me but he spoke before I looked up. 'I never saw the parents alive but there were plenty of photographs. They looked nothing like the kid but he had a cleft palate.'

This I hadn't heard. Flanagan's eyes were shining. He could be off on one again but I nodded and rubbed my lip. The skin was noticeably warmer than elsewhere on my face and I felt a sense of something, disappointment maybe. Because if Flanagan was right and Adam had had a cleft pallet, it would blow the cosmetic surgery and vanity angle out of the water. Rumours had circulated before but if the kid had treatment for a harelip then that was much more understandable.

It was a more serious condition than my own. It would make Adam a figure of sympathy, which could complicate things and I knew a bit about it. Boy must have been in and out of hospital for years. He was twenty-four now and he could easily still be having treatment as the initial operations, designed to close off the roof of the mouth and seal the nasal passages, tended to be followed by years of fine tuning to improve the symmetry of the lips and nostrils. I rubbed my lip again.

Certainly not cosmetic. Not by a long way it wasn't. Again, I could feel Flanagan looking at me. I didn't want to screw with a disability but I was going to be left with fuck all at this rate. Drunks, liars, thieves, lunatics and a dead woman lined up against one fuck-off rich bastard who could take the moral high ground and corner the sympathy angle.

Dead parents. Physical deformity. He'd have covered the bases. He wouldn't need to spin anything that I threw at him and he could take me to the cleaners. He'd be a winner in his own right so maybe I should just call it quits?

I was one driving license and a few hundred quid down the toilet and I had nothing. Worse than that, I had a hundred nothings. My maths wasn't good but seemed to me that a hundred nothings added up to less than nothing and no publisher in this or any other country would touch it as it stood.

But the prize was simply too large to ignore. I managed to give Flanagan a smile but couldn't hold his gaze. I fancied another pint. Might even buy the disreputable lying thief across the table another one into the bargain before I tried to change his flights and get him out of the country as rapidly as possible but, looking back at the photograph, I felt I had to let him down gently. 'He had red hair?'

It was a weak shot. Even if he was adopted we would probably never know and it proved nothing either way but Flanagan laughed aloud. 'Hell Spencer, I'm Irish. Red hair's like weeds in the garden. Keeps coming back. Can cause a scene in the maternity ward, that's a fact. Red's just there. It's in the genes.'

'In the genes?' I frowned but I was talking nonsense and going nowhere. 'Could Adam have believed that he was adopted, even if he wasn't?'

The expression on Flanagan's face told me that this was a tighter line. I felt encouraged and continued. 'Could it have alienated him? Could he have been taunted? Were his parents disappointed in him? They had him late, they produced an only child that looked like that –'

'Maria checked where she could but found nothing.' Flanagan looked away and I could feel it coming. Some sort of dismissal. 'No evidence of abuse, of police or social services' involvement of any sort. Perhaps he'd just got the hump because he was so fucking ugly.'

The American was helping me to back away but I raised my hand to my lip, I couldn't stop myself. 'Could he have felt isolated, driven to do something like this?'

'You tell me.'

Flanagan had nodded towards my birthmark and I flushed. I calmed myself before I spoke and changed the direction of the conversation. 'Even his build is different. His father and mother were both slim and he's well, he's –'

'Built like a tree?' said Flanagan. 'Yeah and that's eight and a half years ago. He won't have shrunk.'

I picked up another picture. In it a younger detective Flanagan was standing next to Adam. An attractive woman was standing behind them, slightly out of shot.

'Crime scene snappers know the score,' said Flanagan twisting his head to one side to see the photograph. 'That shot was to show what he was wearing. The blood on his shoes and so on. I put myself in there to put some scale to him. I'm five ten. I was about 195 pounds then. Puts him at about six two, six three. Even then he would have weighed more than me. Two-twenty. Perhaps two-thirty. That's Maria in the background.'

I looked back at the photo and remembered some of the string-beans that I'd known at school. Lads who'd matured to weigh fifty or eighty pounds more than me and had played rugby at county level. Adam would be a lot bigger now. I tilted the photo in my hand.

Adam Reid's face was known across the world but he had looked different as a child and there had probably been more surgery. The likeness was there but his face was narrower now and more angular. His posture was different. He had been hunched then, more rounded.

Probably nothing more than the shedding of puppy fat and a teenager slouch and I asked the question. 'Could this be a different person?'

'It's possible,' said Flanagan. It still felt as though we were warming down and that I would be dropping the story but he appeared to weigh the suggestion seriously. Didn't dismiss it out of hand but his body language said that he didn't believe it. Maybe he felt guilty about the birthmark crack. 'The surgery probably continued in England. On his palate I mean. Could have changed his appearance. Some of the work might not have started until he was full-grown. Knew a guy on the force had the same problem. Operations went on for years. His teeth and what not.'

I rubbed my top lip again. It wouldn't hurt to let him know I didn't appreciate being called a cripple and I wasn't ready to let the cosmetic angle drop. 'These are big changes we're talking about here.'

Flanagan glanced at me then looked away. 'Can't see how it's a different guy. Sure he's much bigger now but he had a lot of growing to do from fifteen. And he doesn't want to show it. Hell, short guys, film stars and the like surround themselves with other short guys. They're only photographed from certain angles. You know the score. Reid's the other way around. He doesn't want to look too intimidating. He's a businessman after all.'

Eleven
21:30 – Friday 11th June
Fermanagh Mansions, Belsize Park, London

Pushing back my chair, I eased the stiffness in my neck and felt the vertebrae crack as I stretched and looked out of the darkened window.

So much for grabbing another drink. I hadn't been able to just bin the story. There was too much at stake and I rubbed my eyes, opened them again and tried to blink away the flashing stars.

I'd done Flanagan the courtesy of wading through his file and tracking through the photographs in the detective's stolen dossier. Had effectively following the forensics team around the Reids' apartment and it had all looked deceptively ordinary.

An expensive but relatively normal home. But the Christmas decorations and the rather tasteful baubles here and there and the classy furniture and the like didn't prepare you for what came when the team made it into the living room.

I had felt dirty. Like some sort of voyeur groping his way through an underwear drawer but I'd taken my time and followed the re-ordered photographs through the doorway into the apartment and then across the harmless hallway and into the room where the bodies had been found.

Initially I had missed the smoke stains curling above the door but Flanagan had pointed them out. The hallway had a couple of smudged handprints by the light switches but as we made it into the living room the first thing that had caught my eye had been the foot.

I'd turned away. Flanagan hadn't gloried in it although he was more used to this sort of stuff than I was but I had had to look.

It was awful. But also it was somehow clinical and it was possible to remain detached. The blood that Flanagan had described was there. Mrs Reid had looked strangely tranquil, pale and composed but the Professor had looked ghastly.

A real mess. He had slumped unnaturally. He seemed to have been absorbed into the pool of congealing blood and gunge that spread out around him until he had become a part of it. In fact he seemed to grow out of it, his face alabaster white and in the headshots his stupid, unseeing eyes staring at nothing and then there were the shots of the knife.

The images that would never make it into print. They were too graphic and too keenly illustrative of the indignity of death and now they were burnt onto my memory forever.

Long shots and close ups and detailed photographs of the blade taken after the autopsy but still I could not believe it. How could a child, how could anybody plunge a weapon like that into the body of another human being?

Perhaps if driven by fear I would be capable of lashing out but this was different. It was one human being doing something so gross as to be almost unbelievable to another and what about the cloying, stinking blood? Anyone with an ounce of humanity could never have been the same again after this and I shook my head.

'I need something to eat,' said Flanagan. He took off his reading glasses. Slipped them into the top pocket of his jacket and leaned back in his chair and patted his stomach. He looked at the uppermost gory photograph in front of me and smiled.

I think I grimaced but he was right, we should eat.

We needed to as the hours since we'd booted up my laptop and the spare that Flanagan was using had flown by. We'd trawled the 'net. Not much added value but necessary stuff. Background information on the Professor and some ideas as to who and what he was. We'd printed out a mass of information. I looked at the clock on the toolbar of my computer. It was almost 10pm and I found myself speaking. 'Indian?'

Flanagan smirked. 'You name it, I'll eat it.'

I believed him. I rose to my feet. Felt the blood rushing to wherever it rushes when you stand up too quickly and I stretched again, there wasn't a lot to say. We wouldn't need coats and if the American couldn't work that out for himself then that was his problem. I gestured towards the door and Flanagan picked up a pile of printouts as I led the way into the hallway and out of the flat and I scratched my chin. I wouldn't say that I believed Flanagan any more than I had previously but I didn't believe him any less. 'So why keep the father alive?'

I'd spoken quietly, almost to myself and Flanagan, puffing slightly on the stairs behind me, seemed not to hear. There was no one in the stairwell and I continued. 'Why would an adolescent boy use his dead mother, even his dog to try to control his dying father?'

I stopped walking. Let the older man catch up and Flanagan drew level. 'Information.'

That was helpful as far as it went but Flanagan didn't seem to have anything to add. We left the main entrance of the mansion block and I let the silence build, drew together some of what we had learned.

Adam's father had received his knighthood at a relatively young age. He'd been in his early forties. His services to medicine had earned it for him and there had been no shortage of flattering material on the web.

Working on vaccines, he'd helped to save the lives of thousands of people and had pushed a number of diseases to the very fringes of humanity. But there had been some gaps.

He had been a young man in the sixties. He'd completed the first of his handful of degrees at Cambridge and had collected more on the Continent and in North America. He'd then returned to England, working first at Cambridge University's science labs and then in the private sector.

He had worked alongside the brilliant geneticist, Rebecca Bennett, and the couple were married in West London. Bennett had been one of the few women at the forefront of her field but, after six or seven years of marriage, the couple were still childless and she was no longer working. The reports had been very discrete but it was there between the lines; problem pregnancies.

The blare of a car's horn brought me back to reality and I took a deep breath. If Flanagan was intimidated by the North London traffic then he was doing a good job of hiding it and we took a right into Fermanagh Road, a dogleg in this direction, and then swung left and out onto Haverstock Hill. We struck off to the right but there were restaurants aplenty.

We remained silent but I reckoned that Flanagan had suffered enough. He'd travelled all this way just to hear me speak and though he was hiding his distress well, he deserved a few words from me. I spoke as we waited for a gap in the traffic. 'What did you make of the Professor?'

'He was dead.'

Thanks. That was my reward for being considerate. I briefly considered pushing him under a passing taxi but thought better of it. 'I know that.'

'We dug a bit,' he said. If he regretted being a smart arse, he wasn't going to show it. 'He seemed to be clean, at least in the US. Maria wanted more time but we didn't have the resources. Everybody wanted an end to it, even me. Only Maria went against it.'

Flanagan was drifting off but I'd spotted a gap and stepped into the street. 'Here we go.'

The American had probably been looking the wrong way but we made it to the opposite side of the road without event and Flanagan wrinkled his nose. He was brewing one up, a witticism. I waited for it. After all, I was his host for the evening. 'Smells interesting.'

Poor effort. I grunted and opened the restaurant door and a waiter gestured towards a table near the window but I was having none of it. He wanted to put us on show and use us to tempt in passing trade but it would be windy, noisy and dusty and we'd have drunken punters pushing past us for the next hour. I indicated the back of the restaurant instead and the waiter pouted.

I stared him out and he managed a passable smile then led the way to a table further into the restaurant and I ordered our drinks and a pile of food as we took our seats.

We were here to eat not read the menu for forty minutes and Flanagan had said himself that if I chose it, he'd eat it. Even though I'd managed to avoid the temptation to order one of the triple-chili dishes for him, he would have his work cut out to keep that promise just the same.

The waiter left and Flanagan put the large heap of documents, some read and others yet to be read, onto the table with the uppermost face down and I broke the ice. 'So what do we know?'

'Adam offed his parents,' said Flanagan.

I winced as our beers arrived. It seemed to confuse the waiter. I waited for him to disappear and leaned forwards again and had a stab at explaining the facts of life for Flanagan's benefit. 'I'm not going to accuse a man with the resources of Adam Reid of murder. Race is bad enough but it's simpler. It's easier to allude to but even there I've got next to nothing to go on and if we hadn't heard the tape, we really would have nothing –'

'I didn't hear the tape,' said Flanagan. I looked at him and he shrugged and repeated himself in case I was even more of a moron than I looked. 'I didn't hear it.'

I hadn't made a recording of the brief conversation but I knew what I had heard. Still, it felt lonely being the only one who had heard the words but it was Flanagan was the proven liar, not me. We fell into an uneasy silence. The starters arrived and I shovelled a bit of something brown into my mouth. Turns out I was hungry and I took another mouthful. 'Why did he call them Africans?'

Flanagan was sucking at something that appeared to be stuck in his teeth. He showed no signs of having heard me. He looked up, caught my eye and shrugged.

Brilliant. But Flanagan was jet lagged and I cut him a bit of slack, gave it another go. 'Why call them Africans? There are plenty of other racial epithets.'

'Epithets?'

'You know what I mean,' I said. I told Flanagan word-for-word what I'd heard on the phone and continued. 'And there's nothing on the web alleging racism. Maybe it meant nothing, just a few random words.'

'Sure,' said Flanagan. He shrugged again and tore up one of the Nan breads. He swilled it down with a mouthful of beer and looked back at me. 'Why not get in touch with Simon, ask him?'

Not a bad idea. Pretty obvious, in fact. It was number twenty-six on his phone but I'd left the thing in my flat. Maybe Flanagan had one too. 'How did he get in touch with you?'

'Got me through the DEA, the Detectives' Endowment Association,' said Flanagan. 'A lot of the guys use it to get back in touch with each other. It wasn't a big surprise when I got a message. I'd had them on other cases –'

'Saying something about picking up a mobile phone and a note to ring one of the stored numbers?'

Flanagan nodded. 'Spoke to him a couple of times then he said to put the phone back in the pigeonhole at the DEA reception. Never saw it again.'

The restaurant was filling up and our main course was arriving. It piled up on the table as two waiters unburdened themselves of a variety of stainless steel containers and I leaned forward. 'We'll try Simon when we get back to the flat. Tell him that we need more if I'm going to take this further.'

Flanagan was concentrating hard on getting his food into his mouth with the minimum of delay and I followed his example, got stuck in. Between mouthfuls, I managed to get a few more words out. 'So the father worked with animals?'

Flanagan remained focused on his food. And there was plenty in his mouth but he managed to speak. 'Large farm animals, you see the articles?' The American pushed his plate to one side and pulled over the papers. A few moments later he had the sheet that he was looking for. "Professor Promises Jumbo Surprise'.'

Tabloid stuff and I looked at the grainy photograph. The text was only just readable. I gave the photo another look and held it up to the light. A tall man in a white coat was standing next to a large animal.

In fact they didn't get much bigger. Not on land, anyway as it was an elephant and Flanagan took the sheet from me. He'd put his glasses on and he tilted back his head in order to look through them. ''English embryologist George Reid has promised Montana meat-mogul James Jimbo Jamieson a Jumbo Christmas Surprise.' He knocked up the guy's elephant. Not personally, you understand.'

I gave him a nod and looked at the heap of papers that was now mixed in with the food on the table between us. 'Anything after the birth?'

'Couple of stories,' said Flanagan. He reached towards the papers but scowled and turned the uppermost printout face down as a waiter cleared some of the emptied kitchenware. The man brushed half-heartedly at some crumbs on the tablecloth and backed away.

After that we ate quickly and ordered coffees and the bill. It would make more sense to check through the documents in my flat and the coffees came pretty much cold. They didn't delay us for long and I peeled off a few notes and left them on the table as Flanagan gathered up the printouts.

Outside the restaurant, Flanagan lit a cigarette and I could feel him relax. He looked up and squinted against the headlights. 'What happened with your car?'

I shook my head slowly. It still hurt to talk about it so I didn't. Instead I made what I hoped was a pained face and set off towards my flat giving Flanagan little choice but to follow.

It had clouded over and had started to drizzle. A fine, drenching rain and I waited for Flanagan to catch up and we walked to the flat in a reasonably amicable silence. I let us in and we climbed the stairs to my flat at an even, full-bellied pace.

Unlocking the door, I wrinkled my nose and looked at Flanagan. The flat smelt unpleasantly of cigarette smoke. But Flanagan clearly didn't do guilt and he crossed the threshold, walked directly to the computer and gave the mouse a bit of a shake to bring it back to life. He spoke without turning his head. 'So you're not going to fill me in on the car, we're sticking with the elephant, right?'

I took the seat next to him. 'Help yourself.'

'Uh-huh,' said Flanagan. He didn't look up. Instead coaxed a cigarette out if its packet. He lit it and manoeuvred himself through my bookmarks more or less skilfully whilst ignoring my pointed coughing. He typed in a variety of keywords including Reid, elephant and Montana and hit return.

Some coincidental hits but nothing meaningful and Flanagan cleared his throat. 'Got the article?'

He wasn't worth a scowl. Instead, I flipped through the file and crumpled the paper into his hand and Flanagan looked at it as though either the print or the paper itself had insulted him personally. He put his cigarette down on the saucer before him and slipped on his reading glasses. 'Montana Mercury, Professor Reid and an elephant named Naomi. It's all there so why doesn't the link work?'

'I don't know,' I said. 'Put in the full URL.'

Flanagan raised an eyebrow but began to type. It wasn't one of his strengths but the article that we had printed earlier came up onto the screen and Flanagan leaned forward, blocked it from view as he read. 'Boxing Day, 'Christmas Jumbo for Jimbo' it says. 'Naomi the elephant fills Jimbo's stocking."

'Who writes this rubbish?'

'Journalist, I guess,' said Flanagan and glanced at me. He wasn't as jetlagged as I'd imagined and I leaned further over his shoulder as he reached across and tapped the screen. 'Adam's parents died on the elephant's birthday.'

Flanagan continued reading. "-the twenty-two year old Indian Elephant was safely delivered of a female calf weighing in at 240lbs. Pictures and the full story in tomorrow's Marvellous Mercury."

'I can hardly wait,' I said.

Flanagan jabbed a few more keys. His fingers looked like pink carrots and I leaned back in my chair and closed my eyes. I was tired. Important facts could slip me by. I had to keep a grip. I opened my eyes and the following day's newspaper was now open on the screen.

It looked like the material had been loaded from fiches onto the web. Whole pages had been copied together and it wasn't ordered in a story-by-story format as it would have been today.

Flanagan began to scroll through the pages and stopped at an article that filled most of one of the inside pages. The largest photograph, a rather washed-out black and white piece, was of the mother elephant and her calf.

The adult looked proud of itself and very protective of the bundle by its feet. I leaned forward as the grey-brown heap began to take shape. There was a trunk, an ear and a tightly screwed shut eye. Flanagan was scanning the words. 'More of the same. Date of birth and a name for the baby...'

'Calf.'

'-Henrietta. Yes there it is. A reference to Professor Reid –'

'What else?'

Flanagan read from the paper in front of him. 'Not a lot. 'Jimbo Jamieson confirmed that nature had been given a helping hand' it says. Naomi was artificially inseminated. That's about it.'

'Can we follow them forward, see what the newspaper said about them?'

I knew there would be a problem. These articles were from back stories that had been loaded when search engines were less efficient. Cross referencing would have been pretty patchy and there would be gaps. Newspapers might not have archived their data in a searchable form and we could miss things but Flanagan nodded. He already had another article and within minutes had a half dozen or so pieces. A mixture of local papers and something from an academic journal. The Montana Mercury didn't feature and there were no pictures but then Flanagan had something.

Another article was printing out and I stood, walked around the table. It was a large photograph and it printed slowly. I picked it up and saw Naomi. A better shot and still every inch the proud mother, her daughter was by her side but the younger elephant looked different.

I scratched my head. 'Do baby elephants always look like that?'

'Search me,' said Flanagan.

'It looks like he crossed it with something hairy; a camel?'

'Camel my ass,' said Flanagan. He craned his neck to get a better view of the photograph.

'Thank you, but no,' I said but the humour was wasted. Flanagan was going to be a custard pie or fall-down-a-flight-of-stairs man. 'Adam's father did something to her. He must have engineered her to look like that.'

Flanagan looked at me blankly. 'What do you mean?'

'He was a smart bloke, he could he have built her.'

'Yeah, and?'

I put the photograph back on the table, pushed it towards the ex-cop. 'What does it look like to you?'

Flanagan shrugged. 'Hairy elephant?'

'Woolly?'

'Yeah.'

'And another name for a hairy elephant?'

A brief silence.

Flanagan didn't look surprised and I realised that I was being led here. He'd had a little time to think this through. 'A mammoth?'

I said nothing for a few moments. 'Were there stories?'

Flanagan gestured towards the papers. 'Only the ones we see here.'

I was playing catch up again and I didn't like it. 'Any more recent photos?'

Flanagan shook his head. 'None I've found.'

'Could it be done, though?'

'Don't know, Spencer,' said Flanagan. 'But if it was, where would that take us?'

I gave myself a moment. 'If the old man was into something it might be relevant.'

Flanagan was still looking at me. He didn't help. 'Go on.'

'What would you need?'

'Egg, sperm I guess.'

We'd seen the films. DNA from blood-sucking insects sealed in amber. But that was fiction and I rotated the photo back towards myself. 'Maybe only the DNA?'

Flanagan pulled a face. He was still ahead of me but was starting to stumble over the facts. 'Mammoths have been dead what, a million years?'

'A few thousand,' I said. It was one of those useless facts that had stuck somewhere.

'But not yesterday, right?'

Flanagan had a point. 'Could be frozen,' I said. It was the best that I could manage. 'There are stories of the first Russians in Siberia feeding frozen mammoth meat to their dogs.'

Flanagan stifled a yawn and I nodded towards the computer monitor. 'Want to carry on?'

Flanagan looked beat. It was a miracle that he hadn't collapsed already and the elephant could be a dead end, a waste of time. Or it could be the key to everything but my own perspective was slipping. It would be better in the morning but for the moment I pressed on. 'What happened to Henrietta?'

'Don't know.'

I felt a flash of irritation but something else had been nagging at me for some time. 'I'm going to ring Simon.'

‘You got the phone?’

I picked up Simon’s mobile phone from the coffee table. I’d switched it off. Didn’t have a charger for it and didn’t want the battery to run out and I turned it on, waited for the signal to establish itself.

There was no password. It was something that I hadn’t considered and I flicked through to the stored numbers. I hit twenty-six and held the phone away from my head. Flanagan leaned across. A few squawks and then ‘-the number you have dialled is not available, please try again later –’

‘So let’s try again later,’ said Flanagan. He spoke without looking up. ‘You do embryology and cloning and I’ll do mammoths and the Reids.’

It was my flat. He was using my laptop and I’d paid for his flights, his meal and would be providing his accommodation. Flanagan was just the unpaid help but he was right and, within seconds, the printer was in action again.

**

An hour later I pushed back my chair and rubbed my eyes. This was it for the night. It was two thirty in the morning but the stories and photographs were still running through my mind.

I’d used my passwords to get into the archives of a couple of the national majors but had tried the Internet in the past when researching Adam and hadn’t expected this search to add a great deal.

And it hadn’t; information was plentiful but shallow. Truly personal details were scarce but it was an exercise that had to be undertaken on a regular basis.

There had been some references to Adam’s possible plastic surgery and dental work that I hadn’t seen before but it was normal chat-room stuff. Probably untraceable and even then the authors hadn’t directly accused him of anything. But some of the photographs that had been posted seemed to support the view that the man had had work done.

One of the alternative websites, a spiteful and virus-ridden page of the type that sprang up from time to time before being shut down by legal action, had run a series of freeze-frame photographs on a loop, showing the shape of Adam's face altering and mutating into its present form before the viewer's eyes.

'The changing face of capitalism' the website had called it but the quality of the pictures was poor and they proved nothing. A twelve year old could change a face on his laptop and any editor worth his salt would throw out anything sourced so poorly. I needed more but I was running on empty and Flanagan had to feel worse.

I yawned but when Flanagan spoke, he sounded fresh and full of energy. 'So it's possible for mammoths?'

Did I look like a scientist? I felt Flanagan looking at me and I gave my chin a rub. 'Could be,' I said. That didn't add a lot. 'There's the sheep,' I said, glancing again at one of the sheets that Flanagan had passed across earlier. 'Dolly.'

Flanagan looked irritated. 'Yeah but that was under laboratory conditions. Even then only one of the embryos they used survived. They lost nearly three hundred. It says eggs from different mammals react differently even if the techniques used look the same –'

'So cloning a sheep's not the same as cloning a mammoth.' It was a statement rather than a question but I felt as though I should say something.

'You don't say,' said Flanagan. 'What about humans?'

'Don't know,' I said.

'What do you think?'

'Probably, but –'

'No buts, Spencer –'

'There are always buts.'

Flanagan sneered. 'If it's possible then it's been done.'

I didn't reply. I couldn't prove a negative and Flanagan sat back in his chair, coaxed another cigarette from its pack and lit it. 'Could old man Reid have done it?'

'What do you mean?'

'You know what I mean.'

I did but I was flagging. I was unable to think clearly and I lowered my eyes. 'Adam?'

Flanagan looked at me evenly. 'Why not?'

'Why?'

Flanagan drew heavily on his cigarette. 'Wife can't make it to full term and she's not a young woman.'

I'd humour him. And it wasn't impossible. Flanagan could be right. 'So Adam finds out. It unhinges him?'

Flanagan shrugged. 'That or he was wired wrong from the get-go. Either way he's your killer.'

I was too tired to argue but where was the proof? I felt my face flush. It was exhaustion. That and a rising thought. 'Could it be simpler than that? His companies are worth billions. Could he have killed for the information that he needed to make himself rich?'

Flanagan didn't reply and I drifted back to his earlier theory: had Adam Reid's father played God? Had he created Adam? Had he built a human being, the highest of the higher mammals?

How would we ever know? There were well-reported attempts to clone monkeys but there had never been any suggestion of success. Worse, there were some suggestions of massive abnormalities in the slowly dividing cells. Unnatural mutations had led to the deaths of embryos. It was a feature of the higher mammals some of the scientists had said. No monkey embryo had survived past a couple of cell divisions and there had been nothing substantiated with regard to human cloning at all.

And if it wasn't possible now, how could it have been feasible a quarter of a century ago? The Internet reported South Korean expert, Hwang Woo-Suk, as claiming to have successfully cloned a human embryo in 2004. It had been created in order to produce stem cells, the scientists had claimed.

He'd subsequently been charged with embezzlement and bioethics fraud and his work had been tainted but where one scientist had led, others might follow but Adam was born nearly two and a half decades ago. Something intruded on my thoughts and I realised that Flanagan was speaking. 'What?'

It wasn't polite. Flanagan was annoyed but I was too tired to give a shit. 'The mammoth or whatever the fuck it was,' he said. 'Is it possible?'

Flanagan was gawping at me but I didn't want to share everything with him. Not now and perhaps not ever and I played for time, nodded towards the pile. 'Most seem to think it's impossible for higher mammals. They wouldn't even have been close twenty-five years ago.'

He was still looking at me and I felt obliged to continue. 'There's that Japanese guy managed to impregnate cows using sperm that had been frozen and effectively killed.'

'Why the fuck do that?'

Fair question but I ignored it. 'They introduced the sperm into an egg and then tried to persuade it to divide. They passed an electric current through it and it worked.'

'Like Frankenstein?'

'That's what the papers said.'

'Journalists, huh?' Flanagan leaned back in his chair. He flicked the ash from his cigarette into a plant pot and stretched his leg out before him. Didn't the guy ever get tired? 'If the sperm's been dead for an hour or two then why not a million years?'

He was good with the questions. Years of practice but I had to be careful. I wanted his help but I didn't want him as a partner. 'Four or five thousand years,' I said. 'That's when the last of the island pockets of mammoths died out.'

'Whatever,' said Flanagan. 'Is it possible?'

I gave the question a moment or two's thought but stuck to the truth. 'I don't know. You'd need an egg and sperm and where are they going to come from?'

Flanagan turned down the corners of his mouth. 'From the ice?'

‘Could be,’ I said. ‘But could the Professor have been so far ahead of his time?’

That should have held him for a while but Flanagan leaned forward. ‘People are,’ he said. ‘Look at Einstein, da Vinci and others.’

I shrugged. ‘Their achievements were widely reported at the time –’

‘Let’s put it this way,’ said Flanagan. The bastard had cut me off. ‘Given what you’ve read, would you say it’s possible to clone a mammoth?’

‘Not impossible,’ I said. I wasn’t sure but I could audit my responses in the cold light of day.

‘Then it’s been done,’ said Flanagan. He was trying hard to keep the triumph out of his voice. ‘And a human being?’

I looked at Flanagan then pushed back my chair. I rose to my feet. Walked to the window and opened it. It was chilly out there but the room stank and I needed some air. I stretched. I could hardly make it more obvious that I wanted to go to bed but Flanagan was rolling a fresh cigarette between his fingers and I decided any subtlety would be wasted on him. ‘Aren’t you tired?’

‘It’s been a long day.’

A flicker of a smile crossed Flanagan’s face. Perhaps it had been a competition. ‘I need a leak.’

‘Help yourself.’ I was trying to be gracious. If this was a staying awake contest then I didn’t mind losing. Pick your fights. I watched as Flanagan left the room. Pushed the papers around on the table and felt my mind begin to cloud then heard the toilet flush.

Flanagan walked back into the room and made the ‘telephone’ sign with his thumb and little finger. ‘Simon?’

I was losing it. I’d forgotten that we were going to ring him back. I took Simon’s mobile telephone from the table and hit the autodial. Five rings and it was answered. ‘Spencer, is that you?’

Scottish accent. I straightened in my seat and Flanagan leaned towards me as I spoke. He dragged a cloud of smoke across with him and I coughed into my hand. ‘Yes, it’s Beck. I’ve got Daniel Flanagan with me.’

'Interested now?'

'Very,' I said. It didn't hurt to humour the guy. Flanagan scowled. 'What more can you tell us?'

'You're going to the AGM?'

'Yes.' I looked and caught Flanagan's eye. 'We'll be there.'

'He'll expect you but you're not in danger,' said Simon. 'He may not talk. Too many people around but he'll see you in New York.'

I didn't like this 'danger' thing. And what was this about the US? 'New York?'

'Yes,' said Simon and I looked up again. Flanagan was smiling. 'I'll get back to you with the location. Have your questions ready and don't ring this number again. I'll ring you if we need to speak.'

The line went dead. New York? How was I going to swing that? I looked at Flanagan. 'You got that?'

'Yeah. You really laid it out for him, Spencer.' Flanagan smirked. 'So you're coming to the States?'

I nodded. 'I can take it from here on my own, Daniel. You've been a tremendous help.'

It was worth rattling his bars and showing him who was boss and it worked. The smirk slid from Flanagan's face and the pause said it all. 'You're kidding, right?'

Pretty much what I'd expected. 'You've been great but –'

I hadn't expected to be allowed to finish the sentence and I wasn't. Flanagan's face was set. 'After Maria,' he said and I'd swear there had been a catch in his voice. He continued. 'After what I let go for so many years, I've got to be there.'

He wasn't asking for a debate on the subject and despite myself I was pleased. Maybe he was straight. He didn't seem to have any interest in stealing my story and I'd welcome the company. He seemed OK and now that he'd pushed himself on me he could pay his own way. I made a show of thinking about it and considered making him wait until the morning but decided against it. 'I suppose if you want to, why not.'

'Fuckin' A why not,' said Flanagan. Everything was a contest. 'I'll put you up –'

'I don't think that will be necessary.'

I'd said that a little too quickly and Flanagan's face dropped. I hadn't credited him with having any feelings but that may have been unfair and he inclined his chin towards the telephone, changed the subject. 'Do you trust him?'

Another good question. Simon was a critical link. If I couldn't trust him, then everything else would fall away. But I didn't know. I was doing my due diligence and didn't have enough yet to judge him one way or the other. I needed more. 'He hasn't lied to us yet,' I said. 'Do you?'

Flanagan took the cigarette from his mouth but said nothing.

Twelve
08:35 - Monday 14th June
Cambridge, England

Flanagan looked around the small breakfast room. Fortunately, he hadn't sparked up and, muttering something that included the word 'fuck', he put the pack of cigarettes back in his pocket.

It was 8.35am. Monday morning and we were in Cambridge, had stayed over. We'd spent what had been left of the weekend trawling the Internet and pottering around London when it all got to be too much. We'd taken in one or two of the sights that I took for granted and had hacked up to Cambridge across Sunday lunchtime. That way, we wouldn't be late for the two company's AGMs and I looked back at Flanagan. 'You've got food in your hair.'

Flanagan flapped at his head and caught what looked like a few crumbs and examined them but graciously refrained from eating them as I took in the room. Drab was the word that came to mind. Followed by a conciliatory 'but clean'. But I'd wanted to keep the cost down before I knew whether or not I'd be able to stick one of the newspapers that I was talking to with the tab and I took a deep breath – I'd been trying to persuade Flanagan to keep his voice down. It was exhausting and bad for my blood pressure and he looked at me suspiciously while I made a show of patting my pockets.

Money, iPhone, fully charged and Simon's mobile, writing paper and pen. I was tooled up with a cutting edge mix of nineteenth and twenty-first century technology and was ready to go but I felt faintly thick-headed. I'd taken Flanagan to a couple of the pubs that I'd known for years and I hadn't slept well.

The air in the hotel was very dry so I was dehydrated, that was all – because it couldn't be nerves, could it? The tourist thing and the long hours in front of the computer in London and the drive up to Cambridge in the rain had done me in. And Flanagan's snoring and his cigarettes had taken it out of me as well. Left my nasal passages feeling like the inside of a chimney but something else was nagging at me, had kept me from sleep last night.

It was worry and more than that it was fear. I wasn't afraid of Adam Reid himself but I was afraid of being wrong. Of being made to look a fool. I could see the man before me as clearly as if he occupied Flanagan's seat and could still not quite believe that this was happening. Financial journalists had focused on his money and biotech and scientific trade journalists focused on the brilliance of his companies. But the feature writers had been shut out, meaning that there was much less out there to go on than might have been expected.

Flanagan belched into his hand. He looked as happy as a pig in shit but my antennae were twitching. I'd do what I could to prevent it but I could be suckered in, anybody could.

The murder or murders in New York had been real enough. The surgery was likely true. And the interest in embryology, the companies, the financial success and the rest was all there and Flanagan seemed genuine but he could be wrong. Or his strings could be being pulled by a third party; there was always the possibility of a set-up.

Paranoid but was there anyone out there who wanted to bring me down that much? It was unlikely; I was just a lowly hack. I'd made an enemy or two but it was school playground stuff. I wasn't important enough to be targeted but if it wasn't me then could it be somebody using me to get at Adam?

So all I could do was to proceed at a measured pace. I wouldn't do or say anything that would risk my credibility but equally inaction was not an option. I found myself shaking my head in agreement with my own thoughts. I waved away a waitress who'd assumed that I was trying to attract her attention and considered our next move.

The Annual General Meetings were marked as eleven for eleven-thirty. They were a public or at least a semi-public gathering and we had every right to be there. We'd bought a single share each in both Zylagene and Zylapharm in order to ensure that we were on the share registers but I still felt like some sort of criminal.

It was pathetic, really – I was looking around every few seconds to see if we were being overheard. I considered that the tables in the hotel's tiny breakfast room were too close together and I wanted to leave before Flanagan's American accent attracted too much attention, or he said fuck or shit, or mentioned mammoths, murders or groin injuries once too often. I stood up and made a show of checking my watch. 'Time to leave.'

Flanagan looked up at me as though I was some sort of idiot and glanced at his own watch. We were early, yes but I didn't want a debate and I turned before he could say anything and headed for the door when the wallpaper in the hotel's small lobby assaulted my senses again.

It was lively to say the least. And I had to half-close my eyes but we'd left our overnight bags behind the reception desk and I wanted to ensure that we could pick them up after the meeting. Having done so I took a seat in the hotel's lobby and waited for Flanagan to finish up whatever it was he was doing and I tried to put some finishing touches to the day ahead.

I should be able to get something out of it, whatever happened. I could cover the AGMs at the very least. And I could do a human interest piece and comment on the great man's fan club. The devotees that I imagined were going to pack out the meeting and I picked up a couple of newspapers, skimmed the headlines.

Mostly rubbish. Celebrity gossip and whatnot filled the redtops. And sundry financial scandals and low level drug wars in South America dominated the headlines in the couple of broadsheets that lay, well-thumbed on the coffee table. Killings seemed to be positively correlated to the price of cocaine and both were on the up but drug volumes were down and Police Chiefs from Miami to Washington State were claiming successes whilst probably wondering like the rest of us just what was going on.

**

An hour and a half later Flanagan and I left Trinity Street and entered King's Parade. The magnificent fifteenth century college chapel, which had taken ninety years to build and which was deemed to be a gift to God, loomed to our right and the pavement was heavy with tourists.

Nonetheless, we'd had a pleasant enough walk through the Backs though now Flanagan was getting antsy and had fallen silent. He was keen to get to the meeting and I knew how he felt because I had a lot riding on it. Because, whilst Flanagan could slink off back to New York, I was gambling with my career, my reputation and any hope I might have of a future.

If anything went wrong I'd be left the butt of a thousand jokes. And I'd never been a believer in the saying that what didn't kill you made you stronger and I wasn't heartened by the fact that historians and better journalists than me had fallen for the Hitler diaries and no end of other tripe.

They'd been blinded by their desire that something be true. They had tumbled into making a commitment and I knew how powerful a temptation that was. Combine the desire to discover something and to report its existence to the world with flattery and it could become a force that was almost impossible to resist.

So we would progress cautiously. I would insist on it. Didn't want any obvious errors or inconsistencies to embarrass us in the blinding light of day and I kept asking myself if a billionaire could really be a killer?

Stupid question, really. Of course he could. William the Bastard had been a billionaire. They reckoned him to be one of the half dozen richest men in English history and he'd killed hundreds of thousands but that was then. And this was now and we weren't talking about killing with the stroke of a pen or a whispered word but up close and personal.

I could feel the pull on my reasoning. If it were true, then I couldn't let a story like this slip through my fingers. If I didn't write it and somebody else did then I'd have no choice, I'd simply have to kill myself so it was a gamble worth taking and we'd be careful.

I looked across to my companion and saw that Flanagan had acquired a toffee apple from somewhere. He was waving it in tune to a distant brass band. It seemed to be keeping him happy so I left him to it and we made for Queen's College. Headed towards the Fitzwilliam Research Institute, the University's centralized science facilities and the location for today's AGMs. I slowed us down, we had time and I wanted to clear my head, but that was more easily said than done.

Professor George Reid had been an enigma. We'd dug up a bit more and certainly the man had been a brilliant embryologist, geneticist, call it what you will but that had not been the field in which he had initially made his name. He had been an immunologist by training and had worked for the British Government. Much of his work was classified but he'd effectively withdrawn from public view and had thereafter devoted his life to genetics away from the public eye.

But none of what he'd done subsequently seemed to have made it into the journals. He'd been credited in a couple of articles and I got some sense that he'd been held in awe by those that mentioned him but he hadn't contributed directly himself and I turned my attention back to cloning.

We knew that nuclei could be transferred into de-nucleated eggs. The sheep proved it. Others had been produced since and, using what might be called more traditional methods, cattle had been reared using dead sperm and maybe Flanagan had been right. The length of time that the sperm had been dead might be of consequence. If it had been dead for five minutes then why not for five thousand years?

In which case the mammoth would be a real possibility; in theory at least. I could feel the strands of the story coming together but Flanagan was leaning towards me, threatening to tangle the toffee apple in my hair. 'You sure we'll get in?'

I gave myself a moment to judge whether or not he was taking the piss. I'd told him about my troubles up in Yorkshire but he seemed to be playing it straight and I considered his question. I might only have one share but I should be on the share register and I felt a flush of confidence. 'We'll be fine.'

Flanagan raised an eyebrow.

'I've been to dozens of these things,' I said and I could feel him watching me. My voice was steady. I didn't twitch or touch my nose but nor did I look at him directly. 'We won't have a problem.'

'And you're sure about that?'

'Daniel, I've never been refused access to an AGM in my life,' I said. So much was true but there could always be a first time. My little misunderstanding in Ranulfskelf may have earned me a place on some sort of blacklist but I had to convey a sense of confidence. 'Reid doesn't want a row with the Press.'

**

Bold words indeed but on this occasion I was right because, forty minutes later and after a lengthy and rather fretful wait in the queue to get in, Daniel Flanagan and I were seated in the huge lecture hall that was to serve as the setting for the Annual General Meetings of both Zylagene and Zylapharm.

And there had been no problems. Our names were checked and our invites, downloaded from the Internet, were scanned. Very high tech and impressive. I once again looked around the hall. It had been busy when we came in and had got busier since.

The coffee was excellent and the croissants that had been made available as we moved slowly through what had served as an entry-hall-cum-buffet area had been even better and I'd had a couple. And I'd given serious consideration to a third but had let it lie and had watched as Flanagan outdid me, putting away the best part of a dozen before I wrestled to pull him away.

And then we'd managed to bag aisle seats. We'd braved the hard stares of the countless people forced to squeeze by us to take the seats that we'd cut off from the aisle but we needed to be able to make a swift exit if necessary.

The mutterings and mumblings in the hall were still at a high pitch but I sensed that we were about to start and I scoped out the room once more. The raised stage was eighteen or twenty rows away to the front but a huge screen had been erected as a backdrop at head height, halfway between the speaker's podium and the felt covered table reserved for the companies' Boards of Directors.

I couldn't quite make out the nameplates.

But judging by the length of the names, Adam's was blessedly short at four letters by four letters whilst most of the others seemed to be the honourable this, that or the other, it looked as though the key man would be sitting in the centre of the table.

Three stuffed shirts would be seated to either side of him and, as if something had been reading my mind, the screen behind the table came to life and the image on it panned from the audience to the podium and to the director's table. The names were clearly readable and it was confirmed, Adam would be seated at the centre of his Board.

As the audience's attention was drawn to the screen, the noise in the hall subsided. Nothing tangible was happening but conversations were being wound up in anticipation. Soon only a faint background buzz remained and I could feel it, the desire of the hundreds and hundreds of private clients and fund managers made wealthy by Adam Reid to see him and to pay their respects or to simply to be in the same room as the great man.

And, whilst private clients seemed to make up the majority of the audience, the financial community was also here in force and I watched with interest as the image on the screen panned around and played across the seated rows of attendees.

I recognised several of the faces but there were other suited guests I didn't. They looked like money managers, pension fund advisers, financial analysts and there were not a few journalists. They would be as keen as I was to get past the formal nonsense that always accompanied AGMs and to find out just how much money the twin companies were likely to make going forward. And the entire audience would want to know how the various drugs were coming on, whether to expect any announcements in the near future and whether the companies, as had often been rumoured, were to be merged.

I found my eye drawn to the journalists because they were the competition. Some freelancers were in evidence alongside quite a number of staff writers. Many of them would also be shareholders and all of them were looking for an angle, a story, something to make a routine AGM just that little bit more interesting for their readers.

And I wanted them all to fuck off and die, of course. In the nicest possible way but a rustling beside me intruded on my thoughts and I pursed my lips, looked across at Flanagan.

He had produced another croissant. God knows how he had smuggled it past me and I certainly didn't want to ask. He gave me a leery smile and ate it almost whole before returning his attention to the cup of coffee that he'd placed on the floor and which had thus far not been kicked over.

I looked back at the screen and considered my next move. I wasn't going to ask a question in front of such an audience because a question asked was an answer shared and I didn't like public speaking at the best of times. I would drop the microphone or clam up or have a coughing fit or sound like a six year old girl or all of the above so, if I wasn't going to ask any questions, then just what was I doing here?

I could kid myself that it was background research but what I really wanted was the chance to see the man in the flesh. Simon had said that Adam would see us in New York and I was happy to play today as it came.

I'd certainly talk to him if I got the chance but I knew that was unlikely. The door to the side of the Director's table at the front of the hall suggested that the Board would enter and leave the AGM without having to walk the gauntlet of their shareholders. They would preserve their mystique but Flanagan had finished his food and broke my train of thought as he spoke again. He seemed to have been reading my mind. 'So remind me why we're here.'

I looked at him. 'Research, Daniel.'

Perhaps that would sound scholarly enough, shut him up. He leaned towards me and I was treated to a waft of coffee flavoured croissant which, though better than stale smoke, I didn't welcome. Flanagan nodded vaguely towards the back of the hall. 'It's being webcast. Why are we here?'

'I've never seen him in person before,' I found myself saying. It was a nothing comment but it was true.

Flanagan was holding onto the seat in front of him and must have been giving it a bit of a shake because the female occupant, middle-aged, well dressed as though for a wedding, turned and scowled at me. Not that I'd done anything but she seemed to be implying that Flanagan was my responsibility. Some sort of pet so I went on the offensive. 'Would you mind taking your hat off please, Madam?'

That shut her up. It was a horrible pink thing. It wasn't really getting in my way but the woman's bosom swelled dangerously as she processed her outrage and that cheered me up immensely. I blanked her, spoke directly to Flanagan. 'I want to see how he presents,' I said. 'See if he's as impressive as they say.'

'Un-huh,' said Flanagan. He had either caught on or was naturally rude. 'Be at the front of the queue to kiss his ass?'

The woman in front of him quivered with outrage and I looked at her directly whilst replying to Flanagan. 'I'll leave that to some of our fellow guests,' I said and was pleased to see another angry frisson. It was the little things that made life worth living but the hat was still in position so I guess the lady was hanging on for a draw.

'Hey,' said Flanagan a few moments later. I wasn't deaf but I was slow to turn and he jabbed me with his elbow. He raised his arm, pointed. 'Lady seems to know you.'

I looked up and saw a round face looking at me, the hand that was attached to its body making unattractive, jerky motions in order to attract my attention. It was Shelley Mitchum and she was no more than eight rows ahead. She smiled broadly and I groaned. Flanagan coughed into his hand. 'Love interest?'

'Fuck no,' I hissed through what I hoped was a Shelley-facing smile.

'Language, Spencer,' said Flanagan. I heard him chuckle.

The woman in front of us shuddered once again but she had a right to be upset because my language was on the slide. I blamed Flanagan. But the thought of being romantically involved with Shelley was enough to make anyone swear and I had an unpleasant vision of a post-coital Mitchum naked, trying to decide which rolls of blubber belonged in her bra. I spoke from the corner of my mouth. 'She's a hack, a real cow.'

Flanagan smirked but I should have expected her. I suppose that I probably did. She might be a sleazy bitch but she was a professional. I'd have to keep her away from Flanagan otherwise she would smell a story. I lowered my voice. 'She's written on Reid before. Shallow stuff. Nothing in it for us.'

Flanagan smirked again.

He clearly didn't believe me but what could I do? I waved and Mitchum made some sort of 'who is he?' gesture that I chose not to understand. I did my best baffled, made a telephone with my hand followed by a drink gesture and spoke from the corner of my mouth. 'Ignore her. We're here for Reid. He needs us. The financial community including journalists I mean. People like Mitchum and me, particularly if he's trying to do something. Raise new money or combine the companies.'

'Yeah,' said Flanagan. He gave Mitchum what I hoped was a final wave before folding another croissant into his mouth. He wiped the crumbs from his moustache and leant down. Picked up the coffee cup from beneath his chair and drained it. At least his attention had moved away from Shelley and he craned his neck, looked around the hall. 'How many guests, you figure?'

I shrugged. It was a good question. I'd have to have a stab at a number for any piece that I wrote but I caught the eye of the woman in front of us again. Unfortunately that gave her the satisfaction of turning away huffily and put her one up in our little contest. I had a stab at the number of rows, the number of attendees in each row. My mental arithmetic let me down but it was a hell of a crowd. 'I don't know.'

Flanagan raised a frowned and I had another go.

It looked as though the hall's dividing walls had been removed as several subsidiary halls were combined into this larger room and, unless I'd got the decimal point in the wrong place, there were sixteen, seventeen hundred people in it. 'You saw the screens in the reception room? There'll be more people out there, probably a good two to three thousand here in total.'

Flanagan's eyes wandered to the back of the hall, the buffet and he grunted. 'So what about New York?'

'What about what about New York?'

'What's the plan, skipper?'

I raised my shoulders. 'Follow Simon's lead. Go there and try to meet with Adam.'

It sounded weak but we had to go. It meant that I would be joined to Flanagan at the hip for a little while longer but he could be useful.

Because it was his home town and he knew the ins and the outs. He would still have contacts of one sort or another and we had managed to bring his flight time forward. Now we were flying tomorrow afternoon.

That would get us into JFK in the early evening. It would still be Tuesday and the New York meeting was set for 4pm Wednesday at the American Museum of Natural History so I could spend the morning having a sniff around. And Flanagan could harass homeless people or do whatever he did when he was back home and I could still be back in England before the weekend. 'Whether Simon is full of shit or not, we've got to be there.'

'Agreed,' said Flanagan. I'd used the 'we' word by accident and he hadn't missed it. I didn't reply and Flanagan sucked at his empty coffee cup then patted the packet of cigarettes in his pocket. He took them out but scowled and returned them to his pocket.

A buzzer sounded from the reception room behind us and I looked at my watch. It was just shy of 11.30am. The show was about to commence and this was the last call. The doors to the reception room opened and a wave of stragglers swept in. It threatened to overwhelm the ushers who had otherwise been doing a good job head-counting and directing guests to available seats but gradually the general bustle died down and was replaced by an expectant hush because Adam Reid, one of the richest and most powerful men in the world was about to address an audience.

This audience. And I could feel it too. There was a charge in the air, the excitement palpable. My breathing was shallow and I found myself wondering if he would keep us waiting like a rock star or an evangelical preacher. Would he play us like an instrument and allow the anticipation to prepare the ground for him?

He might well do because Adam was a champion. He was an idol but to the people in the audience he was more than that because he had made them rich. He was at the top of his game and he could stay there for the next forty, fifty, sixty years. He was a presence, a real phenomenon and the people around me sensed it.

I sensed it. Even Flanagan seemed to sense it and he leaned towards me. 'This is unreal.'

'Pretty intense.'

'They gonna dim the lights or what?'

Nuremburg rally or not I couldn't allow myself to get swept up in it. I told myself that I'd seen it all before. And that I had a job to do.

Only I knew damned well that I hadn't seen it all before and then the music began.

It wasn't a triumphal march but rather soft and by no means tasteless and I felt rather than heard the intake of breath around the hall. It had come from behind us. The board wouldn't be taking their seats from the front of the hall after all. A thick knot of people had entered the rear of the hall and was moving slowly towards us.

The attendees were rising to their feet and I found myself standing as the wave of guests getting to their feet broke over us and then the audience began to applaud.

A ripple at first but within seconds the hall was a sea of noise. Cheering and clapping. Whistling and the stamping of feet greeted the great man's arrival and I'd never seen anything like it. It was worship of a sort, a mania had descended upon the audience.

This was religious devotion if ever I'd seen it and I had to distance myself from it if I was to do my job. Reid's entourage was making steady progress towards us and I realised that the man was going to pass right by me.

I would be inches from him and I couldn't speak. I was clapping. I couldn't help myself. I may even have been stamping my feet and then the man was there, within touching distance. And just for an instant he was looking straight at me. Adam Reid, the billionaire, a good five, six inches taller than me and his eyes, brilliant blue and full of intelligence and understanding, were concentrating all of their attention on me and then he was gone and I felt drained, physically exhausted.

One of many, I sat down. Slumped more like. I had only held the man's eyes for an instant but Reid had spoken to me. He had somehow communicated with me but I shook my head, had to clear it of such thoughts because the whole audience probably felt the same way.

There was no doubt that the man had something special. In a couple of seconds he had left me with the firm impression of probity but if I wrote that down they would drag me off to a white van and I felt a fool. And that was a risk as well because I couldn't let it develop into a resentment that could prevent me from remaining detached but I did feel as though I had been played in some way. I had been read by the man in a split second and now I was coming down from a high.

I knew the feeling but it was all an illusion, it had to be. I had just been dazzled by his money. I looked back at the group as it neared the podium and that's when I saw Nosey.

The bastard from Ranulfskelf Hall was moving with Adam, was standing towards the back of his group and he was looking at me. He raised two fingers to his head in a salute to me and the adulation fell away; Reid might be a killer and I was here to do a job.

I tried to summarise my initial thoughts. Reid was a large man. Big but not fat. Certainly he was solid and he was as broad as his minders. He wasn't dwarfed by them in any way and he'd conveyed the impression of tremendous strength. He was quite something. I looked at Flanagan and realised that I wasn't the only one having trouble remaining detached. The American's mouth was hanging open.

Flanagan felt me looking at him and shrugged. 'Wow.'

I tried to look nonchalant.

'Wow,' said Flanagan again. 'He's some piece of work.'

I watched the board's progress. Reid had reached the steps to the podium and the chosen few in the front rows were doing everything short of touching his cloak. I knew that not thirty seconds since I had been a part of that myself but this was moving to the next level now because some of them were bowing to him. There was a curtsy or two while others tried to shake Reid's hand and I managed to take a breath.

‘He’s got those people eating out of his hand.’

I felt Flanagan look sideways at me. ‘Not you though huh, Spencer?’

‘He’s got a presence.’

‘Wipe your chin.’

I raised my hand to my chin without thinking. ‘I’ll admit that.’

‘Looks different,’ said Flanagan after a moment’s silence. ‘To when I last saw him, I mean. Only the eyes are the same.’

I let the words sink in and looked up. The large-bosomed woman with the pink fruit cocktail hat was all smiles. She looked as giddy as a schoolgirl, turned around. ‘Wonderful, simply wonderful –’

I tried a cynical, fuck-him sneer but couldn’t carry it off and settled for watching Adam as he sprang up the stairs and onto the stage. He walked towards the single podium whilst the other directors took their positions behind their chairs at the main table where they too remained standing and applauded as their companies’ founder acknowledged them.

Adam Reid turned to face his audience and held up his left hand. The applause died. No hesitation, no fading splutter, it just died and was replaced by the rustle of clothing and of papers as the members of the audience looked as one at Adam who, his face huge on the screen above the heads of the Board behind him, smiled back at them.

The Chairman and Chief Executive of two of the most dynamic companies in the world ran his fingers through his thick hair. He looked young. I felt another stab of jealousy and looked around, trying to gauge the mood of the other attendees. For the most part they appeared to be in a trance and it all made sense.

Nuremberg, Jonestown, the demagoguery and the charismatic leadership found at the head of any one of a number of crackpot sects may well have been similar. Their people may have been equally helpless in the hands of a visionary leader, a man who provided them with a feeling of oneness and a reason to be.

Not that I could put that into words. The screens above Adam Reid’s head were now displaying the logos of Zylagene and Zylapharm and

Adam held up his hand again. The logos above his head melted away to be replaced by an image of the man himself.

He was handsome, in a way. My hand had risen to my lip. Reid's face was unblemished. It was broad and open, crowned by a full head of thick, red-blond hair. I pictured the man's father and saw no similarities as the massive, sky-blue eyes on the screen scanned the audience once more. I felt as though the great man was looking at me and I felt a physical vibration running through me.

Another vibration and I realised that my mobile phone was vibrating against my leg and I laughed with relief. It vibrated again and I killed the call. It would go to voicemail. The thing would vibrate again to tell me if the caller had left a message, would do the same if I got a text. I breathed again and looked back at the image on the screen.

Adam's eyes seemed to hold on mine and then the camera panned out and I had to admit that it was being expertly done. Not triumphal or tasteless. Simply professional and it was getting the message across. This was a team and the camera cut to a wider shot. Adam with the board behind him and he held up his hand once more. 'I'd like to welcome you all here today,' he said. His voice was assured, mid-Atlantic.

Perhaps somewhat more English than American but I'd seen most of the very few television interviews that he'd given and knew what he sounded like. He swept the audience up with his arm and then addressed one of the several cameramen who had been scuttling across the front of the stage before him. 'And not only those of you that have been able to attend in person today in Cambridge but also to those joining us for the webcast. We'll be in New York in person on Wednesday but, for the moment, I'd like to extend a warm welcome to you all.'

Adam paused and took a sip of water. He might be young but he had done this before. He knew his audience and was working it well. They were already breathless. Shit, I was already breathless and the room was deathly quiet.

'Your company,' said Adam. He placed the glass of water on the lectern before him with care. 'We, your Board of Directors and I personally would like to thank you for your continued support.'

A murmur rippled around the room. Nods of approval and Adam continued. 'For without it, we would have achieved nothing.'

A smatter of applause but Adam waved it down. 'So the key message from today, more important than the detail to follow is that we value and need you. And we recognise the vital help that you have provided us in our journey to date.'

Adam paused. This was bollocks. Adam owned the vast majority of the shares in his companies. He could easily have sourced what little capital he required externally from the banks. He scarcely needed the support of his smaller shareholders but heads around the room were nodding and what harm could it do? Throw them a bone from time to time. The need to be needed was a powerful thing.

So Adam was spinning a web. Inclusivity was important to the man. And he may need these people going forward and I had to admit it, he was doing a good job of humouring them. He had achieved so much at such a young age and yet here he was, thanking his audience, the group of private and institutional shareholders who owned the thinnest sliver of his companies. He was making them feel wanted and doing a good job of sounding as though he really meant it.

Maybe he did. Because I was a journalist and cynicism came with the territory but certainly the audience, the heterogeneous individuals that Adam was weaving into a homogenous mass, wanted him to mean it. They wanted to believe that they had pleased their Chairman and felt the desire to applaud themselves. They did so but Adam spoke again and the clapping died. 'There is some formal business to attend to here but, for my part, I'd like to take the opportunity of introducing you to your companies' Boards of Directors.'

Adam turned and included his fellow directors, men that all of us knew were little more than puppets, in his conversation with a sweep of his arm. 'And we'd like to run you through some of the highlights of the last year before covering what we see as some of our major opportunities for the future.'

He was using the 'we' word. He was still pushing the inclusivity button and the audience approved as charts appeared on the screen above Adam's head. I wasn't concentrating so much on the words he was using as the tone, the feel. There was much to celebrate, Adam was saying and, as he ran swiftly and professionally through the main events of the year to March, his shareholders remained transfixed by the presentation and felt themselves to have played an important part in the companies' success.

And then Adam stepped it up. He spelled out how it had been a year of breath-taking achievements. Zylagene had broken new drugs. It had replenished the pipeline for Zylapharm, which had taken the patent-approved products and had marketed them successfully worldwide. The company had opened on time and on budget new production plants in Pennsylvania, the Czech Republic, Indonesia and Colombia.

I knew all of this. Or rather, if I was a little sketchy on the detail I had access to it as it was historic information, but this was genuinely impressive stuff. And the man on the stage, who was gently embracing his audience and relentlessly drawing it in, was not yet twenty-five years old. It was almost impossible to believe and still Adam went on, handling his audience magnificently. Even I could feel something tugging at me. I was anchored to my rock of cynicism but I was listening to his celebratory rhetoric and I could have easily succumbed completely.

I knew it. The man was a marvel. Success had bred success, said Adam. Together he, his directors, his company and this audience had built something to be proud of. They had created something that would make a lasting impression on the world around them. It would shape its very development and, when Adam finally walked back to his fellow directors and sat down amongst them, the dam within the hall burst and the audience leapt to its feet, exploding into a round of applause so loud and so energetic that it shook the walls and drew the breath from my lungs.

And I was clapping, Flanagan too.

My hands were beginning to hurt but, as the company's finance director, Naylor Tyndahl took the podium and began to speak, I could feel the charge begin to ebb.

Not that Tyndahl did a bad job. He ran through the formal business of the meeting efficiently. All of the motions were approved on a show of hands. Had a vote been demanded, Adam's shares would have carried the day whatever had happened in the hall but then Tyndahl returned to the figures and outlined in greater detail the financial state of the company.

And again Tyndahl performed well. I'd been to a few meetings where finance directors had put their audiences to sleep but that wasn't going to happen today. Indeed Tyndahl even managed to inject some excitement and, as he built towards what I was sure was going to be a handover to Adam, ripples of polite applause spluttered from time to time around the room. Finally, the finance director raised his hand. This was his big moment but the audience was ignoring him and I felt a flash of sympathy as the anticipation built and Adam Reid once again rose to his feet.

Adam graced Tyndahl with a smile as the two men crossed by the podium. Any words exchanged between them were lost to the noise in the hall and Adam turned to face his audience once more. He surveyed the room, unspeaking. He didn't need to say it but this was a team. And Adam was simply the first amongst equals. When he spoke, his voice was soft but heavy with meaning.

The company was strong, he said. I found that the words themselves did not register but I knew what he meant and the rest of his audience understood too. Hell the world knew what he was talking about, words were unnecessary.

The companies had made unprecedented progress. In the five short years of their public life they had each put down deep roots. Zylagene broke new ground and Zylapharm was truly in a class of its own with manufacturing operations in sixteen countries and products that sold in a hundred and fifty.

The approval of the audience was almost palpable and Adam played it well. 'Ladies and gentlemen,' he said. The hushed words got through to his audience. 'There is much more to come. We have achieved a great deal, certainly we have. But I can promise you, absolutely promise you that, in the current year, we will deliver to you and to the people of the world much, much more.'

Adam paused and sipped from his glass. He looked up. 'Because this, ladies and gentlemen, will be the most exciting, the most interesting and the most rewarding year in the history of your company. I can promise you that this year, your companies will shake the world.'

Well that did it. Adam Reid, the leader, had spoken. As he held open his arms and encompassed the room it exploded into applause the like of which I had never heard or seen before because we were a team. Every one of us, including myself with my single, solitary share in his companies, had a role to play and Adam was thanking us. His eyes, pale-blue on the huge screen above his head, caught the light and shone down on us and no words were needed because we all knew, individually, that he was speaking to us.

Some in the audience were shaking with emotion. Others were hugging each other. The walls were shaking and Adam waited patiently for silence to return, continued mouthing the same two words: 'Thank you, thank you, thank you.'

Slowly, the noise began to abate. Some in the audience folded, exhausted and utterly spent into their seats and, as I sat down, I felt empty, drained. I had been on a high but exhaustion was just beneath the surface and I looked around me. The room as a whole was quietening down. The audience seemed to be hoping for an encore and I glanced at Daniel Flanagan.

He managed a world-weary shrug but he couldn't carry it off. He had been swept up in it too. As the last of the clapping and whistling and whooping died away, Adam Reid swept his arm across the audience. 'Fellow shareholders. Colleagues. Friends. Let's eat.'

Momentary confusion then the words sunk in and I rose to my feet, stepping into the aisle. I knew what these things could be like. There had been no shortage of nibbles with the coffee but this was the food proper and, at a more typical AGM, the stampede could sweep you out of the room.

But this crowd was different. The people had genuinely come to hear Adam Reid speak and for once the food was incidental. Even Daniel Flanagan was quiet and I began to edge towards the side of the hall. The ex-cop followed but said nothing until we made the back of the room and he gestured towards the now empty stage. 'Not bad.'

Not a lot I could add. We exited the hall and were shepherded along a short corridor, down some steps and into the room where the buffet had been laid out. I caught Flanagan's eye, gestured back towards the main hall with my chin. 'You were immune?'

It broke the spell. I knew that he'd felt it and Flanagan held the sandwich that had somehow appeared in his hand suspiciously to the light. 'Yeah, totally.'

Flanagan took a bite then spoke through the food in his mouth. 'No, I felt it.'

'He's good,' I said. 'He's very, very good and he's just a kid.'

Flanagan grunted, turned back to a second sandwich. Two bites and it was gone. I looked around, decided to give the food a miss. I'd try to catch Adam if he worked the room. Would try to keep Shelley Mitchum away from Flanagan too but that wouldn't be easy as she'd be cruising the room herself within a minute or two. She'd be looking for Adam or for one of the other Board members first. Then she'd look to the B-list and then she'd begin to wonder who Flanagan was. I tapped the man's shoulder and nodded towards the exit.

The American looked momentarily annoyed then crammed something white into his mouth before picking up another sandwich and a napkin. He dabbed his face. The finality of the gesture was reassuring and he spoke. 'Did your cell phone ring?'

Flanagan had this eating-and-speaking-together thing honed to a fine art. He was right though, I'd forgotten the call. I fumbled for the telephone in my pocket and took it out, holding it away from prying eyes.

One missed call, number withheld. On a whim I took out Simon's phone and hit number twenty-six. 'I told you not to ring this number again,' said a voice almost immediately. He didn't sound happy. 'I'll ring you in New York, stay in the Voyager Hotel. We'll organize a room and Reid will see you personally. Plane tickets will be in your flat by the time you get back there. You know the place.'

The line went dead.

'The Voyager, huh?' said Flanagan. 'Nice.'

The man had good ears but just how many people were breaking into my flat? It must be like a fucking railway station in there. Flanagan raised his eyebrows, seemed to require a response but I ignored him. The flights were free and we had to pack.

Thirteen
16:44 - Tuesday 15th June
John F Kennedy Airport, New York

I could see it, my case. The large mauve stickers on its sides singled it out in the sea of black, dark blue and grey luggage moving slowly around the carousel and I congratulated myself on my foresight.

First off the carousel, I dumped my case onto the waiting trolley. Immigration had been a bit of pain. It often was these days but the lines had been efficiently managed and the officials had been polite. But that was ancient history now, I was in. I located customs and pushed off with the trolley because there was no reason to hang around.

I'd travelled alone as Flanagan had been unwell. They'd been quite accommodating on his ticket. He would follow on when he was up to it but I had to make the meeting tomorrow and, after having seen him straining and puking as we'd pulled over on the M11 on our way back to London, I'd had to accept that leaving him behind had been for the best.

I felt a degree of sympathy for the man but I was hardly surprised. He had consumed a large breakfast. Then upward of a dozen croissants followed by chicken sandwiches, strong coffee and God knows what else yesterday and all before lunch. It would have been enough to upset anyone's stomach but his cramps had persisted and, back in London, he'd sunk into the settee and begun to complain of chest pains.

I'd called the doctor out and Flanagan had been taken into the Royal

Free. The hospital had wanted to keep him in for observation and I could hardly blame them. He had looked dreadful and I wished him a speedy recovery but for now, it was clear that I was alone.

I took the green channel. I usually felt vaguely guilty when I did that but this time it was different. I was too busy worrying about Flanagan to consider whether or not I had any bacon or tobacco or apples or whatever in my luggage and I had a job to do. The meetings wouldn't wait and I hadn't asked him to stuff his face will all sorts of crap but if the roles had been reversed, would Flanagan have abandoned me so readily?

I'd never know but one thing I did know was that I needed some sleep ahead of the appointment in New York. I'd determined to ring the hospital the first chance I got and, with customs now behind me and the ugly queue for taxis not going anywhere fast, I took out my mobile and turned it on.

The thing began searching for a signal. It was probably costing me an arm and a leg while it roamed around and did whatever mobile phones did but shortly it flashed up the name of an operating system and I hit the number that I'd stored for the Royal Free.

'Flanagan, yes,' I said some moments later. 'Daniel Flanagan. American. Male, late fifties, admitted late on Monday evening. I need to find out how he's doing.'

'Hold for a moment please,' said the voice. 'I have another number for you.'

'Where is he?'

'Here's the number.'

'Where is he?'

'The number?'

Well she was insistent, I'd give her that. I didn't want to run up the mother of all bills arguing with a receptionist in London so I took down the number. The 0208 suggested that it was in the suburbs somewhere and I heard myself thanking the woman on the other end of the phone before I rang the number that she'd given me.

‘Hello?’

‘This is Spencer Beck,’ I said. I sounded self-conscious. But a number of people in the taxi queue around me were shouting into mobiles in a variety of languages so I had no reason to feel singled out. ‘I was hoping to get some information on a Mr Daniel Flanagan.’

‘Are you a relative?’

‘No,’ I said.

That didn’t sound good. The worry welling in my stomach left me with no words and the silence grew. I suddenly found it difficult to breathe and the woman spoke again. ‘Then may I ask what your interest in Mr Flanagan is?’

‘He’s a friend,’ I said. I sounded much better than I felt. ‘He was staying with me in London.’

‘Would you be able to attend the hospital in person, Mr Beck? It could be very important.’

‘No, I can’t do that,’ I said a little too quickly. This wasn’t getting any better. Surely they would tell me if Flanagan was seriously ill? They wouldn’t put a friend or relative through hours of uncertainty while they travelled to the hospital. ‘I’m out of the country. I can’t get there for a few days. How is he?’

‘When are you coming back, Mr Beck?’ said the voice.

‘How is he?’

‘Mr Beck,’ said the woman. ‘We need to know when you are coming back to the UK.’

I hung up. I didn’t quite know why. I didn’t even know if he was still in hospital. I’d ring back later, give another name. Something Flanagan maybe, could even try an American accent. I pushed my trolley forwards and closed up the gap in the taxi queue lest someone nip in front of me then I looked around and for the first time registered the heat.

Most of the queue was in the shade. Of course it had to be otherwise litigious travellers would be keeling over with sunstroke. But I was now in the sun myself and the steaming air all around me filled the gaps between my clothing and my skin.

I felt my back begin to prickle with sweat. My chest was damp, even my head. A cluster of cabs arrived at once and presently I found myself in the back of one of the large yellow cars and now my shirt had a choice, stick to my back or to the still moist broken vinyl of the car seat. It decided to do both.

So this was summer in New York. I gave the taxi driver, a turbaned Southern Asian, the name of my hotel and the tyres squealed on the hot tarmac as he pulled from the curb. No air conditioning so I wound down the window. Better that than nothing.

The draft had my damp hair flapping in my face immediately but letting the air get to my scalp was worth the new hairstyle. Queens flashed past as we overtook a lorry on the inside then swerved into the middle lane of three before shooting between another lorry and a camper van.

Then the outer New York sights. Flushing Meadow. Basketball courts with black youths moving fluidly whipped past to either side of the freeway. The traffic wasn't too heavy and we made good progress. The driver was going to have to try harder if he wanted to force a collision. He seemed to have the hang of this driving in New York thing. Lean hard on the horn and swear in whatever language came naturally to you. I closed my eyes.

I couldn't doze because, as the car slowed and it sought us out, the heat made relaxation impossible. But the towers of the Manhattan skyline were now looming before us, glinting silver, copper and gold in the bright afternoon sun and they still had the capacity to take my breath away. I looked at the back of the taxi driver's head. 'Been here long?'

The head nodded from side to side in an uncertain gesture. The rest of the journey passed in an uneasy silence that I felt no inclination to break. White guy questions immigration status. Nice start but we were into Manhattan without delay and, less than fifteen minutes later, the cab pulled up outside the New York Voyager.

I watched as an old, liveried doorman, stupid hat sitting on his head at a jaunty, I'm-one-of-the-guys angle, pushed the gum to the side of his mouth and stepped forward to open the cab door. The cab's boot sprang open at the same time and my case was whisked inside and there I was, already wondering what, and who, I should be tipping.

It had begun and I hated it. Jesus it was worse than Cairo. Not that I'd ever been to Cairo but I winced. I knew that I had no small change. Plenty of notes but no one or five dollar bills and ten dollars couldn't be the right price for taking a case out of the boot.

I paid the cab fare but that was a fixed sum, it didn't provide me with any small change. I got a receipt and made a show of slipping a pound coin into the gloved hand of the doorman and avoided the man's eye. But a pound was a pound and if I got a quid every five seconds, I'd be happy.

Even if I had to chew gum for fifty five seconds and work for five every minute, sixty quid an hour was plenty for a sorry looking wash-up. But foreign coins were a bummer at the best of times and I walked into the interior of the hotel without looking back.

It was dark after the bright sunlight outdoors. My eyes took a few seconds to adjust and, once I'd put a bit of distance between myself and the doorman, I slowed because there was little upside in walking quickly into something solid.

After a few seconds I could see well enough to avoid the larger objects and people that occupied the lobby. It comprised a marble, dark wood and uniformed bellboy combination. With plenty of those brass trolleys that populate hotel lobbies along with the sounds of rustling paper, the click of heals and the aroma of wood polish, leather and coffee.

A sweeping staircase and the more distant sounds of cutlery and the chink of glasses further added to the well-to-do ambience. I was glad that I wasn't paying for this myself. It was too rich for my pocket. I'd have been just as happy in a budget hotel provided the sheets were clean but hey, when mixing with billionaires, why not push somebody else's boat out?

I could raid a mini-bar with the best of them but the smile that had crept onto my face faded quickly as I once again thought about Detective Flanagan. I had to reassure myself that he was OK and, maybe not as important but of more immediate concern, I had to check in and get a bit of rest.

I swaggered up to the check-in desk in my sixty quid jacket and supermarket shoes. 'Spencer Beck,' I said when the woman behind the counter looked up. 'I have a reservation?'

She slid a form across the counter, on top of it a key. 'Ah yes, Mr Beck,' she said. I was a guest so she had hit the 'polite' switch. I felt sure she could have done a pretty good 'frosty' under other circumstances. She flashed her perfect teeth at me then glanced at the form between us. 'If we could just take a moment of your time?'

I filled in the form. Passport number, that sort of thing and knew that I had to ask. 'The bill?'

'The room's paid for, sir,' said the woman. She gave me another sweet smile. 'It'll just be room service when you leave.'

So I'd better ease off on the room service then. Still, it was a good result and, with the financial side of things settled, I could relax and chase down Flanagan but nonetheless a gloved hand reached for my room key.

I beat it by an inch. Not bad for a jet-lagged old hack straight off the plane. I pried my case from the bellboy's other hand for good measure and flipped it onto its rear wheels, pulling it over to the lifts.

How hard could it be to find my room, for God's sake? It was eight-eleven. Eighth floor, presumably. And I could switch the lights on and work out the air-con for myself, so I waited for the lift, then entered and hit the button for the eighth and was swept upwards smoothly.

The music in the lift was only mildly annoying and finding the room was no problem. The lock worked and I dumped my case onto the bed and checked the room. It was functional but nothing special. The posh reception area had hinted at more. It looked clean enough but it faced the glass-fronted wall of another hotel or office block and I could see the street below only by craning my neck. The window didn't open. Jumpers would be bad for business. They would lead to messy pavements and even messier law-suits and I looked at my watch.

Almost 6pm. That meant 11pm back home. It would be simpler to stay on English time for a two day trip. On that basis the 4pm meeting tomorrow was 9pm English time so if I got a bit of shut-eye in an hour or two, I could get up in the middle of the American night and treat it like daytime.

Best laid plans and all that but I'd give it a go. I slung my jacket on the back of the desk chair then opened my case and pulled out a shirt. In fact I pulled out the shirt. It looked as though the last person to wear it had been dragged through a hedge shortly before being beaten to death with a dirty stick. But it hadn't been exposed to a New York summer complete with perspiring wearer yet so it had to be better than the one I was wearing. I walked through to the small bathroom and hung it on the shower rail. The steam might help.

I considered how best to spend the next couple of hours. Should I be preparing for the meeting, having a beer or zoning out in front of the television? I returned to the bedroom. I picked up the remote and turned on the TV. Left a news channel playing and clocked the mini-bar. It wouldn't be cheap but I deserved a beer. I opened the fridge, grabbed a bottle of Heineken and took a sip.

'The New York Voyager Hotel would like to welcome Mr Beck,' said the banner scrolling across the bottom of the TV screen. 'You have 1 message at reception.'

Flanagan? I left the room and took the lift down to Reception where I picked up what turned out to be a package and ordered a couple more beers and a light meal to be sent up to the room around 8pm.

So that was my evening planned and a couple of minutes later I was back in eight-eleven. I'd find out how Flanagan was tomorrow. Could spend the rest of the evening checking out whatever was in this envelope, reviewing my notes and drinking as much beer as I felt I could afford.

I held the package at arm's length and shook it. It was light and flexible, my name and room number typed neatly on the address label. Not a bomb then. And nor was it a bag full of poisonous snakes but still I gave it a bit of a squeeze then sat on the bed and worked my finger between the flap and the package proper and tore the envelope open.

Old and faded newspaper cuttings spilled out of it and onto my knees. Some of them were crumbling and all smelled like the papers used to line drawers that had been peed on by countless generations of mice. As I struggled to keep the papers in the order that they had arrived, a burgundy pamphlet followed them onto the bed.

It was old, too. The writing was in a dated-looking font with Latin numerals here and there. It was some sort of scientific paper. I checked that the envelope was empty and then put it to one side and focused on the pamphlet. The pages crackled and protested as I opened the document and began to read.

**

I awoke with a start and banged my head against something solid. I had been back in my grandmother's house, surrounded by old photographs, dusty papers, old certificates and ancient school reports. It had been the smell that had taken me there but the knock at the door had roused me and dragged me back to the present. I shouted something to buy myself a few seconds.

I could have sworn I'd only rested my head on the pillow for a second or two but a look at my watch confirmed that I'd lost an hour and a half. It was 8pm. Room service. I made it to the door and looked through the peephole. I couldn't see much but I opened the door nonetheless and stood back as a white-gloved, expensive-looking young man pushed a trolley into the room.

This was overkill. I'd only ordered a sandwich but what I was faced with was a major salad. A thick chunk of bread and what looked like the hind leg of a well-covered pig alongside some other garnishes completely filled a large plate.

The food was accompanied by orange juice, bagels, a pot of coffee and two beers and I mumbled my thanks as the food was unloaded onto the desk and I fumbled in my pocket.

It was either $5 or another £1 coin. No contest. I slipped the £1 coin into the outstretched hand and I couldn't help catching the look of horror and disgust on the man's face. I braced myself to be handed the coin back but as it was, he wasn't quick enough to snub me and I turned away and busied myself with the envelope and some of the cuttings.

I ignored a bit of throat clearing and felt the waiter give up on me and I was alone again, suddenly hungrier than I had imagined possible. I hit the food hard then went for the orange juice, the coffee and the beer in that order.

More sleep would have to wait because the pamphlet had been a game-changer. I had recognised a number of the newspaper articles as originals of the pieces that Flanagan and I had downloaded from the Internet in London while most of the others seemed to be from contemporary Montana newspapers. Little new there but the pamphlet had contained information on a different level altogether.

Credited to Professor George Reid himself but apparently never published, it was dated the November before his death and outlined his work with Henrietta. It had been written with his peers in mind and the vocabulary was pretty esoteric but I had followed it. More or less at least and, unless I was getting completely the wrong end of the stick, Professor Reid seemed to be confirming in the pamphlet that Henrietta was a clone.

And she was a mammoth.

The document looked genuine enough. The best fakes probably always did but there were more Latin names than you could shake a stick at. Mammuthus Primigenius, Loxodonta Africana and the rest. Jargon heaped upon jargon but the claim as to what had been done seemed to be plain enough. The nucleus from a cell taken from the carcass of a frozen mammoth had been introduced into a de-nucleated elephant's egg and bingo, Henrietta.

So she wasn't an elephant or even a creature of mixed blood, but rather an exact replica of an animal that had been dead for millennia. I rose to me feet and rubbed my warming lip hard wondering what, if anything, this told me about the professor's son.

I considered my position. I could quit while I was ahead and run with the Henrietta story. But if I could tie in Adam, then a good story would become great. If he had been manufactured by the person we thought of as his father then this was my big moment. I would need proof and, as I took another sip of beer, my hand began to shake.

Fourteen
16:55 - Thursday 4th October, nine years earlier. American Museum of Natural History, Central Park West, New York City

The boy stood motionless, his eyes glazed.

People were passing him on either side and Adam Reid registered their presence but he had time for only one thing, the mental image of the huge animal that had become his friend.

He brushed away the moisture that had begun to gather in the corner of his eye and took in the area around him. The small museum shop. The clock with its black numerals against the stark white of its face and, above all, the ant-like people scurrying around him.

He welcomed the familiar smell of paint and other chemicals. He had visited here often and he knew that his father would not be late. He was never late. He was perfect in almost every way and sometime in the next sixty seconds, ninety at the most, and no matter whether he had journeyed by foot, by car or by train, whether he was completing a journey of a couple of hundred yards or a couple of hundred miles, Professor George Reid would arrive on time.

But Henrietta would still die.

They would kill her or she would die a shambling wreck but still his father would not let him in, would not allow him to help in the search for a solution.

Adam needed answers and he would have them.

He pictured his father hopping steps. Leaving the sunlight for a darker place and then his heels clicking on tiles and Adam knew that he was here. Twenty seconds and Adam opened his eyes. They shone brightly as he scanned the crowd. He sifted what information he needed but his mind was elsewhere. He had realised a long time ago why his father had requested that they meet this afternoon. Henrietta must already be dead.

Late-blooming imperfections in the cloning process, undetectable at the embryonic and foetal stages, were her death sentence. Higher mammals did not develop in the same way as sea urchins or frogs because their cells were more complex. Initially healthy cloned cells deteriorated as the chromosomes within them detached from their nuclei to float free and become scattered unevenly throughout the animal's cell as a whole.

And this triggered the suicide of the cells as they turned upon themselves and brought about their destruction rather than allow the horrific malformation that would otherwise have occurred. They died in their billions and even Adam's father had not been able to control the process or to accurately predict what effect such deviance would have upon an adult animal.

Adam shook his head and closed his eyes. His father was here. Adam could feel him but the older man did not approach and Adam looked up. He allowed his pale blue eyes to sweep the room and settle on Professor George Reid.

Father and creator. The man smiled and Adam singled out the footsteps in the sea of noise as his father approached. He could feel the man's presence long before the hand fell upon his shoulder and he did not resist as his father drew him to his chest.

For a moment, the two embraced. 'I'm sorry Adam. I'm so, so sorry.'

'I know you are, father.'

But sorrow was not an absolute state; it came in degrees. People could be sorrier. And then they could be sorrier still but what was the absolute state, was it misery?

Adam felt his father look away. He sensed the older man's

embarrassment and allowed his chest to heave, huge and solid against the old man's bones but his doubts had gone. His fear had been harnessed. He would take what he needed.

Professor Reid stepped back and Adam raised his head. The older man gestured towards the stairs. 'Shall we?'

Adam nodded. He rose to his feet and followed his father. They exchanged no more than a handful of words as they worked their way steadily through the exhibits that both knew so well. They moved quickly as the Professor led his son through the section devoted to vertebrate origins; fish and amphibians and then through the selected dinosaur exhibitions and on to those dealing with the evolution of the mammals.

They had traversed hundreds of millions of years in minutes but now they were in the Hall of Advanced Mammals and Professor Reid stopped. 'She'll always be with us, Adam,' he said softly. He looked at the boy before him but averted his eyes when Adam raised his head.

'I know, father.'

Professor Reid's eyes flickered over the exhibits. 'What I mean is that she's going to be with us forever, both in spirit and –'

Adam's legs weakened. He almost fell and his father struggled to support his son's weight but Adam could see it. Here, surrounded by the higher mammals, the old man wanted to put Henrietta on show. He wanted to scrape her skin and tear out her eyes and fill her with garbage and make her a curiosity, something to amuse. 'No father, you can't.'

'She's not going on display,' said Professor Reid and Adam heard the relief in his father's voice. The older man was relieved to be able to say something, anything that would not cause further distress. 'I mean the donor.'

Adam said nothing and his father inclined his head towards the bone and plaster reconstructions behind him, to the scraped and desiccated skin and Adam had it. 'She's here?'

Professor Reid picked out an exhibit, a mammoth, with his eyes. 'She's been here for some time.'

Adam moved. He rolled from foot to foot. Measured the thick glass with his hands and narrowed his eyes. 'And Henrietta; she's –'

'Dead,' said the Professor. 'She died this morning.'

Adam digested the fact and moved on. 'And you're going to publish?'

The older Reid finally spoke, as Adam knew he would. 'I'm considering it. I might have to.'

'Have to?'

'It would raise awareness Adam,' said the Professor. He looked away and Adam knew that he was struggling with his words. 'It might help.'

Adam closed his eyes. Words were dangerous. Because, once spoken, they could never truly be taken back and he opened his eyes, observed the Professor closely until he spoke. 'We slowed the process, Adam. She could have lived for years but –'

So they had chosen to end her life. The old man's voice had trailed and Adam spoke. 'She could have lived or endured?'

'Adam, please –'

'You said she was better off dead, father. Were you wrong?'

Henrietta had changed. Nature had rebelled against the unnatural. Her condition would have killed her as surely as his father had but she would have died hard. The Professor had eased her suffering and Adam looked at his father. The time was right. 'I need to know, father. I'd like –'

'We'll talk.' Professor Reid said. 'I promise we will.'

Adam closed his eyes but he could not keep it out. The distrust. And then, like a torrent of rats spilling across a hillside, he felt the hatred overflow within him. It took him over and he welcomed it as he sensed his father rise to his feet.

He felt the hand on his shoulder once more. The feeble shake was meant to reassure. He heard his father walk away and raised his hand to his face, tracing the line of scar tissue beneath his chin.

The changes were on-going. They may alter his appearance but they could not change what he was and what he knew he must become and he rose to his feet.

Heads turned as he stretched to his full height. And more heads would turn once he was fully grown.

Adam crossed the hall and left the building. Autumn laced the breeze but still-warm sunshine fell onto West 81st Street and he sniffed the air. He saw that his father was waiting patiently for him but now was not the time to speak.

'There are things we can do,' said his father softly as Adam approached him.

But there were not.

'We have time.'

But they did not.

'We can win.'

But they could not and Adam contemplated his words. He weighed them against the old man's previous comments and he analysed the lie. He did not feel insulted by it. Merely discounted it and he spoke. 'I'd like to have children of my own one day.'

His father looked away. 'We need help, Adam –'

Any doubts were gone and Adam knew. His father would publish. The older man would plead for support and for help. The Professor's mouth was moving again but Adam missed the words. His head was thumping. He allowed his father to guide him to a bench and they sat down. He forced himself to listen. 'You can read it before, before –'

'Don't publish, father,' said Adam. His voice was detached.

It was coming from another place. The old man could still save himself. Adam watched as the words tumbled from his father's lips. 'Siberia...carcass...cells...nucleus...we had the money.'

Adam knew all of this. He struggled against the pounding in his head. He wanted to reach out and crush something but he did not. He wanted to beat somebody. To kill them and throw them lifeless into the traffic but he did not and he turned once more to the words spilling from his father's lips.

Adam nodded and looked at his father but the older man was distant.

He had slipped into a rehearsed speech. Adam let him talk.

He listened out for only the key words, the relevant passages. 'Initially we hoped to find sperm cells,' said the older man. 'Deep frozen. Possibly still alive but at the very least preserved by the cold and still capable of triggering cell division but we were unfortunate.'

Adam had to let the words slip by once more but he caught a few and he didn't need them all. 'Foraging animals...best cells were always likely to come from deep within the animals' bodies but they were fully differentiated; and then we were lucky –.'

Just words but Adam's father smiled and the younger man waited for him to continue. 'It was a fine balance. Quite an ask. We needed the body to have frozen before it could decompose but not so quickly as to allow the frost to destroy the cells within it. We needed it to be buried away from other animals. Preferably quickly and certainly by the time the next summer arrived. It needed to have sunk in something and to be preserved and then we found her.

'Henrietta,' the Professor said. His eyes misted. 'An adult female. She was worth a small fortune but I believe the Russian authorities gave the miner that found her a watch. She'd fallen into a pit of partially-frozen silt. Several of her ribs were broken. She damaged her forelegs in her efforts to get out. Not a pleasant way to die but for our purposes it was ideal. The silt swallowed her up and she was frozen solid for more than five thousand years. We think she died in August. That's late autumn in that part of the world –.'

His father's words became mere noise. Adam could see the thrashing animal. He could feel her pain. He could feel her broken ribs tear through her skin as the weight of her body drove them against her and the panic as the suffocating mud forced its way into her mouth and trunk. She had died horribly once. And now she would have died horribly again had not his father killed her and he raised his eyes. 'The cells?'

The professor looked away as he spoke. 'We resisted the temptation to go for uterine cells and took them from around her heart. We introduced the nucleus to an egg. Stimulated division by the application of an electric current, the rest I'm sure you know.'

Adam did know. He allowed the silence to build before he spoke. 'What about me?'

Fifteen
03:04 – Wednesday 16th June
New York Voyager Hotel, Manhattan, New York

I snorted and bit my tongue for good measure. Whatever dreams had been there faded instantly and I checked the time on my phone. It was just after 3am so 8am London time.

I'd been asleep in a chair in the New York hotel room. It was night time here but the light was on and then the hotel phone rang again. It had woken me and I reached across, picked up the handset. 'Yes?'

'Good morning.'

It was a Scottish voice. I screwed my eyes closed then opened them again and gave my face a brisk rub. 'Simon?'

'You got the package?'

I nodded. Realised nobody could see me. 'Yes, I got it...'

'Adam is expecting your call. Have you got a pen?'

I stood up. Looked around the room then took the pencil and notepad from the bedside table. Simon read out a number and then continued. 'Now would be good.'

It was 3am. I looked at the handset then raised it to speak. 'How can I get in touch with you?'

'I'll ring you,' said Simon.

The line went dead and I returned the handset to its cradle. I stared at the notepad in my hand then put it down, walked to the bathroom and poured myself a glass of water. I returned to the bedroom and sat on the bed.

So the great man wanted to talk? I looked at the number on the notepad and then the pamphlet. I was ringing at his invitation so he must have an agenda. I'd be on the back foot but it wasn't an option not to ring. I lifted the hotel phone before I could change my mind and dialled the number.

The ringing telephone was answered almost immediately. 'Adam Reid.'

'Mr Reid?' I had anticipated a secretary or at the very least an answerphone or some sort of automated switchboard. I stood up. 'This is Spencer Beck. Simon suggested that I should ring you?'

'I believe that you have something that belongs to me?' The voice sounded right. It was educated. More English than American and Adam spoke again. 'Mr Beck?'

Whatever I had expected, it wasn't this. 'I, well –'

'You have some of my personal papers that I hold most dear. My father gave them to me as a child and I would like them back.'

When in doubt say nothing. I stared at the wall but finally felt obliged to speak. 'It's possible. I had a package delivered.'

'I'm not accusing you of theft,' said the voice at the other end of the phone. 'And I'm happy to meet you in person but I would like the papers returned. I'll have somebody there at six thirty.'

The phone went dead and I listened to the tone for several seconds. I was getting used to people hanging up on me. But I'd just spoken to one of the richest men on the planet and that was a first. True, I'd said no more than a handful of words, most of which implicated me in a possible theft, but it was a start.

I looked at my watch and tried to think. I was being told to take a step backwards, to surrender a document albeit in exchange for a face to face meeting. The newspaper clippings were old news. They could be replicated but the scientific paper may well have been irreplaceable and I looked at the document.

It had been given to me. I may have inadvertently handled stolen property but I wasn't sure of the legal implications. But the reality of the situation was that Adam Reid was a powerful man and I was a long way from home. A copy would probably suffice and, if giving back the original bought me some face-time, then the exchange might be worthwhile.

I grabbed up the burgundy covered paper and slipped on my shoes and a moment later I was standing by the lift. I jabbed the call button and, shifting from foot to foot, I considered whether I should simply take the document and move out of the hotel, get some legal advice?

But it wouldn't hurt to get a copy anyway and, when the lift arrived, I got in and rode the car down to a deserted reception hall where a night porter's bowed head was just visible behind one of the counters. As I approached the man looked up and slipped something under what was presumably the signing in book. 'Can I help you, sir?'

'You have a photocopier?'

'In the courtesy office, sir,' said the porter indicating a bank of doors across the lobby. His smile needed some work and I could smell food. 'It's locked.'

I followed the man's eyes to the doors. 'The key?'

The porter pursed his lips. He refreshed his smile and rose to his feet. He was very short and, when he picked a key from a rack of hooks behind him, he had to stretch. He walked around the counter. 'If you'd like to follow me?'

The porter made a big job of unlocking the door to the office and then he turned on every light and machine in the room. I registered a couple of desks complete with chairs along with a bank of telephones, a fax machine and a photocopier. The night porter had already switched the copier on and he appeared to note down a number. 'It'll just take a minute to warm up, sir. Your room?'

'Eight-eleven,' I said to the smile and the man left. He hadn't held his hand out for a tip, which made a pleasant surprise, and he managed to close the door behind him. I had plenty of time and I spread Professor Reid's article on the glass of the whirring photocopier.

**

The machine was slow and, by the time I had the copies that I needed and had returned to my room, it was 3.55am.

I had two and a half hours left before Adam's messenger arrived. If I was going to move hotels I would have to get a move on. I put my case on the bed but a knock at the door disturbed me almost immediately.

Middle of the night and my room was like Grand Central Station. I walked to the door and looked through the spy hole. It was one of the bellboys. I didn't recognise him but, if he'd been sent by Adam Reid, then he was two and a half hours early. It was more likely that I'd left something in the courtesy office and I opened the door.

'Sorry to disturb you, sir,' said the Bellboy. He didn't look in the least bit sorry. 'You have a package?'

I stared at the boy blankly. 'Another one?'

'One for a Mr Reid?'

'Yes,' I said lamely. This was rather a blow. 'But you're early.'

The bellboy held out a package of his own and my heart sank. 'Mr Reid said to serve you these documents in the event that you were unable to give him what he asked for. Said that he would be taking immediate action if he didn't get satisfaction.'

Sounded like the man was challenging me to a duel but I'd been outmanoeuvred. And if it came to a bellboy-tipping contest then the pharmaceutical billionaire was always going to have me beat.

I was floundering when it occurred to me. I could say that I'd left the documents downstairs and then leave the hotel in a hurry but then the bellboy looked over to the bed and spied the burgundy pamphlet.

He smiled, walked over and picked it up, ignored everything else. He flicked it open and seemed to check the page numbers and then looked up. He took a postcard out of his pocket. It looked thin and harmless and he put it on the bed. 'Thank you, sir.'

If the boy had expected a tip then he would just have to carry on expecting. I ignored him as he left the room. He closed the door behind him and I crossed to the bed, picked up the postcard that he had left behind.

I was tired. Focusing was an effort and I blinked at the tiny font. The words looked lost on what was a rather formal note from Adam Reid's office informing me that we had a meeting scheduled for later today and I sat down hard.

It was 4am. The man was as good as his word but I had a meeting with him sometime today and I felt a flutter in my stomach. Sleep would have to wait as I had to prepare.

Adam would know that I had read the pamphlet. He may even suspect that I'd made copies but any journo worth his salt would give their right arm to meet Adam Reid and I was being offered the chance to do just that. I turned the card in my hand. There was a reply number on the back. It had a small '24hr' printed under it so I picked up my iPhone, keyed in the number.

The iPhone had probably been roaming around costing me a fortune for hours but it could be useful to have the reply number for Adam stored in its memory for future use. The phone rang and was answered almost immediately. 'Onesius Global,' said a woman. 'How may I help you?'

Onesius Global? Simon had mentioned the name but I couldn't remember the context. 'This is Spencer Beck. Mr Reid would like to arrange a meeting?'

'Is eight o'clock convenient, Mr Beck?' said the woman. She didn't show any sign of waiting for an answer. 'It'll be in lower Manhattan. We'll get back to you with the venue.'

'My telephone number?'

'We have it already.'

The dead line was already burring in my ear and I sat back in the chair and I wondered just how many people were going to hang up on me before this week was over.

It was 4.12am. So 9.12am in England. I walked to the tiny desk; I had questions to prepare. I opened the background file that I'd put together and shuffled the papers in what I hoped was a meaningful way because the secret to a good interview was preparation but I was tired. Still, I was where I was and three hours' kip wouldn't make much difference either way. Better to spend it doing something useful. I had to give myself the best possible chance of keeping my head above water however the conversation developed.

I tapped my pencil on the desk and beat out a tune. Started visualising how the day would play out. Adam could arrive mob-handed and set his lawyers on me. He might even conjure up some technicality and try to do me for the theft of the journal but as the thing had come to me unsolicited and I'd given it back I wasn't sure that would stick. Of course he might get me thrown in jail for a couple of hours but in comparison to what I could get out of the meeting, all of that amounted to nothing.

I had to go for this and I didn't want to screw it up. I had to work the angles and Simon kept coming up. So much of what had followed hung on his words but I still had no idea who he was or whether he was working alone.

He could be a part of Adam's organisation but I knew one thing for certain and that was that I was being used. And whoever was pulling my strings was better-prepared than I was but that was fine by me. Most people planted stories with journalists for a reason but why me?

Maybe I'd just been in the right place at the right time but still the questions crowded in. Plenty of questions, few answers and no sleep. It was a potent mix. I could be over-thinking the whole thing then, for no particular reason, Flanagan came to mind.

He should be here with me. And provided he didn't intrude on the journalism then he deserved to be and he would certainly have a view. He was perceptive and to-the-point. I walked through to the bathroom and examined my face in the shaving mirror.

The creased shirt would have to do. I'd worn worse and, after I'd taken a shower, filled the bathroom with steam and had a shave, both the shirt and I looked a shade less creased.

And the hot water flushed away some of the cobwebs. I felt somewhat sharper. I looked a little less like an exhausted tramp and, back in the bedroom, I picked up my mobile and disconnected it from its charger. I rang the number for the Royal Free.

A few peeps and squeaks and then a voice. 'Hello?'

'Hello, this is Spencer Beck,' I said. 'I'd like to inquire about Mr Daniel Flanagan.'

The phone clicked. 'Mr Beck?'

'Yes?'

'Where are you Mr Beck?'

Here we go again. I held the phone from my ear and considered hanging up. 'I'm in New York. I'm ringing to inquire –'

'This is the police, Mr Beck. We'd like to speak with you as soon as possible.'

'You're speaking with me now. How's Flanagan?'

A pause at the other end of the line. 'I'm not at liberty to say, Mr Beck. When will you be back in the UK?'

'At the end of the week,' I heard myself saying.

Another pause. I tried to figure out what that signified but hadn't got very far when the voice was back. 'We thought that you might be able to tell us what happened.'

I said nothing.

'Mr Beck?'

Still nothing. I tapped the pencil on the desk. It didn't help.

'Mr Beck?'

'How is he?'

'We need to speak to you –'

'Speak to me about how what happened?'

'Mr Beck, could you come back sooner?'

This was becoming a circular conversation and I decided it was my turn to hang up on somebody. I cut the call and leaned back in the chair.

I felt something weird. More than unease, it was a sort of dread.

Hospitals and police, what was going on? I'd be going back to London. Of course I would. I had work to do here but I couldn't put Flanagan out of my mind.

I could ring Simon. I was shaking my head. Not yet. I hit the number for the Financial Times' news desk instead. I hadn't worked there for years but I still did the occasional piece for the paper and knew most of the staffers. The desk was always manned. Maybe one of them could tell me what the fuck was going on. The phone rang twice before a female voice answered. 'Terry Dubonne?'

Theresa Dubonne. Early thirties. Australian. She'd been there three or four years. Was a bit territorial but that wasn't a bad trait in a journo. A good hack and I knew her pretty well. I was about to speak but was distracted by a knock at the door.

It was probably a marching band. I couldn't think of anyone else who hadn't been in the room already. Another knock and I spoke into the phone. 'Sorry, I'm going to have to ring back.'

'Spencer, is that you? Don't hang up – '

I hung up. I was getting the hang of it and I checked my watch. It was 4.35am and I walked to the door, looked through the spy hole. The bellboy, the smirking piece from earlier, was standing outside my room and I opened the door.

'Message, sir,' said the youth. Unless I misread him he was scrutinizing me intently. 'Gentleman at the desk said to make sure you got this. Told me to bring it right on up.'

I took the proffered envelope, fished in my pocket. No small US bills had made their way onto my person overnight and I'd lost my pound coins, had sixteen pence. I couldn't offer anybody sixteen pence. Not even the individual standing before me so I closed the door in his face instead.

I had nothing to lose. I couldn't sink any further in his opinion and it didn't feel as though the door actually hit him and in any case he was young. He'd heal quickly.

I sat on the bed and weighed the envelope in my hand. It was very thin. I opened it and pulled out a single sheet of paper. It bore the name, location and telephone number of a restaurant on Wall Street, and was signed 'Adam'.

**

Two and a half hours and a light breakfast later, I'd set off downtown. I had plenty of time and didn't feel as badly as I might have done. But I'd had no sleep and the bright, slanting sunlight and the flashing yellow cabs, honking their horns above the din of the thousands and thousands of people that were crowding around me, had left me feeling more than a little light-headed.

It was 7.40am. I detached myself from the flow of pedestrians, blinked hard and rubbed my eyes. Tiny stars sparkled and died behind my eyelids. I needed to catch my breath but a fresh surge of work-bound commuters forced me back into the mainstream and, the walk light thankfully illuminated, I was propelled into the road.

So much for crossing the street Manhattan-style. I was swept up in the flood of people but was moving in the right direction. I was heading south, Wall Street's various towers reaching for the sky and creating a canyon ahead of me.

And now I was three blocks away from the restaurant. I was ahead of time when I heard it. 'Mr Beck?'

I had to complete my crossing of the entire road before I could look back and locate the voice but, when I managed to turn my head, I could see nothing.

'Spencer Beck?'

A loud voice but cultured. Somehow familiar and then I saw the man himself. It was Adam Reid. Half a head taller than the commuters around him and not thirty yards distant on the opposite side of the road. He joined the tail end of the crush that swept me across and I shielded my eyes from the sun.

One of the world's leading industrialists was fighting his way through a scrum of rush-hour commuters to see me. I'd thought that these people were whisked around in helicopters but it would appear that I was wrong. Adam Reid made good progress and smiled as he approached. There were still pedestrians between us but he gestured towards an office doorway, away from the pull of the tide and I pushed towards it. It was a struggle but I got there and almost instantly, Adam was by my side. He held his hand out and I waited for the look.

In fact I half-raised my hand to my face but read nothing in Adam as he introduced himself. 'Adam Reid. I'm pleased to meet you.'

It was so every-day, which made it all the more bizarre. We were just two men meeting on the street. The hack and the billionaire but I went with it and shook Adam's outstretched hand.

Or rather, I tried to shake it but didn't succeed. After a second or two of eye contact, the hand began to move slowly up and down and I spoke. 'Same here, Mr Reid.'

I may have sounded overawed. Probably not the first time Adam Reid had come across that reaction upon first meeting and he broke the silence. 'It's Adam, please. I hear you're keen to see me?'

'You could say that,' I said. Thankfully my voice didn't let me down. 'I believe that we have some friends in common.'

Slightly cheeky and certainly probing but Adam's reaction gave nothing away. 'Do we?'

I felt myself fumbling for a response as Adam's intensely blue eyes focused on mine. I glanced back at the road and played for time. 'How did you know it was me?'

Adam's smile didn't falter. But nor did he answer the question. He patted the slim attaché case that I hadn't previously seen he was carrying. 'Thanks for the papers, a minor misunderstanding.'

I nodded as the crowd around us surged again. Somewhere a 'walk' sign must have illuminated and the weight of bodies pressed in and crushed me against Adam's chest. It made further conversation difficult as the pressure squeezed the air from me and I felt the first flutter of panic as Adam didn't move in the slightest.

He simply stood there solidly but then the crowd ebbed and spilled to either side of us and I could breathe again. I pushed myself back and was left with an impression of mass.

Adam could have been a professional rugby player. He had five or six inches on me. That would make him six-three or six-four and he and I were simply built along different lines. I would have to spend my life being blown around like a leaf on the wind and Adam simply wouldn't. I registered what looked like amusement on his face as we climbed a few steps further up towards the entrance of one of the towers in order to get away from the worst of the suited mob and I took a couple of deep breaths.

This had been sprung on me. We should've been meeting fifteen minutes from now. I would have had more time to gather my thoughts and I didn't want to sound and look even more of an idiot than was strictly necessary. 'I'm working on a financial piece,' I said. I sounded firm and confident, my voice relatively steady. 'And I wondered if you'd have time to give me a few insights.'

'We could talk at least,' said Adam. It had been a safe opener and Adam's smile evolved from open and friendly to sincere and professional. 'And I'm very happy to do so but as far as insights are concerned, I'm sure the Securities and Exchange Commission would have a view on what I should and shouldn't say.'

We shared knowing smiles. I hadn't phrased the question too well. I was tired and I was going to lose any verbal fencing match. I had my sights set on a bigger prize but we had to get the niceties out of the way and, if that entailed letting Adam know that he had the measure of me, then so be it. I smiled and looked at the younger man and gave him the once over.

He was massive though he hid it well. His suit was of the highest quality. European I would guess, probably Italian. Not English and certainly not American. It blurred his shape but where it was meant to hang loose, it didn't.

Because Adam filled every inch of it and he wasn't your business-man-pear-shape. Far from it but nor was he built like a body-builder type. He didn't have the pumped-up physique associated with prison yards or gyms. He looked more like the stump of a tree.

A thickset, solid six foot four stump and I nodded to myself as I considered how I could work that image into my piece. But while I was measuring him, Adam was measuring me. He was checking out my facial blemishes at the same time as I was looking for scar tissue and the man smiled, seemed to recognise what was going on and he spoke again. 'I'm glad that we were finally able to meet.'

'It's entirely my pleasure,' I said. When in doubt, fall back on flattery. 'I was hoping to be educated on the workings of your companies.'

'We'll see what we can do,' said Adam. He did not blink but for a moment his blue eyes lost their focus. A second or two later, the man was back. 'You look tired, Spencer. May I call you Spencer?'

It was better than Alfred. 'Please do.'

'Why don't we forget the restaurant, travel back uptown to the Museum? Food's not bad and we both have to be there later.'

'That would be great,' I heard myself say. I think I was probably grinning like an idiot. But I was too tired to care overmuch and I was swept up in the moment. I'd deny it later of course but here we were. Just good friends and Adam was right. We needed to be at the Museum of Natural History for the speeches – a reassuringly public place.

Adam raised a hand to his mouth.

He managed a piercing whistle and a yellow cab immediately detached itself from the flow of traffic in the road before us. It carved its way across several lanes and drew to a halt beside us. Adam opened the door, slid his attaché case across the seat and got in. He left the door open and I recognised that I was at a crossroads. But turning my back on what could be the story of a lifetime was not an option and I clambered in.

Sixteen
08:16 – Wednesday 16th June
American Museum of Natural History, Central Park West, New York City

Of course the man might kill me.

I might disappear into the concrete foundations of a building or be recycled as dog-food or whatever but I'd get my story first. It might not get published but I would worry about that later. I felt my face beginning to flush in the heat of the taxi and raised my hand to my lip as mid-town New York flashed past.

I was nervous but didn't regret going with it because I could live a hundred lifetimes and never come close to a story remotely as big as this. I just couldn't pass it up. The Museum of Natural History was hardly a mist-laden graveyard at midnight, so what could go wrong? I turned to my companion. 'Adam, I know this may strike you as an unsubtle question, but could I ask you about the money?'

It was a poor question. Stale and worn but perhaps necessary because a million pounds would be a foreign country to most of my potential readers and a billion would be out of this world altogether. And they would want to know what a man with that sort of cash thought about so it wasn't altogether without merit.

But Adam was still looking out of the window. He hadn't given the least indication that he'd heard the question, far less that he was inclined to answer it. So I took the opportunity to look at the back of his head because I'd had enough of the buildings and pedestrians.

A busy city was a busy city but a billionaire's head you don't see too often and I found myself looking for scars. I looked closely at the great man's ears. Nothing to be seen and Adam shifted and half-turned in his seat and I looked away. He smiled and spoke. 'It means very little to me.'

I'd pretty much forgotten the question and that wouldn't do at all. I fumbled in my jacket pocket and pulled out my iPhone. Adam was now facing me and he shook his head. I put it away. The features on the thing weren't getting much use these days. Adam continued. 'It's what money can buy that I find interesting.'

That was understandable. And it begged a follow-up question and I made a mental note to return to the subject of what money could buy later. At least he hadn't said that he lived to search out more challenges or that he was blighted by a continued desire to succeed. And nor had he suggested that he wanted to leave his mark on the world or to help people. I needed another sighting shot. 'The companies, Zylagene and Zylapharm –'

'That would be them,' said Reid, his smile broadening.

'Is it possibly they'll be merged?'

Adam's smile now looked a little stale and I had to accept that it was another poor question. Boringly standard stuff but it was only question two or three and I might be able to claw it back. Adam looked past me and his eyes misted then locked onto something that the cab quickly left behind. 'Most things are possible,' he said. 'Not everything, it has to be said. But you'll find that most things are possible if you exert the right degree of force.'

'And the logic behind any such move?'

That was slightly better I thought as I watched the question sink in. A one word answer wasn't possible. Adam would have to say something more substantive. I felt him moving past the question and perhaps preparing for what he saw as the next one.

'I'll keep it short,' he said looking once more past me at the sliding world beyond. 'Nothing's changed.'

I hoped the irritation didn't show on my face but Adam seemed to read me. 'I don't want to be trite about it,' he said. 'I don't want to be an arse as you might say but the skills required to produce and develop drugs are very different to those required to sell them.

'Hence the people and the culture, the very companies in their early stages of development need to be different. True, many larger companies undertake both activities but they have sufficient critical mass to do so and, in our opinion, they risk failing in both ventures.

'We've chosen to keep the two vehicles separate and I think you'll accept that we've been successful to date. In fact most observers concede that we've been responsible for fully a quarter of all therapeutic discoveries of any size made globally in the last four years. We would appear to be doing something right. But we do acknowledge that size is a feature and hence, as we grow, a merger remains a constant possibility.'

Well, that was a pretty full answer. One that I would have liked to have recorded in order to accurately source a quote or two later. Instead I had to pull out a grubby notepad from my jacked and I raised my eyebrows. Adam nodded and I held the book away from him. Wrote down trite, arse and merger possible and then raised my eyes. 'So it's an on-going debate?'

Adam looked past me at the passing traffic. 'I find it somewhat hot.'

I didn't know how to respond to that so I kept it non-committal. 'Quite.'

I threw in what I hoped was a sage nod and Adam continued. 'New York at this time of year, I mean.'

Billionaires were allowed to ramble I supposed and I wrote down the words hot, ramble and nutter. Eccentricity provided colour and my readers would probably expect it. The mega-rich shouldn't be normal. It would simply be too boring. I didn't have anything to add and the silence stretched. I occupied myself by underlining the word nutter but I was on the clock and had to maintain momentum. Nonetheless, my attention was wandering and I noted that we were making good progress against the work-bound traffic. We were almost at the Museum.

To cue, the cab slewed across the road and stopped sharply and gestured vaguely outside. 'Shall we?'

I opened the door and the steamy heat hit me. It was bloody hot. I got out and Adam slid across the seat and rose beside me. He swept an arm towards the building before us and began to walk towards the steps leading to the Central Park West entrance of the Museum. I took the opportunity to set the iPhone to record before looking at the Museum proper.

It was a magnificent pile. But I knew less about architecture than I did about fossils. To me, the museum looked like a cross between a Roman Senate building and something from Albert Speer's Berlin. The huge, pillared entrance towered above us but something was nagging away in my mind. Like the grain of sand in your sock, I couldn't find it but it wouldn't go away.

Then I had it. Adam hadn't paid for the taxi. I looked back but the cab had gone and Adam was getting ahead of me. He was approaching the entrance of the building and I jogged a few paces and put the thought to one side.

Adam paused at the top of the steps and I took a second to look around, tried to absorb some detail. I could get street-views from Google and could overlay whatever I wanted to say with period detail. The Museum's website or Wikipedia would supply the details later as there was little to keep the sun from the deserted pavement and I was heating up rapidly.

There were no crowds and Adam caught my eye. 'It's closed to the public. We've taken it for three days.'

Of course you have. Adam inclined his head towards the interior of the building and spoke. 'Shall we go in?'

There was no going back. I would have my story. I walked past Adam and crossed the threshold into the cool interior of the building.

'As you see, money does have its compensations,' said Adam. He was following closely behind me. 'This place for example. The hire might not be cheap but I love it and know it well. A quick look around?'

'Yes, I'd be delighted,' I said. Depended on his definition of quick but my nonchalance surprised me. I was here now and would ensure that I got the most out of my time alone with the man. I pulled my sleeve back from my watch. 'How much time do we have?'

Adam Reid did not turn. 'I don't think you'll be disappointed.'

I'd have to take him at face value there and I tried to relax. I didn't want to come over as overawed or humbled and I looked around me, took in the hallway. 'I've never been here before.'

'Then you've missed a treat,' said Adam absently. I looked at him. I had the impression that Adam Reid was rarely absent. 'This is the Teddy Roosevelt Memorial Hall.'

'Uh-huh?'

Buildings were not my thing. Museums left me cold and I preferred my animals served with chips but if the meter wasn't running I was happy for Adam to talk. There was plenty to learn.

'It's all rather politically correct these days,' he said. He pointed to a sign. 'Hall of Bio-diversity, African Peoples etc. but it's still a fascinating place, truly fascinating. We won't let time get in the way, Spencer. We've got a lot to talk about. Shall we?'

I'd go with it because what choice did I have? 'Yes, let's,' I said. I immediately felt like an idiot but Adam, his arm frozen in mid-sweep, seemed satisfied with that as an answer. He moved towards a staircase.

The mention of African Peoples struck a chord but there had been no edge to Adam's voice. No patronizing hint of racism but I could work on it and I watched the billionaire as he walked over to the stairs. He took the first flight of steps two at a time, was remarkably light on his feet for such a big man.

And whether it was arrogance or intuition, he hadn't even looked back, he knew that I would follow. I could be leaving the Museum now, making a break for it but Adam was on the half landing. He was rolling from foot to foot as he moved and, when he did turn, he did not seem to be in the least surprised that I was only a dozen or so steps behind him.

Adam continued to climb and I set off after him. 'Where's the AGM going to be held?' I asked the back of his retreating head. I'd have preferred to take the lift, wanted a moment to get my breath back.

'It's not strictly an AGM,' said Adam. It had been a slip of the tongue. I knew it wasn't an AGM but Adam's voice was now less accented, more English and he turned to face me. 'We're registered in the UK. The Cambridge meeting was the AGM. The formal stuff's finished. No admin here, it's more of a teach-in.

'More than that really,' he continued. He turned and bounded up another half flight of stairs two at a time and I felt my shoulders sag. 'About two thirds of our free floating shares are held over here by US investors and it could make sense to relocate one or even both of the companies over here at some point. There's been speculation to the effect in the Press.'

I had run stories along those lines myself. I felt rather than saw Adam Reid's eyes swing towards me and I was flattered. The man must have read a number of my articles or at least been briefed on them. 'I've mentioned it in passing,' I managed to say. 'But most of the research facilities are in England. Surely they're going to stay there?'

'Any move is just a possibility at this stage,' said Adam, a smile in his voice. He appeared to be enjoying himself. He pointed past an exhibition devoted to the Big Bang. 'Let's take a walk, shall we? The meeting will be outside, on the Arthur Ross Terrace. We'll have standing at the back, shading from the sun. I hear that we can fit in a couple of thousand. There will be others in the auditorium inside. Let's cut through here. Another two flights I'm afraid.'

I smiled and tried to look as though I meant it. 'No problem.'

Adam walked quickly through a small gallery then through the African Peoples exhibition and I looked at the entrepreneur. Scrutinized him as best I could for any reaction to the African art and culture all around us but there was nothing. And he didn't stop. He walked through another exhibition, this one entitled 'Birds of the World'.

I was struggling to keep up and Adam was gone again. He was moving fluidly up another flight of stairs but I had to stop and I wasn't going to apologise for it. It had been hot outside. I hadn't slept and my head was swimming.

I recovered my composure and climbed the remainder of the way to the fourth floor where Adam was waiting for me. He was more than a decade younger than me but he didn't seem in the least tired and he held up his hand. A sort of magnanimous gesture and he waited for me to catch my breath. 'Just the short tour, Spencer. No more climbing.'

I nodded, struggled to speak. 'Great.'

I wasn't bent double and I hadn't thrown up and that was a victory of sorts and I took the opportunity to have a look around. A café now faced us and I looked to my right. An orientation centre.

Adam followed my eyes. 'The floor is arranged on a timeline,' he said. His accent was now pure English. Perhaps it was a chameleon-like affectation that I'd come across before. It was harmless but it could represent a desire to fit in, to be accepted and I could use it in the article. 'There's a certain order to things, wouldn't you agree. Let's start at the beginning.'

'Vertebrate Origins' said the sign above the entrance to the room. Ancient swimming and crawling things with backbones. Dirty has-beens. Not my cup of tea but Adam seemed interested and I looked at the back of his head again. It was certainly the view with which I was becoming most familiar. 'These are what, fish?'

Adam looked around and I got to see his face. That made a change. 'Yes Spencer, these are fish.'

He wasn't far from patronising me. We walked slowly past the exhibits. Adam stopped a couple of times to read an exhibit's description. He seemed to know them well. He read very quickly. Or at least he seemed to but it was sometimes the English description, sometimes the Spanish or French.

He may have wanted me to ask him about his language skills but I held my tongue then noticed that Adam appeared to be reading one of the signs in Japanese. The final straw but it would look good in the book. it wasn't the sort of thing that I could just let go. 'You read Japanese?'

'Yes,' said Adam, he looked up. The smile was gone but there was no hint of embarrassment on his face. 'I can follow it pretty well but that wasn't Japanese.'

I tried not to frown but didn't do a very good job of it. 'It wasn't?'

'It was Korean,' said Adam.

I could use a snippet of information like that but Adam was already moving on. Now there were bones to either side of us. As a boy, I'd been fascinated by dinosaurs. They had just the right mixture of grandeur and violence but I wasn't interested in the Latin names, the lineage etc. It was the horror that had drawn me to them.

That and their huge teeth and the associated fearsome stories of ripping flesh, splintering bones and broken bodies. I followed Adam into the large hall before us and took a look around. 'These are the Saurischian dinosaurs,' he said. 'Their name means 'lizard-hipped'. The pubis points forward and downwards.'

'Quite,' I said. Whatever a pubis was.

'And they've got hands,' said Adam. 'Much more like us, don't you think?'

'Yes, I suppose so,' I said.

Adam glanced at me. I had tried to sound neutral but he seemed to have picked up on something. He continued: 'Don't you feel the bond beginning to grow? Just the first seeds of an identification with these creatures?'

Not in the least. Maybe stand a lizard next to a jellyfish and I might side with the reptile but I decided to go for honesty. 'Maybe I lack your imagination, Adam.'

'I'm not sure it's a matter of imagination,' said Adam. He gestured towards another series of exhibits. 'Here you'll find the Sauropoda. The herbivores and the Theropoda. The two-legged carnivores, Velicoraptors, Tyrannosaurus and the others.'

I studied Adam's back again as walked towards one of the exhibits. I wanted to be sure exactly when I was being observed and when I was not. I was here to gather information and not to give it away but Adam had at least given the conversation a bit of direction and it was time to chance a question. I cleared my throat, did rather telegraph it. 'Why do you believe that some people find it easier to identify with creatures such as these?'

Adam faced me and a spotlight caught his eyes. They were a dazzling blue, truly remarkable. Paler than any I could remember seeing before, they were hard but not threatening. He inclined his head to one side and his smile broadened. He knew that I'd been staring at him. 'Maybe some people simply feel closer to them than others, Spencer. Shall we continue?'

I had a view of the back of Adam's head again and he didn't wait to see if I was going to follow him. I fell into step and he picked up the pace. We were passing the exhibits too rapidly to read about them but I tried to take it in. Adam was into all this and there might be a test at the end. There were skeletons and drawings. Models and the odd TV reconstruction and I could see that it was interesting but at the end of the day, these creatures had come and gone.

They had had their shot at the big time and they weren't even warm-blooded. Let alone remotely human but Adam was leaving the room and I was jogging to keep up. We cut past another flight of stairs and entered the next exhibition. I focussed on the Latin, it was something about birds.

'These are the Ornithischian dinosaurs,' said Adam. 'Bird-hipped. The pubis points backwards and they have some other bird-like qualities. They first appeared around the early Jurassic period. You're familiar with the differences?'

'I know a little about the various types of dinosaurs,' I said. I didn't want to elaborate. Better to say nothing and let him think that I was an idiot rather than open my mouth and prove it beyond doubt.

'There are a few Thyreophora in here,' said Adam. He seemed satisfied with my earlier comment and waved his broad hand slowly to encompass a glass case. 'And a couple of Hadrosauridae. The so-called duck-billed dinosaurs but do you know what? My real interest tends to be in the somewhat more modern.'

He'd turned away again and I was treated to the now-familiar view of the back of his head. It was getting tiresome but I suddenly felt uneasy and Adam stopped. 'Do these creatures make you shudder, Spencer?'

I shook my head, added a non-committal grunt. It wasn't so much the animals that were giving me the creeps as my host. Adam continued. 'Do they repel you, these base, unpleasant creatures?'

Again I shook my head. 'Not really.'

The answer seemed to suffice and Adam led the way through the exhibition. We walked past the last of the Ornithischian dinosaurs and I had to concede that Adam might have had a point. Because the creatures' evil little eyes were birdlike and repellent. We entered the next hall I felt an immediate sense of relief.

But it was short-lived. The half-lit hall was much less bright than elsewhere in the museum and I looked around at a totally different habitat. I became aware of a piped squeaking as squeals and a hurried shuffling of feet filled the air.

'Primitive Mammals,' said Adam. 'Milk-producing creatures. Warm blooded of course. Like you and me. We're getting closer to home.'

Maybe it was Adam's voiceover but my skin began to crawl as the reconstructions of long-dead, rat-like creatures spied on me from the undergrowth. Various rodents crowded the reconstructed jungle floor and bug-eyed lemurs peeped from behind trees. The creeping, scratching foliage all about us felt dark and primitive and the sound-track kicked in as a blood-curdling scream tore the air along with the distant roar of a dinosaur.

The sound shook the very leaves on the trees and shrubs growing behind the glass. It temporarily drowned out the sounds of the smaller animals, the scurrying, furtive mammals, the ancestors of man.

'Do you feel it?' asked Adam Reid. His eyes were shining. He could tell.

'I feel something,' I said. It was the least I could grant him and I looked around again. The flashing eyes were dimly visible and I tried not to shiver. 'This was how long ago?'

'Don't worry,' said Adam. That smile again. I suppressed a scowl as he swept a hand to take in the massive glass exhibition cases around us. 'There are millions of years between these creatures and us. The dinosaurs are still present, as you can hear from the audio-feed, but the first mammals are here too. They're ready to take over and exploit any weakness.'

I was impressed. This little tour was illuminating a millennia-spanning fight for life. And, despite the plaster, the plastic and the glass and the long-dead bone, I was finally beginning to feel something for these strange ghosts.

This was nature red in tooth and claw. One species or one whole group of species, cunning and low in the undergrowth, was waiting for the least sign of any weakness in another. I shuddered as the half-hidden bead-like eyes of our ancestors followed me from case to case.

'Vicious little beasts weren't they?' said Adam quietly. He was speaking almost to himself. 'We can't see them here but they were waiting for the collapse of the old order. Maybe it was ever thus.'

I said nothing. Adam knew that it had got to me and we walked on through the exhibition with its twitching undergrowth and the sly, squealing mass of animals, of sub-humanity and I told myself that they were just reconstructions.

I knew that. Adam and I were the only two creatures in the room with a heartbeat. The others were either recreations or long-since dead skin and bone but they were disturbing and I was comforted by the presence of the thick glass between us. I considered Adam's last words and weighed them for meaning.

Of course the law of the jungle survived in some parts of society. Perhaps Wall Street was a prime example as was business in general. And amongst the drug-dealers and the underclass it was dog-eat-dog but overall, surely things had changed for the better?

I realised that I was asking a question rather than making a statement and I threw off a shiver. These vicious little creatures were programmed to kill without mercy and to survive at all costs and Adam was right. They seemed closer to home, more human.

'This is my favourite exhibition,' said Adam as he stopped and turned to face me. His body was obscuring the entrance to the next area and the dead and stuffed animals within. He nodded his head. He was affirming his comment and I could feel it, the tension. I fought against a tremble in my leg as Adam continued. 'Of course you read the paper.'

'I, well, I thought it was a gift.'

'That's fine,' said Adam. 'It made for interesting reading but it was only the first of several.'

This must be the exhibition that featured Henrietta. I backed off a pace but Adam appeared calm. 'I had my doubts at first,' he said. 'Henrietta died and Jamieson had the carcass destroyed but she's still here, in a manner of speaking at least. You don't have to take my word for it, you can see for yourself.'

Adam stood aside and I could read the signage. We were standing outside the Hall of Advanced Mammals and Adam spoke again. 'I loved her you know.'

It was a statement but I had to clarify it. 'Henrietta?'

Adam looked away. When he spoke, I strained to pick up his words. 'Death is so final but extinction is the end, don't you think?'

I was considering a reply when Adam turned sharply to face me and I jumped. I was half expecting a blow but I immediately felt foolish. I hadn't realized that I had moved so close. 'Do come in. There's someone here I'd like you to meet.'

I clenched my fists. The knuckles shone white but I had crossed the Atlantic to be here. To experience this moment and I had already taken an unaccompanied taxi ride with a man I believed may be a killer. Touring the building with him was surely less of a challenge but still I felt my stomach heave as I followed Adam into the large display hall and looked around me.

It was a massive chamber. I wondered once more if this was cutting edge journalism or whether I was simply putting myself in harm's way. I looked at Adam closely. He rolled his shoulders as he moved and I felt the panic begin to build and flutter within me.

He was a businessman. I knew that but he looked every inch the killer. Powerful, his languid movements put me in mind of a huge cat. My breathing slowed and I felt the blood begin to bang in my ears. Adam stopped. He faced me and I felt his eyes on me. 'I'd like to introduce you to Henrietta.'

I remained silent, my pen hovering stupidly over my notepad.

'The donor animal at least,' Adam continued. 'I'm sure that you got that far.'

I may have nodded. The gesture seemed to suffice. Adam's eyes did not leave my own and he spoke again. 'My father was going to tell the world.'

I felt as though my feet had been bolted to the floor.

'He never did of course. It wouldn't have been wise.'

Then Adam looked away and I found that I could move again. I took a step backwards at the same time as Adam moved a step away from me and at once I could see the huge mammoth clearly. She was still some distance away, encased in a massive glass display. Despite my misgivings both Adam and I edged closer. 'Why?'

The words were mine. Adam spoke. 'Why what, Spencer?'

'Why did he want to publish?'

Adam turned away, ignored my question and I focused on the mammoth. I could feel Adam's approval as he took in the exhibit himself.

‘Impressive, isn’t she?’

I nodded in response. Realised Adam could not see me but he continued nonetheless. ‘Henrietta was genetically identical to the animal that you see before you. They were effectively one and the same. But Henrietta and her donor were delivered from different wombs. There were always going to be micro-mutations as a result of their different pre and post natal environments.

‘Even identical twins are not absolutely identical to the eye. They have dissimilar fingerprints but they’re genetically the same and here, to all intents and purposes, we’re looking at the Henrietta that I knew. The animals shared the same life, separated by ten thousand years.’

I raised my hand to the glass and cupped it to cut out the ambient glare. I found that I had ventured further into the display. The first plaque had been in Spanish but there was the English translation. The text was larger and I read it quickly as I approached.

She was an adult female. Approximately 35 years of age at the time of her death. Around 3.2 metres tall, weight around six tonnes. This specimen had been found in Siberia but as a species, mammoths had inhabited most of Eurasia and the North American continent as far south as Mexico with an outlying population in Colombia, of all places.

The suggested lineage was given along with the similarities and differences between mammoths and modern day elephants. It was nothing too heavy but Adam was looking at me, moving towards me. His body language confused me, he was expecting something.

Discovered in the Kirgilyakh Valley, the verbiage went on. Parts of the display had been found in Siberia and the Italian Tyrol. The artefacts were replicas of those found in Hochdahl, Germany –’

What artefacts?

I cupped my hands to the glass once more and Adam walked slowly past me. He brushed against my shoulder and I could feel him, smell him.

Hochdahl meant nothing to me. I looked up from the information plaque. The animal was there. Along with rocks and the dried vegetation and then I found myself staring into the glassy eyes of another exhibit, a man who was not a man.

Standing by the side of the mammoth, he had previously been obscured. I felt my knees begin to weaken. I supported my weight against the glass and looked at the sign again.

'Hochdahl is near Düsseldorf,' said Adam softly. He was standing immediately behind me. 'It's in the Neander Valley.'

'He's a hominid,' Adam continued.

I could hear the smile in his voice and the hairs on my neck and arms prickled up. The Neander Valley. This was a Neanderthal man and I looked back at the figure. My legs began to move. I edged around the glass and passed Adam in order to secure a better view.

I heard the words as I spoke them. 'It can't be.'

'Can't be what, Spencer?'

I was now no more than ten feet from the preserved hominid. I forced myself to take a breath, looked wordlessly at the exhibit. The finer details might be nothing more than the guesswork of a museum technician, so I tried to look past them.

I put to one side the crown of shaggy dark-brown hair and the chocolate-brown skin. I discounted the dark, mahogany eyes and tried to concentrate on the hominid's core features. Its powerful legs. Its thick, heavy trunk and the massive, barrel-chested upper body. The muscular arms and the hands with their heavy, blunt fingers.

The hominid radiated strength and latent menace. It looked tremendously solid and I tried to keep the thought from my mind but I couldn't. I could see how the exhibit would walk. I could see that it would roll from foot to foot and my eyes found Adam's, the billionaire once more by my side.

'You were going to say something?' said Adam. A smile played on his face. He looked from me to the hominid and back again.

I shook my head. 'No.'

‘Nothing?’

I remained silent.

‘Say it, Spencer.’

‘I can’t...’

‘You can,’ said Adam. ‘Say it.’

I said nothing but my eyes, my hesitation and my entire body had already betrayed me.

‘Say it, Spencer.’

‘It’s just that it –’

‘Yes?’

‘It looks like –’

I couldn’t finish the sentence. I didn’t need to. Adam spoke. ‘Like me?’

I nodded and Adam‘s piercing blue eyes drifted lazily from mine to the exhibit of the man behind the glass and he spoke. ‘Spencer, it is me.’

Seventeen
09:20 – Wednesday 16th June
American Museum of Natural History, Central Park West, New York City

The world had stopped spinning and I stared blankly at the glass before me. I fumbled for the iPhone in my pocket. I had no idea if the thing had recorded Adam's comments but I was certain that I had heard him correctly.

I leaned forward against the glass of the display cabinet and supported myself as the hominid came slowly back into focus. Round shouldered and hugely powerful, built like the stump of a tree. It was him.

'I know it's a shock,' said Adam. The words registered but I did not react. 'Try to imagine how I felt.'

I moved my mouth but no sound emerged and Adam continued. 'I'd suspected something for some time.' I was floundering, couldn't keep up. Adam raised his hand to the glass in front of him and took a deep breath. 'The body was found in the Italian Alps,' he said. He sounded casual, matter-of-fact. 'So maybe I'm Italian but the tools were replicated from finds near Hochdahl.'

And the weapons. I could see the axe and a stone knife but Adam simply nodded towards the exhibit and continued. 'And having met me I'm sure you'll agree that the researchers know much less about Neanderthals than they think they do.'

He turned towards me. I didn't know if he expected a reply but I was still a long way from being able to speak. Adam continued. 'Decent finds are rare. No soft tissue has ever been found.

'Officially, that is,' he said and he smiled. 'But my father had already taken what samples he needed before the exhibit here was handed over. Now only its bones are truly genuine and a bit of hair. The whole thing had been sitting in a frozen peat bog for thousands of years. That doesn't do wonders for the skin, as I'm sure you can imagine.

'So there were a lot of blanks. They didn't know how hairy to make him for example.' Adam turned from the exhibit to face me and I could feel him reading me. 'They didn't know whether to give him clothes. Didn't know what colour his skin was or even his eyes.'

Adam seemed to be inviting comparison with the exhibit and his ice-blue eyes held mine. 'So they guessed,' he said. 'And as I said, sunk in a freezing bog for thirty thousand years, most things come out brown. They added hair and some scraps of clothes. They made him look like a moderately intelligent gorilla don't you think?'

I had to agree. I nodded weakly and Adam spoke again. 'So should I be insulted, Spencer? Well let's just say I'm hardly flattered. And they assumed that these monkey-men couldn't speak. It wasn't possible, the researchers said. Inadequately evolved larynx. I find that rather amusing.'

My eyes flickered between the exhibit and the man before me. Adam's eyes were no longer smiling and my eyes widened. I was standing shoulder to shoulder with a Neanderthal man but Adam didn't seem to want or expect anything from me. I didn't contribute, was happy simply to let Adam continue. 'It was the Victorians, of course. They twisted the truth to suit their own purpose. They bent the Neanderthal's limbs.

'They gave him a sub-human stoop and ignored the fact that his brain was larger than an anatomically modern human. About thirteen per-cent larger on average. They made him appear more apelike. It simply wasn't convenient for their theories to assume otherwise. Where would that leave man having been made in the image of his God?

'The Neanderthal might not have been the missing link. They knew from the early days that his was a parallel branch of humanity rather than an ancestor of man but he was certainly deemed to be an inferior branch. A brainless hulk, it's a wonder I've done as well as I have, don't you think?'

I looked from the Neanderthal to the businessman beside me. Adam looked so human. His face was not unusually broad and his chin, though a little shallow, was normal. His appearance may have been altered by surgery but his eyes in their dazzling and natural blue, shone with intelligence and his skin colour was unmistakeably northern European.

'Of course we shouldn't blame them,' said Adam. He seemed to be enjoying himself. 'Product of their time, the Victorians, and they twisted the facts to suit their infant theories.

'Most examples that were found were relatively small. But as you can see, I'm rather large myself, so their lack of stature was merely a dietary issue rather than genetic but the anthropologists had to guess at so many things. I suppose they didn't make too bad a job of it overall.' Adam inclined his head to one side and looked at the exhibit. 'They knew for sure that his bones were much thicker than those of an AMH – that's an anatomically modern human. A great deal heavier. They were much denser and the muscle attachments were much larger.

'So they knew that this was a powerful hominid but then so too is a gorilla. Gorillas stand around five foot ten and tip the scales at four hundred pounds, that's a powerful beast, Spencer. And gorillas aren't made in God's image either so it must have seemed natural to make this latest hominid look stupid too.

'They slightly overdid the brow. Made him chinless but got the other physical features right. He was proportionally short-limbed. Was made for the cold, was much less gangly than other hominids, than the Africans.'

AMHs had pushed north into Europe from Africa but I still didn't trust myself to vocalise my thoughts. Instead, I focused on the Neanderthal man in the glass case. Hunched, his lips drawn back and his teeth showing, the dull-eyed exhibit looked back. The spark of human intelligence was missing. This was most certainly an animal. Not a human being and I turned to Adam who was as human as any man I had ever met.

'So the end-result isn't too flattering,' he said. He seemed to be reading me again and he held out his arms, beckoning me to look at him. 'Not a patch on the younger model, which would be me.'

Adam pointed and I followed the course of his blunt finger to the sharpened rock in the exhibit's left hand and the huge leather-bound stone axe in its right. 'Other little things,' he said.

'We think they were all left-handed. Like the old story about polar bears so the axe is in the wrong hand. It's an excellent replica that we donated to the museum. The head weighs more than two kilos. Rather heavy but I like it. It's a good, strong wooden handle. A new one but the head is modelled on an original find. It's chiselled from flint. I've held it you know, used it. I thought that it was appropriate.'

'Neanderthal?'

'Yes that's right,' said Adam almost gently. 'You're not wired are you?'

Wired? I shook my head. 'No, I'm not wired.'

'Just the phone?'

Adam was holding out his hand. I didn't know if it was legal to tape conversations in New York. I lifted my iPhone out of my pocket and Adam took it. It disappeared from view and I knew that I would never see it again. I still had Simon's Nokia but had no idea if that could record a conversation. I'd have to use my scrappy powers of recall and I waited for Adam to speak. 'We haven't got the metal detectors set up yet. But so few people wear a wire on a first meeting. They feel that they have to establish a rapport. They need to create a trust before they breach it. So rude, don't you agree?'

'I don't know,' I said. I was too tired to worry. The image of Adam's blood-drenched father came into my mind. Then there were the stories about Maria Alvarez but when I spoke, my voice was level. 'It never occurred to me to wear a wire.'

'Do you know, I believe you,' said Adam. He looked away. 'Did you think that I might hurt you?'

'I, well –'

'It's OK, you needn't worry,' said Adam. He was facing me and he looked suddenly very young. I thought back to the diary pieces that I'd penned about the man and felt a flush of guilt as Adam gestured towards my face with his chin. 'Debilitating isn't it? The treatment is working though. You should be pleased.'

I nodded, wondered if I should thank him but said nothing.

'It's no longer the violent purple of your youth,' Adam continued. 'But it still sets you apart. It brands you and differentiates you from other people. You can never be the same as them, can you Spencer? I thought that you of all people might understand what I've had to go through, what I'm still going through.'

Adam Reid raised his hand. His fingers outstretched, he touched my face. He traced the lines of the port-wine stain. His touch was remarkably gentle and I managed not to recoil. 'I'm not going to hurt you,' he said. 'I can only guess at what you might have heard about me but you have my word, I will never hurt you.'

I heard the words but I was somewhere else. I couldn't be here, in the centre of one of the largest cities in the world talking to the billionaire Adam Reid, the man who was a leader in his field and now by his own words, a liar, a lunatic or a Neanderthal man. I felt my head begin to spin. A supporting hand gripped my elbow as I struggled to remain upright and I blinked hard.

I brushed away Adam's hand. My own disfigurement had made me what I was. I hated it but it was a part of me and maybe Adam was the same. He was staring at me intently. He raised his head and stroked the whiter skin, the scar tissue beneath his own chin. 'I know what it's like to be different, Spencer,' he said. 'And I know what you may have heard about me but I have powerful enemies. They're people who would stop at nothing in their attempt to destroy me. They would use anything against me, even you. They will lie to you and try to mislead you.'

I said nothing. It seemed like the safest course of action and Adam continued. 'And we have to be careful, Spencer. They might even kill you as they did my parents, the policewoman and the others. They'll distort the truth. They'll use anything or anybody they can. Don't believe what you've been told about me. Check everything and anything that they tell you before you let them use you as a tool against me.'

I didn't appreciate being called a tool any more than the next man but I held my tongue and waited for Adam to speak. 'They're setting me up for something, something really huge. I know it's confusing but they'll tell you that they represent the authorities. They've been using Flanagan but you have to keep an open mind.'

This wasn't what I'd been expecting. As a story it was bigger, much bigger than anything that I could have imagined. I mumbled something that even I couldn't make out.

'Can I trust you Spencer?' Adam's eyes were imploring and I looked at him. He wasn't an idiot. I was a journalist. I felt the hot exhibition lights beating down on me and finally I could see the scarring on his face clearly. Under the chin and around the man's ears the skin shone white, a testament to the pain that he had suffered. Adam spoke again. 'Can I trust you?'

What Adam had said made sense. In the absence of proof, remove those things that are incredible and what is left has to be the truth. There was nothing the man had said that was inconsistent with the facts. Evidence could always be planted. It was consistent with the harassment that I'd suffered. Someone had been setting me up but that person could be someone other than Adam.

But Nosey had scratched the Porsche the first time and he was Adam's man. And where did Flanagan stand in all this? I was more confused than enlightened and Adam continued. 'I can deal with my enemies within the law, Spencer.' His voice was small, imploring. 'I swear it. There'll be no bloodshed if it can be avoided but I need time. Can I trust you?'

Once again I felt myself removed from my body. I was watching a confused and pitiful journalist struggle with his choices. I was being swept along and had to let myself go. I was reeling but I felt my mouth open and the words began to form. Before me was a man in pain. And that man was appealing to me on the most basic of levels. But it was my ambition that spurred me on. A favour granted to Mr Reid could be repaid a thousand fold. I could see the money, the influence and the power standing before me but above all, I could see a story, one that could be bigger than any that had ever been written.

In one moment, I saw it all: the accolades and the feting and the guest appearances and the crowning success. And I saw the wide, open and honest face of a vulnerable man and I wanted to help. Looking at the piercing and tear-moistened blue eyes, I saw the real distress of another person, another human being and I looked directly at Adam Reid and I inclined my head.

'Yes Adam,' I said. 'You can trust me.'

Eighteen
10:10 – Wednesday 16th June
American Museum of Natural History, Central Park West, New York City

He could trust me.

What was I saying?

But at the time I said it, I meant it and Adam lowered his eyes and paused before he spoke. ‘Let’s get away from here, Spencer. I’ll tell you about Henrietta. Perhaps it will help you to understand.’

It would be a relief to leave the exhibits. Better still to leave the museum altogether and feel a breeze on my face. We descended to the second floor in silence and continued out of doors onto a large terrace where a table and two chairs had been set apart from the main seating area.

And there were other people around. Adam picked up the attaché case that I’d seen him with earlier from one of the seats and we sat down. A large umbrella shaded us from the strengthening sun and he put the case on the table. I looked at it but it scarcely registered.

I was still an observer rather than a participant in the events that were taking place around me. Adam had left me floundering and the real world seemed a distant memory. On the terrace, men in overalls were setting up outdoor furniture while white jacketed waiters made the final adjustments to the seating for the meeting later that afternoon. Above our heads, the mechanics of a huge sunscreen were being tested.

Drinks arrived. I was thirsty. I gulped down an orange juice then hit the coffee and managed a question. 'You were saying Adam, your father's work?'

Adam Reid reached down and span the attaché case in his hands, clicking open the twin locks. He lifted the lid of the case but its contents were hidden from view. He shuffled some papers and spoke as he was doing so. 'Henrietta was a clone,' he said. 'But you already know that. The nucleus of a mammoth cell was transferred into the egg of an elephant. She was born a year or so before me, in Montana.

'Given the different gestation periods for elephants and humans, she'd been implanted into the womb of her surrogate mother two years before my mother fell pregnant with me.'

Adam looked at me and gently, almost reverently, lifted out the burgundy covered paper that I had photocopied earlier from the case and put it on the table between them. 'Henrietta was normal and healthy, at least in the early days. Not that my father or anybody else had had anything against which to compare her, but her appetite, her behaviour and even her cell structure were what he had expected. That is until she began to mature at which point things started to change.'

Adam looked away and I followed his eyes. We watched as his staff busied themselves beginning at the furthest corner of the terrace. They were business-like and professional and I could imagine the whole thing shot in time-lapse photography. The workers would be scurrying like ants. The tables and chairs would be planting themselves and spreading like a white mould across the terrace. It would not take them long but Adam's eyes had misted so I stole a look at my watch. I had to move things on. 'I heard that she was put down?'

'Put down,' said Adam. And not for the first time I wondered how I'd survived for so long as a journalist asking provocative questions. Adam had loved her and I'd known that before I'd asked the question. Adam pursed his lips and spoke again. 'Yes, put down.'

I fought hard against a shudder. I tried not to show my discomfort and

Adam continued. 'She was destroyed, yes. She had begun to deteriorate and my father feared the worst. He was a generation ahead of his time. Aside from my mother, he had no one to turn to. He was almost certainly correct in his projections but he had no one in whom he could confide. Scientifically he was out there on his own. You have to respect what he did, he was a great man.'

I didn't want to interrupt Adam and presently he continued. 'He didn't tell me of course. He never went into detail. I was a child but I could pick up some of what was going on. Henrietta had begun to suffer from some nervous disorder, some sort of degenerative brain condition.

'Scanning her brain pre-mortem was never going to be easy,' said Adam. I had questions flooding in now but I said nothing, let the man before me talk. 'The signs were there,' he said. He did not seem to be fully engaged. 'She was delusional. She became paranoid and her behaviour at times was extremely violent. Somehow he managed the scan and the outcome confirmed what he knew to be true.

'There was massive white tissue damage to her brain. The frontal lobes were in tatters and it was irreversible. She was not going to recover, she was going to die.'

Cocooned in the building and sheltered from the pressing weight of the millions of New Yorkers around us, we could have been alone but outside a car sounded its horn. Adam's eyes were glazed but I remained fascinated, gripped by his story and now I began to feel something else in the younger man; I could feel his fear. Where Henrietta had led he might follow.

I had to be professional and dispassionate. I was exhausted and could make mistakes. I would have to check that the facts were the facts but Adam's fear was real, I could feel it building before me. He spoke. 'He considered a lobotomy at one point.'

I nodded.

'You know what that means?'

I did but I didn't. I shrugged and shook my head. Some sort of brain operation? 'Not really.'

'The brain's an odd thing,' said Adam. He allowed the words to sink in. More for my benefit I imagined than his own. 'It's crucially important but so little about it is truly understood.'

I nodded again.

The pause lengthened before Adam continued. 'You've heard of Phineas Gage?'

I shook my head. If Adam was disappointed by my ignorance, he didn't show it and continued. 'He was a US railway worker. In the late 1840s he was tamping down gunpowder into a hole with a three feet long iron rod. The powder exploded and shot the pole clean through his head. It landed twenty-five yards behind him.

I didn't like the sound of that at all. And I liked Adam's stabbing gestures with his thumb even less. He moved his finger slowly from his left cheek to the top of his head. 'It punched a hole the size of a silver dollar from here to here and he lived.

'For nearly twelve years as a matter of fact,' continued Adam. 'But the frontal lobes of his brain were badly damaged. His very character changed. He became a foul-mouthed liar and a cheat. He no longer knew the difference between truth and fiction or between right and wrong. The contact between parts of his brain had been disturbed and it had affected his behaviour.'

I didn't know what to say but Adam did nothing to break the silence and I had to say something. 'So what happened to him?'

Adam's eyes focused upon me. 'He stumbled on, Spencer. What's important is that his behaviour led doctors to believe that no contact within the brain between the frontal and prefrontal cortex might be better than the wrong sort of contact.'

I was hot, tired and my mouth was dry but Adam's lesson in carving up brains wasn't over yet. He continued. 'Early experiments were carried out on animals. Not elephants of course but the subjects were lobotomised. The lobes allowing contact between the two parts of the brain were severed. Do you know how that's done?'

I didn't have a clue. Reid reached for the shaft of the parasol that emerged from the centre of our table and adjusted its position. The shade caught me and I immediately felt cooler and Adam spoke. 'In the early days, a lobotomy involved trepanning the skull.'

Adam smiled without humour. 'That's opening it up, Spencer. They would remove the hair, peel back the scalp and then shave away slivers of the skull until the brain was exposed. Then these early pioneers simply sliced around with a knife.'

Adam's voice betrayed no discernible emotion and I did not comment. The image was too vivid and I waited for the man to continue. 'It was hard to judge results with animals, of course. It was hard to tell if they were more or less paranoid than they had been before the operation but over time the doctors got hold of human subjects.

'They were seen as hopeless cases,' continued Adam. 'And that was perhaps just as well because the post operation mortality rate was very high. Attrition, they called it. About 40% of the subjects died before a Portuguese neurosurgeon, a psychiatrist by the name of Moniz, who had been shot and crippled by a pre-lobotomy patient, developed a method that involved passing a length of wire through the brain, which was then used to cut it like a piece of cheese.'

I had an unpleasant watery feeling in my bowels. Adam continued. 'It was less invasive than the knife. It resulted in much less trauma and a degree of success. In fact it looked as though it had reduced paranoia and anxiety but patients exited surgery more apathetic and sluggish than they had gone in and the mortality rate remained significant.'

This was just getting better. I edged further into the shade of the parasol and took a sip of water. Adam nodded, apparently to himself. 'Work carried on into the twentieth century. In the US in the 40's Walter Freeman popularised a quicker and less dangerous method which became known as the ice-pick lobotomy.'

I could picture an ice-pick only too clearly. Adam was watching me intently. 'Yes, that's right Spencer. Freeman spent the rest of his career hammering metal spikes into the brains of his patients.'

'He used an ice-pick?'

Hardly an insightful or cutting remark but Adam seemed not to care. 'Absolutely,' he said. 'Freeman's only tools were an ice-pick, a hammer and a little local anaesthetic.'

I stood up. Horror films, screaming victims strapped into chairs, came into my mind. Grinning, maniacal doctors swung hammers at ice picks and I caught Adam's eye before he looked away. His half-smile masked a deeper sadness. I felt foolish and I lowered myself back into my chair. Adam continued with his story. 'The ice-pick was hammered into the brain through the roof of the eye orbit and was then swept from side to side. The whole operation could be done in seconds. The procedure was carried out on thousands of human beings but Henrietta was more fortunate. My father decided to have her put to sleep.'

I looked at Adam. For him this was real. This could be his future. As I looked at the younger man I found it hard to believe that this was the person that Daniel Flanagan and I had been discussing only a few days earlier. I heard myself speak. 'So what does this mean for you?'

I hadn't meant it to sound so cold. Reid did not reply. He looked instead at the attaché case before him. It was open but its contents were still shielded from me. Adam took out a second report, another pamphlet. Purple covered and similar in size to the burgundy pamphlet already on the table, this one was thicker and more carefully bound. It had Roman numerals, probably a date, at the top, and a logo that I had seen before at the bottom. Adam slid it to the centre of the table.

I tried to read the title upside down but the font was too small and the logo still escaped me. I looked up sharply as Adam spoke. 'My father was murdered.'

I found myself nodding.

'You know that don't you, Spencer? He had worked at a weapons facility the UK Government has in Wiltshire.' Adam paused and I finally recognised the logo on the pamphlet. It was Porton Down, the UK Government's centre for research into bacteriological and chemical weaponry. 'The people who killed him needed information. They needed to know what my father knew, what he had told the others.'

What others? I was getting drawn in. This could be paranoia. I would have to be careful. 'He was deeply involved in genetic research,' continued Adam. 'He maintained links with the organisation long after he left and he was worried in the weeks before his death. He thought that he might have information that others would kill for.

'What information; and who would kill for it?'

I had sounded brusque and business-like and Adam lowered his eyes. 'I don't know.'

As a journalist, I had to remain detached. Most conspiracy theories were bullshit. I looked at the report and tried to consider what I knew to be true. I only had Adam's word that Henrietta had gone mad. I gave him some more rope. 'And these people are targeting you?'

Adam raised his eyes. 'I don't know.'

In many ways that was better than a totally paranoid 'yes'. I looked away, watched the stewards moving slowly towards us. They were ignoring us absolutely and beside me, Adam took a deep breath. 'My father also worked overseas on several occasions on government business. After his death they came to see me, MI6. They were concerned about something. They were worried about some sort of breach and had to change their working procedures.'

'Because of what your father might have told his killer?'

I wasn't being particularly sensitive but Adam said nothing and I wiped my brow on my shirt sleeve. The sun was creeping around again and I was warming up. I'd be a sweaty mess before too long and I scraped the chair back into the shade of the umbrella. It placed me closer to Adam. He didn't look as though he was going to speak so I chanced a question. 'The second paper, could I see it?'

'All in good time,' said Adam. He looked up and exhaled. It was almost a sigh and he continued. 'I fell into a depression after my mother and father died. I don't mind admitting it. My father meant more to me than you can imagine and I missed him terribly. I still do. But more than that, I respected him and I needed him. After his death, I found myself utterly alone.

'His work with Henrietta may have helped me but she was gone and then he was gone and I considered suicide,' said Adam. 'Either that or going to the authorities. I could have thrown myself on their mercy. But they would have treated me like some sort of freak and would have used me. My life would never have been my own again.'

Adam stretched and continued. 'No, I had to work on the problem myself. That's the reasoning behind Zylagene and Zylapharm but first I needed the money. So I gambled. Or rather I invested if you prefer to use that word but the funds that I ran did well.

'In fact they performed more strongly than I could ever have hoped. But the money that I was making was only ever going to be a means to an end. I had to focus on molecular biology and I had to move quickly in case, well –'

Your brain began to deteriorate? I managed not to say the words but Adam also fell silent. I took the opportunity to ask another question. 'Once you had refocused yourself on science, the allegations of corner-cutting and of unethical experiments?'

A direct approach but this was my one shot at the big time and Adam did not appear to bristle. 'They were just that,' he said. He did not look up. His broad fingers traced out some of the lettering on the purple cover of the second report. 'There was never any substance to them but I won't deny that I was in a hurry. I had a tremendous incentive to make progress but the only subject that I've ever abused has been me.'

Adam looked up. His crystal-clear blue eyes sparkled and he continued. 'My rivals know that I'm driven to succeed but they don't know why. And they can never know why so they have had to invent reasons.

'Greed they say. Or maybe I'm driven by an insatiable thirst for power or simple megalomania. But they know nothing. They try to dirty my companies. Add in a healthy dose of professional jealousy and is it any wonder that they plant evidence and start what rumours they can about me? They're all untrue.'

More paranoia? Perhaps. But if I could rely on even a part of what Adam had said in the last hour then he had reason to be worried. He raised his head. He looked directly at me and I had never seen a more open, honest and trustworthy face in my life.

But then what did I know? I was in a vulnerable position because I was tired and I so wanted the story to be true. I was in danger of becoming a part of it when I should remain a detached observer.

And I was being fed line after line. Each one was no less plausible than the last but the story was becoming increasingly bizarre in aggregation and I would not be in a position to investigate any of the allegations until long after this meeting was over.

'I want to believe you Adam,' I found myself saying. I expected to see a flash of irritation on the man's face but I did not. Instead, Adam looked resigned and disappointed. 'But this is all too much for me to take in.'

'I can understand that, Spencer,' said Adam. 'In time I can prove to you that what I'm saying is true. I'm in danger and I know that you can empathise, that you know it's not easy being trapped inside a body that sets you apart.'

Adam's eyes were pleading and I found myself nodding as he inclined his chin towards my face. 'You've decided to have the birthmark removed and I don't blame you. It's the right decision but if you could have removed it without having to resort to surgery wouldn't you have done so?

I felt myself agreeing with the man and Adam continued. 'And take it a little further. If your disfigurement could have been dealt with at source –'

'What are you talking about?'

This time the irritation showed but Adam quickly had it under control.

'Dealt with at source. If you could reprogram your genes to remove it for you wouldn't that be a step forward, a real advance?'

I couldn't bring myself to nod this time. I was having trouble keeping up. Adam measured me before he continued. 'It's worse for me, Spencer. It's much worse than you could possibly imagine. I'm a freak and I've been through enough.

'I've had bone shaved from the front of my skull. I've had the ridges of my eyebrows filed down and bone from all over my body has gone to build up this chin. I've had my jaw broken and re-set a dozen times and hell, I'm only six-four, but I weigh more than three hundred pounds. Could you walk a mile in my shoes, imagine a day in my life?'

Could I empathise? Well possibly. But I was neither a billionaire nor a Neanderthal man and there were limits. Fortunately, Adam didn't seem to expect an answer and he spoke again. 'But more importantly can you imagine the scale of the threat that's hanging over me? It's a threat to my sanity and to my life. You know what happened to my father. I'm on my own now and I've told you what happened to Henrietta but I can beat it, I just need the time.'

'I can sympathize, Adam –'

'Don't add the 'but',' said Adam and his eyes held me. 'We're almost identical you and I. Much, much more than 99% of our DNA is identical but that's not enough, we're still different. Just try to imagine how I feel. And since my father was murdered I have no-one in my life and I have nowhere to go. My life, what I have left of it, is a permanent hell.'

I looked at Adam and felt myself drawn to his plight. I could understand at least some of what he was going through but I was worried once more and I didn't know why. Adam must have given up on me speaking because he continued. 'We've mapped the human genome. You probably know that but recording something is not the same as understanding it.

'It certainly doesn't imply that the data recorder is able to create the building blocks from scratch. But that's what I have to do. I want to create cells for myself because I want to be normal, Spencer. I want to be human.'

Nineteen
10:55 - Wednesday 16th June
Central Park West, Manhattan, New York

I want to be human. The words had resonated. They had struck a chord deep within me as Adam must have known that they would and he had said that he needed my help.

I was flattered and confused. And not a little afraid and I wanted time to think. I had made my excuses and, heavy legged, and more tired than I could ever remember being in my life before, I had left the Museum of Natural History. Underneath the blazing sun and an unbroken azure sky, I shaded my eyes and looked around.

I was drawn to the leafy Park and, as I walked towards the shade, I began to flush. I could understand the desire to be normal but this was more, much more than that. I would attend the meetings this afternoon and then see Adam this evening privately when he would give me access to the second paper. But for now, I headed south. I had to get some rest.

I wanted to put a bit of distance between myself and the Museum but I was running on empty and I knew it. After a couple of minutes I saw a diner and fell through the door and into its air-conditioned interior. I needed a drink, something long and cold. No alcohol and maybe a coffee as well and then I could take a cab back to the hotel.

My mind began to clear away from the heat and the air seemed to have lightened. I took a seat, ordered a Coke and a coffee. Both came quickly and I drank the Coke, ordered another and set about the coffee.

I knocked it back in a hurry and began to feel better. It might not last long but I felt almost human again and I smiled at the thought. Then the smell of bacon and burgers got through to me and my stomach rumbled. I'd been burning off calories all morning and I ordered what looked like the nearest thing to a full-English breakfast from the all-day menu.

The meal was comprised of bacon, eggs and bagels, toast and a few black and brown things of indeterminate origin. I ate quickly then pushed the empty plate away from me and sat back in my chair. It was wonderful to be able to think again and not to be pushed too quickly, to have at least some time to reflect.

My career would hinge on what I did over the next few hours and on how I chose to exploit or not to exploit this goldmine of a story. I drank a second coffee and ordered another. Put my elbows on the table and cradled my head in my hands. The draft from the air-con was pleasing on my bare neck and I closed my eyes.

The question was whether to go with what I'd got or stick with Adam and try to get more. Publish and be damned or try to make a friend of one of the richest men in the world? Put like that it seemed obvious. I'd have to stick with it. That would keep my options open because to go with what I had now might be to go with nothing at all.

I had nothing tangible from Simon, Flanagan was discredited and the pamphlet and my iPhone were gone.

If I could substantiate what I'd heard today, it was mind blowing. There would be no way of softening the blow for my readers because Adam Reid was not a man. He was not like the other seven billion two legged apes that walked the planet, because he was a Neanderthal.

Either that or he was totally full of shit and I was too tired to decide which. I needed somebody to talk to and not for the first time Daniel Flanagan came to mind. Adam had cast doubt on at least some of what the American had told me but I wasn't prepared to write the ex-cop off just yet. He might have been used, as I had been, but I wanted him to be genuine, needed someone in whom I could confide.

I would ring the hospital again from the hotel. Catching the waitress's eye, I gestured to her to bring me the bill and held out my credit card as she approached. She took it and I considered whether Flanagan might be well enough to come to the phone.

I marvelled at just how well I felt after having had the chance to cool down and to rehydrate and I smiled at the waitress as she walked towards me. She did not smile back. She wore an expression that I couldn't place and shook her head as she reached my table. She was holding out my credit card as though it had been dipped in something unpleasant. 'It won't clear, sir.'

A couple of heads turned and she gave me a worn smile. I noticed that she'd placed herself between me and the door and one of the cooks was keeping an eye on proceedings. The words took a while to sink in. 'What do you mean?'

The young waitress's face hardened. 'What's not to understand?' said her face. She refreshed her smile. 'They gave me a number for you to call. Or do you have another card?'

I shrugged. I wasn't packing any other plastic but I'd only given the girl a card in order to avoid splitting a hundred. I took out my wallet and peeled off a bill.

I scratched my head. I'd been good regarding overspending recently. I'd paid my bills on time so there should have been plenty of room on the card. Just a bit of petrol and a couple of meals and then I remembered Flanagan's plane tickets. Not that the cost would have been enough to breach my limit so perhaps someone had cloned the thing and had been charging purchases to it, it had happened before.

'Your change, sir,' said the waitress a moment later. She held out a saucer, several bills and coins on it. I noticed that one of the tens was split into singles to give me plenty of flexibility tip-wise and I scooped the bulk of the cash up.

'Thanks,' I said. I sounded awful. I tried to pull myself together. 'Sorry for the mix-up. You mentioned a telephone number?'

'I'll get it for you, sir,' said the waitress. She glanced at the change in the saucer before returning to the cash-desk and retrieving a piece of paper.

I'd use Simon's Nokia. Might cost him a fortune but Adam had my iPhone so I had no choice. The waitress handed over a slip of paper and I dropped a third and fourth dollar into the saucer. She'd left it for me to consider my options and what the hell; I was in the big league now. I could afford four dollars and I'd leave her the quarters and dimes too. It was her lucky day.

I left the diner and the heat hit me. I began to leak from every pore. I wouldn't have believed it was possible to warm up so quickly but it was and I stayed on the Park side of the road, moved to the shade of a tree. I propped myself against its trunk and took out Simon's Nokia. It looked straight forward enough and I dialled the number that the waitress had given me. I tapped in the credit card number at the request of some over-polite robot and was put in a queue.

More expense for Simon's people to deal with but I waited on the line. Peak time New York to the UK, just one more thing to worry about. After what seemed like an age, a woman with a northern Irish accent introduced herself.

I was tired. I couldn't remember my password or even my own date of birth. I couldn't possibly have sounded more suspicious. I was routed through to an account controller and gave the second woman my date of birth, postcode and whatnot. I managed my mother's maiden name, all the usual shit and she confirmed that I'd breached my limit. It was all in a day's work for her but I wasn't pleased and I was left to ask the obvious question. 'Have there been any unusually large transactions in the last few days?'

I was quite proud of that. It went some way to portraying me as a victim rather than some credit-addict. 'Yes,' said the voice. The woman sounded quite happy. 'There have been a number as a matter of fact.

United Airlines, two thousand eight hundred and forty nine pounds – '

'Nearly three grand?'

'That's correct, Mr Beck,' continued the voice.

Something was troubling me. I needed time to think. 'Just a moment please.'

'Certainly.'

What was it? Thinking at ten quid a minute or whatever phone calls like this cost was difficult. I wasn't at my best and then I had it; United Airlines. Flanagan had flown American. He had been on the American Airlines 9.30pm getting into Heathrow. So this was either a genuine error or something worse.

'You said United?'

'Yes, sir.'

'And the dates?'

'I'm afraid I don't know the dates for the flights themselves but the tickets were purchased on the 14th June.'

The 14th June was Monday. Only two days ago and my mind was spinning. Flanagan had arrived in the UK the previous Friday. The eleventh so these weren't his tickets but could they be my own? I cleared my throat. It gave me another second or so before I spoke. 'And what else is on the bill? Just the larger items please.'

'There's the £2,849 to United, a £399 charge to American Airlines and £625 to the New York Voyager Hotel...'

'The New York Voyager?'

'Yes, sir,' said the woman. She was sounding somewhat more sympathetic. 'It was also charged on the 14th June. Is there a problem, Mr Beck?'

'No,' I said. What I meant was yes. I tried to clear my head but the incessant honking of the cars around me blurred into one grey noise and it was a struggle. 'I'll get back to you, thanks.'

I hung up. What was happening? Simon was going to take care of the bills yet I'd been stuck with them. Was this a mistake or the result of a lie? Simon had been an ally and my best source of information but now my paranoia levels were rising and the world began to spin. I looked at my watch.

It was 11.28am. That was half past four in the afternoon in England. I hadn't slept for almost 36 hours and had had a pretty turbulent ten days or so before that. So I wasn't in the best shape mentally but I had to consider my options. I'd got four and a half hours before the Zylagene and Zylapharm meetings and I crossed the road, walked back into the diner.

Inside the place the cooler air was a blessing and the waitress seemed to recognise me as she approached. 'Another coffee?'

My four dollar tip hadn't been wasted and I managed a smile. Another coffee might be a mistake but I decided to go with it. 'Please.'

'Coming up,' she said. 'You OK.'

'I'm fine thanks,' I said. I was falling apart but I was still proud enough to deny it to strangers. Presently a generous mug of coffee appeared on the Formica table in front of me and I settled down to try to work out a plan of action.

Putting paranoia to one side there was only one theory that immediately fit the facts and that was that Simon was a fraud and that I was being set up. Simon had been instrumental in getting me up to Yorkshire, he'd said the flights and hotels would be paid for so where did that leave Adam?

In the cool of the diner, away from Adam and his open and honest face and his piercing blue eyes, the doubts that I'd had about him resurfaced and I tried to drill down to what I knew to be irrefutably true.

Adam's parents had died. The death of Flanagan's partner was a matter of record and an elephant or mammoth by the name of Henrietta seemed to have existed but nothing else was beyond doubt and even the centrepiece of my story, the suggestion that Adam had been cloned, that he was a Neanderthal, could be rubbish.

It could be a fantastic, unbelievable lie that would finish me as a journalist and render useless anything else that I might say about Adam. It would weaken allegations that I may make regarding his involvement in the deaths of his parents. Any such comments could be discounted as the ramblings of the idiot journalist who had thought the Chief Executive of two of the UK's most dynamic and progressive companies, was a monkey.

Reid had waved some purple covered pamphlet in front of my eyes and my desire to believe him had done the rest so I had to line up my options.

I would chase up Flanagan first. Ring my flat and see if he was there, judge his reaction if I challenged him. I took out Simon's Nokia, rang my own number in the UK and heard a series of clicks.

It could be the answer-phone. I would leave a message. Flanagan didn't have to be the best detective in the world to think of listening to the machine if he ever returned to Fermanagh Mansions. He would ring me back but then the telephone was answered. 'Good afternoon,' said a voice that I did not recognise. 'Who is this?'

I looked at the phone in my hand, checked the number on the LCD display. It was my London number and I should be asking the questions. 'Who the hell are you?'

'Mr Beck?'

'Yes, who are you?'

'This is the police, Mr Beck. We need to talk to you. You're –'

I hung up. I took another mouthful of coffee and considered Julian Broadbent. He might have some ideas. At the very least he was a solicitor and his one of the very few numbers that I carried in my head. It was still late afternoon in the UK and I punched in his number.

'Broadbent?'

Julian was a pushover but he managed to sound tremendously fierce on the telephone. 'Julian? It's Spencer...'

'Spencer, what the fuck have you been up to?' said Julian. He rarely swore. That he chose to do so now didn't fill me with confidence. 'Where in God's name are you?'

I answered the easier question first. 'New York.'

'New York?'

If Julian was going to repeat every answer then I'd be running Simon up quite a bill. 'What's going on?'

I sounded like an exhausted and tearful eight year old. Hopefully Julian would put it down to distortion on the line. 'The police are all over the place, that's what's going on. Your friend's dead –'

That wasn't a word I'd wanted to hear. I said nothing.

'Did you hear me, Spencer?'

'Flanagan?'

Now it was me asking the stupid questions. Sod the bill. 'Who?'

I shook my head. Something flickered in my brain. Maybe the coffees were having an effect. 'Flanagan, the American?'

'No,' said Julian. 'Not him. You know, your friend. That horrible woman, God rest her. Shelley Mitchum...'

'Dead?'

'Yes and the police want to talk to you about it. Now don't panic, we can arrange things –'

'What do you mean don't panic?' I said. It was the first thing that came into my head and my words caught the waitress's attention. I swivelled away from her in my seat and lowered my voice. 'Panicking comes naturally at times like this, have you got any better ideas?'

'Spencer, let's –'

'How did she die?

'I don't know. Police involvement doesn't look good and the American, the guy that was staying with you, I think he's in hospital.'

The information was sinking in but I was aware of the pause. The hesitation before Julian continued. 'You didn't do anything, right?'

'Like what?'

'Like poison them for instance?'

'Is that some kind of joke?'

'No, it's –'

'Of course I didn't poison them.'

My voice didn't carry quite the conviction that I'd hoped. Partly because I'd had to whisper but Julian hesitated before he spoke. 'I believe you, Spencer.'

'You're a fucking awful liar, Julian.'

'Well look, you've got to come back. It would look bad if you didn't and we can organize it, do a handover.'

I hung up. I think I was ahead in the hanging up game. But that was a minor victory and just how was I meant to react to a phrase like 'do a handover'? It sounded like something out of a John Le Carre novel. Spies crossing each other on a moonlit bridge, but I wasn't a spy. I wasn't a criminal, either. Not in any meaningful way and I most certainly wasn't a murderer. But it sounded as though Julian was already working on a diminished responsibility plea on my behalf and I took another mouthful of coffee.

It had gone cold. I gestured for another, the most ridiculous thoughts flooding my mind. If I went to prison, for example, then who would feed my fish? And would the prison authorities allow me to finish my course of laser treatment to remove my birthmark?

I rubbed my eyes again. What I needed was twelve hours in a bed. Fourteen would be even better but that wasn't going to happen. Eye rubbing and caffeine were all that I had at the moment and I tried to graft the information that I'd picked up from Julian onto what I already knew.

Who could I trust? Pretty much nobody was the answer. There was me. I was pretty sure about that. And just possibly Flanagan. But he was in a hospital on the other side of the Atlantic so what about the husband of Flanagan's partner Maria Hernandez, no Alvarez?

A good man, Flanagan had said. A lawyer in the Bronx DA's office. Hector. I raised my head from my hands. I couldn't remember having put it there a second time but I managed to catch the waitress's eye. I put a few coins onto the table where another coffee had materialised and asked for the telephone directory.

Twenty
12:50 – Wednesday 16th June
161st Street, the Bronx, Manhattan, New York

There were dozens of H. Alvarez's working for the City of New York.

I'd been on hold for an age. Transferred from department to department, the Nokia's battery was beginning to run down and I must have cost Simon a small fortune. The calls would have been bouncing from New York, to the UK and back to New York in order to allow me to speak to a person not a couple of miles from where I was standing but I'd got hold of Alvarez in the end and it had been Daniel Flanagan's name that had got me the meeting.

The D Train, unthreatening and clean and efficient, had whisked me up to the Bronx and delivered me to the front of the massive bulk of the Yankee Stadium safely and I took in the scene. The cars were older and shabbier here and there were fewer of them. And the people mirrored the cars but the 161st Street entrance of the Bronx County Building looked safe enough.

Officials were buzzing here and there and I'd arranged to meet Alvarez on the steps. As it was, he pushed out from one of the shaded doorways and called out my name as I passed. Sensible to stay out of the sun but just how the man had spotted me, I didn't know.

Hector Alvarez was slightly built. No more than five six. Perhaps 140 pounds, smartly dressed. Early forties, dark featured and balding his expensive, rectangular glasses were fashionably thin and mixed emotions registered on the man's face; curiosity and fear.

I'd had a day and a half without sleep and had been boiled by the sun. I tried to steady my breathing and concentrated on looking a little less unbalanced but Alvarez did not offer me his hand. Undeterred, I offered mine and we shook as the man moved backwards slightly. He seemed keen to stay more than an arm's length from me and I couldn't blame him. He nodded fractionally and backed off further. 'You mentioned Maria?'

'Reid had her killed.'

Blunt. I felt dirty but the last time I'd looked in the mirror I was a journalist and it was an occupational hazard. Besides which it was what he wanted to hear, it may well be the truth and I didn't have time for niceties. Alvarez let this sink in and then spoke. 'You know this for certain?'

I hadn't come here with proof, if that's what he was asking. I spoke nonetheless. 'She was in his way. He got rid of her and now he's targeting me.'

Hector Alvarez took off his glasses. He polished them on his tie. I was getting the impression that he would be an easy man to underestimate. He glanced up at me. 'If that was the case, do you expect me to believe that you'd still be in New York talking to me?'

This wasn't going at all the way I'd planned. He seemed sharper than me, which wasn't helpful. I'd have to work on his curiosity and perhaps his desire for revenge. 'I may be being used by others.'

That at least was true. I was going to have to give Alvarez something. The lawyer slipped his glasses back on and blinked at me. 'And how does this concern me?'

I tried to dredge something up, decided that the truth or at least a version of it would have to do. 'I want to find out what really happened to Maria.'

It was all going wrong. Alvarez looked at me steadily. 'Guy that killed

Maria died in prison. Maria's over.'

He sounded like he meant it. Maybe a few years in therapy had persuaded him that he had to move on. I considered using the unborn child. But there were limits to even my behaviour and I shook my head. I was wasting my time. 'I'm sorry, Mr Alvarez. I shouldn't have bothered you,' I said. 'I'm sorry for your loss.'

Alvarez looked at me evenly. He didn't try to prevent me leaving and I headed back to the subway. I descended to the platforms and found myself on the southbound D. Hector was no use, Flanagan was three thousand miles away and I was alone. I needed something tangible and that could only mean the papers, the pamphlets.

I'd seen the first one and made a copy but what good was that?

I could have knocked it up on a PC, soaked the paper in tea and produced a half decent hoax in a couple of hours but Adam's fingerprints would be on the original and that would be better than nothing.

The second pamphlet Adam had simply waved at me. It had looked genuine but I had no idea what was in it. Sight of it would be useful. A copy would be better and the original better still because it would give me some idea as to whether or not the Neanderthal stuff was rubbish.

I left the train. I must have done. I couldn't remember actually getting off but I was climbing the stairs, the bright sunshine bleaching the upper steps and I emerged into the light back at the American Museum of Natural History.

A pedestrian bumped into me. He mumbled something and I swore at him. Another one caught me and I told her to watch where she was going. People were beginning to stare and I tried to focus on my watch. I shielded the dial from the glare, noted that it was just after two.

It took me several seconds to work out that I had a couple of hours before the presentations. That wasn't particularly impressive. I looked up at the imposing façade of the Museum towering above me. I'd left the train at the right stop but it occurred to me that I shouldn't use the same entrance as I had earlier.

With the heat pressing in on my head and no shade to speak of, I walked around the building. It was huge but I found another entrance, this one fronted by an area where burgundy ropes had been set up to shepherd a queue that had not yet formed.

I approached the door where a gold-lettered notice declared that the museum was closed for a private function. I knew that already – I was a guest. Adam had said that he would see me again personally. The door was open and I peered in.

There was no sign of life. The guests that were expected later in the day had not yet begun to arrive and I checked my watch again. The first arrivals should be here long before 4pm. Not all of the seats had been pre-allocated. There would be a degree of competition for the best remaining places. The museum wouldn't be empty for long and the thought both spurred me on and comforted me.

I entered the building and my head began to clear in the cool air. I felt the tiniest flush of confidence. It didn't last long but I felt better for it. I could function in a crowd. It was where I worked best and, if Cambridge was anything to go by, the place would be packed. I walked further into the building and raised my head, tried not to skulk.

I was a guest after all but I wanted to get the documents and get out. The papers would give me something tangible before the guests arrived. Once I'd got them I could either leave the building or lose myself amongst the other attendees. I could sit out the presentations and perhaps even get a rest.

The museum was gloriously cool. My mind was clearing and I considered my options. I could still leave. It wasn't too late but who was I kidding? My legs were carrying me further and further into the Museum and there was no way that I was going to turn my back on the story at this stage.

So I would press on. And that meant playing it by ear. So the plan was that I didn't have a plan. I looked around the entrance hall. To my right were the lifts and to my left a small café. Last seen, Adam and the documents had been on the second floor terrace. That seemed like a logical place to start and, as a guest, it was one of the places where I'd have least trouble explaining my presence.

If Adam had moved the case, then I'd have to reassess my options from there. I walked over to the lifts but thought better of it and took the stairs. I was satisfied that I'd thought through the problem and had set myself a course of action. It might be the wrong one, but at least I was doing something and, for the moment, I had to concentrate on getting up the stairs, which seemed suddenly extraordinarily steep.

I didn't need the exercise and the blood was thumping in my head again. It would derail my plans if I collapsed in a heap before I'd achieved anything. I took a breather and walked up at a measured pace to the 2nd floor.

The stairwell was quiet. The traffic was a distant hum and I was at the opposite side of the building to the terrace and there were no signs of preparation. Nor could I smell food but I had no conception of what food for several thousand people smelled like or looked like, so maybe I was overanalysing the situation.

I walked into the Birds of the World exhibition and looked ahead into the adjoining room. To the jungle scenes, where vengeful, vicious creatures ruled the forest floor and the hairs on my arms began to rise. I paused to catch my breath once more.

'Spencer,' said a voice. I stood still. 'Been back to Africa I see.'

I turned. Nothing. I span on my heels and there he was. 'Adam?'

'Hello again,' said Adam. He was motionless against the glass of the exhibit. He blended somehow with the flora behind him, maybe the fauna too. The smile last seen was still in place. 'Did you forget something?'

I tried to sound casual. 'I'm just a little early.'

Adam shook his head slowly He looked genuinely pained. 'That's rather poor, Spencer. But I suppose I have been careless, taken a few risks.'

I frowned. I had no intention of saying anything further and Adam spoke. 'They were calculated,' he said. 'But they were risks nonetheless and this wasn't what I'd intended.'

I think I shrugged and Adam continued. 'So where do we go from here?'

I returned to my frown. I took a step backwards but Adam pushed off from the glass behind him and took a step towards me. He made an expansive gesture with his hand. 'African Peoples,' he said, smiling again. His pale blue eyes caught the light. 'Do you feel at home? Maybe you should. I'd like to show you something. We'll use the stairs. Your visit to the terrace can wait.'

I could feel the adrenalin coursing through my sluggish body. But it wasn't going to help me run far and I didn't fancy my chances in a fight. I felt myself begin to flush and Adam took another couple of steps. He was still thirty or forty feet away, but I'd seen him move. He could be on me in seconds. I looked at his large, blunt-fingered hands and imagined them around my throat.

Outside, cabs were honking at each other and life went on. Maybe danger rarely made its presence felt until it was too late but guests would be arriving soon and the building would be busy. My fear subsided a fraction. Adam took another step and a second figure emerged from behind a glass case to his right.

Another guest. Perhaps the moment of danger was passing. I looked toward the new arrival but the face staring back at me was stony and unsmiling. I'd seen this man before. Mid to late thirties, forty at a push and heavily built. Square headed, large but broken nose. He'd been at Ranulfskelf Hall back in Yorkshire. He'd barred my access to the building, had scratched my car and had saluted me in Cambridge. It was Nosey.

I registered footsteps behind me. I turned. Another man grabbed at me and Nosey sneered as he pushed me towards the stairwell.

'Don't be alarmed,' said Adam. He was by my side and was now holding my arm. His eyes were warm. 'My friends are your friends.'

I'd need to work on that. I looked around. There were two more of them. Four goons and Adam, crowding around me and they were big, almost as big as Adam himself and the man gestured with his hand. 'Shall we?'

My feet moved.

I had a flashback to my time on one of the local papers that I'd worked on in my youth; a slaughterhouse that I'd reported from. I remembered the vacant and resigned expression on the faces of the doomed animals and knew that my face was a mirror of theirs. Adam spoke again. 'I'm disappointed that you doubted me, Spencer.'

This wasn't going the way I'd hoped. The bad guy held all the aces but what was he talking about? I think I mumbled something about forgotten documents and Adam nodded. I stumbled again but hands supported me. We made the two flights of stairs and we entered the Hall of Advanced Mammals. The huge mammoth reared up before us once more, the still and solid Neanderthal man by its side. Adam turned and followed my eyes to the ape-man, the hominid.

'Yes,' he said and I could swear that I felt him. He was reading me. He was inside me. 'I told you the truth.'

Adam smiled. Friendly and open but the hand in my back pushed me on and propelled me past the display and behind Adam, into a much smaller room, the door thick, metal lined. A desk faced us and Adam tapped at a keyboard. 'If you'd worn a wire, you might have been able to prove at least some of what you've heard.

'As it was you needed the pamphlet. I'm not surprised that you came back. And it is genuine, if that's what you're wondering.' Adam gestured towards a bank of displays. 'This is an observation room.

It's also a panic room. A refuge from fire within the building, but it's the cameras that I wanted you to see.'

Adam's broad hand swept the air and I followed its progress. Several video screens blinked at me from a desk pushed up against the wall opposite us. They flickered from scene to scene as Adam manipulated them. He spoke. 'I'd like to show you something.'

I looked around the small, bare room. There were no artefacts. No books, no brochures, just the desks several chairs and the video equipment. The screens went blank before one flickered back into life and I squinted at it. I struggled to make out the off-white script at the bottom of the image. It was the 77th Street entrance to the museum. An entrance hall shot and to the top right was a timer. It was 13:55. Just a few minutes ago now. I saw an image of myself as I crept into the building. I seemed to hug the wall before furtively moving across the marble floor to the staircase.

Adam wagged his finger. 'Bit cloak and dagger don't you think?'

The scene cut to the grainy image of a small café on the first floor. I couldn't remember passing it but it `was my image on the screen. My stomach fluttered as I looked around once more, tried not to move my head too rapidly. It was clear that I wasn't going anywhere fast. Adam, Nosey and his three other goons and myself were crammed into the room and I couldn't even see the door through the press of bodies.

'This is my favourite bit,' said Adam. He had turned his back on me. He seemed happy. He inclined his head towards the screen and I watched as the camera cut to a staircase. I rubbed my eyes. One of the goons had raised his hand to mine. He was attentive and seemed to have expected a blow. I looked back at the image. A greenish grey, it was hard to see what was going on but as my screen-self entered the Hall of African Peoples, the buckle on my belt showed up a brilliant white.

'It's the widespread fear of terrorism that made them necessary,' said Adam. 'They're everywhere now. Sensors built into the doorways of public buildings. Into the entrances to some of the exhibitions here in the Museum, for example. In fact, I donated some of the funds needed to make it possible myself and as it shows clearly, you're not wearing a wire and you've got no weapon. I've got your iPhone and you'll find that you've lost Simon's phone. We know you've got nothing.'

Adam was no longer smiling. His body language was different. He looked bigger and more threatening. 'Weren't you tempted to bring a gun, Spencer?'

I'd never seen or touched a gun in my life. Adam tilted his head slightly to one side, his brow furrowed. 'It needn't have come to this.'

'Sorry?'

So there I was. I could speak but I was apologising to a criminal and quite possibly a murderer. Adam spoke again. 'We could have parted friends. Well friends of a sort, at least. When did you first feel the line?'

"Line? '

'Yes the line,' said Adam. I'd have to expand on my one-word answers but Adam seemed unconcerned. 'The hook was in from the early days but you didn't feel it. You swallowed the bait whole and still nothing.'

'I don't know what you mean, Adam,' I said.

'I think you do.'

Adam paused the video. 'You came back. And that suggests to me that you felt something. I'm curious to know what.'

The room was becoming hot and oppressive. No trace of humour on his face, Adam inclined his head. 'I said I'd like to know, Spencer. You might be a lot of things but I know you're not deaf.'

'It was the air fare,' said a voice. It was my own. Quiet but steady and I looked at my feet. In my current mental state Adam was two of me. And physically, he was three. I was in a tight spot. 'It was charged to my account; the business class flight, United Airlines.'

Adam pursed his lips. 'Paying for business class tickets made it so much more likely that you would come. But I wanted the bills to be in your name, Spencer. I was painting a picture. You were fleeing the country, took the first flight out of the UK.'

That was news to me. I was sure that my lack of comprehension was showing on my face but I changed the subject. 'And Flanagan?'

'He's genuine,' said Adam. He nodded slowly. 'Only a small player in our little drama, but he's the real deal. So the airfares led you to Simon?'

'Flanagan, he's –'

My voice failed me. Adam ignored the interruption. 'Concentrate, Spencer. I asked you about Simon?'

I raised my eyes, opened my mouth. Adam was watching me closely but I was finding it hard to breathe. It was all becoming clearer to me. I could see the man before me standing above the body of his father. A knife in his hand and it frightened me but there was more than that. I felt something wash over me.

It was defeat. I'd get my story but it would never be written. I was going to die here. And the story would die with me and who's to say that an unwritten story was ever a story at all? 'Simon didn't work,' I heard myself say. 'It was just too neat. It led back to you.'

Adam was smiling. 'Call me Simon,' he said. His voice had altered, it was totally different. 'The stories are true,' he said, his accent familiar, Scottish. 'Reid has touched your life.'

I raised my hand. I wanted to support my head but one of Nosey's goons grabbed my arm and prevented me. Adam spoke again. The words washed over me but some stuck. 'It was difficult choosing just how long a charge to give the mobile phone's battery. Too little and you might not have taken the bait but too much and you might have worked it out. 'Don't ring me' I said, 'I'll ring you."

Adam arched an eyebrow. 'Simon says go to New York. Simon says Adam will meet with you. Simon says. Didn't you get it?'

His words scraped like a knife on bone and I felt my face redden. I remained silent. I would take my fears and my disappointment with me wherever I was going. Adam continued. 'Flanagan might have worked it out. He's much less trusting than you, Spencer. But I really thought that you might have caught on earlier.'

I could see little point in trying to find any words and Adam spoke again. 'Didn't you find it odd that you and Flanagan, one dead-end journalist and a washed up cop, would find evidence on the Internet linking Adam Reid's father to a cloned mammoth after all these years? The New York police might have been slow but they were never stupid. You found what I wanted you to find.'

Adam moved closer. I tried to take a step backwards but couldn't. 'But this isn't a game, Spencer. Not for Hector Alvarez, it isn't –'

'What?' I'd spoken. I felt that I had to continue. 'What about Hector?'

'He's dead. A rational man; he would have gone to the police in time and I couldn't allow that.'

I sagged. Once again, Adam had read me. 'Did a part of you think that they were coming?'

Adam continued. 'So you argued with the man in the Bronx. You threatened him and then you killed him. That's what the papers will say. He's been found now. What's left of him is at the morgue and he's got Simon's phone in his pocket. We took it from you on the subway. Your prints are on it. You stabbed him. I've got the knife here. I'll let you hold it later –'

'You bastard.'

Adam's eyes flashed. He was covering the angles. He inclined his head to the side. 'Parents not married at the time of my birth? True enough, I'm a bastard. And if you're lucky, you'll live to see just how much of a bastard I can be.'

'You'd already killed his wife – '

'I've killed many people's wives,' said Adam. 'I'm sure I'll kill many more. What made him so special?'

My head felt too heavy for my neck to support and I slumped within myself. Hector had been harmless. A bright guy but Adam was right. The crazy Englishman standing in front of him only a couple of hours ago had got the man killed.

'You did a number on him,' said Adam. A reflective smile played on his face. 'Very messy at the end but I think he actually believed you, Spencer. I really do. They'll come after you for it but even if they don't, then it will just have been another fucked up mugging in the Bronx and there's no-one left to care.

'They'll find drugs in his pockets. More in his apartment. Hector was a broken man after the death of his wife. Maybe this was a release for him, suicide by drug dealer.'

‘Go to hell, Reid.’

‘Not yet,’ said Adam. He looked down and steepled his fingers. ‘Onesius?’

I hadn’t given the name a lot of thought and Adam continued patiently. ‘I thought not. He was the Greek god of retribution. Not a pleasant fellow but it was all there for you to work out. Onesius, Simon and all of the other coincidences. The hook was tearing the lining from your mouth. It was screaming at you that you were being used but still you could see only the story.’

Adam raised his hand and I flinched. He stroked my chin. ‘You saw what you wanted to see. Big mistake for a journalist. You heard what you wanted to hear. ‘I want to be normal’ I told you. ‘I want to be human.’ It was all I could do not to laugh in your face. I don’t want to be like you, Spencer. I never did.’

Adam’s eyes hardened. To my knowledge, I had never fainted but my legs were quivering. This could be a first. Adam continued. ‘I’m not an unnecessarily violent man,’ he said. ‘In the light of what I’ve done and what I’m about to do, you may find that hard to believe but it’s true.

‘Shelley had to go. She was a part of the wider picture. She was what tipped you over the edge. You’ll find items of her underwear in your case and some of her doodlings regarding me. A mixture of sexual frustration and professional jealousy led you to kill her with the same knife that you used on Hector.

‘And I considered removing your solicitor friend, Broadbent. Perhaps your editor too and that woman at the FT but you were perfect. They’ll remember you as flustered, frustrated and mad. They’ll testify to it with a genuine sincerity so you can be proud of that, Spencer. You saved their lives.

‘Maybe it was your visit to Yorkshire, they’ll say. It all started to go wrong for you up there. Drinking too much, scraping your car, getting into all sorts of trouble but let’s try to look on the bright side, shall we? You won’t face the needle. There’s no death penalty here in New York.

You might even get to spend the rest of your life in a prison hospital. Could experience a lobotomy first hand.'

I looked at Adam then tried to turn my head away to avoid his eyes. Nosey gripped my chin hard and pulled my head around. It hurt. 'Why me?'

'We'll get on to that.'

'You're insane.'

The man's face was a blank. I was disappointed that I hadn't provoked a reaction but that didn't last for long. Adam nodded fractionally. Nosey let go of my chin and I pulled away, opened my eyes in time to see the open hand coming back apace.

It struck me hard across my face and I crumbled to the ground. I gave the floor a nasty crack with my knees. The rest of my body wasn't far behind them but hands supported me beneath my arms and I was pulled back up.

My legs were rubber. I could taste blood. I hadn't been hit in the face for twenty years. I needed to take the count, give myself a few seconds. Possibly even sink further and let the darkness take me for a while but that wasn't going to happen. Nosey raised his hand again and I pulled away but the blow didn't come and I opened my eyes.

'You're not the action-man type,' said Adam. 'So let's keep the unpleasantness to a minimum. Think of what I've done and what I'm about to do as an extended act of self-defence or justifiable homicide. These are not the actions of a mad man.'

Adam paused. I tried to spit out a mouthful of blood and other gunk but whatever it was, it didn't make it past my chin. It can't have enhanced my appearance much as it dripped nastily onto my chest. I wanted to cry. More from a frustrated impotence than from fear. My story was gone, my legacy with it. I couldn't even manage to spit on the floor.

Adam approached me and gestured towards the door. 'Let's join Henrietta. She'd enjoy the company.'

Twenty-One
14:32 – Wednesday 16th June
American Museum of Natural History, Central Park West, New York City

I had no idea how I'd managed to remain upright. I was swaying but lacked the strength to fall. I tried to concentrate as the hand on my shoulder bunched into a fist and drew in a clump of my jacket. It made movement difficult and escape impossible and I was tired, disorientated.

I became aware that Adam was speaking. 'I said they're fascinating animals, Spencer,' he said. His eyes were once more on mine and he placed what appeared to be an earpiece into his ear. He smiled tolerantly. 'Mammoths rather than the Neanderthal, that is. There were six sub-species spread over the best part of the globe but over time they came to favour the tundra.

'They look like elephants and they are closely related but there are some differences.'

So here I was. Isolated, scared and receiving a lecture on hairy elephants from a fucking monkey. I kept the thought to myself. I stared at Adam blankly and said nothing. This was his show. 'The two animals split from each other much earlier than did the hominids. They're less similar than are you and I.

'Mammoths had less broad skulls than do modern day elephants. They had four toes rather than five and their tusks were different, tending to slope inwards and down. Henrietta's certainly did. It was rather a giveaway. They also had a flap of skin protecting their anus from the cold. Not pleasant to have a freezing arse all day.

'They were doing nicely but then something happened,' he continued and I found myself hanging on his words. 'You and I happened, Spencer. And the various territories of the mammoths shrank and shrank until they became extinct eleven millennia ago.'

I was drifting. Considering how convenient it would be if Adam too were extinct but he was regarding me directly. 'You have a question?'

I had a thousand questions but I held my tongue. My anger had to be a positive thing. And anything that focused my attention away from my bowels and from the shame of failure could only be good and I forced myself to speak. 'You said you weren't a violent man?'

Adam smiled. 'Everything's relative.'

Adam waited for me to continue. 'You mentioned the things you'd done?'

'Yes.'

Ask a closed question and get a one word answer but this was the hard part. 'And something that you were about to do?'

Adam's smile became distant. 'All in good time, Spencer.'

I tried to follow Adam's eyes.

He was looking at the mammoth, its tusks spiralling towards the floor and the Neanderthal man beside it and then I felt his breath on my face. 'I didn't mean to sound so melodramatic,' he said. 'I know you doubt me and I can't blame you.

'My father had succeeded with Henrietta and he couldn't resist pushing further. He was like all scientists, and I include myself in that regard. He didn't recognise limits. Because he could do it, he did do it. He just had to push on and he stopped to ask no-one, least of all me.'

I took a breath. There was another lecture coming. Every minute that I managed to draw breath took us closer to the presentations and closer to the crowds and to the safety that I sought. I wanted Adam to speak and he continued. 'Of course it was never announced that he'd found an almost entire Neanderthal cadaver.' Adam was regarding me as one would a lunatic behind bars. Not the slightest concern that I might attack him or make a hostile move of any description. He nodded towards the exhibits. 'Enough scraps made it to the museum to reconstruct the hominid that you see here but that wasn't my father's primary concern.

'He didn't want a hybrid. No, I'm the real deal. Nuclear transfer. He'd done it with Henrietta. You've read the mammoth's story and mine's very much the same. Donor animal was killed by a rock-fall, died in winter and was quickly buried in silt and subsequently frozen.

'When the ice retreated, many of the thousands and thousands of bodies that there were out there were exposed and eaten by scavenging animals. Torn limb from limb, Spencer.' At this Adam looked at me without expression. Hairs prickled on my neck as he looked at my arms and legs and snapped them mentally. He continued. 'Mammoth carcasses are still being found in the permafrost of Siberia and some Neanderthal corpses remained frozen in the mountains of eastern and central Europe and the Caucasus. I'm not boring you, am I?'

I shook my head and Adam took a deep breath. I felt him weigh me. 'I know you're tired but there'll be plenty of time to catch up on your sleep later. My father transferred the nucleus from a well-preserved cell into a de-nucleated Homo sapiens egg. It came from my mother of course. His wife, I should say. She was never my mother but you probably guessed as much.'

I made a feeble noise then cleared my throat and spoke. 'I don't know what to say, Adam.'

'Then say nothing, Spencer. Do you have time for a little anthropology?'

Another lecture would help to pass the time and I raised myself to my full height. I reached Adam's shoulder and spoke before I'd really considered my words. 'So you'll be going on display in there too?'

Adam smiled and looked at his watch. My heart sank as he shook his head slowly. 'No time soon.'

The blood, metallic in my mouth, tasted like an old coin. I hesitated but had to continue. 'So after your lobotomy, what then?'

'Don't push me, Spencer,' said Adam. He was still smiling but his eyes were not and that gave me more satisfaction than made sense. 'You're going to outlive the presentations but consider what happened to the dog. She loved me. The old bitch wiped her snot on me for twelve years and I loved her back. And I loved my father too and you've read the files, you know what happened to them.'

'Fuck you, Adam –'

'I hate so few people,' said Adam. He slowly looked me over from head to foot. 'And none that are alive.'

I felt removed from reality and freer than I had for days. And I could feel an idea beginning to build. It was crazy. I knew it was. It was something along the lines of dying like a man but it helped me and I felt liberated. That was a good word. I didn't use it often. But I was bone tired and that loosened my fears. I tried to relax and to draw together what strength I could. My mind fell back into my body and I could focus. My entire life had led up to these moments and now there was nothing else. The past was gone. The future may not exist. I had only the present.

Adam was regarding me differently, perhaps with more caution, a little more respect. 'Do you know where we came from, you and I?'

'I've never studied it,' I said. I was calm. I didn't want another smack in the mouth. I didn't mix well with violence but I wasn't going to beg. My eyes flickered to the hominid, to the axe.

'We came from common stock,' said Adam. His eyes had followed mine to the display and he waved a hand. 'Like Henrietta there and her elephant surrogate mother. We're cousins rather than direct descendants, the one from the other. We share common ancestors in homo habilis and homo erectus but that's where the branches split.

'There's some disagreement about when that divergence occurred but it was more than a hundred and fifty thousand years ago. Sounds like a long time but it was effectively the blink of an eye and things went swimmingly for a while. After all, we were both homo sapiens. We were both fully human. Homo sapiens neanderthalensis evolved in Europe and Western Asia and homo sapiens sapiens stuck to Africa but then things changed.'

I looked away. If for no other reason than that I thought Adam wanted me to look at him. But I made the mistake of catching the eye of one of Nosey's goons and had to look away. I could see death in the man's eyes. Adam laughed out loud. 'Do you have any idea how difficult it is to get good help these days?'

Adam didn't seem to know that he was dealing with the new Spencer. Or if he did, he didn't care. He continued. 'Particularly help that really doesn't give a shit. Help that has no interest whatsoever in the rights or wrongs of what one might be doing?

'It's not easy, I can tell you.' Adam looked at his reflection in the glass of the Museum display. He raised his fingers to it and traced the reflection of the scars beneath his chin. 'It's thick, Spencer. I doubt you could break it.'

Did he mean his skin or the glass? Either way, Adam had been in my head. I had been imagining the axe and I could still feel his presence. He turned and looked into me rather than at me. He smiled. 'Could you lift an axe like that? Could you swing it, crush my skull and smite me to the ground? I think not. So I'll continue if you don't mind. Where did it all go wrong, where did our problems begin?'

Adam was enjoying this. I glared at him but it achieved nothing. 'About 40,000 years ago, your ancestors left Africa and crossed into Europe, a new continent. It was open and apparently available and you spread like a stain across Eurasia.

'Poor old small-brained homo erectus, the little bugger that Neanderthals, as you now call us, had lived alongside peacefully for millennia, had no chance at all. So Asia fell quickly but in Europe you faced something of a stiffer test, you faced us. And we were an altogether tougher nut to crack.

'We'd occupied Europe and Western Asia for nearly a quarter of a million years. We were pretty well established. We were a major challenge so perhaps we should have shared the continent?

'A nice thought, Spencer. But we're a product of our time. Or at least you are and sharing things is such a twenty first century idea. It isn't natural and it's not what happened all those millennia ago.

'Still, the two branches of humanity lived alongside each other in what had been our homeland for 10,000 years or more. A thousand decades. That's hundreds of generations, centuries of toil until the last of the Neanderthals died, probably in Croatia, around thirty thousand years ago and homo sapiens won. You had killed us, Spencer. You had wiped us out.'

Adam sounded resigned rather than annoyed and I smirked. 'No need to be a sore loser, Adam.'

Adam graced the comment with a smile. 'Who said I'm a loser?'

I sagged and Adam continued. 'The victory of anatomically modern humans had never been the foregone conclusion that hindsight would suggest, we were too similar for that.'

Adam raised his hand, examined his fingers. I thought that he was going to pick his nails but he didn't. 'Neanderthals, strange that it should be thought of as a term of insult now, were built for the cold. Sometimes shorter, more compact, we were much more heavily built than an AMH.

'And we also had the protruding jawbones and pronounced eyebrow ridges that condemned us to look unintelligent in your opinion. But then the victor gets to choose what looks smart and what doesn't but Neanderthal brains were, or should I say are, somewhat larger on average than those of your people.

'That's not widely known and why would it be? It rarely makes it into the books, after all. And even when it does they say that it might have been indicative of a different type of intelligence, more one-dimensional and animalistic. Not truly human.

'Still, Neanderthal's cared for their injured, even thirty millennia ago. The prolonged survival of the infirm the anthropologists call it, a sign of what they refer to as embedded intelligence, civilisation if you will.'

My flush of confidence was ebbing and with it my strength and still Adam was looking at me, weighing me. He had given me a moment. I could feel that but now he looked away. He glanced at the axe in the hand of the exhibit beyond the glass and continued. 'Both branches of mankind used tools. In fact many of the early artefacts are impossible to tell apart.

'Anthropologists assumed that any sophisticated tool must have belonged to an AMH but they would, wouldn't they? But they could never prove it and both branches of humanity buried their dead and knew how to use fire. They both survived the ebb and flow of the ice as the weather varied and maybe even worshipped a God but then something happened.'

My eyes opened wider. I couldn't help it and Adam read it. He turned back to the display. 'Around the time that the homo sapiens began to move into Europe in larger numbers, there was a big bang.'

I stirred, shook myself. 'That was billions of years ago, the dawn of time?'

Adam nodded. 'I'm pleased to see that you're paying attention, Spencer. It was a big bang, not the Big Bang. It was an anthropological event.'

I tried to shrug and looked at Nosey. I immediately looked away. He really didn't look like a pleasant man. I suppose I had wanted to share my ignorance with another human being. But I had got nothing back and Adam's eyes had followed my own. 'You're wasting your time there, I can assure you. You've read the book, 2001?'

I shook my head.

'Arthur C Clarke?'

'No.'

Adam continued. 'Seen the Stanley Kubrick film?'

This time I couldn't even summon the energy to move. I counted the seconds. 'I haven't seen the film.'

'Well something happened about 40,000 years ago,' Adam said. 'No-one's quite sure what, but something kick-started the movement from a general to a more specific level of intelligence in the AMH branch of our family. I don't subscribe to the alien intervention theory but we still don't know if the same phenomenon was present amongst the Neanderthals. Maybe it wasn't.

'There were no obvious physical changes. Some said the bang was effectively the invention of language. Neanderthals couldn't keep up. The monkey-men couldn't talk due to their restricted hypoglossal canal. As I said earlier, I found that theory quite amusing and I could have told them so but I've said nothing.

'Others considered that it must have been the hand of God but whatever it was, it accelerated the development of one branch of human kind, your branch and it led to the ultimate extinction of mine.'

Adam paused. I could feel him willing me to understand. He continued. 'But you've seen the exhibits in the Primitive Mammals Hall, you get the picture. I saw you feel it, Spencer. I felt you feel it. The brooding menace present in those first mammals; the ever-present plotting and scheming, the moves and the counter-moves at the inter-species level. Each animal may have been mindless in itself but each as a species they were each waiting for their chance.

'The lower mammals needed another species to slip. Or even a huge grouping of species such as the dinosaurs to make a mistake or to fail to adapt and anatomically modern humans did the same. They did no more and no less than their rodent forbears had done and they did it splendidly.'

Adam took a breath. His eyes were shining. He had read me and I could see into his mind too. I could recognise his brilliance but felt the madness behind it that had driven him on. He spoke again. 'Effectively everything,' he said. He made a sweeping gesture with his left hand. 'The whole evolutionary process. The billions of years, the competition in the slime of pre-history through to the victory of the mammals over the dinosaurs sixty five million years ago and everything that followed, was a race up to that point some thirty thousand years ago. And, though it went right to the wire, your branch of humanity defeated mine.

'There were no rules,' he said. I found the smile upon his face more chilling now that the eyes behind it were cold. 'There never are. Whatever drove you, be it your newly acquired language or your more primitive instincts, to slake your hunger or to drive for sex or avoid danger, we are here today, spinning around on our little ball of rock, one Neanderthal man still drawing breath alongside seven billion of your people.'

I remained silent. An apology would be rather too little and much too late. Adam continued. 'Of course I'm somewhat biased here,' he said. 'But it seems to me that the Palaeolithic period was split into the Middle and the Upper specifically to exclude Neanderthals from modern history.

'It allowed the surviving humans to believe that it was them, the AMHs, who had brought the first light of civilization to Europe. It allowed you to overlook the fact that many of the artefacts discovered predated your arrival on the continent.'

I felt the blood throbbing in my face but my head was clear and my voice steady. 'It's in the past Adam.'

'No it isn't,' said Adam. He looked at me squarely. His blue eyes shone bright. 'It's in the present. I'm back, Spencer. I'm lonely and I'd like to have children one day but I'm back and that's a start, don't you think?'

My eyes narrowed. God knows in my position I didn't mean it to look aggressive. But nor did I want to give Adam the satisfaction of seeing that he had rattled me. 'What do you mean?'

Adam looked at me and curled his lip. I couldn't have looked a pretty picture but he smiled. 'As you might imagine, I'm backing the underdog,' said Adam. 'I want to give him a chance, level the playing field. I may have the time to go through the specifics later but for the moment we're still in the past.

'By 40,000 years ago, anatomically modern humans probably outnumbered Neanderthals six or seven to one globally. But in Europe, the numbers were broadly even. My ancestors still peopled the continent from Gibraltar to the Black Sea but populations on both sides were small, existence was fragile.

'During the hundred centuries, the five hundred generations that your ancestors and mine shared the continent, populations of both probably averaged no more than 100,000 or so individuals. Famine and natural disasters were common enough to seriously threaten a number that small. On several occasions it's thought that the combined populations fell as low 10,000. That's a modest football crowd, Spencer. And it's a number that had to be spread thinly over the whole of Europe meaning that, at such times, all branches of humanity could have squeezed easily into this museum.'

Adam moved silently closer to me and I could feel his power. Violence buzzed in the air around him and then it abated. He continued. 'It was so tenuous a thread. So fine a filament separating us from the nothingness of extinction. We could both have shared the fate of the 99% or so of species that have at one time or another existed and which now do not, so how did we hold on?

'Well sadly one branch did not hold on. Perhaps a billion Neanderthals lived and died on this rock during the quarter of a million years of their existence and now, aside from me, they're all gone.

'Gone but not forgotten because I knew from the earliest days just what I was. My parents never told me the truth and let me tell you why. After my arrival, and face it, Spencer, I'm almost identical to you, they could scarcely bring themselves to admit it. But they had initially intended to create a laboratory animal more similar in its physiology to anatomically modern humans on which scientists could conduct experiments.

'They wanted to bring back Neanderthals simply to kill them again and they felt guilty. So they protected me from the truth. They began the process of moulding me, of making me into one of you. They cut me and shaped me. They tried to make changes but I knew who I was and I could feel the pull. I knew what I had to do.'

I felt myself try to turn. Didn't know why I'd done it but the goon's grip on my shoulder was too firm and I scarcely moved. 'You see, Spencer,' said Adam. 'I feared that I was the last of my species and the prospect horrified me. But as I grew in strength, I could see that I was only the first.'

Adam paused. I tried to back away from him again but found myself wedged between one of Nosey's thugs and the thick glass of the massive display cabinet behind me. Adam placed his hand on the glass. He leaned in toward me and once again I felt the barely suppressed violence in his movement as he scanned the exhibits. 'I also began to ask other questions,' he said and the smile that had been playing on his face slowly melted away. In its place there was nothing. 'Did you kill them all, for example?

'Not just one of them. Not even a thousand or a million of them but every last man, woman and child? And did you kill them with your spears and clubs or did you starve them and drive them to the frontiers of the world and make them die? An interesting question but I don't know the answer and I never will.'

The man's misted eyes were focused on nothing. Adam looked as though he may slip into a trance but then his eyes cleared and he looked down at me. My back pushed up against the display glass, I felt my insides turning to liquid as he spoke again. 'Some say that interbreeding hastened the end. They say that it led to a reabsorbing of Neanderthal blood into a single human gene pool. They believe that Neanderthals are all around us, that some may even be of almost pure blood in the Carpathian Mountains but I doubt it. I've been there and I favour the simpler answer, the obvious answer. That good guys finish last, that the Neanderthals were exterminated.'

'Regrettable,' I said. My voice was firm. It was almost as though someone else were speaking. 'But as I said, it's in the past.'

'Tell that to the Native Americans,' said Adam and his brilliant blue eyes flashed in the glare of a spotlight. 'Tell it to the Jews or the Kurds or the Armenians or to the Aboriginal people of Australia or to the victims of the slave trade. Tell it to the countless millions of victims of your own homicidal tendencies. Tell it to any number of now dead species. But you'd be wasting your breath because you won't change humanity. You're killers, Spencer. It's just what you are'

Adam raised his head and sniffed the air. He closed his eyes and then opened them slowly. 'Do you believe in racial memories?'

Adam could go fuck himself. 'Go fuck yourself, Adam.'

I expected a blow but none came. When I opened my eyes, Adam was smiling. 'I take it that's a no?'

I tried to shake my head and Adam continued. 'I'm talking about inexplicable thoughts. Memories based upon experiences that you simply have not had. They may be indistinguishable from instinct perhaps. Effectively memories that are hard-wired into the brains of a whole species, an unthinking ability to do or to know something?'

I managed to stare at him blankly enough that he continued. 'I believe in such memories. I've carried these thoughts with me from the day I was born. And believe me, whilst there is breath in my body, I'll be guided by them and will do what I have to do.'

So Adam was hearing voices. Maybe he was simply mad. He could have fabricated everything. But whether he had or he hadn't, my present position was unchanged. The man's eyes left the figure of the Neanderthal man. They slowly focused on my own. 'Questions?'

I took the opportunity to speak. 'As far as being driven by our instincts is concerned, it's different now. We're more –'

'Mind your words, Spencer,' said Adam, his eyes hard blue stones. 'Some are overused. Others are used without thought or are simply inappropriate. Civilized for example? It's impossibly vague, means nothing, you must be more precise. Do you mean civilized like the Nazis? Like the Conquistadors or the Inquisition?'

'You know what I mean,' I said. The man could run verbal rings around me. I wasn't going to play that game.

'No,' said Adam. 'That's exactly the problem. I don't know what you mean. You're an anatomically modern human, Spencer. Do you ever stop to think what you're hardwired to do?'

'Hardwired?'

Adam ignored the interruption. I knew what he meant, was playing for time. 'I don't blame you or your kind for your behaviour,' he said. 'I simply recognise it for what it is. Like the cuddly chimps that grow into thieving, murderous and sexually violent adults, your behaviour is simply hardwired onto your psyche. It's dictated by your genes, forced upon you by your experiences in the primeval swamp.

'Your men want sex,' he said. 'They want to fight and to kill. Your women want babies and the species lives on. You get what you want. Evolution; it works, so why change it?

'Because we can, of course, that's the whole point. I'll cover that later but you would protect your blood-line with your lives. No surprise there but what about your community, would you die for that? I think you would. And what's your country if not a super-large community but then what about your species?

'Would you die for it? Would you kill for it? If the answer to both questions is yes then you shouldn't be surprised if I'm prepared to do the same.'

Adam's body language and the tone of his voice, everything about him had said that these were important words. He was moving towards some sort of conclusion but my tiredness was edging back in and I lowered my eyes as Adam glanced at his watch again.

That wasn't good. I felt the urgent need to talk. 'We're more than a collection of instincts, Adam. We always have been –'

'You're so wrong, Spencer. We're nothing but a collection of instincts,' said Adam. He was speaking slowly. He was lecturing an imbecile. 'You'll do what your instincts tell you to do. Why do you exterminate cockroaches, for example? Why do you hunt down and kill rats? I don't blame you for it. I kill them too but I do it with my eyes open. I don't claim that they have a lesser right to life than do I.'

'I simply kill them because they get in my way. And I kill them because I can and face it, Spencer. You kill them for the same reason. You don't like them. And you feel justified in killing them because they're not like you.

'So what's the difference between targeting a rat or a Neanderthal man? In the final analysis, perhaps very little. Both are warm blooded vertebrates. Neither of them shares all of your genes. Neither of them is you and, in the end, that's what it comes down to. I can understand why you hunted us down and killed us and drove us to extinction. You did it because you could and all I ask is that you judge my actions in the same light.'

'What are you going to do, for God's sake?' I said. I was trying to keep up but my voice let me down. A thin wedge of panic had been driven in there. It was unmistakeable. Adam smiled and looked at Nosey. The man left the room.

'It's been a day of surprises,' said Adam. 'Let's go and say hello to Mr Flanagan.'

Twenty-Two
15:15 – Wednesday 16th June
American Museum of Natural History, Central Park West, New York City

Flanagan?

I tried to remain calm, expressionless. Adam's eyes glittered. 'You thought he was dead? Or are you asking yourself if he's working for me?'

Adam had followed my thoughts. He was a difficult man to lie to. 'I thought you'd killed him.'

His lips pursed, Adam continued. 'I can understand why you might think that. But we'll keep that to ourselves because the wider world will believe that you poisoned him. You've been on quite a spree.'

'I don't know what the hell you're talking about.'

Adam smiled. 'That's the truth. You were a driven man, Spencer. Shelley Mitchum beat you to the book and you couldn't stand it. You killed her. You lured Flanagan to the UK. You pumped him for information and tried to kill him lest he share it with anyone else and then you fled to the US. I was your target but you tracked down Alvarez, threatened him. You couldn't understand why he wouldn't support you and you killed him, too.

'Still, I should thank you,' Adam continued. 'You missed Flanagan but you've helped me tidy up. Alvarez has been a minor irritation for years but he lacked the courage to actually do anything. You both gave purpose to his life and caused his death.'

'You're mad, Adam.'

'Not yet,' said Adam. 'But examine your own actions. The chicken in your fridge laced with arsenic? It was in the ant-killer you bought on Friday –'

'Ant killer?'

I frowned, and Adam continued. 'You used your credit card, Spencer. The girl at the checkout won't remember you but that hardly matters. There's no CCTV but your prints are on the bottle and we can get your prints to the shop –'

'Why frame me?'

It came out as a whimper and Adam talked over me again. 'I wonder if Mr Flanagan has ever put anyone in the frame. We can ask him...'

'You bastard.'

Still Adam did not raise his hand to me. Instead, he looked tired. 'You're repeating yourself, Spencer. We have so little time together. Let's not waste it on insults.

'You were acting irrationally in England. Your friends will testify to that. The live ones, that is. Paranoid tendencies. Pursuing imaginary enemies and rambling. Is it such a big leap to conclude that you attempted to kill your house guest and fled the country?'

'Why bother, Adam?'

'I have my reasons.'

'I'm just some bloke off the street –'

'You're underselling yourself, Spencer. You've been more helpful than you might imagine.'

I could feel my head shaking from side to side, an unconscious movement. This was a nightmare and I struggled for the words. 'How can you do things like this?'

'It's not difficult,' said Adam. His face took on a different expression and he looked much younger. 'Flanagan intrigues me. He must have quite a constitution –'

'The croissants –'

Adam raised his eyes, looked directly at me. 'Pay attention, Spencer. It was the chicken. Whatever other junk he ingested would have slowed things down but there should have been sufficient to see him off. He wasn't asymptomatic. He was in toxic shock at one point, hyper-acute poisoning –'

'He was sick,' I said. This was unreal. I looked at the stony faces around me and at Adam's youthful features and shook my head hard. My mind was clearing but Adam did not flinch. He did not fear me in the slightest.

'Arsenic's terrible stuff, you know,' said Adam. 'I certainly wouldn't recommend it. Our friend should be suffering from multi-organ failure by now but it would appear not. Maybe he's as tough as old Henrietta here but even she's extinct and it would appear that Mr Flanagan isn't. Not yet at least.'

A movement to Adam's right and I followed his eyes. One of Nosey's thugs was making a gesture of some sort and Adam nodded. He pointed back towards the observation room. 'Mr Flanagan's on Central Park West. He'll be here in a moment. Shall we?'

Adam snapped out a few words. They weren't in English and one of the guards took a firm grip of my right shoulder, crushed it through my jacket. Another took my left hand and pushed me in the back. There wasn't a lot that I could do to slow my progress. Inside the observation room, the video monitors were scrolling from screen to screen.

'One of the outside camera's, that's West 77th,' said Adam. He repeated himself in another language and the phrase sounded almost comical. Some meaningless babble with the words 'West 77th' stuck in the middle. I was tempted to laugh. It couldn't put me in a worse position than the one I already occupied but a slap in the face I did not need. The screen cut to another view. 'That's better,' said Adam. 'There he is.'

I moved forward to look more closely at the flickering light. The restraining hand did not leave my shoulder. The screen showed several figures, moving purposefully. They had somewhere to go but then I had him. The size and build was right. Familiar walk but he was moving more slowly than the others around him.

'Doesn't look too well does he, Spencer?' said Adam. He shook his head sadly. 'Bit of a tummy upset I'd say. We'd better keep an eye on him.'

I didn't believe in any of that psychic mumbo-jumbo but Adam had read my thoughts as easily as he would have an open book. I tried to clear any expression from my face and watched as the figure walked the remaining few yards to the Central Park West entrance of the Museum.

It was Flanagan, I was sure. I could see him much more clearly as he looked about him before entering the building where another camera picked him up immediately. He was in the Theodore Roosevelt Memorial Hall.

Adam smiled. 'Do you think he'll take a tour? He might find the stairs a bit of a challenge. I'm not sure that he'll be able to make it to the fourth floor. We might have to help him up but something's clearly driving him. Maybe he thinks he's going to be able to right some terrible wrong. What do you think, Spencer?'

I shrugged. Adam could be fucking with my head. Flanagan could still be on his team but I was beginning to think not and I couldn't help it, I so wanted the ex-cop to be the man I'd taken him to be. I wanted him as an ally and a friend and I had to warn him.

But that was more easily said than done. I looked to my side and opened my mouth but I was slow, much too slow. The goon had been expecting it and a large hand closed over my mouth.

'Now, now,' said Adam quietly. He lowered his voice and addressed Nosey's men and a second thug left the room. 'He couldn't hear you from here but we wouldn't want to spoil his surprise now, would we?'

I could barely breathe but I forced myself to look back at the screen. Flanagan was leaving the stairwell now. He was hugging the wall on the third floor. The stairs looked to have taken a lot out of him. He was scarcely moving. He leant against the wall and then bent double before straightening slowly.

He looked spent but then he pushed off from the wall and moved on. The blurry figure returned to the stairwell and Adam whistled gently. 'Good effort, Daniel.' He looked at his watch. 'We should still have time to talk.'

I had never felt more impotent in my life.

'Do you think he's armed?'

My eyes did not leave the screen. Flanagan was going to be taken. Any moment now he would be caught. Even killed. He should run from the building, pick up a telephone, anything.

But Daniel Flanagan did not run. The ex-cop exited the stairwell on the fourth floor and looked to his right but turned and walked through the arched doorway and into the Hall of Advanced Mammals. Now he was close and the hand on my mouth clamped down harder.

'Mr Flanagan how could you?' said Adam a moment later. His voice was rich with mock-horror as he regarded the screen. On it, Flanagan's image was materially altered. It was greener and less sharp. He was being viewed in a different light. We were seeing his image through the eyes of the metal detector. I could see clearly that he had what looked like a set of keys and there was a second, brighter object clearly visible by the ankle of the grey-green figure.

'A concealed weapon?' said Adam. He wagged his finger. 'Are you sure that's legal in New York, Daniel?'

I could not move or speak. I refused to meet Adam's eyes, didn't want him to see my fear but the man saw straight through me and smiled as he looked away. He barked a couple of words and another of Nosey's goons left the room. Now only one man remained alongside Adam and I.

And Flanagan was in the room outside. He was only a matter of feet away and I raised my foot, tried to stamp it down heavily on that of the man holding me but the foot behind me had gone.

I made a noise at least and I tried again but strong arms tightened around my body and my feet left the floor.

As the breath hissed from my body I expected a blow but it did not come.

Instead bright lights flashed before my eyes and I threw my head backwards, tried to smash the face of the man holding me but again nothing. He was ahead of me and I couldn't breathe. I thrashed my feet and hit something but it was a feeble blow and, as I hovered on the edge of consciousness, the arms loosened and I sucked in a lungful of air as I fell to the floor in a heap.

**

I opened my eyes. I was facing an array of feet and I looked up. Adam was smiling good-naturedly and he pointed with his chin towards the monitors. 'You haven't missed much, Spencer.'

Fuck.

I couldn't even faint properly and the on-screen Flanagan appeared to have heard nothing. Any flapping and banging that I'd managed to accomplish would have been drowned out by the noise from the Primitive Mammals exhibition. The sounds from the undergrowth. The mewling and the squeaking would still be audible from where Flanagan now stood and my feeble efforts had achieved nothing.

The grainy image of Flanagan passed the shadow of the mammoth outside the panic room and then he froze. I was pulled to my feet and a hand clamped once more across my mouth. I could do nothing as the image showed Flanagan cocking his head and then moving sharply.

His hand reached down towards the floor. But he was too slow. He was old and ill and, behind him, a shape approached and then another and another. Flanagan had done well to reach his ankle. He had something in his hand but he was still bent double when Nosey grabbed his arm and locked it, held it firmly pointing towards the ground and then the others were upon him.

I wanted to weep. I could feel the tears of frustration welling in my eyes but I held them back. I did not look at Adam though I could feel his eyes upon me.

But Flanagan was alive. I was no longer alone. That was good news but as the figure on the screen was pushed from sight, I couldn't help but catch Adam's eye. The younger man nodded sympathetically. 'Just wasn't to be, was it? Let's go and say hello.'

My feet were back on the floor but I couldn't support my own weight. One hand beneath my shoulder, another in my back and I stumbled forward, out of the observation room and into the Hall of Advanced Mammals where Daniel Flanagan looked pale and drawn.

And he appeared very small next to Nosey and two of his men, his moustache looked much darker against his pallid skin. I probably fared little better myself but I managed a smile.

Flanagan's eyes flared. He didn't smile back, there was still a spark there. 'You're a fucking monster, Reid.'

Adam grinned broadly. 'Define monster.'

If Adam failed in whatever megalomaniac scheme he was putting together he could make it as a script-writer. Flanagan's mouth was moving soundlessly as Adam continued. 'And definitions change over time. And they vary according to the perception of the observer.' Adam reached out his hand, took the old policeman's pistol from Nosey's men and held the weapon to the light. 'You brought a twenty-two, Daniel? Dear me, who do you think you're dealing with here, a small child perhaps?'

I looked at Flanagan and willed him to face me but he did not. His skin was stretched across the bones of his face. It was almost translucent in the harsh light. He looked weak and washed up but his eyes were alive. They flickered from Adam to Nosey and his heavies and then to me and I caught the flash of recognition. I had an ally. Flanagan puffed himself up, looking back at Adam. 'You stopped taking your medication?'

'Now, now Daniel,' said Adam patiently. 'Do you mind if I call you Daniel?'

'Yes I do mind,' said Flanagan. He was struggling weakly. The goon gripping his arm did not appear to notice. 'You hallucinating, Adam?'

Adam did not respond immediately. He tilted his head. 'Finished?'

'Get these apes off me,' said Flanagan. He flapped an arm. He succeeded only in drawing the thug's attention to the fact that he was trying to worm it free.

'Apes, Daniel?' said Adam. Was he irritated, a momentary reddening? 'I suppose that's accurate in a way but I can smell your fear. It's tangible. I could almost touch it. I can understand it and you're right to be afraid. You're in a place that you don't want to be.'

'You threatening me, asshole?'

'Why, yes, Daniel,' said Adam. He smiled warmly. 'I believe I am.'

'You think you can frighten me?'

Adam looked at Flanagan for several seconds in silence. 'I know that I can.'

'Don't kid yourself, Reid,' said the ex-cop. But he looked away. I was proud of him and when his eyes settled on mine I tried to tell him as much but he quickly looked away, glared at Adam. 'I knew you, Reid.'

Adam refreshed his smile. 'Tell yourself that, Daniel, if it helps you to sleep at night and to keep the demons away, the ones that tell you that you abandoned Maria when she needed you.'

'Maria was on to you –'

'And it did her a lot of good,' said Adam. His eyes glittered in the light. 'But you're right, she was indeed. However, Ms Alvarez is no longer with us. And her baby, a boy I hear. He would have been what, coming up eight?'

Flanagan's already white face seemed to whiten further and Adam continued. 'Whether she was right or wrong, she brought about her own death. She killed herself and her child and now her husband...'

'Hector?'

Adam waved his hand. 'Hector, Henry, whatever. He bled out on the sidewalk. Spencer did it.'

Flanagan glanced at me. He looked away and then back again. 'You OK, Spencer?'

Not the sort of question that required an answer but Adam gestured toward the goon holding me and the man drew his hand away from my mouth. 'I didn't do anything.' Flanagan nodded and I continued. 'And you're right, he's a monster –'

'He's no fucking oil painting,' said Flanagan.'

I could feel the tears well in my eyes. I was happy, light headed. I had a friend and I felt like crying for joy but my voice did not betray me. 'How's your stomach?'

Flanagan kept his eyes on Adam. 'Been better.'

'Sweet,' said Adam. 'Daniel, you shouldn't have come –'

'What and miss this?' Flanagan looked at the exhibits. 'This all about that senile old elephant?'

'She was neither senile nor an elephant,' said Adam. 'But then you know that, don't you? No Daniel, this is about something altogether different, altogether more interesting.'

'He feels aggrieved,' I said.

'So would I if I looked like that,' said Flanagan. 'Schizophrenic paranoia, Reid? Your Thorazine not doing the job anymore?'

'I own a drug company,' said Adam. 'We make our own anti-psychotics but I prefer to stay clean.'

'Clean?'

Adam nodded to Nosey who was standing by Flanagan's side and the American winced as the grip on his arms tightened. He blinked hard. 'You got a problem with the world, Reid?'

'No,' said Adam without looking up. 'Just with a number of the people in it.'

I watched the killer raise his eyes. Distant and cold, they were hard and they moved from my own to Flanagan's. I looked at the pistol in Adam's hand, felt my bowels churn.

'A Beretta 89,' said Adam. He was staring blankly at Flanagan. Was looking right through him. 'Not a bad piece. Point two-two calibre. Eight round magazine but better suited to a woman. Like being poked with a knitting needle –'

'Give it back then.'

Adam weighed the pistol in his hand. 'I think not, Daniel. Fully loaded I should say. They're not blanks are they? I would be so disappointed if they were.'

'Point it at your head,' said Flanagan. 'Pull the trigger's one way to find out.'

'True enough,' said Adam. 'But I think I'll shoot Spencer instead. He tries to poison you and you pop him? That sound about right?'

'They're not blanks, Reid,' said Flanagan. 'And let Spencer go, he's a civilian.'

Adam showed no sign of having heard Flanagan's words. He turned the gun in his hand and I noticed that it was pointing at me. I tried to take a step backwards. I may as well have attempted to fly. 'Quite a useful bit of kit in the right hands, Spencer,' said Adam. 'But this looks like a street piece and if you buy it there, the chances are, it's there for a reason.

'Often they're too hot to handle,' said Adam. He spun the weapon in his hand. Once more it ended up pointing at me. 'See here? No serial number. It could have quite a history. Have you ever fired a gun?'

I tried to speak. He knew I hadn't. Had never knowingly been in the same room as one before and Adam raised the weapon, straightened his arm. He smiled. The barrel a black circle, the gun was pointing at my eyes. Adam pulled the trigger.

Nothing happened. 'Silly me, safety catch –'

Adam swung his arm away from me and pulled the trigger a second time. A report rang loud around the room. I had expected it but still flinched and Nosey grinned. A puff of dust drifted from the forehead of an exhibit beyond a heavy burgundy rope, a giant bear.

The animal rocked slightly on its stand. 'Make quite a noise don't they?'

Adam Reid looked at me in the way that I imagined a lion with a full belly would regard a zebra with a broken leg. It was not yet my time to die. Adam raised the gun again and pulled the trigger three times in rapid succession. Dust flew from the head of the bear and it rocked again but did not fall. Adam slipped the safety catch back on.

'Not blanks,' he said. 'Both your prints will be on it guys. We can make sure of that but where should the remaining bullets go, maybe into Mr Flanagan?'

Adam's head inclined slightly to the side. 'Cat got your tongue, Spencer?'

'No,' I said. Adam didn't care about the noise that the gun was making and that was disturbing.

'I suppose not,' said Adam. He walked towards me and stooped, our faces very close. 'Not yet anyway.

'Well placed, a two-two bullet will do the job. But small guns lack stopping power. And from time to time that's what you need, believe me.'

Adam turned to Flanagan. 'Would you have shot me, Daniel? Emptied the magazine into me? Because that's what you would have needed to do. I have eight inches of flesh and a chest full of ribs in front of my heart. My head is like a hardwood block so would you have had the guts to take an aimed shot? Would you have shot me in the eye?'

'Give me the gun,' said Flanagan. 'Let's find out.'

'Perhaps not,' said Adam. He'd read it. The edge in Flanagan's voice. The fear. He slipped the magazine out of the gun, held the barrel to the light and put the magazine in his pocket. Adam checked his watch. I didn't like it when he did that. But he didn't seem to care whether I liked it or not. He inclined his head towards observation room. 'Shall we?'

Again a hand in my back. I staggered and saw Flanagan stumble then straighten himself up and raise himself to his full height. 'Been talking to the elephant, Adam?'

Reid smiled.

'She talking back to you?' Flanagan's head jerked backwards as he took another shove in the back. 'Anybody at home, Reid?'

Adam's hand began to close on the small gun. The noise was neither loud nor sharp. Not the cracking of a nut but rather the crushing of a fresh apple and when Adam opened his hand, the handle of the gun was splintered and broken. It fell to the floor.

'So you got a thing for the elephant, huh?' said Flanagan. 'Maybe the monkey over there, too?'

My senses sharpened. Flanagan was seconds from death. He had dragged himself halfway around the world for this moment but I knew what Adam was capable of and Flanagan's tongue could kill us both. I tried to communicate with him but it was Adam's eyes that I found. 'Mr Flanagan is a deeply disturbed man, Spencer,' he said and I felt him draw strength from my fear. 'It was the death of his wife that did it –'

'You piece of shit, Reid.'

Adam observed Flanagan. 'Tell me Daniel, how is Sean? He's still in Miami?'

Flanagan stumbled again, almost fell. He was hurt. I knew it and Adam knew it. The American was wordless, floundering. 'To have a child,' said Adam softly.

We were directly in front of the exhibits. The huge mammoth was once again looming above us and I spoke. 'He's a clone –'

Flanagan's brow creased as he managed a creditable sneer. 'Figures.'

'He's a Neanderthal man.

Twenty-Three
15:30 – Wednesday 16th June
American Museum of Natural History, Central Park West, New York City

Flanagan looked from Adam to the reconstructed hominid behind the glass and shrugged. 'Monkey, huh?'

Why not? 'Yes, he's a monkey.'

Flanagan clearly had some sort of death-wish but I felt light-headed enough to go with it. Still I shut my eyes as Flanagan continued. 'So what's he do now, cross himself with an ape?'

I had no idea and I turned to Adam. I wanted to hear the answer from the monkey's mouth, as it where, but Adam simply smiled and looked again at the gun in his hand. Apparently satisfied that it was useless, he let the remaining pieces slip to the floor.

It wouldn't be easy getting our prints on it now. Perhaps Adam was slipping?

'They're not my cup of tea,' said Adam. The sound of the gun striking the marble floor echoed around the room and he continued. 'Not an insoluble problem. But we're a bit short of females, don't you think?'

'Go fuck yourself.'

Flanagan was pushing it. Adam radiated menace but said nothing. 'Now that isn't altogether a bad idea.'

Flanagan's sneer had lost its edge and Adam nodded. 'But the planet's a little crowded at the moment, don't you think? Maybe we should clear some room first.'

'What do you mean?'

The words were mine but Adam's eyes remained focused on Flanagan. 'You were a cop, Daniel. You can see the justice in settling old scores?'

'You're fucking mad, Reid.'

'I'll take that as a yes.'

'Take what you like.'

'You've done it yourself. Perhaps you'd like to help me do the same?'

'I'd rather die,' said Flanagan.

I shook my head. There were words there that I didn't like the sound of. Adam's smile did little to warm his icy eyes. 'That's not your choice, Daniel.'

Flanagan held steady. 'You interrupted me, Reid. I'd rather die than help you.'

'You could do both,' said Adam.

Flanagan was scared. And he was the only person in the room who didn't know it but his fear was infectious and it was becoming a living, growing thing. 'Just fuck you, Reid –'

'Daniel, please. That's both rude and repetitive.'

Flanagan had developed a tick in his right eye. He managed to keep his voice even. 'So monkey-boy thinks we're here to help him does he?'

'Spencer doesn't know,' said Adam. He glanced at me and then swept an arm to encompass the Museum. 'But it's time that you both did. You've been to plenty of these things in the past, haven't you, Spencer?'

The turn in the conversation had thrown me but I managed a nod. Adam seemed satisfied and he continued. 'People come from all over the country, all over the globe. Don't you find it amazing just how many of them seem to come for the food? I certainly do but today we've got something more than sandwiches for them, we've got something really rather special.'

'You're going to poison them?' said Flanagan. He frowned. 'Just a few hundred poor bastards out to hear you speak?'

'Not a few hundred, not poor, not bastards and not poison, Daniel,' said Adam. 'No, there should be three thousand or more here today and we're going to give them something of a gift.'

Flanagan opened his mouth to speak but no words emerged and Adam spoke. 'Yes, the attendees include brokers, fund managers and wannabe millionaires but there'll be others, people who've come because of the subsidized travel –'

I coughed but I got the words out. 'Give them something?'

Adam ignored me. 'We paid some attendees' expenses, I wanted them here. I'll be able to look out over the audience this afternoon and see representatives from every corner of the world. Every creed and every colour. I want them to return home and help me spread the good work.'

'What are you going to do, you crazy son of a bitch?' Flanagan had decided to join in and to bring his own questioning techniques to the conversation. His face was reddening.

The added colour made him look a little less sick but Adam smiled at him and let the jibe pass. 'I'm going to do very little, Daniel.'

'You know what he means.'

Adam turned slowly to face me. I immediately wished that he hadn't. 'My guests will do most of the heavy lifting as they say these days, have you seen the list? No of course you haven't but people have made their way here from every state in the Union and from more than a hundred and twenty countries –'

'Smallpox?'

Adam's expression did not change. 'Variola, Spencer? It certainly got a lot of publicity after nine-eleven. Any outbreak would cause a hell of a scare. That's not what I'm after but you know I presume that the World Health Organization voted not to destroy the last of the Smallpox virus in 2001? It showed more consideration to the virus than your ancestors showed to mine –'

'You can't –'

'I think you'll find I can,' said Adam. The finality of the words and the tone of his voice did not suggest that Adam expected a debate. The temperature in the room had fallen. 'But that's not to say that I will. I know the virus well but I find it too brutal, too unattractive –'

'You're mad,' said Flanagan.

'Been working on that comment for some time, have you?'

'You'll never –'

'Get away with it?' said Adam. His head was once again inclined to one side. He looked boyish, harmless. 'That's not very original. And you should choose your words more carefully. We all should, to be fair, because any single one could be our last.

'So as I was saying, smallpox.' Adam rolled the word and looked from Flanagan to myself. The ex-cop looked awful and I was sure that I looked little better. 'It's fatal in about 30% of cases and it's contagious but not spectacularly so and it's easy to immunise against.

'Significant quantities of the vaccine are stockpiled on every continent. Indeed that's the official reason why the Americans and the Russians kept the virus alive, in order to manufacture more of the vaccine against it. But that's a circular argument and it's really rather a boring disease.

'However, there are others that are much more interesting. Streptococcus, for example. A dynamic killer. A flesh-eating bug but can you can imagine the outcry? No, I needed something altogether more subtle –'

'The police are on their way,' said Flanagan.

'Then they'd better hurry, hadn't they?'

'They know everything...'

'Considerably more than you, then?'

'Just don't do anything stupid before they arrive,' said Flanagan. The ex-cop looked around him. He was flagging. 'We can still –'

'Work something out?' said Adam. 'You really think so? Did you not feel my guiding hand on your shoulder, Daniel? I was with you in New York, London, Cambridge and back here. I know that you haven't been in contact with the police for months.

'Still you did well in England, I must say. You should have died. You probably wished you had. At points you certainly looked dead. You didn't have a telephone with you, did you? You didn't use one at the airport or on the plane. And you went straight to your apartment earlier today to pick up your gun but you didn't use the phone there either.

'Maybe you should have done but you were too keen to confront me, maybe even shoot me weren't you? Well you've confronted me. So well done but no, the police are not on their way.'

Flanagan shifted his weight. I hadn't thought it was possible for my heart to sink any further. But it was and it did and Adam had his answer. I was a journalist. Occasionally, quite a good one and I could read Flanagan without difficulty. But Adam was operating on a completely different level. And if he'd had any doubts as to whether the police were on their way or not, he now knew for certain that they were not.

'Yes, getting back to smallpox. I could have changed it somewhat,' said Adam. 'The virus gentlemen. Please try to keep up. I could have made it more interesting. Perhaps more intelligent or adaptable. Could have bound it to a protein so that it passed through your genes to the next generation and became a real nuisance but that wasn't what I had in mind. I was working on something quite different and I've got you to thank for bringing it over, Spencer.'

I looked at Flanagan, was sure that his uncomprehending face mirrored my own. 'It wasn't quite ready for the Cambridge meeting,' said Adam. 'It was delayed. Human error apparently. Ironic that a human error could have bought some time for humanity as a whole. But that's all it bought, just a little time.

'And New York was always the fall-back. You were a mule, Spencer. And you played your role extremely well. Encouraged by Simon, of course, don't you remember? Simon says Adam will see you in New York?'

'Simon says,' said Flanagan. His mouth twisted into a grimace. I hoped that it made him feel better because it did precious little to lift my mood.

'Simon said a lot of things, Daniel,' said Adam. 'But I don't remember him saying to bring a gun to our little meeting?'

‘He’s Simon,’ I said and nodded towards Adam for Flanagan’s benefit.

The American looked as though he’d picked up a bad smell. ‘That works.’

‘You brought it over in your case,’ said Adam. ‘The large one, purple patches?’

The conversation was taking too many turns. My head was reeling but I felt something inside of me crumble and I couldn’t keep up. I’d been comprehensively outmanoeuvred. My body was shot and my mind was going the same way. My knees were wobbling uncontrollably but strong hands once again supported me.

At Heathrow they’d asked me if I’d packed my own case. Of course I’d packed it but I hadn’t locked it, never did. Why would I? To the best of my knowledge I’d never locked a suitcase in my life but all I ever carried was clothes and toiletries. Clean going out and dirty coming back. Hardly the crown jewels. But that wasn’t the point and I noticed that Adam was watching me minutely. He smiled. ‘Did you, Spencer? Did you pack your own case?

‘I suppose you did but could it have been tampered with? Something added or something taken away? Perhaps things would have developed differently if we’d been ready to go in Cambridge. But we weren’t and life’s like that. A small change here leads to a larger change there. You’ve been a minor irritant for some time, Spencer, but you clearly wanted to be centre-stage and that’s where you are, I hope you’re happy. Until recently, I simply needed to keep you close, make sure you didn’t become too much of a problem but then I saw a role for you and it suited me to keep you interested.

‘I might have been somewhat brusque at Ranulfskelf.’ Adam glanced at Flanagan. ‘A little rude perhaps but I needed you. I wanted the hook firmly in place and it worked. You co-operated magnificently and now here we are, having this little chat. It’s been in your shaving foam for a couple of days, Spencer.’

Adam Reid’s eyes caught the harsh light and shone fiercely blue as he turned his head towards me. 'And I see you've been shaving. Did you manage it without nicking the skin? I doubt it. You'll still be the first but you'll hardly be the last.'

I glanced at Flanagan. Saw something in his eyes that caused a flutter in my stomach. Adam had poisoned me and Flanagan was sizing me up for a coffin. But Adam looked happy. He brought his fingers to his lips. 'Delicious, don't you think? Mystery illness strikes down suspected poisoner? Will they assume that you engineered the disease? Perhaps you had the inclination to move on from murder to genocide?'

'You're putting this on him?'

'Just stating the facts, Daniel,' said Adam. 'I'm not seeking to interpret them. There will be plenty only too eager to do that and I'll admit that it's not a particularly good frame. It may not be up to your standards but it will hold for a while and afterwards? Well there will be no afterwards –'

I felt my stomach heave. Tears were stinging my eyes. The words washed over me in a blur but some of them remained painfully clear.

There will be no afterwards.

'You son of a bitch, Reid,' growled Flanagan. I couldn't see him. Bile was rising in my throat and I had a mouth full of something unpleasant. I tried to rub my eyes. Flanagan was straining against the arms that held him when Adam once more faced him. 'No Daniel, I may be a bastard but I'm not a son of a bitch.'

'What have you done to him?'

'What's the fuss about, fat-boy?' said Adam. Violence crackled around him.

'You crazy fucker –'

'Daniel –'

'What have you done?'

Adam did not respond but the veins on his temple were showing. His hands were bunching into fists. This didn't look good but slowly the smile returned. Flanagan had walked the cliff-edge again but he still hadn't fallen off. Adam turned towards me. 'Spencer, you don't look well.'

I tried to spit but I couldn't. Something warm hit my shirt.

'There's blood in your vomit –'

'You fucking bastard.'

I closed my eyes tight, the light suddenly painful and I heard something. A sickening thud, it was me hitting the floor. I was pulled up and opened my eyes then screwed them half-closed against the light.

'Are you disappointed in me, Spencer?' said Adam. He was very close to me. Flanagan was in a heap on the floor. He wasn't moving and Adam continued. 'Upset maybe because I said that I wouldn't hurt you?'

Adam nodded to himself and brought his hand up to my face. I felt him trace the damaged skin of my cheek as he spoke. 'I can understand that. But don't let it twist you out of shape. Some things are so much more important than the truth.

'Ask any of the great figures from your past. I'm sure they would agree. But perhaps that's because they wrote your history. They got to define the truth. Maybe I'll live to do the same.'

I felt Adam's breath hot on my cheek. 'So concentrate, Spencer. This isn't a hypothetical question, will you do it?'

I struggled to support my weight. I didn't have a clue what he was talking about. I tried to shrug my shoulders but lacked the strength. 'Will you kill yourself to protect your species?'

My knees wobbled but I did not fall. I heard Flanagan speak. 'It doesn't have to be this way, Reid.'

Thick-voiced, the old man was trying to stand when Adam faced him. 'I'm afraid that I must disagree, Daniel.'

'You'll be stopped, Reid.'

'You really think so?'

'You're crazy.'

'Is that the best that you can do?'

'You can't –'

'Oh but I can. And what's the problem? It's only Varicella.'

'Varicella?'

'That's chickenpox –'

'Chickenpox?'

'Not deaf then, Daniel,' said Adam. 'Not yet anyway. But if you insist on repeating every word that I say this will take longer than necessary; chickenpox, yes. My father did tweak it somewhat and I've given it a bit more of an edge. A bit more bite but essentially it's the childhood disease.

'A shorter incubation period, though. Only a day or two rather than the more usual two weeks and that's a pity as it could slow the spread. Guests will know that they're ill around the same time they become contagious but, with air travel and all, they could be anywhere in the world by then. Don't worry. There will be plenty of Typhoid Marys out there.

'I suppose Spencer will be the first to find out just what the big deal is. Outside the lab, that is, but simultaneous outbreaks of such a commonplace disease are hardly likely to provoke panic. It's an everyday thing. But Varicella, unlike Variola, really is contagious.'

Adam tilted his head to one side. 'I expect you actually liked it when you had it as a child, didn't you, Spencer, with its mild, flu-like symptoms? A few spots here and there. The odd dab of Calamine Lotion from mother and a fortnight off school?

'And a one in forty thousand chance that you would die wasn't something for your parents to be unduly afraid of was it? That's if they knew anything about the mortality rate in the first place but sadly I don't think you'll find this variety half as agreeable –'

My knees were gone and I was down again but I was pulled upright. My legs trailed beneath me and immediately I began to wheeze. I couldn't get any air into my chest. My peripheral vision was going when Adam barked something rough and guttural. The hands were pulled from beneath my shoulders and I hit the floor.

'Don't be so dramatic, Spencer,' said Adam from somewhere above me. He had the measured air of a doctor talking to either a very young or a very old patient. 'You don't look too well but hanging around like that can make it very difficult to breathe.'

My vision began to improve and I sat up. My shoes scraped the floor as I struggled to support my weight. Something slipped from my chin. I'd been sick again. I struggled to get a grip and straightened up. Adam was speaking again. 'Bloody vomit and severe diarrhoea,' he said and pointed at me. 'Looking at Spencer, I think we've worked that one out. Dehydration could be an issue. It's an altogether more interesting disease than the original chickenpox and the subsequent shingles could be quite spectacular.

'But your chances are quite good. You may have picked up a bigger dose than most people will but you're relatively young and not completely unfit. I don't think you'll die.'

I spluttered and spat something out of my mouth. I felt it dribble onto my chin and Adam frowned as he turned away. 'Spencer, must you really do that?'

'It's not your most attractive habit. Where was I? Ah yes, I wanted something really contagious and chickenpox fits the bill. My father confirmed the nineteenth century findings with regard to smallpox. Found that every infected person in an unvaccinated population will infect on average, another five people. . That's the 'R' rate, Spencer. You've probably heard of it. This rises to more than ten in a crowded city environment. Ironically, hospitals are one of the most efficient conduits.

'But chickenpox is much more effective. One carrier should infect more than a dozen people on average and twenty-five or thirty in a crowded city and it won't be reported. No contagious disease alarm bells will be going off in the early stages so it will have a head start.'

'Why?'

Flanagan had struggled to his feet but his voice was steady. Adam smiled before raising his eyes. 'Payback, Daniel. Surely you, of all people, can understand that?'

Flanagan grimaced but remained silent and I spoke. 'Why did you keep your father alive, Adam?'

Adam sighed. 'Why do you think?'

'Information?'

It was Flanagan who had spoken. It was both a question and a statement and Adam said something that I did not catch. Nosey raised a hand and cuffed Flanagan hard across the face. He folded at the knees and hit the ground again. I felt Adam's eyes on me. 'Rude to interrupt. Please continue Spencer.'

'Not the cloning,' I said. The words came out pretty well. I had to keep it up and win us a few more minutes. 'He wouldn't tell you how to slow down your decline?'

'Uninspired, Spencer,' said Adam, his eyes on the middle distance. 'He loved me. He really did. He'd have done anything, literally anything within his power, to help –'

'He worked at Porton Down.'

'That's much better.'

'Military science park, weapons grade viruses?' It came out as a hiss. I sounded like a punctured gas bottle but still, Adam nodded.

He was looking directly at me. No he was looking through me and I could feel myself being defiled, the information being sucked out of me. 'Bizarre, don't you think? My father was knighted for his pioneering work on vaccines but his real expertise lay elsewhere.

'As I've said, he was a genius, he really was. He was a viral engineer of the first order, one of the world's first dark biologists –'

'Fucking mumbo-jumbo –'

Flanagan's mouth was working again but Adam ignored him. 'He was involved in the kidnapping and debriefing of scientists from Biopreparat, the former Soviet Union's biological weapons facility. They had refined smallpox but he was way ahead of them. They could teach him nothing. It took me years to catch up with him. And I'm smart so believe me, that's quite a compliment.

'Hot agents, they were called. He lived for viruses. Nurtured them, encouraged them to mutate. I think he even loved them. He produced some of the most frightening weapons-grade material that the planet has ever seen. So it's fitting, I suppose, that he died for them.

'His work saved thousands of lives and he deserved the accolades. He made great strides in immunology but the thing is, Spencer, he studied vaccines only to learn best how to prevent them from working. He devoted much of his life to engineering viruses, into making them resistant to vaccines and to that end he had information that I needed to have –'

'Don't do it Adam,' I said. My stomach contracted and I retched again. It undermined my attempts at authority. 'Don't play –'

'God?' said Adam. I'd been too slow and his eyes left mine and settled on an invisible horizon. 'It was like a glorious game of chess. My father was a grand master. Perhaps he was the best the world had ever seen but then I came along.'

Adam was momentarily lost momentarily in his own world of dark agents and weapons-grade bugs but then he continued. 'Refining viruses was the least of my tasks. Most of them are just itching to refine themselves. Much more challenging is targeting them.

'They need to be guided through the chaff of humanity to strike at one's true target whilst at the same time they must be protected against attack either from the body's immune system or from vaccines. And they mustn't surrender any of their potency whilst doing so. If you divert all your power to the shields, then you can't fire your photon torpedoes. It's not what civilized countries like to talk about but it's what my father knew. And he was good at it.'

Adam's eyes flickered over to Daniel Flanagan. The ex-cop had dragged himself into a sitting position. He was bleeding from his nose and mouth. The front of his white shirt was heavily stained and he coughed. It built from deep within his body and he winced. His lips bubbled red and he spat on the floor.

'Daniel, you're such a fucking pig,' said Adam. But his eyes were misted. He was elsewhere, wasn't inclined to judge the winner in the disgusting mess competition that Flanagan and I were having. 'But there was so much blood and he was surprised, you know? He was unaware that I knew so much. But then again he wasn't. Had he known what I was capable of, what he had made me capable of, then he would have saved us both a great deal of trauma –'

'And your mother Adam?'

'She was my host, not my mother,' said Adam. 'She was no more my mother than the specimen dish that held me before her womb. But I did respect her. I respected them both. I still do. They'd made some strides but with hindsight they still had a long way to go –'

I looked at Flanagan and then at Adam. 'Why?'

'Isn't that the biggest of little words?'

'So indiscriminate –'

Adam looked back at me. He covered the few paces that separated us and held out his hand. I recoiled as his blunt, powerful fingers made contact with my upper lip. 'We could have been friends you and I.'

I shook my head. I'd seen what happened to Adam's friends.

'Don't deny it, Spencer. I respect you and you're right. As a weapon Varicella is sub-optimal. It can't be targeted, isn't ideal. But then again, it was never meant to be.'

I spoke before the thought had fully formed in my mind. 'The disease isn't the weapon.'

Twenty-Four
15:40 – Wednesday 16th June
American Museum of Natural History, Central Park West, New York City

'Clever, clever boy,' said Adam.

'Is this a scam?' said Flanagan. His words were slurred. More flecks of blood spattered from his upper lip and dripped from his moustache onto his shirt and the floor in front of him. He grimaced. 'Spread some disease and sell the vaccine? You cheap bastard.'

'Hardly cheap,' said Adam. He let the words hang then looked directly at me. 'I'll make billions. But I've already got billions. Think bigger.'

'It's not the money,' I said. 'It can't be –'

'No, not the money,' said Adam. He sounded detached. 'But tell me. Do you think that killing someone brings you closer to them?'

'I don't know –'

'Indeed you don't but what do you think?' Adam stooped. His breath was sweet, hot against my face. 'Does it create a bond, could it forever cement in place one that was already there?'

'You tell me –'

'I may do more than that, Spencer,' Adam whispered. His powerful fingers held my chin to the light and I knew that I was flushing. 'I may show you.'

I tried to pull away but Adam simply smiled. 'Were you bullied? Were there those who told you that you were different and that you didn't belong?'

Adam didn't wait for an answer. He continued. 'Of course there were. But did you hate them for it? Did you really hate them, the name-callers? Did you want to kill them or did it spur you on and keep you going when all around you could go no further?

'I think perhaps it did. But I can feel the hatred in you, Spencer. Disfigured from birth and different. Did you raise your hand against them, did you strike back?'

'Bit late to be trying to bond with him, Monkey boy.'

Adam let his hand drop from my face. He walked across to Daniel Flanagan who had somehow made it back onto his feet. The American tried to back away but Nosey effortlessly prevented him from doing so.

'Don't kill him.' I couldn't explain it but I'd been in the man's head. I could see Flanagan as a lifeless corpse. 'He, he –'

Adam looked at me intensely. 'Very good, you're coming along nicely.'

Flanagan struggled, tried to spit but Adam ignored him. 'We'll have the pleasure of Mr Flanagan's company for a little while longer but money is a tool, Spencer. It should be used as such.

'It can influence people, change things. And I really want to change things.' Adam's eyes were shining. He raised his hand to his chin and rubbed the scar tissue gently. 'As I said, I want to give you something.

'So few people truly give but that's what I want to do. I want to add something to the human gene pool. As you say, it's in the vaccine. The disease is simply a means to an end.

'It won't touch everybody. Diseases never do but the vaccine might. I had to make the disease benign enough not to trigger any of the anti-terrorist systems active in many US hospitals in the early days, but I also had to make it virulent and nasty enough for there to be a real demand for the vaccine. I thought that a mortality rate of anything more than 1% would do the trick so that's what you're looking at, Spencer, about a one in ninety chance that you'll die.

'Not bad odds but that's four or five kids even in a small school and what parent would take that risk? Demand for the vaccine will be huge.

Everyone will want to be inoculated.' Adam paused before addressing Flanagan. 'No more jokes, Daniel? Do you think the greens will like me? Sure, it's only going to remove a hundred million people from the last count, but they may see that as a useful start, don't you think?'

'Then the vaccine?'

Looking at Adam, I could see the man beneath the plastic surgery. I could see the body mass and the bone structure. He watched me observing him and smiled. 'Yes the vaccine,' he said. He rolled the words with something like respect. 'But don't judge me before you judge yourself.'

'We would never do this.'

'Really?'

'We're not like that –'

'Rubbish, Spencer,' said Adam. 'Sanctimonious shit. Your ancestors killed mine. Your churches have killed and burnt and tortured in the name of their God. The Nazis made an industry out of it and they and no end of other dictators all believed that they had right on their side. Most of them tucked their children up in bed every evening and even now wars are being waged in the name of the common good.'

'Your parents raised you,' I said. We needed time. String together enough minutes and we would survive. 'What about your aunt in Yorkshire, your staff and your colleagues? How could you turn on them?'

Adam's eyes once again caught the light. He drew his words like a blade from a sheath. 'If I'm licked by a dog -'

'You owe them everything -'

'- should I be grateful?'

'Yes, Adam.'

Adam looked away. I felt that was a victory of sorts but when he continued I felt the violence of his words. 'Do you really think they put me in the womb of a barren woman for my benefit? Consider your answer before you speak, Spencer. Or might they not have done it for themselves? Driven by the selfish desire to have a child, achieve something that they knew would never be open to me? I was an experiment and I did what I had to do and –'

'What's in the vaccine?'

'- I will continue to do so.'

'The vaccine Adam?'

'I'm impressed,' said Adam. He looked at his watch once more. Not a good sign. 'You've retained focus. That's uncommon. I needed a disease where I could corner the market for the vaccine. I can't afford to completely ignore the competition but they won't catch me on this one and I'll give it away for free to those that can't afford it. I don't need or want their money.'

'What does it do?'

The billionaire moved closer and I felt my hair begin to prickle. 'I really was in danger of underestimating you, Spencer.'

'Tell me.'

'I want to have children.' The words threw me. The room was deathly silent. A sticky gob of spit and blood slid from my chin and Flanagan grunted but Adam ignored him. 'I'd like to have lots of them. There are not many young ladies of my choosing at the prom tonight, but the vaccine will help.'

'What do you mean?'

Adam rose to his full height. From my angle, sitting in an unpleasant puddle of my own making he blocked the light. 'Don't you see? The vaccine is intelligent. It can do amazing things –'

'What?'

'It'll fight off the pox," said Adam, ignoring the interruption. 'That's the easy part. That's not in doubt but it will do a lot more. It can differentiate between males and females. It's your women –'

'What've you done?'

It was Flanagan again and Adam turned to face him. 'I could have had you killed a thousand times, Daniel. You deserved to die for letting Maria down. You know that don't you? You'll spend what's left of the rest of your life carrying that burden but I wanted you to live, to realize what you'd done.

'And I had a gap in preparations with fat, corrupt, washed up cop written all over it. That's you, Daniel. You provided the credibility that an otherwise potentially unbelievable story lacked. You brought Spencer to me. You played your part well and I'd like to thank you.'

Flanagan strained against the goons holding his arms. If it had been physically possible, I'd have been sick again. Adam continued. 'I haven't got time for a science lesson but it's a refinement of my father's work. It's an aggressive vaccine, one that will bind itself to the proteins of certain cells and will encourage micro-mutations within them.'

Some of the words were making it through. Adam was talking about bio-engineering and he was smiling. But I couldn't get any words out and he continued. 'I could so easily have made the disease, or the vaccine for that matter, fatal. I could have programmed either agent to prevent the production of red blood cells for example. Could have watched you cough and choke yourselves to death but to wipe out seven billion humans of whatever persuasion seemed like such a waste.'

Adam waved his arm. He drew the room around him into his world and managed to keep me with him. 'But then reproduction itself is so wasteful. All those millions of sperm cells and hundreds of wasted eggs and cloning too –'

'You're rambling Reid,' said Flanagan.

'No, I think not,' said Adam. Seconds were passing. And the seconds were becoming minutes. A minute here and a minute there, it was beginning to add up. I thought that I could hear movement, voices elsewhere in the building. Adam seemed oblivious. He gestured towards Nosey and his men. 'And it's what I think that counts.

'The active elements within the vaccine will sit there, Spencer,' he said. He was not frothing at the mouth. He didn't look mad. Not even angry and I found myself strangely disappointed. 'They'll lay there dormant but they've got stamina and real patience. No-one will notice the effects for some time but the menstrual cycles of your females will be changed. Their eggs will be subtly reprogrammed and will look for something new, something hitherto not present in sufficient quantities in the human gene pool.

'Without the correct trigger their eggs will reject human sperm cells and human females, all of them, not just the odd one or two, will become barren. That's where I come in.'

I glanced at Flanagan through filmy eyes. His body language suggested that he was boiling with anger and I managed to speak. 'You?'

'Children,' said Adam softly. 'Lots and lots of them. Existing sperm banks will be useless but nature is so bountiful, don't you think?'

'You been jacking off for years then, Reid?' said Flanagan.

'Haven't we all?' said Adam. Flanagan pulled an unpleasant face. He wasn't amused but nor was he able to conjure up a reply and Adam continued, his tone conversational. 'The number of frozen fertile eggs is statistically insignificant but, as I was saying, many researchers believe that Neanderthals and modern humans interbred.

'The two branches of humanity may have merged. There may be some genetic continuity although the more obvious Neanderthal characteristics have been lost. It's just a theory, but the vaccine will put it to the test. Fertility levels in some areas may be maintained –'

'Neanderthal women,' said Flanagan. 'Sounds like Brooklyn.'

Adam managed a smile. 'You might think of that as an insult –'

'You're mad Adam.'

They were my words. Adam turned towards me. 'And you're a dead man, Spencer. Which would you rather be?'

I couldn't manage a response and Adam spoke to Nosey. His movements brusque and business-like, he was preparing to leave the exhibition. 'Mustn't keep our guests waiting. They'll be hungry. The sooner we get the formal business out of the way, the sooner they can eat.'

'Don't do it Adam,' I said. Exhaustion and a deeper resignation had permeated my voice. The guests had arrived. I hadn't even heard them and they would change nothing. 'There must be another way...'

Adam's smile did not falter. He turned and left the exhibition.

Twenty-Five
16:00 – Wednesday 16th June
American Museum of Natural History, Central Park West, New York City

So that was it, game over. I felt a release. I couldn't control events anymore; what would happen would happen. As the Museum's loud speakers crackled into life I could see things for what they really were.

Adam was a lunatic. He was brilliant, certainly, but he was also mad. He was going to do something terrible and he was going to kill me. Shudders swept the length of my body as my strength ebbed away.

'Good afternoon ladies and gentlemen,' said a voice over the PA system. It was Adam. I wished I'd had the foresight to at least puke on him and put him off his stride. As it was he sounded utterly confident in his role as global entrepreneur. 'Thank you for joining us for what we hope will be a most rewarding and interesting afternoon –'

The voice washed over the dry and rock-like bones of the fish and the reptiles. It echoed past the Saurischian and Ornithischian dinosaurs and around the Hall of Advanced Mammals. It reached into the furthest corners of the building as one of the museum's own; a long-dead creature drew breath and spoke once more. 'I'd like to say a special thank you to those attendees who've travelled a great distance to be here with us today. And to those of you away from the main hall, elsewhere in the building. I hope that you can hear me well enough. I'll be up to see you as soon as the formalities are over and I can assure you there'll be plenty of food for everyone.'

A pause. Presumably for applause and gentle laughter. But the microphones had not picked it up and I looked at Flanagan. His face crusted with browning blood, the American was squatting on his haunches. He looked beaten. He'd given his repertoire an outing. He'd tried violence, threats and verbal abuse and he had nothing left to give. He looked old.

He was no threat to the two men either side of him, Nosey close in attendance. I decided to risk a dig from the fourth man who was by my side and chance a question. 'When's the food?'

Flanagan looked at the floor and then raised his head and when he spoke he opened a cut on his lip and winced. 'He's going to kill us.'

'I know,' I said.

I felt liberated. I was free. It was infectious and Flanagan tried to smile. 'Do you believe these goons don't speak English?'

'Nosey does,' I said. I jerked my chin towards the thug-in-chief four or five yards from Flanagan and continued. 'The good looking one there with the nose. I don't know about the others. Besides, Adam might have an ear-piece.'

'Spencer?' I raised my head and Flanagan continued. 'You remember what I said in England?'

What was I, a tape recorder? The man had spewed forth a river of verbiage. He had only fallen silent when he was eating or smoking. But there had been something in Flanagan's voice and I looked at him, tried to concentrate. 'What?'

'Don't make me shout,' said Flanagan. He had a point. 'The things you learn as a cop?'

I shook my head. Adam Reid was speaking again. It was something technical. It meant nothing to me but his tone seemed to change. Flanagan had heard it too. We were only a second or two from any one of these goons shutting us up and preventing further communication. 'You've got to back up your brother officer?'

That rang a bell. 'Go on.'

'Back up your brother officer, you remember?'

I forced a nod. I could recall a part of it at least but what else had he said? Never rely on a single chest shot? Some other macho bullshit but that wasn't it. Then I had it.

Carry a second gun. Carry a throwaway; it could save your life. Flanagan cocked his head to one side as the voice of Adam Reid echoed once again around the Museum.

The applause was beginning to build now. I felt it resonate around the building. The words were similar and the reception was every bit as warm as the one that Adam had received in Cambridge. 'I can assure you that we'll do more,' the man was saying. 'We'll do much, much more. We've made great strides and we'll continue to do so in the years to come.' A pause. More clapping. Adam's audience was going to go home sore handed. 'And ladies and gentlemen,' he said with a passion that silenced his audience. 'If I'm sure of one thing and one thing only, it's that the best is yet to come.'

More clapping. The floor was drumming. Flanagan licked his lips. He was going to either shit or bust trying and I had to help but my head was thumping as I watched the American closely. I waited for the least sign of movement as the applause built still further and then fast, very fast for a man of his age, out of shape, recently beaten, poisoned and jet-lagged, Flanagan reached down towards his feet.

Time froze into a series of single frames. I could almost hear them clicking by and then the reaction began as the goons to either side of Flanagan started to bend with him. Perhaps they were trying to support a frail old man as he fell but the thug by my side could see what the others could not and he was twisting around.

And now I could see it too. The gun at the ex-cop's ankle. The hand on my shoulder pulled away as the goon that had been holding me moved to help his colleagues and I ducked down sharply. Momentarily free, I kept my eyes on Flanagan.

Still bent double, the American had the small gun in his hand and was twisting his wrist, trying to get the angle for a shot. The barrel of the insignificant-looking piece was swinging around and the thug to Flanagan's left, his hand fumbling at his breast pocket, began to pull back.

And then I heard it. A single tiny hand-clap lost in a sea of applause. The man who had been back-peddling was now clutching at his face, blood spilling from between his fingers.

Flanagan was swinging his arm, choosing his target. Another crack and the second man, now also moving backwards, was clawing at his throat and Flanagan was away.

I pushed myself backwards on the polished marble floor as Flanagan scuttled to his side. I slid into something and grabbed at it. Three feet high and a foot or so in diameter, it was light and hollow. I rose to my feet and summoned what strength I had left and swung the litter bin hard.

The crash as it connected with the head of the man who had been holding me echoed around the room. It was a huge, satisfying sound but the bin was empty and weighed very little. Dented and useless, it spun from my hands and fell to the floor while the injured thug, a thin trickle of blood creasing his forehead, had murder in his eyes.

I couldn't move. I watched as the man pulled a short knife from his waistband and then shut my eyes. I heard the crack of a pistol and then a second retort and felt no pain.

Cowering like a whipped dog, I opened my eyes. The guard still standing above me had been hit twice. One shot had passed through both cheeks, while a second had opened up a third eye on his forehead. He looked surprised and swayed but did not fall.

Head like a cement block, his eyes were clearing. He looked directly at me and raised his knife hand when another shot rang out. A splash of red from the man's throat and he crumpled inwards and to the ground. The knife skittered away.

The applause over the loudspeakers faded and Nosey, his hands partly raised, was backing away. I looked at Flanagan. The two men nearest to him were now down. One was crawling towards the exit, the other was still frothing and bubbling on the floor and the man next to me had taken three shots and was a motionless heap.

That left only Nosey and I could feel him doing the maths. Maybe he knew what model the gun was, how many bullets it held but I had no idea and I scrabbled backwards, bumped into the glass of the mammoth exhibit.

More words from Adam but something was different. The man had paused in mid-sentence and I felt a flutter of panic. He had heard something. 'We can achieve more,' said the voice over the PA. It might have lacked enthusiasm and then it faded into the applause. Some in the crowd were whistling and shouting. Stamping their feet and the exhibits in the Hall of Advanced Mammals began to quiver but Adam's voice had gone.

He was coming. I could feel him. Nosey was only feet from the exit and Flanagan raised his arm. The thug raised both hands and showed his palms. He opened his mouth but no words emerged as Flanagan's gun spat yellow-red flame.

The noise was lost in the applause. Nosey's hands scrabbled at his face and his legs buckled. His knees hit the ground hard and he pitched forward, smacking into the marble floor. I pushed any feeling of sympathy for the car-scratching bastard from my mind and looked at the injured guard who had almost made it to the exit.

This time I did hear the sharp crack and the man shuddered and lay still. 'Jesus, Flanagan. What now?'

The ex-cop walked to the nearest prostrate shape and kicked it. 'I'm out of bullets. Check them for weapons. Might find a gun but watch the one that's still moving. Then we get to a phone, call the cops.'

A vision of Adam flashed into my mind. I could feel his anger. 'He's coming.'

'I know.'

'He heard us, I'm sure of it,' I said. 'His speech was shorter.'

'I said I know,' said Flanagan. He pulled his hand from Nosey's jacket. In it he held a knife. 'What've you got, Spencer?'

I didn't know where the dropped knife had gone. I looked down at the crumpled pile nearest to me and forced myself to kneel beside it. I avoided the man's face and reached into his jacket. The chest was rigid. He was wearing an armoured vest but there was no gun. I pulled out another knife and held it up.

'The Beretta?' said Flanagan.

'Adam broke it.'

'Where did he put the bullets?'

They could still be in Adam's pocket. But that had to be unlikely. I pointed out the panic room. 'Observation room?'

I had no idea whether the guns took the same bullets but Flanagan seemed to know and he nodded. He rose to his feet and walked towards the observation room. He moved rapidly but was stooping and looked to be in pain.

'He'll be here within a minute,' I said. I'm not sure that that added a lot but Flanagan re-emerged from the observation room a moment later. He held up what I presumed was the magazine from his first gun and began popping out the bullets.

'Can't you just put the magazine in?'

Flanagan, who was pushing hard at a small bullet with his thumb, did not raise his head. 'Leave the guns to me, Spencer.'

I held the knife in my hand to my chest and pictured Adam Reid. I could see the huge, three hundred pound lump of bone and gristle mounting the stairs three, four at a time. I moved hesitantly to the exit, but could hear nothing. I slipped out of the exhibition hall. The lifts were stationary and there was nobody in sight but then I heard them, hurried footsteps.

More than one person was moving quickly towards us and I stumbled back into the exhibition 'On the stairs. More than one of them.'

Flanagan clicked the final bullet into place as I reached his side and he slapped the magazine home with his left hand. He slid the barrel of the gun forward and back again and raised his arm as the first man, one I'd never seen before, flew into the room.

Flanagan shot him in the face. The man fell to his knees as a second and third entered the room and then Adam. Flanagan's arm traversed the two upright thugs and sought out Adam. He fired without hesitation but Adam was moving fast and the shot went wide. Adam reversed direction effortlessly and Flanagan's arm swung back as Reid bent and grabbed one of the prostrate thugs by the entrance.

I heard the sound of ripping cloth as he lifted the body and turned it towards Flanagan in one smooth movement. Another shot rang out from the ex-cop's tiny gun. The bullet tugged at the body's clothing and Adam began to move backwards.

I had no idea how many shots he had left. Would Adam know? I looked at him. I had a clear view but no weapon. Flanagan had the opposite. I wondered if I would be able to pull the trigger if I had a gun and Adam spoke. 'Well would you, Spencer?'

Adam continued to edge towards the exit as the two uninjured men that had entered the room with him fanned to his left and right. 'One bullet left, Daniel. How's that going to work?'

Flanagan hesitated but as the thug to Adam's right drew a gun of his own the decision was made for him and his arm swung around and the tiny weapon, so insignificant against the darker background of the mammoth's hide, spat red for the last time.

The man's head jerked backwards and he fell, the gun spilling from his hand and sliding across the tiled floor. Adam immediately dropped the body in his hands. He was betting his life on Flanagan having spent his bullets. The remaining goon continued to flank us as Adam concentrated on closing the distance between himself and Flanagan.

This was it. Time had slowed again and the heavy gun, sliding across the marble struck my foot. I bent quickly, picked it up without thought and raised my arm. 'Adam.'

Adam Reid ignored me.

But he knew.

Quickly, a cat-like fluidity in his movements, he scooped up a dead man by his feet and turned towards me as I slipped off what I hoped was the safety catch and pulled the trigger.

A tremendous pain shot up my arm as the gun reared into the air. The sound was deafening. As the swirl of smoke in front of me cleared, Adam raised an eyebrow. 'Spencer, you surprise me.'

I straightened my arm and steadied the gun. I was trying not to vomit.

'Would you do it, Spencer?'

Flanagan threw the empty Beretta to the floor. 'Shoot him, Spencer.'

'Shoot me in cold blood?'

I had a shot now. But I pictured an Adam scrabbling at a wound and then a dead Adam on the floor, and later on the mortuary slab and I knew that I could not pull the trigger. Adam Reid smiled. 'I thought not...'

At the periphery of my vision I sensed movement. The remaining goon was reaching to his chest and I swung my arm, pulled the trigger. The sound from the gun reverberated around the room and the man went down. He was clawing at his groin. The material of his dark trousers was immediately shiny and wet under the bright lights.

'I think you've killed him, Spencer,' said Adam. He might have been discussing the choice of bedroom wallpaper. He looked briefly at the writhing man. 'I'd give him four, maybe five minutes. Torn artery, dislocated hip, massive trauma. Aren't you going to get help? You've killed a man. It's a lot to carry on your conscience and believe me, I would know.'

'Shoot him, Spencer.'

'That's not very kind, Daniel,' said Adam. He glanced at Flanagan.

'For fuck's sake shoot him,' said the American.

No doubting what Flanagan thought. Adam looked calmly at him and at the tiny pistol on the floor. 'All done, Daniel?'

‘Spencer?’

Adam’s eyes blazed blue in the light and they were back on mine. He was holding the body of one of his men before him as he continued to move towards me. The gun in my hand was getting heavy and it began to sag. It waved from side to side and Adam regarded me coldly. I didn’t have much of a shot. I could only see a foot and a bit of leg. Perhaps an inch or two of head and a blue eye every now and again and I knew that I wouldn’t be able to pull the trigger.

And what I knew, Adam knew.

‘Just back off, ape-man,’ said Flanagan.

Flanagan glanced at me as Adam’s eyes flickered between him and the gun in my hand and for the first time I saw it. It was fear. Not the fear of death or of pain or of humiliation, but the fear of failure. Then it was replaced by something without a name; determination or a deep, abiding hatred. I pictured it as a crimson wash darkening through burgundy to black and Adam took another step towards me. He kicked a body out of his way but did not bend or present a target for an instant.

The body slid stickily to one side and Adam spoke. ‘No more wise-cracks, Daniel?’

‘Leave him alone, Adam.’

I could feel Flanagan’s fear. It filled the room and Adam smiled. ‘No more jokes?’

Flanagan’s voice betrayed him. He was close to panic. ‘Just pull the fucking trigger, Spencer. He’s going to kill us both.’

I could not pull the trigger. I felt Adam’s eyes boring into me and I closed my mind, thought of nothing. Adam knew what I could and could not do and I watched as the big man shifted the body in his hands, gripped it and rammed its head hard against the glass of the huge display case by his side.

The glass shattered and dead man’s head imploded. A frothy pink mush spilled onto the floor and Adam spoke. ‘Oops.’

He dropped the torn body and turned his back on me. I had a clear target. I could feel Adam's contempt and Flanagan's imploring eyes on me. But my gun hand was shaking uncontrollably and I lowered it to my side as, with the glass crunching beneath his feet and his huge shoulders rolling from side to side, Adam Reid walked towards the mammoth.

He stopped and stroked the beast's trunk. 'Everyone has to die, Daniel,' he said. 'Some sooner than others, it would appear. Spencer could no more shoot me in the back than he could drown a baby –'

Flanagan let out a racking sob. 'Spencer?'

Which means that you've got a problem,' said Adam. He sounded amused. He could so easily have been relating an after-dinner anecdote. 'Because I'm stronger than you, I'm smarter than you and here's the bad news; I really want to kill you.'

Adam moved further into the interior of the huge glass case and placed his hand on the squat, powerfully built Neanderthal's arm before him. 'Will you run, Daniel?'

Flanagan looked to his left and right. He was old and sick but he wasn't like me. He wouldn't give up until the last breath was wrenched from him and Adam knew. 'Or will you die where you stand, piss-wet and shaking?'

I tried to raise the gun but I couldn't. I started to cry. 'I can't do it.'

Flanagan's wide eyes flickered from mine to Adam as Adam gently took the wooden-handled stone axe from the hand of the Neanderthal. He weighed it, allowed it to swing free. Flanagan flinched. 'Yes it probably will, Daniel,' said Adam. 'But only for an instant.'

He began to walk towards Flanagan as I recovered some sort of control over my limbs and I raised the gun. Adam tilted his head and savoured the air as he watched Flanagan begin to shuffle sideways towards me. Then he moved to close down his angles.

I still couldn't pull the trigger and Flanagan bolted, ran for the door. But Adam had anticipated his move and he reached down, picked up a heavy, football-sized rock from the floor of the display with his left hand and swung his weight from his left foot to his right.

The huge rock shot through the air and tore through the reinforced glass of the display case, catching Flanagan on his shoulder. The old man spun helplessly into the stuffed recreation of an exhibit, some long-dead horse, and fell to the floor.

Adam's eyes sought out mine and then he looked back at Flanagan. He began to walk briskly towards the prone body. He had a job to do but my own legs were moving, I was running towards Flanagan myself, the gun waving wildly before me.

Adam saw me and slowed and then I was there. I was by the American's side. Flanagan was groaning but alive. He was struggling to focus on movement behind me and I rose to my feet.

Adam Reid was moving fast. He was almost on us and I raised the gun, pulled the trigger. The huge sound swept the room and, smoke from the first discharge still swirling before me, I pulled the trigger again. My arm shot into the air a second time and then fell back as the roar of the discharge tumbled upon the first.

The exhibits quivered and I sucked in a lung full of tainted air. The smoke cleared. Adam was still standing not twenty paces away. He looked mildly surprised. I'd hoped for more but he nodded behind him. 'You shot the mammoth, Spencer,' he said. No gasp of pain, no blood flecked lips. I hadn't hit him. 'What did she ever do to you?'

I shook my head and raised the gun again. 'You wouldn't kill to save yourself,' said Adam. He took a step backwards. I so wanted him to sound afraid but he didn't. 'Yet you'd kill me to save this sick old man.'

I wanted him dead. I didn't have what it took to make him dead myself but I tried to picture him sprawled and broken on the floor, more for his benefit than mine, and I left the thought in my mind for Adam to see. He inclined his head. 'That's wishful thinking, Spencer.'

'You want to bet?'

'Actually I do,' said Adam and he took a step forward.

My hand fell and I began to gag. Adam had weighed me and found me wanting. And I knew beyond any doubt that he was right and that I was going to die. He took another step and the shaft of the axe slipped comfortably through the fingers of his left hand. He let it slide to its fullest length and I could picture the leverage that he would get when he swung it. He would smash our bones. I shuddered and Adam kicked away the hanging shards of glass that stood in his way and took another step.

Adam moved past the body of one of Nosey's men and then another. He smiled but then, as I pressed the gun, slippery with sweat, blood and vomit into Daniel Flanagan's hand, it froze on his face. The ex-cop's finger settled on the trigger of the gun and Adam spoke, reproach in his voice. 'Spencer, after all I've done for you?'

He was shaken but still not afraid. Flanagan was weak. The gun might slip from his hand. Or he might lack the strength to pull the trigger. Or the bullets might miss or do little damage and Adam would kill us both.

I could feel him weighing the odds. They favoured him but he hesitated and I could see it. He believed he was too important to die. He would not and could not lose his own life. Adam took another step backwards and then reached down, picked up an injured man and held the groaning body before him.

But Flanagan's hand had steadied and his lips began to move. 'Glock?'

'Overrated,' said Adam. His words lacked conviction.

'We'll see,' said Flanagan. He lowered his arm. I didn't know who or what a Glock was but a shot in Adam's foot would do. Better yet his head but Flanagan did not pull the trigger and he spoke without turning his head. 'Hit the alarm, Spencer –'

'No.'

Adam had spoken sharply. Flanagan managed a smile. 'Hit the alarm.'

I rose and looked at Adam. An alarm would clear the building. I checked the walls. Alarms were red in England. There had to be hundreds in a public building like this and then I saw one, a small, glass covered case glinting in the light.

Only a few paces away but a noise drew my eyes to the entrance as two more men arrived. And then more but they saw the gun in Flanagan's hand and slowed. The alarm would change everything.

I began to move. Banged my hip heavily against a display but Adam could not risk Flanagan's weaving gun. 'Spencer,' he said. 'Don't do it.'

'Hit it, Spencer.' Flanagan was on his feet and was almost with me. 'Hit it.'

Adam was still widening the distance between us with the injured guard in one hand and the stone axe in the other and the man groaned, long and low and then the pitch changed. I could hear a cracking. The crunching of bone and the guard screamed. 'Spencer, don't –'

Flanagan's finger tightened on the trigger. An orange-red flash. The gunshot drowned the screams as Adam crushed the man in his hand, broke him apart. Adam spoke. 'There'll be panic, a stampede. People will die.'

'You're full of shit, Adam,' I said and hit the glass. Nothing happened and I hit it again, harder. This time the glass broke and a tremendous wailing filled the room.

Adam's men were drawing guns. I felt strangely relaxed as I braced myself against the shots that would tear through me and end my life. I'd done my bit but Flanagan shoved me hard. I fell backwards and tumbled through the door of the observation room with Flanagan immediately behind me.

I hit the ground. Could hear nothing above the wail and piercing screech of the fire alarm but saw Flanagan's mouth moving in silent outrage as he struggled with the door and yellow and orange muzzle flashes sparked in the display beyond.

Angry bees whipped past my head and the smell of burning hair filled my nostrils. Splinters of wood and glass were flying through the air. Bits of metal and other vicious debris were sticking in me but I was distant and removed, scarcely felt them. Someone had pressed the mute button. Flanagan was screaming in my face as a bullet passed through my shoe. The leather began to smoke and another tore a lump from my sleeve and set the cloth on fire. Then Flanagan was gone. The door to the observation room banged shut and the darkness closed in.

Epilogue
08:30 Sunday 4th July
Corey Hills, Nevada

The blood-spattered sheets were gone. Clean linen was crisp against my skin and I coughed, winced and coughed again. It had not been my time to die. I was drained and utterly spent. I could feel and control my fingers and my toes but I lacked the strength to lift my limbs and knew that I had been to a place from which many do not return.

The images that crowded my mind were coming together. My senses had sharpened but so had the pain. The scabs where they caught and pulled against my bedding, the dull ache where the IV line entered my arm and the pull of the medical tape that held a bird's nest of tubes in place on my chest, were all too real to me now and I knew that I had come through.

I was alive. And I was grateful for that but the drugs that were dulling my pain had left me confused and fearful. I could still feel Adam Reid's presence and knew that my life would be split forever between the monochrome years before I had met the man and the stark and bloody life that I had known since.

I had taken three bullets in New York. I had lasted a lifetime without one and then three in the blink of an eye but I was still here and I could remember very little about the time that we had spent in the museum's panic room. I had a dull recollection of fire fighters and of being pulled from the room and into the light. And of an exhibition room, the glass cases and the exhibits utterly destroyed and I could picture Adam Reid flailed around with his terrible axe and of bone and fur being crushed and torn.

And I remembered that Adam and his people had gone. And that Flanagan had insisted that we be quarantined, but everything else was a blur. I was exhausted and spent and then the disease had filled my life. The pain had built and had spilled over upon itself and built again until it was alone with me, my only companion.

There had been no doctors and no nurses. No night and no day. Only the pain and it had lasted forever. Puss-filled blisters the size of pennies had formed on my body. Huge clusters of them had stretched and torn my skin. They had threatened to suck the very life from me. They had erupted around my groin and under my arms, in my mouth and in my nose and inside the deepest recesses of my body. It had hurt like nothing I had known before.

The drugs dulled the pain but they had depressed my breathing and slowed my heart. Dosages had been cut back and the pain had taken over my world.

And I had become dehydrated. My joints burned. Filthy pus had oozed from my body but I had survived and then I had begun to scratch. It was a sign of life they had said. It was healthy but they had put gloves on my hands and later secured my arms to the sides of the cot in order to prevent it.

I had opened cuts on my face and neck. They had sedated me once again but now I was back and I raised my hand and rubbed my eye, the stab of pain and the sticky blood on my finger something real, tangible proof that I was back amongst the living. I had not seen a mirror. I had registered the looks of pity that the staff had flashed to each other in my presence. That was a worry for the future.

The sound of air rushing to fill the negatively pressurised room suggested that the door had been opened and I watched a muffled figure wearing an anti-bacterial suit enter the room. Its arm in a sling, the figure favoured one leg. It limped towards me before turning back to the door and I frowned.

The figure picked up a chair, slid it under the handle to the door then approached my bed. It was too small to be Adam. Too small and too ugly. It bent closer and spoke. 'You look like shit.'

The pain and the pulling and tearing of my various scabs could not prevent me smiling because I knew that voice and Daniel Flanagan held up his hand. Behind the glass of his helmet his dark eyes twinkled and he glanced towards the door. 'Got to be quick, Spencer. First, there's no trace of the disease. What you've had, they're working on, but there was nothing in the food or in your possessions.'

I tried to speak but could not and Flanagan continued. 'But they seem to know it's real and they need to manufacture a vaccine –'

'Who?'

I could taste blood in my mouth but I was pleased. The word had come out. I could speak and Flanagan had understood me. 'Who will do it?'

I nodded. It hurt like hell but trying to speak was worse.

'Not Reid's companies,' said Flanagan. He looked worried, was not trying to hide it. Behind him a shadow crossed the glass of the door. 'They asked Zylagene to stand aside. To share information but not to get involved. There's something I have to tell you.'

I tried to speak but failed and my eyes began to swim with tears. Flanagan looked towards the door where a helmeted shape was now moving on the other side of the glass. 'I'm wearing a wire, Spencer. Was the only way they would allow me to see you but they're not going to bust in. Too scared. We've got a minute or two.'

Flanagan tore something from beneath his shirt and threw it on the floor. 'They still don't believe us. Not all of it, anyway. They want me to give you up, get you talking.'

I managed to get something out. 'Adam?'

I'd worked out that vowels hurt my throat and consonants hurt my tongue and mouth. There wasn't a lot to choose between the two and Daniel Flanagan looked at the door again. Now there were several figures moving beyond it. 'Just listen. Don't try to talk. Reid's dead.'

I felt my eyes, bloodshot and yellow-tinged widen and it hurt like hell itself.

'They didn't tell me for days, wanted to see if I knew. But I know how it works. Was obvious they had something so I waited them out.' Flanagan took a breath. He didn't look too good himself. 'Spencer, they think that you might have been involved.'

I felt the pillow beneath my head rise up either side of my face as I sank into it. I'd been in custody since the museum, they couldn't be serious. Flanagan continued. 'You know how rich Reid was. His people have spoken to the police, said there'd been threats.

'Short calls to Adam's private mobile the cops told me. Some were traced to the mobile that Reid gave you when he was posing as Simon. The one found with Hector's body and one to your hotel room.'

Reid was Simon and I'd rung him what, four, five times? Maybe more and I tried to lean forward. 'I know, Spencer,' said Flanagan, his hand resting on my shoulder. 'I know. But they said you were thrown out of Ranulfskelf, had been obsessing about him –'

A bang at the door interrupted him and Flanagan turned his head. Another bang and Flanagan held up his hand. 'Ignore them, Spencer. They're not going to risk tearing their suits. They saw what you went through.'

I tried to speak again but it was a whisper. Flanagan talked over me. 'Reid died on the day of the meetings. Car bomb in the parking lot. Crude gasoline and fertilizer job. Big bang and a huge fire and the nitrogen-based fertiliser matched traces in your luggage. Instructions printed from the Internet in your apartment in London. Your fingerprints on them and mine too. Hell of a job Spencer, hell of a job.'

More hammer blows at the door and Flanagan looked away. 'They've got dates, times and bits of conversations. You were named as a volunteer for medical testing. Adam's people say that's how you got ill but that you hated him, blamed him for something?'

I felt sick. The medication held it off but I had to close my eyes. I felt the hesitation in Flanagan's voice as he weighed his words. 'Bodies were burnt. Unrecognisable. Adam and the other guys with bullet wounds. Good frame. Bullets will be from a gun with my prints all over it.'

Flanagan leaned forward and ignored the banging on the door behind him. He poured some water into a glass and lifted it to my lips. I shuffled a little. Managed to take some of the water and coughed. I needed to get the words out and they were recognisable, at least to me. 'Definitely him?'

'Car burnt hot,' said Flanagan. 'And it burnt for a long time. Fire crews were tied up evacuating the museum.'

My back arched and I waited for the pain to pass then leaned forward. 'DNA?'

'Body parts. Fragments and bits of clothing. A couple of teeth and some hair blown clear by the blast –'

I pursed my lips. The hammering at the door was more distant now. It was a sound from another world. Flanagan was still talking but his words were passing me by. They were being drowned out by those of a dead man and I could see him clearly, Adam Reid. He was speaking to me from the grave. I could see the words forming on his lips.

It is me, Spencer.

It's me.

'Spencer, what is it?' The pain stabbed through my body. Flanagan had a hold of my shoulder, was gripping me hard. 'Spencer, you OK?'

'Do it,' I said.

Flanagan pulled away from me. 'Do what?'

I shivered. I could feel a presence. It was Adam. 'Carbon-date the tooth.'

Also from Hit the North

Big Daddy by Mark Brumby

Vikings wake in the tenth century and die in the twentieth. A murderous Nazi platoon massacres civilians in Poland fifty years after the death of Adolf Hitler. A B-29 bomber, lost in 1945, resumes a mission to drop an atomic bomb on Tokyo in 1999. Named 'Big Daddy', the bomb is a little larger than both 'Little Boy' and 'Fat Man', which were dropped on Hiroshima and Nagasaki. At the turn of the 21st century, world leaders, backed by their time-travel scientists, have hours and days to work together to locate and neutralise the scientist responsible a timeless flight's nuclear nightmare.

After the Bridge by Andrew J Field

Two suicidal strangers, failing actor Owen Chard and traumatised Ukrainian refugee Becky Letts, postpone death on the Humber to honey-trap men. They make easy money zig zagging across the north of England until they reach Manchester when a blackmailing civil servant dies on Becky in a hotel room. Owen, seduced by life-changing megabucks, fakes his death and steals the dead man's identity to con a quarter of million quid from a brain-damaged hero's trust fund. His impersonation is good, but doesn't fool a cynical cop, or the deceased's crazy self-harming granddaughter. Putin's pals, in the city sponsoring a world boxing championship showdown, are demanding the blackmailer's sex-pest list with menaces. Will Owen and Becky rediscover their humanity in Manchester or drown in a sea of corruption and criminality?

All Down the Line by Andrew J Field

Cain Bell's proposal to girlfriend April Sands backfires when she claims the hit and run driver who killed his daughter two decades ago wasn't Ted Blake. Before April can explain, she is left in a coma after a mugging by a Castlefield canal in Manchester. Doctors must wait until the sedation drugs wear off to ascertain if she is dead or alive. Cain now knows he was fed lies then and is being duped again. But he is being encouraged to look the other way. If April lives, her ex-husband Bob Ord has booked her into a California clinic to recover or go on ice. Bob has also lined up a top Hollywood PR job for Cain, who can start afresh in America — or stay for a showdown showtime in the Mancunian shadowlands, naming and shaming the people complicit in both the death of his daughter and April's attack, even if it costs him his life.

Without Rules by Andrew J Field

China is fighting back against her abusers. She knows she must win, whatever the cost, otherwise she is mincemeat. Sexually abused as a young teen, China fears her young daughter is next the gang's next victim unless she can finally permanently break free from her abusers. But she can can only do this if she is more ruthless than her evil amoral abusers. When her initial plan ends up in a bloodbath, she must team up a cold-blooded killer suffering from PTSD and forget all the rules if she and daughter are to survive the wicked games of evil men.

www.ingramcontent.com/pod-product-compliance
Lightning Source LLC
Chambersburg PA
CBHW020504310726
48979CB00016B/2774/J
9781068574726